Conduct and Courage

A Story of the Days of Nelson

G. A. Henty

Conduct and Courage: A Story of the Days of Nelson

Copyright © 2019 Indo-European Publishing

The present edition is a reproduction of previous publication of this classic work. Minor typographical errors may have been corrected without note, however, for an authentic reading experience the spelling, punctuation, and capitalization have been retained from the original text.

ISBN: 978-1-64439-265-2

CONTENTS

CHAPTER I

AN ORPHAN

A wandering musician was a rarity in the village of Scarcombe. In fact, such a thing had not been known in the memory of the oldest inhabitant. What could have brought him here? men and women asked themselves. There was surely nobody who could dance in the village, and the few coppers he would gain by performing on his violin would not repay him for his trouble. Moreover, Scarcombe was a bleak place, and the man looked sorely shaken with the storm of life. He seemed, indeed, almost unable to hold out much longer; his breath was short, and he had a hacking cough.

To the surprise of the people, he did not attempt to play for their amusement or to ask, in any way, for alms. He had taken a lodging in the cottage of one of the fishermen, and on fine days he would wander out with his boy, a child some five years old, and, lying down on the moorland, would play soft tunes to himself. So he lived for three weeks; and then the end came suddenly. The child ran out one morning from his room crying and saying that daddy was asleep and he could not wake him, and on the fisherman going in he saw that life had been extinct for some hours. Probably it had come suddenly to the musician himself, for there was found among his scanty effects no note or memorandum giving a clue to the residence of the child's friends, or leaving any direction concerning him. The clergyman was, of course, called in to advise as to what should be done. He was a kind-hearted man, and volunteered to bury the dead musician without charging any fees.

After the funeral another question arose. What was to be done with the child?

He was a fine-looking, frank boy, who had grown and hardened beyond his years by the life he had led with his father. Fifteen pounds had been found in the dead man's kit. This, however, would fall to the share of the workhouse authorities if they took charge of him. A sort of informal council was held by the elder fishermen.

"It is hard on the child," one of them said. "I have no doubt his father intended to tell him where to find his friends, but his death

1

came too suddenly. Here is fifteen pounds. Not much good, you will say; and it isn't. It might last a year, or maybe eighteen months, but at the end of that time he would be as badly off as he is now."

"Maybe John Hammond would take him," another suggested. "He lost his boat and nets three weeks ago, and though he has a little money saved up, it is not enough to replace them. Perhaps he would take the child in return for the fifteen pounds. His old woman could do with him, too, and would soon make him a bit useful. John himself is a kind-hearted chap, and would treat him well, and in a few years the boy would make a useful nipper on board his boat."

John Hammond was sent for, and the case was put to him. "Well," he said, "I think I could do with him, and the brass would be mighty useful to me just now; but how does the law stand? If it got to be talked about, the parish might come down upon me for the money."

"That is so, John," one of the others said. "The best plan would be for you, and two of us, to go up to parson, and ask him how the matter stands. If he says that it is all right, you may be sure that you would be quite safe."

The clergyman, upon being consulted, said that he thought the arrangement was a very good one. The parish authorities had not been asked to find any money for the father's funeral, and had therefore no say in the matter, unless they were called upon to take the child. Should any question be asked, he would state that he himself had gone into the matter and had strongly approved of the arrangement, which he considered was to their advantage as well as the child's; for if they took charge of the boy they would have to keep him at least ten years, and then pay for apprenticing him out.

Accordingly the boy was handed over to John Hammond. With the buoyancy of childhood, William Gilmore, which was the best that could be made of what he gave as his name, soon felt at home in the fisherman's cottage. It was a pleasant change to him after having been a wanderer with his father for as far back as he could remember. The old woman was kind in her rough way, and soon took to sending him on small errands. She set him on washing-days to watch the pot and tell her when it boiled. When not so employed she allowed him to play with other children of his own age.

Sometimes when the weather was fine, John, who had come to be very fond of the boy, never having had any children of his own, would take him out with him fishing, to the child's supreme enjoyment. After a year of this life he was put to the village school, which was much less to his liking. Here, fortunately for himself, he attracted the notice of the clergyman's daughter, a girl of sixteen. She, of course, knew his story, and was filled with a great pity for him. She was a little inclined to romance, and in her own mind invented many theories to account for his appearance in the village. Her father would laugh sometimes when she related some of these to him.

"My dear child," he said, "it is not necessary to go so far to account for the history of this poor wandering musician. You say that he looked to you like a broken-down gentleman; there are thousands of such men in the country, ne'er-do-wells, who have tired out all their friends, and have taken at last to a life that permits a certain amount of freedom and furnishes them with a living sufficient for necessary wants. It is from such men as these that the great body of tramps is largely recruited. Many such men drive hackney-coaches in our large towns; some of them enlist in the army; but wherever they are, and whatever they take up, they are sure to stay near the foot of the tree. They have no inclination for better things. They work as hard as men who have steady employment, but they prefer their own liberty with a crust to a solid meal regularly earned. I agree with you myself that there was an appearance of having seen better times about this man; I can go so far with you as to admit that I think that at some time or other he moved in decent circles; but if we could get at the truth I have no doubt whatever that we should find that he had thrown away every opportunity, alienated every friend, and, having cut himself adrift from all ties, took to the life of a wanderer. For such a man nothing could be done; but I hope that the boy, beginning in vastly poorer circumstances than his father, will some day come to earn his living honestly in the position of life in which he is placed."

The interest, however, which Miss Warden took in the boy remained unabated, and had a very useful effect upon him. She persuaded him to come up every day for half an hour to the rectory, and then instructed him in his lessons, educating him in a manner very different from the perfunctory teaching of the old dame at the school. She would urge him on by telling him that if he would attend to his lessons he would some day be able to rise to a better position than that of a village fisherman. His father, no doubt, had had a good education, but from circumstances over which he had had no control he had been obliged to take to the life of a strolling musician, and she was sure that he would have wished of all things that his son should be able to obtain a good position in life when he grew up.

3

Under Miss Warden's teaching the boy made very rapid progress, and was, before two more years had passed, vastly in advance of the rest of the children of the village. As to this, however, by Miss Warden's advice, he remained silent. When he was ten his regular schooling was a great deal interrupted, as it was considered that when a boy reached that age it was high time that he began to assist his father in the boat. He was glad of his freedom and the sense that he was able to make himself useful, but of an evening when he was at home, or weather prevented the boat from going out, he went up for his lesson to Miss Warden, and, stealing away from the others, would lie down on the moor and work at his books.

He was now admitted to the society of watchers. He had often heard whispers among other boys of the look-out that had to be kept upon the custom-house officers, and heard thrilling tales of adventure and escape on the part of the fishermen. Smuggling was indeed carried on on a large scale on the whole Yorkshire coast, and cargoes were sometimes run under the very noses of the revenue officers, who were put off the scent by many ingenious contrivances. Before a vessel was expected in, rumours would be circulated of an intention to land the cargo on some distant spot, and a mysterious light would be shown in that direction by fishing-boats. Sometimes, however, the smugglers were caught in the act, and then there would be a fierce fight, ending in some, at least, of those engaged being taken off to prison and afterwards sent on a voyage in a ship of war.

Will Gilmore was now admitted as a helper in these proceedings, and often at night would watch one or other of the revenue men, and if he saw him stir beyond his usual beat would quickly carry the news to the village. A score of boys were thus employed, so that any movement which seemed to evidence a concentration of the coast-guard men was almost certain to be thwarted. Either the expected vessel was warned off with lights, or, if the concentration left unguarded the place fixed upon for landing, the cargo would be immediately run.

Thus another five years passed. Will was now a strong lad. His friend, Miss Warden, could teach him but little more, but she often had him up of an evening to have a chat with him.

"I am afraid, William," she said one evening, "that a good deal of smuggling is carried on here. Last week there was a fight, and three of the men of the village were killed and several were taken away to prison. It is a terrible state of affairs."

William did not for a moment answer. It was something

4

entirely new to him that there was anything wrong in smuggling. He regarded it as a mere contest of wits between the coast-guard and the fishermen, and had taken a keen pleasure in outwitting the former.

"But there is no harm in smuggling, Miss Warden. Almost everyone takes part in it, and the farmers round all send their carts in when a run is expected."

"But it is very wrong, William, and the fact that so many people are ready to aid in it is no evidence in its favour. People band together to cheat the King's Revenue, and thereby bring additional taxation upon those who deal fairly. It is as much robbery to avoid the excise duties as it is to carry off property from a house, and it has been a great grief to my father that his parishioners, otherwise honest and God-fearing people, should take part in such doings, as is evidenced by the fact that so many of them were involved in the fray last week. He only abstains from denouncing it in the pulpit because he fears that he might thereby lose the affection of the people and impair his power of doing good in other respects."

"I never thought of it in that way, miss," the lad said seriously.

"Just think in your own case, William: suppose you were caught and sent off to sea; there would be an end of the work you have been doing. You would be mixed up with rough sailors, and, after being away on a long voyage, you would forget all that you have learnt, and would be as rough as themselves. This would be a poor ending indeed to all the pains I have taken with you, and all the labour you have yourself expended in trying to improve yourself. It would be a great grief to me, I can assure you, and a cruel disappointment, to know that my hopes for you had all come to naught."

"They sha'n't, Miss Warden," the boy said firmly. "I know it will be hard for me to draw back, but, if necessary, I will leave the village now that you are going to be married. If you had been going to stay I would have stopped too, but the village will not be like itself to me after you have left."

"I am glad to think you mean that. I have remained here as long as I could be of use to you, for though I have taught you as much as I could in all branches of education that would be likely to be useful to you, have lent you my father's books, and pushed you forward till I could no longer lead the way, there are still, of course, many things for you to learn. You have got a fair start, but you must not be content with that. If you have to leave, and I don't think a longer stay here would be of use to you, I will endeavour to obtain some situation for you at Scarborough or Whitby, where you could, after your work is done, continue your education. But I beg you to do nothing rashly. It would be better if you could stay here for another year or so. We may hope that the men will not be so annoyed as you think at your refusal to take further part in the smuggling operations. At any rate, stay if you can for a time. It will be two months before I leave, and three more before I am settled in my new home at Scarborough. When I am so I have no doubt that my husband will aid me in obtaining a situation for you. He has been there for years, and will, of course, have very many friends and acquaintances who would interest themselves in you. If, however, you find that your position would be intolerable, you might remain quiet as to your determination. After the fight of last week it is not likely that there will be any attempt at a landing for some little time to come, and I shall not blame you, therefore, if you at least keep up the semblance of still taking part in their proceedings."

"No, Miss Warden," the boy said sturdily, "I didn't know that it was wrong, and therefore joined in it willingly enough, but now you tell me that it is so I will take no further share in it, whatever comes of it."

"I am glad to hear you say so, William, for it shows that the aid I have given you has not been thrown away. What sort of work would you like yourself, if we can get it for you?"

"I would rather go to sea, Miss Warden, than do anything else. I have, for the last year, taken a lot of pains to understand those books of navigation you bought for me. I don't say that I have mastered them all, but I understand a good deal, and feel sure that after a few years at sea I shall be able to pass as a mate."

"Well, William, you know that, when I got the books for you, I told you that I could not help you with them, but I can quite understand that with your knowledge of mathematics you would be able at any rate to grasp a great deal of the subject. I was afraid then that you would take to the sea. It is a hard life, but one in which a young man capable of navigating a ship should be able to make his way. Brought up, as you have been, on the sea, it is not wonderful that you should choose it as a profession, and, though I may regret it, I should not think of trying to turn you from it. Very well, then, I will endeavour to get you apprenticed. It is a hard life, but not harder than that of a fisherman, to which you are accustomed."

When William returned to his foster-father he informed him that he did not mean to have anything more to do with the smuggling.

The old man looked at him in astonishment. "Are you mad?"

6

he said. "Don't I get five shillings for every night you are out, generally four or five nights a month, which pays for all your food."

"I am sorry," the lad said, "but I never knew that it was wrong before, and now I know it I mean to have nothing more to do with it. What good comes of it? Here we have three empty cottages, and five or six others from which the heads will be absent for years. It is dear at any price. I work hard with you, father, and am never slack; surely the money I earn in the boat more than pays for my grub."

"I can guess who told you this," the old man said angrily. "It was that parson's daughter you are always with."

"Don't say anything against her," the boy said earnestly; "she has been the best friend to me that ever a fellow had, and as long as I live I shall feel grateful to her. You know that I am not like the other boys of the village; I can read and write well, and I have gathered a lot of knowledge from books. Abuse me as much as you like, but say nothing against her. You know that the terms on which you took me expired a year ago, but I have gone on just as before and am ready to do the same for a time."

"You have been a good lad," the old man said, mollified, "and I don't know what I should have done without you. I am nigh past work now, but in the ten years you have been with me things have always gone well with me, and I have money enough to make a shift with for the rest of my life, even if I work no longer. But I don't like this freak that you have taken into your head. It will mean trouble, lad, as sure as you are standing there. The men here won't understand you, and will like enough think that the revenue people have got hold of you. You will be shown the cold shoulder, and even worse than that may befall you. We fisher-folk are rough and ready in our ways, and if there is one thing we hate more than another it is a spy."

"I have no intention of being a spy," the boy said. "I have spoken to none of the revenue men, and don't mean to do so, and I would not peach even if I were certain that a cargo was going to be landed. Surely it is possible to stand aside from it all without being suspected of having gone over to the enemy. No gold that they could give me would tempt me to say a word that would lead to the failure of a landing, and surely there can be no great offence in declining to act longer as a watcher."

The old man shook his head.

"A wilful man must have his way," he said; "but I know our fellows better than you do, and I foresee that serious trouble is likely to come of this."

7

"Well, if it must be, it must," the boy said doggedly. "I mean, if I live, to be a good man, and now that I know that it is wrong to cheat the revenue I will have no more to do with it. It would be a nice reward for all the pains Miss Warden has spent upon me to turn round and do what she tells me is wrong."

John Hammond was getting to the age when few things excite more than a feeble surprise. He felt that the loss of the boy's assistance would be a heavy one, for he had done no small share of the work for the past two years. But he had more than once lately talked to his wife of the necessity for selling his boat and nets and remaining at home. With this decision she quite agreed, feeling that he was indeed becoming incapable of doing the work, and every time he had gone out in anything but the calmest weather she had been filled with apprehension as to what would happen if a storm were to blow up. He was really sorry for the boy, being convinced that harm would befall him as the result of this, to him, astonishing decision. To John Hammond smuggling appeared to be quite justifiable. The village had always been noted as a nest of smugglers, and to him it came as natural as fishing. It was a pity, a grievous pity, that the boy should have taken so strange a fancy.

He was a good boy, a hard-working boy, and the only fault he had to find with him was his unaccountable liking for study. John could neither read nor write, and for the life of him could not see what good came of it. He had always got on well without it, and when the school was first started he and many others shook their heads gravely over it, and regarded it as a fad of the parson's. Still, as it only affected children too young to be useful in the boats, they offered no active opposition, and in time the school had come to be regarded as chiefly a place where the youngsters were kept out of their mothers' way when washing and cooking were going on.

He went slowly back into the cottage and acquainted his wife with this new and astonishing development on the part of the boy. His wife was full of indignation, which was, however, modified at the thought that she would now have her husband always at home with her.

"I shall speak my mind to Miss Warden," she said, "and tell her how much harm her advice has done."

"No, no, Jenny," her husband said; "what is the use of that? It is the parson's duty to be meddling in all sorts of matters, and it will do no good to fight against it. Parson is a good man, all allow, and he always finishes his sermons in time for us to get home to dinner. I agree with you that the young madam has done harm, and I greatly fear that trouble will come to the boy. There are places where smuggling is thought to be wrong, but this place ain't among them. I don't know what will happen when Will says that he doesn't mean to go any more as a watcher, but there is sure to be trouble of some sort."

It was not long indeed before Will felt a change in the village. Previous to this he had been generally popular, now men passed without seeing him. He was glad when John Hammond called upon him to go out in the boat, when the weather was fine, but at other times his only recourse was to steal away to the moors with his books. Presently the elder boys took to throwing sods at him as he passed, and calling spy and other opprobrious epithets after him. This brought on several severe fights, and as Will made up for want of weight by pluck and activity his opponents more than once found themselves badly beaten. One day he learned from a subdued excitement in the village that it was time for one of the smuggling vessels to arrive. One of his boyish friends had stuck to him, and was himself almost under a ban for associating with so unpopular a character.

"Don't you come with me, Stevens," Will had urged again and again; "you will only make it bad for yourself, and it will do me no good."

"I don't care," the former said sturdily. "We have always been good friends, and you know I don't in the least believe that you have anything to do with the revenue men. It is too bad of them to say so. I fought Tom Dickson only this morning for abusing you. He said if you were not working with them, why did you give up being on the watch. I told him it was no odds to me why you gave it up, I supposed that you had a right to do as you liked. Then from words we came to blows. I don't say I beat him, for he is a good bit bigger than I am, but I gave him as good as I got, and he was as glad to stop as I was. You talk of going away soon. If you do, and you will take me, I will go with you."

"I don't know yet where I am going, Tommy, but if I go to a town I have no doubt I shall be able in a short time to hear of someone there who wants a strong lad, or perhaps I may be able to get you a berth as cabin-boy in the ship in which I go. I mean to go for a sailor myself if I can, and I shall be glad to have you as a chum on board. We have always been great friends, and I am sure we always shall be, Tommy. If I were you I would think it over a good many times before you decide upon it. You see I have learnt a great deal from books to prepare myself for a sea life. Miss Warden is going to try to get me taken as an apprentice, and in that case I may hope to get to be an officer when my time is out, but you would not have much chance of doing so. Of course if we were together I could help you on. So far you have never cared for books or to improve yourself, and without that you can never rise to be any more than a common sailor."

"I hate books," the boy said; "still, I will try what I can do. But at any rate I don't care much so that I am with you."

"Well, we will see about it when the time comes, Tommy. Miss Warden was married, as you know, last week. In another three months she will be at Scarborough, and she has promised that her husband will try to get me apprenticed either there or at Whitby, which is a large port. Directly I get on board a ship I will let you know if there is a vacancy in her for a cabin-boy. But you think it over well first; you will find it difficult, for I don't expect your uncle will let you go."

"I don't care a snap about him. He is always knocking me about, and I don't care what he likes and what he don't. You may be sure that I sha'n't ask him, but shall make off at night as soon as I hear from you. You won't forget me, will you, Will?"

"Certainly I will not; you may be quite sure of that. Mind, I don't promise that I shall be able to get you a berth as cabin-boy at once, or as an apprentice. I only promise that I will do so as soon as I have a chance. It may be a month, and it may be a year; it may even be three or four years, for though there is always a demand for men, at least so I have heard, there may not be any demand for boys. But you may be sure that I will not keep you waiting any longer than I can help."

One day Will was walking along the cliffs, feeling very solitary, when he heard a faint cry, and, looking down, saw Tom Stevens in a deep pool. It had precipitous sides, and he was evidently unable to climb out. "Hold on, Tom," he shouted, "I will come to you."

It was half a mile before he could get to a place where he was able to climb down, and when he reached the shore he ran with breathless speed to the spot where Tom's head was still above the water. He saw at once that his friend's strength was well-nigh spent, and, leaping in, he swam to him. "Put your arms round my neck," he said. "I will swim down with you to the point where the creek ends." The boy was too far gone to speak, and it needed all Will's strength to help him down the deep pool to the point where it joined the sea, and then to haul him ashore.

"I was nearly gone, Will," the boy said when he recovered a little.

"Yes, I saw that. But how on earth did you manage to get into the water?"

"I was running along by the side of the cliff, when my foot slipped. I came down on my knee and hurt myself frightfully; I was in such pain that I could not stop myself from rolling over. I tried to swim, which, of course, would have been nothing for me, but I think my knee is smashed, and it hurt me so frightfully that I screamed out with pain, and had to give up. I could not have held on much longer, and should certainly have been drowned had you not seen me. I was never so pleased as when I heard your voice above."

"Can you walk now, do you think?"

"No, I am sure I can't walk by myself, but I might if I leant on you. I will try anyhow."

He hobbled along for a short distance, but at last said: "It is of no use, Will, I can't go any farther."

"Well, get on my back and I will see what I can do for you."

Slowly and with many stoppages Will got him to the point where he descended the cliff. "I must get help to carry you up here, Tom; it is very steep, and I am sure I could not take you myself. I must go into the village and bring assistance."

"I will wait here till morning, Will. There will be no hardship in that, and I know that you don't like speaking to anyone."

"I will manage it," Will said cheerfully. "I will tell John Hammond, and he will go to your uncle and get help."

"Ah, that will do! Most of the men are out, but I dare say there will be two or three at home."

Will ran all the way back to the village, which was more than a mile away. "Tom Stevens is lying at the foot of the cliff, father. I think he has broken his leg, and he has been nearly drowned. Will you go and see his uncle, and get three or four men to carry him home. You know very well it is no use my going to his uncle. He would not listen to what I have to say, and would simply shower abuse upon me."

"I will go," the old man said. "The boy can't be left there."

In a quarter of an hour the men started. Will went ahead of them for some distance until he reached the top of the path. "He is down at the bottom," he said, and turned away. Tom was brought home, and roundly abused by his uncle for injuring himself so that he would be unable to accompany him in his boat for some days. He lay for a week in bed, and was then only able to hobble about with the aid of a stick. When he related how Will had saved him there was a slight revulsion of feeling among the better-disposed boys, but this was of short duration. It became known that a French lugger would soon be on the coast. Will was not allowed to approach the edge of the cliff, being assailed by curses and threats if he ventured to do so. Every care was taken to throw the coast-guard off the scent, but things went badly. There was some sharp fighting, and a considerable portion of the cargo was seized as it was being carried up the cliff.

The next day Tom hurried up to Will, who was a short way out on the moor.

"You must run for your life, Will. There are four or five of the men who say that you betrayed them last night, and I do believe they will throw you over the cliff. Here they come! The best thing you can do is to make for the coast-guard station."

Will saw that the four men who were coming along were among the roughest in the village, and started off immediately at full speed. With oaths and shouts the men pursued him. The coast-guard station was two miles away, and he reached it fifty yards in front of them. The men stopped, shouting: "You are safe there, but as soon as you leave it we will have you."

"What is the matter, lad?" the sub-officer in charge of the station said.

"Those men say that I betrayed them, but you know 'tis false, sir."

"Certainly I do. I know you well by sight, and believe that you are a good young fellow. I have always heard you well spoken of. What makes them think that?"

"It is because I would not agree to go on acting as watcher. I did not know that there was any harm in it till Miss Warden told me, and then I would not do it any longer, and that set all the village against me."

"What are you going to do?"

"I will stay here to-night if you will let me. I am sure they will keep up a watch for me."

"I will sling a hammock for you," the man said. "Now we are just going to have dinner, and I dare say you can eat something. You are the boy they call Miss Warden's pet, are you not?"

"Yes, they call me so. She has been very kind to me, and has helped me on with my books."

"Ah, well, a boy is sure to get disliked by his fellows when he is cleverer with his books than they are!"

After dinner the officer said: "It is quite clear that you won't be able to return to the village. I think I have heard that you have no father. Is it not so?"

12

"Yes, he died when I was five years old. He left a little money, and John Hammond took me in and bought a boat with that and what he had saved. I was bound to stay with him until I was fourteen years old, but was soon going to leave him, for he is really too old to go out any longer."

"Have you ever thought of going into the royal navy?"

"I have thought of it, sir, but I have not settled anything. I thought of going into the merchant navy."

"Bah! I am surprised at a lad of spirit like you thinking of such a thing. If you have learned a lot you will, if you are steady, be sure to get on in time, and may very well become a petty officer. No lad of spirit would take to the life of a merchantman who could enter the navy. I don't say that some of the Indiamen are not fine ships, but you would find it very hard to get a berth on one of them. Our lieutenant will be over here in a day or two, and I have no doubt that if I speak to him for you he will ship you as a boy in a fine ship."

"How long does one ship for, sir?"

"You engage for the time that the ship is in commission, at the outside for five years; and if you find that you do not like it, at the end of that time it is open to you to choose some other berth."

"I can enter the merchant navy then if I like?"

"Of course you could, but I don't think that you would. On a merchantman you would be kicked and cuffed all round, whereas on a man-of-war I don't say it would be all easy sailing, but if you were sharp and obliging things would go smoothly enough for you."

"Well, sir, I will think it over to-night."

"Good, my boy! you are quite right not to decide in a hurry. It is a serious thing for a young chap to make a choice like that; but it seems to me that, being without friends as you are, and having made enemies of all the people of your village, it would be better for you to get out of it as soon as possible."

"I quite see that; and really I think I could not do better than pass a few years on a man-of-war, for after that I should be fit for any work I might find to do."

"Well, sleep upon it, lad."

Will sat down on the low wall in front of the station and thought it over. After all, it seemed to him that it would be better to be on a fine ship and have a chance of fighting with the French than to sail in a merchantman. At the end of five years he would be twenty, and could pass as a mate if he chose, or settle on land. He would have liked to consult Miss Warden, but this was out of the question. He knew the men who had pursued him well enough to be

13

sure that his life would not be safe if they caught him. He might make his way out of the station at night, but even that was doubtful. Besides, if he were to do so he had no one to go to at Scarborough; he had not a penny in his pocket, and would find it impossible to maintain himself until Miss Warden returned. He did not wish to appear before her as a beggar. He was still thinking when a shadow fell across him, and, looking up, he saw his friend Tom.

"I have come round to see you, Will," he said. "I don't know what is to be done. Nothing will convince the village that you did not betray them."

"The thing is too absurd," Will said angrily. "I never spoke to a coast-guardsman in my life till to-day, except, perhaps, in passing, and then I would do no more than make a remark about the weather. Besides, no one in the village has spoken to me for a month, so how could I tell that the lugger was coming in that night?"

"Well, I really don't think it would be safe for you to go back."

"I am not going back. I have not quite settled what I shall do, but certainly I don't intend to return to the village."

"Then what are you going to do, Will?"

"I don't know exactly, but I have half decided to ship as a boy on one of the king's ships."

"I should like to go with you wherever you go, but I should like more than anything to do that."

"It is a serious business, you know; you would have to make up your mind to be kicked and cuffed."

"I get that at home," Tom said; "it can't be harder for me at sea than it is there."

"Well, I have not got to decide until to-morrow; you go home and think it over, and if you come in the morning with your mind made up, I will speak to the officer here and ask him if they will take us both."

CHAPTER II

IN THE KING'S SERVICE

Before morning came Will had thought the matter over in every light, and concluded that he could not do better than join the navy for a few years. Putting all other things aside, it was a life of adventure, and adventure is always tempting to boys. It really did not seem to him that, if he entered the merchant service at once, he would be any better off than he would be if he had a preliminary training in the royal navy. He knew that the man-of-war training would make him a smarter sailor, and he hoped that he would find time enough on board ship to continue his work, so that afterwards he might be able to pass as a mate in the merchant service.

Tom Stevens came round in the morning.

"I have quite made up my mind to go with you if you will let me," he said.

"I will let you readily enough, Tom, but I must warn you that you will not have such a good look-out as I shall. You know, I have learnt a good deal, and if the first cruise lasts for five years I have no doubt that at the end of it I shall be able to pass as a mate in the merchant service, and I am afraid you will have very little chance of doing so."

"I can't help that," Tom said. "I know that I am not like you, and I haven't learnt things, and I don't suppose that if I had had anyone to help me it would have made any difference. I know I shall never rise much above a sailor before the mast. If you leave the service and go into a merchantman I will go there with you. It does not matter to me where I am. I felt so before, and of course I feel it all the more now that you have saved my life. I am quite sure you will get on in the world, Will, and sha'n't grudge you your success a bit, however high you rise, for I know how hard you have worked, and how well you deserve it. Besides, even if I had had the pains bestowed upon me, and had worked ever so hard myself, I should never have been a bit like you. You seem different from us somehow. I don't know how it is, but you are smarter and quicker and more active. I expect some day you will find out something about your father, and then probably we shall be able to understand the difference between us. At any rate I am quite prepared to see

15

you rise, and I shall be well content if you will always allow me to remain your friend."

Will gratified the sub-officer later by telling him that he had made up his mind to ship on board one of the king's vessels, and that his friend and chum, Tom Stevens, had made up his mind to go with him.

The coxswain looked Tom up and down.

"You have the makings of a fine strong man," he said, "and ought to turn out a good sailor. The training you have had in the fishing-boats will be all in your favour. Well, I will let you know when the lieutenant makes his rounds. I am sure there will be no difficulty in shipping you. Boys ain't what they were when I was young. Then we thought it an honour to be shipped on board a man-of-war, now most of them seem to me mollycoddled, and we have difficulty in getting enough boys for the ships. You see, we are not allowed to press boys, but only able-bodied men; so the youngsters can laugh in our faces. Most of the crimps get one or two of them to watch the sailors as the boys of the village watch our men, and give notice when they are going to make a raid. I don't think, therefore, that there is any fear of your being refused, especially when I say that one of you has got into great trouble from refusing to aid in throwing us off the scent when a lugger is due. If for no other reason he owes you a debt for that."

Three days passed. Will still remained at the coast-guard station, and men still hovered near. Tom came over once and said that it had been decided among a number of the fishermen that no great harm should be done to Will when they got him, but that he should be thrashed within an inch of his life. On the third day the coxswain said to Will:

"I have a message this morning from the lieutenant, that he will be here by eleven o'clock. If you will write a line to your friend I will send it over by one of the men."

Tom arrived breathless two minutes before the officer.

"My eye, I have had a run of it," he said. "The man brought me the letter just as I was going to start in the boat with my uncle. I pretended to have left something behind me and ran back to the cottage, he swearing after me all the way for my stupidity. I ran into the house, and then got out of the window behind, and started for the moors, taking good care to keep the house in a line between him and me. My, what a mad rage he will be in when I don't come back, and he goes up and finds that I have disappeared! I stopped a minute to take a clean shirt and my Sunday clothes. I expect, when

16

he sees I am not in the cottage, he will look round, and he will discover that they have gone from their pegs, and guess that I have made a bolt of it. He won't guess, however, that I have come here, but will think I have gone across the moors. He knows very well how hard he has made my life; still, that won't console him for losing me, just as I am getting really useful in the boat."

The lieutenant landed from his cutter at the foot of the path leading up to the station. The sub-officer received him at the top, and after a few words they walked up to the station together.

"Who are these two boys?" he asked as he came up to them.

"Two lads who wish to enter the navy, sir."

"Umph! runaways, I suppose?"

"Not exactly, sir. Both of them are fatherless. That one has received a fair education from the daughter of the clergyman of the village, who took a great fancy to him. He has for some years now been assisting in one of the fishing-boats and, as he acknowledges, in the spying upon our men, as practically everyone else in the village does. When, however, Miss Warden told him that smuggling was very wrong, he openly announced his intention of having nothing more to do with it. This has had the effect of making the ignorant villagers think that he must have taken bribes from us to keep us informed of what was going on. In consequence he has suffered severe persecution and has been sent to Coventry. After the fight we had with them the other day they appear to think that there could be no further doubt of his being concerned in the matter, and four men set out after him to take his life. He fled here as his nearest possible refuge, and if you will look over there you will see two men on the watch for him. He had made up his mind to ship as an apprentice on a merchantman, but I have talked the matter over with him, and he has now decided to join a man-of-war."

"A very good choice," the officer said. "I suppose you can read and write, lad?"

"Yes, sir," Will said, suppressing a smile.

"Know a bit more, perhaps?"

"Yes, sir."

"Well, if you are civil and well behaved, you will get on. And who is the other one?"

"He is Gilmore's special chum, sir. He has a brute of an uncle who is always knocking him about, and he wants to go to sea with his friend."

"Well, they are two likely youngsters. The second is more heavily built than the other, but there is no doubt as to which is the more intelligent. I will test them at once, and then take them off with me in the cutter and hand them over to the tender at Whitby. Now send four men and catch those two fellows and bring them in here. I will give them a sharp lesson against ill-treating a lad who refuses to join them in their rascally work."

A minute later four of the men strolled off by the cliffs, two in each direction. When they had got out of sight of the watchers, they struck inland, and, making a detour, came down behind them. The fishermen did not take the alarm until it was too late. They started to run, but the sailors were more active and quick-footed, and, presently capturing them, brought them back to the coast-guard station.

"So my men," the lieutenant said sternly, "you have been threatening to ill-treat one of His Majesty's subjects for refusing to join you in your attempts to cheat the revenue? I might send you off to a magistrate for trial, in which case you would certainly get three months' imprisonment. I prefer, however, settling such matters myself. Strip them to the waist, lads."

The orders were executed in spite of the men's struggles and execrations.

"Now tie them up to the flag-post and give them a dozen heartily."

As the men were all indignant at the treatment that had been given to Will they laid the lash on heavily, and the execrations that followed the first few blows speedily subsided into shrieks for mercy, followed at last by low moaning.

When both had received their punishment, the lieutenant said: "Now you can put on your clothes again and carry the news of what you have had to your village, and tell your friends that I wish I had had every man concerned in the matter before me. If I had I would have dealt out the same punishment to all. Now, lads, I shall be leaving in an hour's time; if you like to send back to the village for your clothes, one of the men will take the message."

Tom already had all his scanty belongings, but Will was glad to send a note to John Hammond, briefly stating his reasons for leaving, and thanking him for his kindness in the past, and asking him to send his clothes to him by the bearer. An hour and a half later they embarked in the lieutenant's gig and were rowed off to the revenue cutter lying a quarter of a mile away. Here they were put under the charge of the boatswain.

"They have shipped for the service, Thompson," the lieutenant said. "I think they are good lads. Make them as comfortable as you can."

"So you have shipped, have you?" the boatswain said as he led them forward. "Well, you are plucky young cockerels. It ain't exactly a bed of roses, you will find, at first, but if you can always keep your temper and return a civil answer to a question you will soon get on all right. You will have more trouble with the other boys than with the men, and will have a battle or two to fight."

"We sha'n't mind that," Will said; "we have had to deal with some tough ones already in our own village, and have proved that we are better than most of our own age. At any rate we won't be licked easily, even if they are a bit bigger and stronger than ourselves, and after all a licking doesn't go for much anyway. What ship do you think they will send us to, sir?"

"Ah, that is a good deal more than I can say! There is a cutter that acts as a receiving-ship at Whitby, and you will be sent off from it as opportunity offers and the ships of war want hands. Like enough you will go off with a batch down to the south in a fortnight or so, and will be put on board some ship being commissioned at Portsmouth or Devonport. A large cutter comes round the coast once a month, to pick up the hands from the various receiving-ships, and as often as not she goes back with a hundred. And a rum lot you will think them. There are jail-birds who have had the offer of release on condition that they enter the navy; there are farm-labourers who don't know one end of a boat from the other; there are drunkards who have been sold by the crimps when their money has run out; but, Lord bless you, it don't make much difference what they are, they are all knocked into shape before they have been three months on board. I think, however, you will have a better time than this. Our lieutenant is a kind-hearted man, though he is strict enough in the way of business, and I have no doubt he will say a good word for you to the commander of the tender, which, as he is the senior officer, will go a long way."

The two boys were soon on good terms with the crew, who divined at once that they were lads of mettle, and were specially attracted to Will on account of the persecution he had suffered by refusing to act as the smugglers' watcher, and also when they heard from Tom how he had saved his life.

"You will do," was the verdict of an old sailor. "I can see that you have both got the right stuff in you. When one fellow saves another's life, and that fellow runs away and ships in order to be near his friend, you may be sure that there is plenty of good stuff in them, and that they will turn out a credit to His Majesty's service."

They were a week on board before the cutter finished her trip

19

at Whitby. Both boys had done their best to acquire knowledge, and had learnt the names of the ropes and their uses by the time they got to port.

"You need not go on board the depot ship until to-morrow," the lieutenant said. "I will go across with you myself. I have had my eye upon you ever since you came on board, and I have seen that you have been trying hard to learn, and have always been ready to give a pull on a rope when necessary. I have no fear of your getting on. It is a pity we don't get more lads of your type in the navy."

On the following morning the lieutenant took them on board the depot and put them under the charge of the boatswain. "You will have to mix with a roughish crew here," the latter said, "but everything will go smoothly enough when you once join your ship. You had better hand over your kits to me to keep for you, otherwise there won't be much left at the end of the first night; and if you like I will let you stow yourselves away at night in the bitts forward. It is not cold, and I will throw a bit of old sail-cloth over you; you will be better there than down with the others, where the air is almost thick enough to cut."

"Thank you very much, sir; we should prefer that. We have both been accustomed to sleep at night in the bottom of an open boat, so it will come natural enough to us. Are there any more boys on board?"

"No, you are the only ones. We get more boys down in the west, but up here very few ship."

They went below together. "Dimchurch," the boatswain said to a tall sailor-like man, "these boys have just joined. I wish you would keep an eye on them, and prevent anyone from bullying them. I know that you are a pressed man, and that we have no right to expect anything of you until you have joined your ship, but I can see that for all that you are a true British sailor, and I trust to you to look after these boys."

"All right, mate!" the sailor said. "I will take the nippers under my charge, and see that no one meddles with them. I know what I had to go through when I first went to sea, and am glad enough to do a good turn to any youngsters joining."

"Thank you! Then I will leave them now in your charge."

"This is your first voyage, I suppose," the sailor said as he sat down on the table and looked at the boys. "I see by your togs that you have been fishing."

"Yes, we both had seven or eight years of it, though of course we were of no real use till the last five."

"You don't speak like a fisherman's boy either," the man said.

"No. A lady interested herself in me and got me to work all my spare time at books."

"Well, they will be of no use to you at present, but they may come in handy some day to get you a rating. I never learnt to read or write myself or I should have been mate long ago. This is my first voyage in a ship of war. Hitherto I have always escaped being pressed when I was ashore, but now they have caught me I don't mind having a try at it. I believe, from all I hear, that the grub and treatment are better than aboard most merchantmen, and the work nothing like so hard. Of course the great drawback is the cat, but I expect that a well-behaved man doesn't often feel it."

The others had looked on curiously when the lads first came down, but they soon turned away indifferently and took up their former pursuits. Some were playing cards, others lying about half-asleep. Two or three who were fortunate enough to be possessed of tobacco were smoking. In all there were some forty men. When the evening meal was served out the sailor placed one of the boys on each side of him, and saw that they got their share.

"I must find a place for you to sleep," he said when they had finished.

"The officer who brought us down has given us permission to sleep on deck near the bitts."

"Ah, yes, that is quite in the bows of the ship! You will do very well there, much better than you would down here. I will go up on deck and show you the place. How is it that he is looking specially after you?"

"I believe Lieutenant Jones of the Antelope was good enough to speak to the officer in command of this craft in our favour."

"How did you make him your friend?"

Will told briefly the story of his troubles with the smugglers. The sailor laughed.

"Well," he said, "you must be a pretty plucky one to fly in the face of a smuggling village in that way. You must have known what the consequence would be, and it is not every boy, nor every man either, if it comes to that, that would venture to do as you did."

"It did not seem to me that I had any choice when I once found out that it was wrong."

The sailor laughed again. "Well, you know, it is not what you could call a crime, though it is against the law of the land, but everyone does a bit of smuggling when they get the chance. Lord bless you! I have come home from abroad when there was not one of the passengers and crew who did not have a bit of something hidden about him or his luggage—brandy, 'baccy, French wines, or knick-knacks of some sort. Pretty nigh half of them got found out and fined, but the value of the things got ashore was six or eight times as much as what was collared."

"Still it was not right," Will persisted.

"Oh, no! it was not right," the sailor said carelessly, "but everyone took his chance. It is a sort of game, you see, between the passengers and crew on one side and the custom-house officers on the other. It was enough to make one laugh to see the passengers land. Women who had been as thin as whistles came out as stout matrons, owing to the yards and yards of laces and silk they had wound round them. All sorts of odd places were choke-full of tobacco; there were cases that looked like baggage, but really had a tin lining, which was full of brandy. It was a rare game for those who got through, I can tell you, though I own it was not so pleasant for those who got caught and had their contraband goods confiscated, besides having to pay five times the proper duty. As a rule the men took it quietly enough, they had played the game and lost; but as for the women, they were just raging tigers.

"For myself, I laughed fit to split. If I lost anything it was a pound or two of tobacco which I was taking home for my old father, and I felt that things might have been a deal worse if they had searched the legs of my trousers, where I had a couple of bladders filled with good brandy. You see, young 'un, though everyone knows that it is against the law, no one thinks it a crime. It is a game you play; if you lose you pay handsomely, but if you win you get off scot-free. I think the lady who told you it was wrong did you a very bad service, for if she lived near that village she must have known that you would get into no end of trouble if you were to say you would have nothing more to do with it. And how is it"—turning to Tom—"that you came to go with him? You did not take it into your head that smuggling was wrong too?"

"I never thought of it," Tom said, "and if I had been told so should only have answered that what was good enough for others was good enough for me. I came because Will came. We had always been great friends, and more than once joined to thrash a big fellow who put upon us. But the principal thing was that a little while ago he saved me from drowning. There was a deep cut running up to the foot of the cliffs. One day I was running past there, when I slipped, and in falling hurt my leg badly. I am only just beginning to use it a bit now. The pain was so great that I did not know what I was doing;

I rolled off the rock into the water. My knee was so bad that I could not swim, and the rock was too high for me to crawl out. I had been there for some time, and was beginning to get weak, when Will came along on the top of the cliff and saw me. He shouted to me to hold on till he could get down to me. Then he ran half a mile to a place where he was able to climb down, and tore back again along the shore till he reached the cut, and then jumped in and swam to me. There was no getting out on either side, so he swam with me to the end of the cut and landed me there. I was by that time pretty nigh insensible, but he half-helped and half-carried me till we got to the point of the cliff where he had come down. Then he left me and ran off to the village to get help. So you will understand now why I should wish to stick to him."

"I should think so," the sailor said warmly. "It was a fine thing to do, and I would be glad to do it myself. Stick to him, lad, as long as he will let you. I fancy, from the way he speaks and his manner, that he will mount up above you, but never you mind that."

"I won't, as long as I can keep by him, and I hope that soon I may have a chance of returning him the service he has done me. He knows well enough that if I could I would give my life for him willingly."

"I think," the sailor said to Will seriously, "you are a fortunate fellow to have made a friend like that. A good chum is the next best thing to a good wife. In fact, I don't know if it is not a bit better. Ah, here comes the boatswain with a bit of sail-cloth, so you had better lie down at once. We shall most of us turn in soon down below, for there is nothing to pass the time, and I for one shall be very glad when the cutter comes for us."

The boys chatted for some time under cover of the sail-cloth. They agreed that things were much better than they could have expected. The protection of the boatswain was a great thing, but that of their sailor friend was better. They hoped that he would be told off to the ship in which they went, for they felt sure that he would be a valuable friend to them. The life on board the cutter, too, had been pleasant, and altogether they congratulated themselves on the course they had taken.

"I have no doubt we shall like it very much when we are once settled. They look a rough lot down below, and that sentry standing with a loaded musket at the gangway shows pretty well what sort of men they are. I am not surprised that the pressed men should try to get away, but I have no pity for the drunken fellows who joined when they had spent their last shilling. Our fishermen go on a spree

23

sometimes, but not often, and when they do, they quarrel and fight a bit, but they always go to work the next morning."

"That is a different thing altogether, for I heard that in the towns men will spend every penny they have, give up work altogether, and become idle, lazy loafers."

Two days later, to the great satisfaction of the boys, a large cutter flying the white ensign was seen approaching the harbour. No doubt was entertained that she was the receiving-ship. This was confirmed when the officer in charge of the depot-ship was rowed to the new arrival as soon as the anchor was dropped. A quarter of an hour later he returned, and it became known that the new hands were to be taken to Portsmouth. The next morning two boats rowed alongside. Will could not but admire the neat and natty appearance of the crew, which formed a somewhat striking contrast to the slovenly appearance of the gang on the depot-ship. A list of the new men was handed over to the officer in charge, and these were at once transferred to the big cutter.

Here everything was exquisitely clean and neat. The new-comers were at once supplied with uniforms, and told off as supernumeraries to each watch. Will and Tom received no special orders, and were informed that they were to make themselves generally useful. Beyond having to carry an occasional message from one or other of the midshipmen, or boatswain, their duties were of the lightest kind. They helped at the distribution of the messes, the washing of the decks, the paring of the potatoes for dinner, and other odd jobs. When not wanted they could do as they pleased, and Will employed every spare moment in gaining what information he could from his friend Dimchurch, or from any sailor he saw disengaged and wearing a look that invited interrogation.

"You seem to want to know a lot all at once, youngster," one said.

"I have got to learn it sooner or later," Will replied, "and it is just as well to learn as much as I can while I have time on my hands. I expect I shall get plenty to do when I join a ship at Portsmouth. May I go up the rigging?"

"That you may not. You don't suppose that His Majesty's ships are intended to look like trees with rooks perched all over them? You will be taught all that in due time. There is plenty to learn on deck, and when you know all that, it will be time enough to think of going aloft. You don't want to become a Blake or a Benbow all at once, do you?"

"No," Will laughed, "it will be time to think of that in another twenty years."

The sailor broke into a roar of laughter.

"Well, there is nothing like flying high, young 'un; but there is no reason why in time you should not get to be captain of the foretop or coxswain of the captain's gig. I suppose either of these would content you?"

"I suppose it ought," Will said with a merry laugh. "At any rate it will be time to think of higher posts when I have gained one of these."

The voyage to Portsmouth was uneventful. They stopped at several receiving-stations on their way down, and before they reached their destination they had gathered a hundred and twenty men. Will and Tom were astonished at the bustle and activity of the port. Frigates and men-of-war lay off Portsmouth and out at Spithead; boats of various sizes rowed between them, or to and from the shore. Never had they imagined such a scene; the enormous bulk of the men-of-war struck them with wonder. Will admired equally the tapering spars and the more graceful lines of the frigates and corvettes, and his heart thrilled with pride as he felt that he too was a sailor, and a portion, however insignificant, of one of these mighty engines of war.

The officer in command of the receiving-ship at Whitby had passed on to the captain of the cutter what had been told him of the two boys by the lieutenant of the Antelope, and he in turn related the story to one of the chief officers of the dockyard. It happened that they were the only two boys that had been brought down, and the dockyard official said it would be a pity to separate them.

"I will put them down as part of the crew of the Furious. I want a few specially strong and active men for her; her commander is a very dashing officer, and I should like to see that he is well manned."

The two boys had especially noticed and admired the Furious, which was a thirty-four-gun frigate, so next morning, when the new hands were mustered and told off to different ships, they were delighted when they found their names appear at the end of the list for that vessel, all the more so because Dimchurch was to join her also.

"I am pleased, Dimchurch, that we are to be in the same ship with you," Will exclaimed as soon as the men were dismissed.

"I am glad too, youngster. I have taken a fancy to you, as you seem to have done to me, and it will be very pleasant for us to be together. But now you must go and get your kit-bags ready at once; we are sure to be sent off to the Furious in a short time, and it will be a bad mark against you if you keep the boat waiting."

25

In a quarter of an hour a boat was seen approaching from the Furious. The officer in charge ascended to the deck of the cutter, and after a chat with the captain called out the list, and counted the men one by one as they went down to the boat, each carrying his kit.

"Not a bad lot," he said to the young midshipman sitting by his side. "This pretty nearly makes up our complement; the press gang are sure to pick up the few hands we want either to-day or to-morrow."

"I shall be glad when we are off, sir," the midshipman said. "I am never comfortable, after beginning to get into commission, until we are out on blue water."

"Nor am I. I hope the dockyard won't keep us waiting for stores. We have got most of them, but the getting on board of the powder and shot is always a long task, and we have to be so careful with the powder. There is the captain on deck; he is looking out, no doubt, to see the new hands. I am glad they are good ones, for nothing puts him into a bad temper so readily as having a man brought on board who is not, as he considers, up to the mark."

As they mustered on deck the captain's eye ran with a keen scrutiny over them. A slight smile crossed his lips as he came to the two boys.

"That will do, Mr. Ayling; they are not a bad lot, taking them one for all, and there are half a dozen men among them who ought to make first-rate topmen. I should say half of them have been to sea before, and the others will soon be knocked into shape. The two boys will, of course, go into the same mess as the others who have come on board. One of them looks a very sharp young fellow."

"He has been rather specially passed down, sir. He belonged to one of the most noted smuggling villages on the Yorkshire coast, which is saying a great deal, and he struck against smuggling because some lady in the place told him that it was wrong. Of course he drew upon himself the enmity of the whole village. The coast-guard stopped a landing, and two or three of the fishermen were killed. The hostility against the lad, which was entirely unfounded, rose in consequence of this to such a pitch that he was obliged to take refuge in the coast-guard station. I hear from the captain of the Hearty that the boy has been far better educated than the generality of fisher lads, and was specially recommended to him by the officer of the receiving-ship."

"Is there anything extraordinary about the other boy?" the captain asked with a slight smile.

"No, sir; I believe he joined chiefly to be near his companion, the two being great friends."

"He looks a different kind of boy altogether," the captain said. "You could pick him out as a fisher boy anywhere, and picture him in high boots, baggy corduroy breeches, and blue guernsey."

"He is a strong, well-built lad, and I should say a good deal more powerful than his friend."

"Well, they are good types of boys, and are not likely to give us as much trouble as some of those young scamps, run-away apprentices and so on, who want a rope's end every week or so to teach them to do their duty."

The boys were taken down to a deck below the water-level, where the crew were just going to begin dinner. At one end was a table at which six boys were sitting.

"Hillo, who are you?" the eldest among them asked. "I warn you, if you don't make things comfortable, you will get your heads punched in no time."

"My name is William Gilmore, and this is Tom Stevens. As to punching heads, you may not find it as easy as you think. I may warn you at once that we are friends and will stick together, and that there will be no punching one head without having to punch both."

"We shall see about that before long," the other said. "Some of the others thought they were going to rule the roost when they joined a few days ago, but I soon taught them their place."

"Well, you can begin to teach us ours as soon as you like," Tom Stevens said. "We have met bullies of your sort before. Now, as dinner is going on, we will have some of it, as they didn't victual us before we left the cutter."

"Well, then, you had better go to the cook-house and draw rations. No doubt the cook has a list of you fellows' names."

The boys took the advice and soon procured a cooked ration of meat and potatoes. The cook told them where they would find plates.

"One of the mess has to wash them up," he said, "and stow them away in the racks provided for them."

"Johnson," the eldest boy said to the smallest of the party, "you need not wash up to-day; that is the duty of the last comer."

"I suppose it is the duty of each one of the mess by turn," Will said quietly; "we learnt that much as we came down the coast."

"You will have to learn more than that, young fellow," the bully, who was seventeen, blustered. "You will have to learn that I am senior of the mess, and will have to do as I tell you. I have made one voyage already, and all the rest of you are greenhorns."

"It seems to me from the manner in which you speak, that it is not a question of seniority but simply of bounce and bullying, and I hope that the other boys will no more give in to that sort of thing than Stevens or myself. I have yet to learn that one boy is in any way superior to the others, and in the course of the next hour I shall ascertain whether this is so."

"Perhaps, after the meal is over, you will go down to the lower deck and allow me to give you a lesson."

"As I told you," Will answered quietly, "my friend and I are one. I don't suppose that single-handed I could fight a great hulking fellow like you, but my friend and I are quite willing to do so together. So now if there is any talk of fighting, you know what to expect."

The bully eyed the two boys curiously, but, like most of the type, he was at heart a coward, and felt considerable doubt whether these two boys would not prove too much for him. He therefore muttered sullenly that he would choose his own time.

"All right! choose by all means, and whenever you like to fix a time we shall be perfectly ready to accommodate you."

"Who on earth are you with your long words? Are you a gentleman in disguise?"

"Never mind who I am," Will said. "I have learnt enough, at any rate, to know a bully and a coward when I meet him."

The lad was too furious to answer, but finished his dinner in silence, his anger being all the more acute from the fact that he saw that some of the other boys were tittering and nudging each other. But he resolved that, though it might be prudent for the present to postpone any encounter with the boys, he would take his revenge on the first opportunity.

CHAPTER III

A SEA-FIGHT

As the conflict of words came to an end, a roar of laughter burst from the sailors at the next mess-table.

"Well done, little bantam!" one said; "you have taken that lout down a good many pegs, and I would not mind backing you to thrash him single-handed. We have noticed his goings-on for the past two or three days with the other boys, and had intended to give him a lesson, but you have done it right well. He may have been on a voyage before, but I would wager that he has never been aloft, and I would back you to be at the masthead before he has crawled through the lubbers' hole. Now, my lad, just you understand that if you are ready to fight both those boys we won't interfere, but if you try it one on one of them we will."

The boys' duties consisted largely of working with the watch to which they were attached, of scrubbing decks, and cleaning brass-work. In battle their place was to bring up the powder and shot for the guns. On the second day, when the work was done, Will Gilmore went up to the boatswain.

"If you please, sir," he said, "may I go up the mast?"

The boatswain looked at him out of one eye.

"Do you really want to learn, lad?"

"I do, sir."

"Well, when there are, as at present, other hands aloft, you may go up, but not at other times."

"Thank you, sir!"

Will at once started. He was accustomed to climb the mast of John Hammond's boat, but this was a very different matter. From scrambling about the cliffs so frequently he had a steady eye, and could look down without any feeling of giddiness. The lubbers' hole had been pointed out to him, but he was determined to avoid the ignominy of having to go up through it. When he got near it he paused and looked round. It did not seem to him that there was any great difficulty in going outside it, and as he knew he could trust to his hands he went steadily up until he stood on the main-top.

"Hallo, lad," said a sailor who was busy there, "do you mean to say that you have come up outside?"

"Yes, there did not seem to be any difficulty about it."

"And is it the first time you have tried?"

"Yes."

"Then one day you will turn out a first-rate sailor. What are you going to do now?"

Will looked up.

"I am going up to the top of the next mast."

"You are sure that you won't get giddy?"

"Yes, I am accustomed to climbing up the cliffs on the Yorkshire coast, and I have not the least fear of losing my head."

"Well, then, fire away, lad, and if you find that you are getting giddy shout and I will come up to you."

"Thank you! I will call if I want help."

Steadily he went up till he stood on the cap of the topmast.

"I may as well go up one more," he said. "I can't think why people make difficulties of what is so easy."

The sailor called to him as he saw him preparing to ascend still higher, but Will only waved his hand and started up. When he reached the cap of the top-gallant mast he sat upon it and looked down at the harbour. Presently he heard a hail from below, and saw the first lieutenant standing looking up at him.

"All right, sir! I will come down at once," and steadily he descended to the maintop, where the sailor who had spoken to him abused him roundly. Then he went to where the lieutenant was standing.

"How old are you, youngster?"

"I am a little past fifteen, sir."

"Have you ever been up a mast before?"

"Never, sir, except that I have climbed up a fishing-boat's mast many a time, and I am accustomed to clambering about the cliffs. I hope there was no harm in my going so high?"

"No harm as it has turned out. You are a courageous little fellow; I never before saw a lad who went outside the lubbers' hole on his first ascent. Well, I hope, my lad, that you will be as well-behaved as you are active and courageous. I shall keep my eye upon you, and you have my permission henceforth, when you have no other duties, to climb about the masts as you like."

The lieutenant afterwards told the captain of Will's exploit.

"That is the sort of lad to make a good topman," the captain remarked. "He will soon be up to the duties, but will have to wait to get some beef on him before he is of much use in furling a sail."

"I am very glad to have such a lad on board," said the

30

lieutenant. "If we are at any station on the Mediterranean, and have sports between the ships, I should back him against any other boy in the fleet to get to the masthead and down again."

One of the midshipmen, named Forster, came up to Will when he left the lieutenant, and said: "Well done, young un! It was as much as I could do at your age, though I had been two years in the navy, to climb up where you did. If there is anything I can do for you at any time I will gladly do it. I don't say that it is likely, for midshipmen have no power to speak of; still, if there should be anything I would gladly help you."

"There is something, if you would be so very good, sir. I am learning navigation, but there are some things that I can't make out, and it would be a kindness indeed if you would spare a few minutes occasionally to explain them to me."

The midshipman opened his eyes.

"Well, I am blowed," he exclaimed in intense astonishment. "The idea of a newly-joined boy wanting to be helped in navigation beats me altogether. However, lad, I will certainly do as you ask me, though I cannot think that, unless you have been at a nautical school, you can know anything about it. But come to me this evening during the dog-watches, and then I will see what you have learned about the subject."

That evening Will went on deck rather shyly with two or three of his books. The midshipman was standing at a quiet spot on the deck. He glanced at Will enquiringly when he saw what he was carrying.

"Do you mean to say that you understand these books?"

"Not altogether, sir. I think I could work out the latitude and longitude if I knew something about a quadrant, but I have never seen one, and have no idea of its use. But what I wanted to ask you first of all was the meaning of some of these words which I cannot find in the dictionary."

"It seems to me, youngster, that you know pretty well as much as I do, for I cannot do more than fudge an observation. How on earth did you learn all this? I thought you were a fisher-boy before you joined."

"So I was, sir. I was an orphan at the age of five. My father left enough money to buy a boat, and, as one of the fishermen had lately lost his, he adopted me, and I became bound to him as an apprentice till I was fourteen. The clergyman's daughter took a fancy to me from the first, and she used to teach me for half an hour a day, which gave me a great advantage over the other boys in the school. I was very fond of reading, and she supplied me with books. As I said I meant to go to sea, she bought me some books that would help me. So there is nothing extraordinary in my knowing these things; it all came from her kindness to me for ten years."

"Why didn't she try to get you into the mercantile marine?"

"She got married and left the place, sir, but before she went she told me that it was very wrong to have anything to do with smugglers. So I decided to give it up, and that set the whole village against me, and I should probably have been killed if I had not taken refuge in the coast-guard station. There the officer in charge spoke to me of joining the royal navy, and it seemed to me that it would do me good to serve a few years in it; for I could afterwards, if I chose, pass as an officer in the merchant service."

"You are the rummest boy that I ever came across," Forster said. "Well, I must think it over. Now, if there is anything that you specially wish to know, I will explain it to you."

For half an hour they talked together, and the midshipman solved many of the problems that had troubled the lad. Then with many thanks Will went below.

"Is it true, Will," Tom Stevens said, "that you have been right up the mast?"

"Not exactly, Tom, but I went up to the top of the top-gallant mast."

"But why did you do that?"

"I wanted to get accustomed to going up. There was not a bit of difficulty about it, except that it was necessary to keep a steady head. You could do it just as well as I, for we have climbed about the cliffs together scores of times."

"Do you think it will do any good, Will?"

"Yes, I think so. When they see that a fellow is willing and anxious to learn, it is sure to do him good in the long run. It will help him on, and perhaps in two or three years he may get rated as an able seaman, and no longer be regarded as a boy, useful only to do odd jobs. One of the midshipmen is going to give me some help with my navigation. I wish, Tom, you would take it up too, but I am afraid it would be no use. You have got to learn a tremendous lot before you can master it, and what little you were taught at our school would hardly help you at all."

"I know that well enough, Will, and I should never think of such a thing. I always was a fool, and could hardly take in the little that old woman tried to teach us. No, it is of no use trying to make a silk purse out of a sow's ear. I hope that soon I shall be able to hit a good round blow at a Frenchman; that is about all I shall be fit for, though I hope I may some day get to be a smart topman. The next time you climb the mast I will go with you. I don't think there is enough in my head to make it unsteady. At any rate I think that I can promise that I won't do anything to bring discredit upon you."

The feat that Will had performed had a great effect upon the bully of the mess. Before that he had frequently enjoyed boasting of his experience in climbing, and even hinted that he had upon one occasion reached the masthead. Now no more was heard of this, for, as Tom said openly, he was afraid that Will might challenge him to a climbing-match. The next evening the first lieutenant said to the captain: "That other lad who was brought down from Yorkshire has been up the mast with his chum this afternoon. As I told you, sir, I heard that they were great friends, and Stevens did as well as the other."

"But there is a great difference between them. The one is as sharp and as bright as can be; the other is simply a solidly-built fisher-boy who will, I have no doubt, make a good sailor, but is not likely to set the Thames on fire."

"Do you know, sir, Mr. Forster came to me this morning, and told me that on his talking to the boy he astounded him by asking if he would be kind enough to explain a few things in navigation, as he had pretty well mastered all the book-work, but had had no opportunity of learning the use of a quadrant. Forster asked if I had any objection to his giving him lessons. It is the first time that I ever heard of such a request, and to allow it would be contrary to all idea of discipline; still, a lad of that sort deserves encouragement, and I will talk with the padre concerning him. He is one of the most good-natured of men, and I think he would not mind giving a quarter of an hour a day to this boy, after he has dismissed the midshipmen from their studies. Of course he must do the same work as the other boys, and no distinction must be made between them."

"Certainly not. I think the idea is an excellent one, and I have not much doubt that Mr. Simpson will fall in with it."

The first lieutenant went off at once to find the clergyman.

"Well, he must be a strange boy," the chaplain said when the case was laid before him; "I should not be surprised if a fellow like that found his way to the quarter-deck some day. He appears to be a sort of admirable Crichton. Such an amount of learning is extraordinary in a boy of his age and with his opportunities, especially in one active and courageous enough to go up to the cap of the top-gallant mast on his first trial in climbing a mast. Certainly

33

I shall be very glad to take the boy on, and will willingly give him, as you say, a quarter of an hour a day. I feel sure that my time will not be wasted. I never before heard of a ship's boy who wished to be instructed in navigation, and I shall be glad to help such an exceptional lad."

The next day the Furious, having received all her stores, went out to Spithead. The midshipmen had been all fully engaged, and there were no lessons with the padre, but on the following day these were resumed, and presently one of the other boys came down with a message that Will was to go to the padre's cabin.

"I have arranged, lad," the chaplain said when he entered, "to give you a quarter of an hour a day to help you on with your navigation, and I take it that you, on your part, are ready to do the work. It seems to me almost out of the question that you can be advanced enough to enter upon such studies. That, however, I shall soon ascertain. Now open that book and let me see how you would work out the following observation," and he gave him the necessary data.

In five minutes Will handed him the result.

"Of course, sir, to obtain the exact answer I should require to know more than you have given me."

"That is quite right. To-morrow you shall go on deck with me, and I will show you how to use a quadrant and take the altitude of the sun, and from it how to calculate the longitude, which is somewhat more difficult than the latitude. I see you have a good knowledge of figures, and I am quite sure that at the end of a few days' work you will be able to take an observation that will be close enough for all practical purposes."

He then asked Will many questions as to his course of study, the books he had read, and the manner in which he had got up the book-work of navigation.

"But how did you manage about logarithms," he said. "I generally find them great stumbling-blocks in the way of my pupils."

"I don't really understand them now, sir. I can look down the columns and find the number I want, and see how it works out the result, but why it should do so I have not been able to understand. It seems quite different from other operations in figures."

"It is so," the chaplain said, "and let me tell you that not one navigator in fifty really grasps the principle. They 'fudge', as it is termed, the answer, and if they get it right are quite content without troubling themselves in any way with the principle involved. If you want to be a good navigator you must grasp the principle, and work the answer out for yourself. When you can do this you will have a right to call yourself a navigator. If you come to me at twelve o'clock to-morrow I will show you how to work a quadrant. The theory is easy. You have but to take the angle the sun makes with the horizon at its moment of highest ascension. In practice, however, this is far from easy, and you will be some time before you can hit upon the right moment. It requires patience and close observation, but if you have these qualities you will soon pick it up."

The sailors were the next day greatly astonished at seeing the chaplain take his place at the side of the ship and explain to Will the methods of taking an observation.

In the meantime Will was making rapid progress in the good graces of the crew. He was always ready to render assistance in running messages, in hauling on ropes, and generally making himself useful in all respects. His fight with Robert Jones had come off. Will had gained great confidence in himself when he found that he was able to climb the mast in the ordinary way, while Tom Stevens was able only to crawl up through the lubbers' hole. Goaded to madness by the chaff of the other boys, all of whom had ranged themselves under Will's banner, Jones threw down the challenge. Tom Stevens was most anxious that Will should not take it up except on the conditions stated, but Will proclaimed a profound contempt for the bully.

"I will try it myself, Tom. I can hardly fail to lick such a braggart as that. I don't believe he has any muscles to speak of in that big body of his, while I am as hard as nails. No doubt it will be a tough fight if he has a scrap of pluck in him, but I think I will win. Besides, if he does beat me, he will certainly get little credit for it, while I shall have learnt a lot that will be useful to me in the next fight."

Accordingly, at the time appointed the two lads went down to the orlop deck, a good many of the sailors accompanying them. An ordinary fight between boys attracted little attention, but the disparity between the years of the combatants, and the liking entertained for Will, brought most of those who were off duty to witness it. The difference between the antagonists when they stripped was very marked. Robert Jones was fully three stone the heavier and four inches the taller, but he was flabby and altogether out of condition, while Will was as hard as nails, and as active on his feet as a kid.

"It is ten to one against the young un," one of the men said, "but if he holds on for the first five rounds I would back him at evens."

"So would I," another said, "but I doubt whether he can do so; the odds are too great against him."

"I will take four to one," another said. "Look at the young un's muscles down his back. You won't often see anything better among lads two years older than he is."

The fight began with a tremendous rush on the part of Jones. Will stood his ground doggedly, and struck his opponent fairly between the eyes, making him shake his head like an exasperated bull. Time after time Jones repeated the manœuvre, but only once or twice landed a blow, while he never escaped without a hard return. At length he began to feel the effects of his own efforts, and stood on the defensive, panting for breath. Now it was Will's turn. He danced round and round his opponent with the activity of a goat, dodging in and delivering a heavy body-blow and then leaping out again before his opponent could get any return. The cheers of the sailors rose louder and louder, and Will heard them shouting: "Go in; finish him, lad!" But Will was too prudent to risk anything; he knew that the battle was in his hands unless he threw it away, and that Jones was well-nigh pumped out. At last, after dealing a heavy blow, he saw his antagonist stagger back, and in an instant sprang forward and struck him between the eyes with far greater force than he had before exerted. Jones fell like a log, and was altogether unable to come up to time. A burst of cheering rose from the crowd, and many and hearty were the congratulations Will received.

"What was going on this afternoon, Mr. Farrance?" asked the captain; "I heard a lot of cheering."

"I made enquiry about it, sir, and the boatswain told me that it was only a fight between two of the boys. Of course he had not been present."

"Ah! It is not often that a boys' fight excites such interest. Who were they?"

"They were Jones, the biggest of the boys, and by no means a satisfactory character, and young Gilmore."

"Why, Jones is big enough to eat him."

"Yes, sir, at any rate he ought to have been. He was a great bully when he first came on board, but the other tackled him as soon as they were together, and it seems he has to-day given him as handsome a thrashing as could be wished for, and that without being seriously hurt himself. He has certainly established his supremacy among the boys of this ship."

"That boy is out of the common," the captain said. "A ship's boy newly joined taking up navigation, going about the masts like a monkey, and finally thrashing a fellow two years his senior must be considered as altogether exceptional. I shall certainly keep my eye upon him, and give him every opportunity I can for making his way."

Will received his honours quietly.

"There is nothing," he said, "in fighting a fellow who is altogether out of condition, and has a very small amount of pluck to make up for it. I was convinced when we first met that he had nothing behind his brag, though I certainly did not expect to beat him as easily as I did. Well, I hope we shall be good friends in future. I have no enmity against him, and there is no reason why we should not get on well together after this."

"I don't know," said the sailor to whom he was speaking; "a decent fellow will make it up and think no more about it, but if I am not mistaken, Robert Jones will do you a bad turn if he gets the chance."

No one was more delighted at the result than Tom Stevens, who had cheered loudly and enthusiastically. Dimchurch was also exuberant at Will's success.

"I knew that you were a good un, but I never thought you could have tackled that fellow. I don't know what to make of you; as a general thing, as far as I have seen, a fellow who takes to books is no good for anything else, but everything seems to agree with you. If I am not mistaken, you will be on the quarter-deck before many years have passed."

They were now running down channel, and the boys were astonished at the ease and smoothness with which the ship breasted the waves, and at the mass of snowy canvas that towered above her. As they sat one day at the bow watching the sheets of spray rise as the ship cut her way through the water, Tom said to his friend: "You are going up above me quick, Will. Anyone can see that. You are thought a lot of. I knew it would be so, and I said I should not grudge it you; in fact, the greater your success the better I shall be pleased. But I did not think that your learning would have made such a difference already. The first lieutenant often says a word to you as he passes, and the padre generally speaks to you when he goes along the deck. It is wonderful what a difference learning makes; not, mind you, that I should ever have gone in for it, even had I known how useful it is. I could never have taken it in, and I am sure the old woman could never have taught me. I suppose some

37

fellows are born clever and others grow to it. And some never are clever at all. That was my way, I suppose. I just learned to spell words of two letters, which, of course, was of no use. A fellow can't do much with ba, be, by, and bo, and these are about all the words I remember. I used to think, when we first became chums, how foolish you were to be always reading and studying. Now I see what a pull you have got by it. I expect it is partly because your father was a clever man, and, as most of the people thought, a gentleman, that you came to take to it. Well, if I had my time over again I would really try to learn something. I should never make much of it, but still, I suppose I should have got to read decently."

"Certainly you would, Tom; and when you once had got to read, so as to be able to enjoy it, you would have gone through all sorts of books and got lots of information from them. I am afraid, however, it is too late to worry over that. A man may be a good man and a good sailor without knowing how to read and write. I am sure you will do your share when it comes to that."

"I wonder when we shall fall in with a Frenchman?"

"There is no saying. You may be sure that every man on board is longing to do so. I hope she will be a bit bigger than we are, and I know the captain hopes so too. He is for ever watching every ship that comes in sight."

When running down the coast of Spain one day the look-out at the masthead shouted: "A sail!"

"What is she like?" the first lieutenant hailed.

"I can only see her top-gallant sails, sir, but she is certainly a square-rigged ship bound south, and her sails have a foreign cut."

The first lieutenant swung his telescope over his shoulder and mounted the rigging. When he came to the top-gallant crosstrees he sat down and gazed into the distance through his glass.

After making a careful examination of the ship he called to the captain, who was now on deck:

"She is, as Johnson says, sir, a square-rigged ship, and I agree with him as to the cut of her sails. She is certainly a Frenchman, and evidently a large frigate. She is running down the coast as we are, and I expect hopes to get through the Straits at night."

"Well, edge in towards her," the captain said. "Lower the top-gallant sails. If she hasn't already made us out, I shall be able to work in a good deal closer to her before she does so."

All hands were now on the qui vive, but it was not for some time that the stranger could be made out from the deck.

"You can get up our top-gallant sails again," the captain said.

"She must have made us out by this time, and she certainly has gained upon us since we first saw her. There is no longer any possibility of concealment, so hoist royals as well as top-gallant sails."

The stranger made no addition to her sails. By this time those on board the Furious were able to judge of her size, and came to the conclusion that she was a battle-ship of small size, and ought to be more than a match for the Furious. The vessels gradually approached each other, until at last a shot was thrown across the bows of the Frenchman. She made no reply, but continued on her way as if unconscious of the presence of the English frigate. The crew of the Furious could now make out that she had fifty guns, whereas their own ship had thirty-four.

"Just comfortable odds," the captain said quietly when this was reported to him. "I have no doubt she carries heavier metal as well as more guns. Altogether she would be a satisfactory prize to send into Portsmouth."

The men had not waited for orders, but had mustered to quarters on their own account. The guns were run in and loaded, and the boarding-pikes got ready. In five minutes orders were given to fire another shot. There was a cheer as white splinters were seen to fly from the Frenchman's side. Her helm was put up at once, and she swept round and fired a broadside into the Furious. Four or five shots took effect, some stays and ropes were cut, and two shot swept across her deck, killing three of the sailors and knocking down several of the others.

"Aim steadily, lads," the captain shouted; "don't throw away a shot. It is our turn now. All aim at her centre ports. Fire!"

The ship swayed from the recoil of the guns, and then she swung half-round and a broadside was poured into the Frenchman from the other side.

After this Will and Tom knew little more of what was going on, for they were kept busy running to and from the magazine with fresh cartridges. They were not tall enough to see over the bulwarks, and were only able to peep out occasionally from one of the port-holes. They presently heard from the shouts and exclamations of the men that everything was going well, and on looking out they saw that the enemy's foremast had been shot away, and in consequence she was unmanageable. The crew of the Furious had suffered heavily, but her main spars were intact, and the captain, manœuvring with great skill, was able to sail backwards and forwards across the enemy's stern and rake him repeatedly fore and aft.

So the fight continued until at last the captain gave the order to lay the ship alongside the Frenchman and board. There was no more work for the powder-monkeys now, so Will and Tom seized boarding-pikes and joined in the rush on to the enemy's deck. The resistance, however, was short-lived; the enemy had suffered terribly from the raking fire of the Furious, and as the captain and many of the officers had fallen, the senior survivor soon ordered the flag to be lowered. A tremendous cheer broke from the British. They now learned that the ship they had captured was the Proserpine, which was on her way to enter the Mediterranean and effect a junction with the French fleet at Toulon.

The next day the crew worked hard to get up a jury foremast. When this was done a prize crew was put on board. The French prisoners were confined below, as they far outnumbered their captors. Then, having repaired her own damages, the Furious proceeded on her way.

On arriving at Gibraltar the captain received orders to proceed to Malta, and to place himself under the order of the admiral there. For a time matters proceeded quietly, for the winds were light and baffling, and it took a fortnight to get to their destination. Here the ship was thoroughly examined, and the damage she had suffered more satisfactorily repaired than had been possible while she was at sea.

When the overhauling was completed she received orders to cruise off the coast of Africa. This was by no means pleasing to the crew, who considered that they had small chance of falling in with anything of their own size on that station. They were told, however, that there had been serious complaints of piracy on the part of the Moors, and that they were specially to direct their attention to punishing the perpetrators of such acts.

One morning three strange craft were sighted lying close together. Unfortunately, however, it was a dead calm.

"They are Moors, certainly," the captain said to the first lieutenant after examining them with his glass. "What would I not give for a breath of wind now? But they are not going to escape us. Get all the boats hoisted out, and take command of the expedition yourself."

Immediately all was bustle on board the ship, and in a very short time every boat was lowered into the water. Will was looking on with longing eyes as the men took their places. The lieutenant noticed him.

"Clamber down into the bow of my boat," he said; "you deserve it."

In the highest state of delight Will seized a spare cutlass and made his way into the bow of the boat amid the jokes of the men. These, however, were stilled the moment the first lieutenant took his place in the stern.

The Moors had not been idle. As soon as they saw that the boats had been lowered they got out their sweeps and began to row at a pace which the lieutenant saw would tax the efforts of his oarsmen to the utmost. The Moors had fully three miles start, and, although the men bent to their oars with the best will, they gained very slowly. The officers in the various boats encouraged them with their shouts, and the men pulled nobly. Five miles had been passed and but one mile gained. It was evident, however, that the efforts of the Moorish rowers were flagging, while the sailors were rowing almost as strongly as when they started. Three more miles and another mile had been gained. Then from the three vessels came a confused fire of cannon of all sizes.

Several men were hit, boats splintered, and oars smashed. The first lieutenant shouted orders for the boats to open out so that the enemy would no longer have a compact mass to aim at. At last, after another mile, the Moors evidently came to the conclusion that they could not escape by rowing, and at once drew in their oars, lowered their sails, and all formed in line. As soon as this manœuvre was completed heavy firing began again. Will, lying in the bow, looked out ahead, and, seeing the sea torn up with balls, wondered that any of the boats should escape unharmed.

The lieutenant shouted to the boats to divide into two parties, one, led by himself, to attack the vessel on the left of the line, and the other, under the second lieutenant, to deal with the ship on the right, for the middle boat would assuredly be captured if the other two were taken.

"Row quietly, men," he shouted; "you will want your breath if it comes to fighting. Keep on at a steady pace until within two hundred yards of them, and then make a dash."

This order was carried out by both parties, and when within the given distance the men gave a cheer, and, bending their backs to the oars, sent the boats tearing through the water. The pirate craft were all crowded with men, who raised yells of rage and defiance. However, except that one boat was sunk by a shot that struck her full in the bow, Lieutenant Farrance's party reached their vessel.

The first to try to climb on board were all cut down or thrown backwards, but at length the men gained a footing on the deck, and, led by Mr. Farrance, fell upon the enemy with great spirit. Will was

41

the last to climb up out of his boat, but he soon pushed his way forward until he was close behind the lieutenant. Several times the boarders were pushed back, but as often they rallied, and won their way along the deck again.

During one of these rushes Lieutenant Farrance's foot slipped in a pool of blood, and he fell to the deck. Two Moors sprang at him, but Will leapt forward, whirling his cutlass, and by luck rather than skill cut down one of them. The other attacked him and dealt him a severe blow on the arm, but before he could repeat it the lieutenant had regained his feet, and, springing forward, had run the Moor through the body.

Another five minutes' fighting and all resistance was at an end. Some of the Moors rushed below, others jumped overboard and swam to their consort. As soon as resistance had ceased the lieutenant ordered the majority of the men to return to the boats, and, leaving a sufficient number to hold the captured vessel, proceeded to the attack of the middle craft.

The fight here was even more stubborn than before, for the men that fled from the ships that had already been taken had strongly reinforced the crew of this one. The British, however, were not to be denied. The boats of one division attacked on one side, those of the second on the other, and, after nearly a quarter of an hour's hard fighting, brought the enemy to their knees.

The pirates were all now battened down, the wounded seamen cared for by the doctor who had accompanied the expedition, and the bodies of the dead Moors thrown overboard. When this was done the successful expedition prepared to return to the Furious. They had lost twenty-eight killed, and nearly forty wounded.

"The loss has been very heavy," the first lieutenant said when the return was given to him; "and to do the fellows justice they fought desperately. Well, now we have to get back to the ship, which is a good ten miles away. She is still becalmed, and so are we, and unless the wind springs up we shall hardly reach her before nightfall. I don't like to ask the men for more exertions after a ten miles row at such a ripping pace; still, it must be done. Let two boats take each of the pirates in tow; they shall be relieved every hour."

The sailors, who were in high glee at their success, took their places in the boats cheerfully, but when night fell they were still more than four miles away from the frigate.

CHAPTER IV

PROMOTED

The lieutenant took a boat when it became dusk and rowed to the frigate, where he handed in his report of the fight.

"I will read that later, Mr. Farrance," the captain said. "Meanwhile, tell me briefly what is the result? Of course I saw you returning with the three vessels in tow."

"We had a very sharp fight, sir, and I am sorry to say that the casualties are heavy, twenty-eight killed and nearly forty wounded more or less severely."

"That is a heavy list indeed, Mr. Farrance, very heavy, and we are the less able to bear it since we have some seventy men away on the French prize. The rascals must have fought desperately."

"They did, sir. I am bound to say that men could hardly have fought better. We had very hard work with the two outside ships, and as most of the fellows jumped overboard and swam to the other, we had an even stiffer fight there. In fact, if we had had only one of our division of boats available I am sure we should not have carried her."

"What are the casualties among the officers?"

"Midshipman Howard is killed, sir, and Lieutenant Ayling and Midshipman James very severely wounded. I myself had a very narrow escape. I slipped upon some blood, and two Moors rushed at me and would have killed me had not that boy Gilmore thrown himself between us. He waved his cutlass about wildly, and, principally from good luck, I think, cut down one of them. On this the other attacked him, and I had time to get to my feet again. As soon as I was up I ran the Moor through, but not before he had given the boy a very ugly wound on the arm."

"That is a wonderful boy," the captain said with a smile. "I think he is too good to remain where he is, and I must put him on the quarter-deck."

"I should feel greatly obliged if you would, sir, for there is no doubt that he saved my life. He is certainly as well up in his work as any of the midshipmen. The chaplain told me only yesterday that he had learnt to use the quadrant, and can take an observation quite as accurately as most of his pupils."

"Such a boy as that," said the captain, "ought to be given a chance of rising in his profession. He is quite at home aloft, and may be fairly called a sailor. He is certainly a favourite with the whole crew, and I think, if promoted, will give every satisfaction. Very well, Farrance, we may consider that as settled."

"Thank you very much, sir! I need hardly say that it will be a pleasure to me to fit him out."

The next morning there was a light breeze, and the three prizes, which had remained four miles from the frigate through the night, closed up to her. The wounded were transhipped, and a prize crew was told off to each of the captures, a considerable portion of the Moors being also transferred to the frigate and sent down into the hold.

In the afternoon Will, to his surprise, received word that the captain wished to speak to him. His jacket had been cut off and his injured arm was in a sling, so he could only throw the garment over his shoulders before he hurried aft. When he reached the poop he found that the crew were mustered, and in much trepidation as to his appearance, and with a great feeling of wonder as to why he had been sent for, he made his way to where the captain was standing surrounded by a group of officers.

"Men," the captain said in a loud clear voice, "I am going to take a somewhat unusual step, and raise one of your comrades to the quarter-deck. Still more unusual is it that such an honour should fall to a ship's boy. In this case, however, I am sure you will all agree with me that the boy in question has distinguished himself not only by his activity and keenness aloft, but by the fact that he has, under great difficulties, educated himself, and in manner and education is perfectly fit to be a messmate of the midshipmen of this vessel. Moreover, in the fight yesterday he saved the life of Lieutenant Farrance when he had fallen and was attacked by two of the Moors. One of these the lad killed, and the other he engaged. This gave Lieutenant Farrance time to recover his feet, and he quickly disposed of the second Moor, not, however, before the rascal had inflicted a severe wound on the lad. Mr. William Gilmore, I have real pleasure in nominating you a midshipman on board His Majesty's ship Furious, and inviting you to join us on the quarter-deck."

The cheer that broke from the men showed that they heartily approved of the honour that had fallen upon their young comrade. As to Will himself, he was so surprised and overcome by this most unexpected distinction that he could scarcely speak. The captain

44

stepped forward and shook him by the hand, an example followed by the other officers and midshipmen.

"You had better retire," the captain said, seeing that the lad was quite unable to speak, "and when you have recovered from your wound the ship's tailor will take your uniform in hand. Lieutenant Farrance has kindly expressed his intention of providing you with it."

Will, with the greatest difficulty, restrained his feelings till he reached the sick berth, and then he threw himself into a hammock and burst into tears. Presently Tom Stevens came in to see him.

"I am glad, Will," he said, "more glad than I can possibly express. It is splendid to think that you are really an officer."

"It is too much altogether, Tom. I had hoped that some day I might come to be a mate, or even a captain in a merchant ship, but to think that in less than two months after joining I could be on the quarter-deck was beyond my wildest dreams. Well I hope I sha'n't get puffed up, and I am sure, Tom, that I shall be as much your friend as ever."

"I don't doubt that, Will; you would not be yourself if it made any difference in you. Dimchurch asked me to tell you how much he too was pleased, but that he was not surprised at all, for he felt sure that in less than a year you would be on the quarter-deck, as it would be ridiculous that anyone who could take an observation and be at the same time one of the smartest hands aloft should remain in the position of ship's boy. One of the elder sailors said that in all his experience he had never known but three or four cases of men being promoted from the deck except when old warrant officers were made mates and appointed to revenue cutters."

"Thank Dimchurch very heartily for me, Tom, and tell him that I hope we shall sail many years together, although it may be in different parts of the ship. Now I will lie quiet for a time, for my arm is throbbing dreadfully. The doctor tells me that although the wound is severe it can hardly be called serious, for with so good a constitution as I have it will heal quickly, and in a month I shall be able to use it as well as before."

The agitation and excitement, however, acted injuriously, and the next day Will was in a state of high fever, which did not abate for some days, and left him extremely weak.

"You have had a sharp bout of it, lad," the doctor said, "but you are safe now, and you will soon pick up strength again. It has had one good effect; it has kept you from fidgeting over your wound, and I have no doubt that, now the fever has left you, you will go on nicely."

In another three weeks Will was able to leave the sick bay, and on the morning he was discharged from the sick list he found by his hammock two suits of midshipman's uniform, a full dress and a working suit, together with a pile of shirts and underclothing of all kinds, and two or three pairs of shoes. His other clothes had been taken away, so he dressed himself in the working suit, and with some little trepidation made his way to his new quarters. The midshipmen were just sitting down to breakfast, and, rising, they all shook hands with him and congratulated him heartily both on his promotion and his recovery.

"You are very good to welcome me so heartily," he said. "I know that neither by birth nor station am I your equal."

"You are quite our equal, youngster," said one of the midshipmen, "whatever you may be by birth. Not one of us could have worked half so well as you have done; the chaplain tells us that you can take an observation as well as he can. I can assure you we are all heartily glad to have you with us. Sit down and make yourself at home. We have not much to offer you besides our rations; for we have been out for over a month, and our soft tack and all other luxuries were finished long ago, so we are reduced to ham and biscuit."

"It could not be better," Will said with a smile, "for I have got such an appetite that I could eat horse with satisfaction. I feel immensely indebted to you, Mr. Forster; for if you had not brought my request before the first lieutenant I should not have been able to make such progress with my books as I have done."

"The chaplain is a first-rate fellow—but, by the way, we have no misters here; we all call each other by our surname plain and simple. Even Peters, who has welcomed you in our name and who is a full-fledged master's mate, does not claim to be addressed as mister, though he will probably do so before long, for the wound of Lieutenant Ayling, who, it is settled, will be invalided when we get to Malta, will give him his step. On that occasion we will solemnly drink his health, at his own expense of course."

"That is not the ordinary way," the mate laughed. "I know that you fellows will be game to shell out a bottle apiece—I don't think I can do it—not at least until I get three months of my new rate of pay."

So they laughed and chaffed, and Will felt grateful to them, for he saw that it was in no small degree due to the desire to set him at his ease.

"You will be in the starboard watch, Gilmore," the mate said when the meal was finished. "That was the one Ayling had. The third lieutenant, Bowden, who is now in charge, isn't half a bad fellow. Of course he is a little cocky—third lieutenants on their first commission generally are, but he is kind-hearted and likes to makes himself popular, and he will wink one eye when you take a nap under a gun, which is no mean virtue. The boatswain, who is in the same watch, is a much more formidable person, and busies himself quite unnecessarily. One cannot, however, have everything, and on the whole you will get on very comfortably. I am in the other watch, Rodwell and Forster are with you. They are well-meaning lads; I don't know that I can say anything more for them, but you will find out their faults soon enough yourself."

Will then went up on deck with the others. It seemed strange to him to enter upon what he had hitherto regarded as a sort of sacred ground, and he stood shyly aside while the others fell into their duties of looking after the men and seeing that the work was being done. Presently the first lieutenant came on deck. Will went up to him and touched his hat.

"I cannot tell you, sir," he said, "how indebted I feel to you for your kindness in speaking for me to the captain, and especially in providing me with an outfit. I can assure you, sir, that as long as I live I shall remember your kindness."

"My lad, these things weigh but little against the saving of my life, and I can assure you that it was a great satisfaction to me to be able to make this slight return. I shall watch your career with the greatest interest, for I am convinced that it will be a brilliant one."

Owing to the fact that two officers had gone away in their first prize, and that three had been killed or disabled in the late fight, there was a shortage of officers on the Furious. Three had left in the Moorish prizes, and when, a week later, another Moorish vessel was captured without much fighting, the captain had no officers to spare above the rank of midshipmen.

"Mr. Forster," he said, "I have selected you to go in the prize. You can take one of the juniors with you; I cannot spare either of the seniors. Who would you like to take?"

"I would rather have Gilmore, sir. I feel that I can trust him thoroughly."

"I think you have made a good choice. I cannot spare you more than thirty men. You will go straight to Malta, hand over your prize to the agent there, and either wait till we return, or come back again if there should be any means of doing so."

Will was delighted when he heard that he was to go with Forster. "Will you pick the crew?" he asked his friend.

47

"No, but I could arrange without difficulty for anyone you specially wished."

"I should like very much to have my friend Tom Stevens and the sailor named Dimchurch; they are both good hands in their way, and were very friendly with me before I got promoted."

"All right! there will no difficulty about that; we shall want a boy to act as our servant, and one able seaman is as good as another. I have noticed Dimchurch; he is a fine active hand, and I will appoint him boatswain."

Great was the pride of Will as the prize crew rowed from the Furious to the Moorish galley of which he was to be second in command, but he could not help bursting out laughing as he went down with Forster into the cabin.

"What are you laughing at?" Forster asked.

"I was having a bit of a laugh at the thought of the change that has come over my position. Not that I am conceited about it, but it all seems so strange that I should be here and second in command."

"No doubt it does," laughed Forster, "but you will soon get accustomed to it. It is almost as strange for me, for it is the first time that I have been in command. I have brought a chart on board with me. Our course is north-north-east, and the distance is between two and three hundred miles. In any decent part of the world we should do it in a couple of days, but with these baffling winds we may take a week or more. Well, I don't much care how long we are; it will be a luxury to be one's own master for a bit."

The first step was to divide the crew into two watches.

"I am entitled not to keep a watch," Forster said, "but I shall certainly waive the privilege. We will take a watch each."

Tom Stevens was appointed cabin servant, and one of the men was made cook; nine of the others were told off to each watch.

"I wish she hadn't all those prisoners on board," Forster said. "They will be a constant source of anxiety. There are over fifty of them, and as hang-dog scoundrels as one would wish to see. We shall have to keep a sharp look-out on them, to make sure that they don't get a ghost of a chance of coming up on deck, for if they did they would not think twice about cutting our throats."

"I don't see how they could possibly get out," Will said.

"No; it generally does look like that, but they manage it sometimes for all that. These fellows know that when they get to Malta they will be set to work in the yards, and if there was an opportunity, however small, for them to break out, you may be sure that they would take it. These Moorish pirates are about as ruffianly

48

scoundrels as are to be found, and if they don't put their prisoners to death they only spare them for what they will fetch as slaves."

After three days' sailing they had made but little way, for it was only in the morning and the evening that there was any breeze. Will had just turned in for the middle watch, and had scarcely dropped to sleep, when he was suddenly awakened by a loud noise. He sprang out of bed, seized his dirk and a brace of pistols which were part of the equipment given him by the first lieutenant. As he ran up the companion he heard a coil of rope thrown against the door, so he leapt down again and ran with all speed to the men's quarters. They, too, were all on their feet, but the hatch had been battened down above them.

"This is a bad job, sir," Dimchurch said. "How they have got out I have no idea. I looked at the fastenings of the two hatches when I came down twenty minutes ago, and they looked to me all right. I am afraid they will cut all our comrades' throats."

"I fear so, Dimchurch. What do you think we had better do?"

"I don't know, sir; it will require a good deal of thinking out. I don't suppose they will meddle with us at present, but of course they will sooner or later."

"Well, Dimchurch, as a first step we will bring all the mess tables and other portable things forward here, and make a barricade with them. We will also obtain two or three barrels of water and a stock of food, so that when the time comes we may at any rate be able to make a stout resistance."

"That is a good idea, sir. We will set to work at once."

In a short time, with the aid of tubs of provisions, barrels of water, and bales of goods, a barricade was built across the bow of the vessel, forming a triangular enclosure of about fourteen feet on each side. The arms were then collected and placed inside, and when this was done there was a general feeling of satisfaction that they could at least sell their lives dearly.

"Now, sir, what is the next step?" Dimchurch asked. "You have only to give your orders and we are ready to carry them out."

"I have thought of nothing at present," Will said. "I fancy it will be better to allow them to make the first move, for even with the advantage of attacking them in the dark we could hardly hope to overcome four times our number."

"It would be a tough job certainly, sir; but if the worst comes to the worst, we might try it."

"It must come to quite the worst, Dimchurch, before we take such a step as that."

As evening approached, the Moors were heard descending the companion. There was a buzz of talk, and then they came rushing forward. When they reached the door between the fore and aft portions of the ship Will and his men opened fire upon them, and as they poured out they were shot down. Seven or eight fell, and then the others dashed forward. The seamen lined the barricade and made a strenuous resistance. Cutlass clashed against Moorish yatagan; the Moors were too crowded together to use their guns, and as they could gather no more closely in front than the sailors stood, they were unable to break through the barricade. At last, after many had fallen, the rest retired. Three or four of the sailors had received more or less severe wounds, but none were absolutely disabled. Tom Stevens had fought pluckily among the rest, and Will was ready with his shouts of encouragement, and a cutlass he had taken for use instead of his dirk, wherever the pressure was most severe.

When the Moors had retired, Dimchurch and two others went outside the barricade and piled some heavy bales against the door, after first carrying out the dead Moors.

"They will hardly attack us that way again, sir," he said to Will; "it will be our turn next time."

"Yes, six of their number are killed, and probably several badly wounded, so we ought to have a good chance of success if we make a dash at them in the dark."

They waited until night had fallen. Then Will said:

"Do you think you can lift that hatchway, Dimchurch?"

"I will have a pretty hard try anyhow," the man said. "I will roll this tub under it; that will give me a chance of using my strength."

Although he was able to move it slightly, his utmost efforts failed to lift it more than an inch or two.

"They have piled too many ropes on it for me, sir; but I think that if some others will get on tubs and join me we shall be able to move the thing."

"Wait a minute, Dimchurch. Let each man make sure that his musket is loaded."

There was a short pause, during which all firelocks were carefully examined. When he saw that all were in good order, Will said:

"Now, lads, heave away."

Slowly the hatchway yielded, and with a great effort it was pushed up far enough for a man to crawl out. Pieces of wood were shoved in at each corner so as to hold the hatch open, and the men who had lifted it stood clear.

"Clamber out, Dimchurch, and have a look round. Are there many of them on deck?"

"Only about a dozen, as far as I can make out, sir. They are jabbering away among themselves disputing, I should say, as to the best way to get at us."

"I expect they intend to leave us alone and take us into Algiers. However, that does not matter. You two crawl out and lie down, then give me a hand and hoist me out. I think the others can all reach, except Tom; you had better hoist him up after me."

Each man, as he clambered out, lay down on the deck. When all were up, they crawled along aft to within a few yards of the Moors, then leapt to their feet and fired a volley. Five of the Moors fell, while the others, panic-stricken, ran below.

"Now, pile cables over the hatchway," Will shouted.

The sailors rushed to carry out the order. They were startled as they did so by a shout from above.

"Hillo, below there! Have you got possession of the ship?"

"Yes. Is that you, Forster?"

"Yes."

"Thank God for that!" Will shouted back, while the men gave a cheer. "Why don't you come down?"

"I am going to slide down the mast."

"What for? Why don't you come down by the rattlings?"

"I have cut the shrouds. When our last man fell I made a dash for them, and directly I got to the top I cut them, and half a dozen men who were climbing after me fell sprawling to the deck. Then I cut them on the other side. I thought then that they would at once shoot me, but there was a lively argument among them and shouts of laughter, and they evidently thought that it would be a great joke to leave me up here until I chose to slide down and be killed. Of course I heard their attack on you, and trembled for the result; but when the noise suddenly ceased I guessed that you had repulsed them. Well, here goes!" and half a minute later he slid down to the deck. "How do matters stand?" he asked, when he stood among them.

"We killed six and wounded eight or ten in the first attack upon us, and we have shot five more now. All the rest are battened down below."

"There they had better remain for the present. Well, Gilmore, I congratulate you on having recaptured the ship. It has been a bad

51

affair, for we have lost nine men killed; but as far as you are concerned you have done splendidly. I am afraid I shall get a pretty bad wigging for allowing them to get out, though certainly the bolts of the hatchways were all right when we changed the watch. Of course I see now that I ought to have placed a man there as sentry. It is always so mighty easy to be wise after the event. I expect the rascals pretty nearly cut the wood away round the bolts, and after the watch was changed set to work and completed the job. We shall not, however, be able to investigate that until we get to Malta."

"We have blocked up the door between the fore and the after parts of the ship," said Will; "but I think it would be as well to place a sentry at each hatch now, as they might turn the tables upon us again."

"Certainly. Are you badly wounded, Dimchurch?"

"I have got a slash across the cheek, sir, but nothing to speak of."

"Well, will you take post at the after-hatch for the present. Stevens, you may as well go down and guard the door. You will be able to tell us, at least, if they are up to any mischief. I should think, however, the fight is pretty well taken out of them, and that they will resign themselves to their fate now."

"This is a bad job for me," Forster said, as he and Will sat down together on a gun.

"I am awfully sorry, Forster, but I am afraid there is no getting out of it."

"No, that is out of the question."

"There is one thing, Forster. If you did not put a sentry over the hatchway, neither did I, so I am just as much to blame for the disaster as you are. If I had had a man there they could hardly have cut away the woodwork without his hearing. I certainly wish you to state in your report that you took the watch over from me just as I left it, and that no sentry had been placed there, as ought certainly to have been done when I came on watch at eight o'clock."

"It is very kind of you, Gilmore, to wish to take the blame upon your own shoulders, but the responsibility is wholly mine. I ought to have reminded you to put a man there, there can be no question at all about that, but I never gave the matter a thought, and the blunder has cost us nine good seamen. I shall be lucky if I only escape with a tremendous wigging. I must bear it as well as I can."

While they were talking the sailors were busy splicing the shrouds. When this was done two of the men swarmed up the mast by means of the halliards. Then they hoisted up the shrouds, and fastened them round the mast, making all taut by means of the lanyards. The sails were still standing, flapping loosely in the light breeze, so the sheets were hauled in and the vessel again began to move through the water. Two days later they anchored in Valetta harbour.

"Here goes," Forster said, as he stepped into the boat with his report. "It all depends now on what sort of a man the admiral is, but I should not be surprised if he ordered me to take court-martial."

"Oh, I hope not!" Will exclaimed. "I do wish you would let me go with you to share the blame."

"It cannot be thought of," Forster said; "the commanding officer must make the report."

Two hours later Forster returned.

"It is all right, Gilmore," he said as the boat came alongside. "Of course I got a wigging. The admiral read the report and then looked at me as fierce as a tiger.

" 'How was it that no sentry was placed over the prisoners?'

" 'I have to admit, sir,' I said, 'that I entirely overlooked that. I am quite conscious that my conduct was indefensible, but I have certainly paid very heavily for it.'

" 'It was a smart trick taking to the shrouds,' the admiral said, 'though one would have thought they would have shot you at once after you had cut them.'

" 'That is what I expected, sir,' said I, 'but they seemed to think it was a very good joke, my being a prisoner up there, and preferred to wait till I was driven down by thirst.'

" 'I suppose your men sold their lives dearly?' he asked.

" 'Yes, sir,' I replied. 'Taken by surprise as they were they certainly accounted for more than one man each.'

" 'And doubtless you did the same, Mr. Forster?'

" 'Yes, sir, I cut down two of them, and I did not cease fighting until I saw that all was lost.'

" 'Then I suppose you thought that your duty to His Majesty was to take care of yourself,' he said slyly.

" 'I am afraid, sir,' I said, 'at that moment I thought more of my duty towards myself than of my duty to him.'

"He smiled grimly.

" 'I have no doubt that was so, Mr. Forster. Well, you committed a blunder, and I hope it will be a lesson to you in future.'

" 'It will indeed, sir,' I said.

"Then he started to question me about you.

" 'Your junior officer seems to have behaved very well,' he said.

53

" 'Extremely well, sir,' I said. 'I only wish I had done as well.'

" 'His plan of forming a barricade across the bow so that his little force were ample to defend it was excellent,' he said. 'Also the blocking up of the door of communication through the bulkhead was well thought of, and his final escape through the hatchway and sudden attack upon the enemy was well carried out. I will make a note of his name. I suppose he is not as old as yourself, as he is your junior?'

" 'No, sir, he is not yet sixteen, and he was only promoted from being a ship's boy to the quarter-deck three weeks ago.'

" 'Promoted from being a ship's boy?' the admiral said in surprise.

"Then I had to give a detailed account, not only of the fight that led to your promotion, but also of your life so far as I knew it.

"When I had finished, the admiral said:

" 'He must be a singular lad, this Gilmore, and is likely to prove an honour to the navy. Bring him up here at this hour to-morrow; I shall be glad to see him. There, now, you may go, and don't forget in future that when you are in charge of prisoners you must always place a guard over them.'

"So unknowingly you have done me a good turn, Gilmore, for I expect that if the admiral had not been so interested in you he would not have let me off so easily. You must put on your best uniform for the first time and go up to-morrow."

"Well, I am afraid I should have felt very shaky if I had not heard your account of the admiral. From what you say it is evident he is a kindly man, and after all you have told him about me he can't have many questions to ask."

"Well, I feel a good deal easier in my mind, as you may guess," Forster said. "When I went ashore I felt like a bad boy who is in for a flogging. I dare say I shall get it a little hotter from the captain, but it will be just a wigging, and there will be no talk of courts-martial. By what we saw of the goods on board this craft before this rumpus took place I fancy the Moor had captured and plundered a well-laden merchantman. In that case the prize-money will be worth a good round sum, and as the admiral gets a picking out of it he will be still more inclined to look favourably on the matter. Here comes the boat to take off the prisoners. I have no doubt some of them will be hanged, especially as they will not be able to give any satisfactory explanation as to the fate of the merchantman. As soon as we have got rid of them we will overhaul a few of the bales and see what are their contents."

54

When the last of the prisoners were taken ashore Forster and Gilmore went below and examined the cargo. This proved to consist of valuable Eastern stuffs, broad-cloths, silks, and Turkish carpets.

"It could not be better," Forster said; "she must be worth a lot of money, and it will add to the nice little handful of prize-money we shall get when we return home. They ought to give us a good round sum for the Proserpine; then there were the three Moorish vessels, though I don't think they were worth much, for their holds were nearly empty and I fancy they had only been cruising a short time. This fellow, however, is a rich prize; he certainly had very hard luck, falling in with us as he did. I fancy the ship they pillaged was a Frenchman or Italian, more likely the latter. I don't think there are many French merchantmen about, and it is most likely that the cargo was intended for Genoa, whence a good part of it might be sent to Paris. Well, it makes little difference to us what its destination was, its proceeds are certainly destined to enrich us instead of its original consignees."

The next morning Will put on his best uniform for the first time, and, landing with Forster, ascended the Nix Mangare stairs and called on the admiral.

"Well, Mr. Gilmore," the admiral said as he was shown in, "it gives me great pleasure to meet so promising a young officer. Will you kindly tell me such details of your early history as may seem fitting to you."

Will gave him a fairly detailed account of his history up to the time he joined the navy.

"Well, sir, you cannot be too grateful to that young lady, but at the same time there are few who would have availed themselves so well of her assistance. It is nothing short of astonishing that you should have progressed so far under her care that you were able, after a few lessons from the chaplain of your ship, to use a quadrant. As a mark of my approbation I will present you with one. I will send it off to your ship to-morrow morning."

With many thanks Will took his leave, and returned with Forster to the prize.

On the following morning the quadrant arrived. That afternoon the prize was handed over to the prize-agents, and the crew transferred to the naval barracks, Forster and Gilmore receiving lodging money to live on shore. Hitherto, the only fortifications Will had seen were those of Portsmouth, so he was greatly interested in the castle with its heavy frowning stone batteries, the deep cut separating it from the rest of the island, and its towering rock. Then there was the church of St. John, paved with tombstones of the knights, and other places of interest. The costume and appearance of the inhabitants amused and pleased him, as did the shops with their laces, cameos, and lovely coral ornaments. Beyond the walls there were the gardens full of orange-trees, bright with their fruit, and the burying-place of the old monks, each body standing in a niche, dressed in his gown and cowl as in life.

Will wished that he could get his share of prize-money at once, and promised himself that his very first expenditure would be a suite of coral for the lady who had done so much for him. In no way, he thought, could he lay out money with such gratification to himself.

A fortnight later the Furious came into harbour bringing another prize with her. This had been taken without any trouble. One morning, when day broke, she was seen only a quarter of a mile from the frigate. A gun was at once fired across her bows, and, seeing that escape was impossible, she hauled down her colours without resistance.

Forster and Gilmore, with the officers who had brought in the other prizes, all went on board at once and made their reports. As Forster had predicted, he was severely reprimanded for not having placed a sentry over the prisoners, but in consideration of the fact that he had already been spoken to by the admiral himself the captain was less severe on him than he would otherwise have been. Gilmore, on the other hand, was warmly commended.

"You managed extremely well," the captain said, "and showed that you fully deserved your promotion."

CHAPTER V

A PIRATE HOLD

The Furious was at once placed in the hands of the dockyard people, who set to work immediately to repair damages, while large quantities of provisions were brought off from the stores on shore.

"They are not generally as sharp as this," Forster said; "I should say there must be something in the wind."

Such was the general opinion on board the ship, for double gangs of workers were put on, and in three days she was reported to be again ready for sea. The captain came on board half an hour later and spoke to the first lieutenant, and orders were at once issued to get up the anchors and set sail. Her head was pointed west as she left the harbour, and the general opinion was that she was bound for Gibraltar. It leaked out, however, in the afternoon that she was sailing under sealed orders, and as that would hardly be the case if she were bound for Gibraltar, there were innumerable discussions among the sailors as to her destination. Could she be meant to cruise along the west coast of France, or to return to England and join a fleet being got ready there for some important operation?

"What do you say, Bill?" one of the men asked an old sailor, who had sat quietly, taking no part in the discussion.

"Well, if you asks me," he said, "I should say we are bound for the West Indies."

"The West Indies, Bill! What makes you think that?"

"Well, I thinks that, because it seems to me as that is where we are most wanted. The French have got a stronger fleet than we have out there."

"Well, they have got as strong a fleet at Toulon, and quite as strong a one at Brest."

"Yes, that may be so, but I think we are pretty safe to lick them at either of these places if they will come out and fight us fair, whereas in the West Indies they are a good bit stronger. There are so many ports and islands that, as we are, so to speak, a good deal scattered, they might at any moment come upon us in double our strength."

"Have you ever been there before, Bill?"

"Ay, two or three times. In some respects it could not be better; you can buy fruit, and 'bacca and rum for next to nothing,

57

when your officers give you a chance. Lor', the games them niggers are up to to circumvent them would make you laugh! When you land, an old black woman will come up with a basket full of cocoa-nuts. Your officer steps up to her and examines them, and they look as right as can be. Perhaps he breaks one and it is full of milk; very good. So you go up to buy, and the officer looks on. The woman hands you two or three, and when she gives you the last one she winks her eye. She don't say anything, but you drop a sixpence into her hand among the coppers you have to pay for the others, and when she has quite sold out the officer orders you into the boat to lie off till he comes back. And when he returns he is quite astonished to find that most of the crew are three sheets in the wind.

"Then they will bring you sugar-canes half as thick as your wrist, looking as innocent as may be; both ends are sealed up with bits of the pith, and when you open one end you find that all the joints have been bored through, and the cane is full of rum. But mind, lads, you are fools if you touch it; it is new and strong and rank, and a bottle of it would knock you silly. And that is not the worst of it, for fever catches hold of you, and fever out there ain't no joke. You eats a good dinner at twelve o'clock, and you are buried in the palisades at six; that's called yellow jack. It is a country where you can enjoy yourselves reasonable with fruit, and perhaps a small sup of rum, but where you must beware of drinking; if you do that you are all right. The islands are beautiful, downright beautiful; there ain't many places which I troubles myself to look at, but the West Indies are like gardens with feathery sorts of trees, and mountains, and everything that you can want in nature."

"It is very hot, isn't it, Bill?"

"It ain't, so to speak, cool in summer-time. In winter it is just right, but in summer you would like to lie naked all day and have cold water poured over you. Still, one gets accustomed to it in time. Then, you see, there is always excitement of some kind. There are pirates and Frenchmen, and there are Spaniards, whom I regard as a cross between the other two. They hide about among the islands and pop out when you least expect them. You always have to keep your eyes in your head and your cutlass handy when you go ashore. The worst of them are what they call mulattoes; they are a whity-brown sort of chaps, neither one thing nor the other, and a nice cut-throat lot they are. A sailor who drinks too much and loses his boat is as like as not to be murdered by some of them before morning. I hate them chaps like poison. There are scores of small craft manned by them which prey upon the negroes, who are an honest, merry lot, and not bad sailors either in their way. Sometimes four or five of these pirate craft will go together, and many of them are a good size and carry a lot of guns. They make some island their head-quarters. Any niggers there may be on it they turn into slaves. There are thousands of these islands, so at least I should say, scattered about, some of them mere sand-spots, others a goodish size.

"Well, I hope it is the West Indies. There is plenty of amusement and plenty of fighting to be done there, and I should like to know what a sailor can want more."

There was a hum of approval; the picture was certainly tempting.

After a six days' run with a favourable wind they passed through the Straits without touching at Gibraltar, and held west for twenty-four hours. Then the sealed orders were opened, and it was soon known throughout the ship that it was indeed the West Indies for which they were bound. The ship's course was at once changed. Teneriffe was passed, and they stopped for a day to take in fresh water and vegetables at St. Vincent. Then her head was turned more westward, and three weeks later the Furious anchored at Port Royal. The captain went on shore at once to visit the admiral, and returned with the news that the Furious was to cruise off the coast of Cuba. The exact position of the French fleet was unknown, but when last heard of was in the neighbourhood of that island.

"I must keep a sharp look-out for them," the captain said, "and bring back news of their whereabouts if I do catch sight of them; that is, of course, if we don't catch a tartar, for not only do the French ships carry heavier guns than we do, but they sail faster. We are as speedy, however, as any of our class, and will, I hope, be able to show them a clean pair of heels. In addition to this, I am told that three piratical craft, which have their rendezvous on some island off the south coast of Cuba, have been committing great depredations. A number of merchantmen have been missed; so I am to keep a sharp look-out for them and to clip their wings if I can."

"What size are they?" asked the first lieutenant.

"One is said to be a cutter carrying eight guns and a long-tom, the other two are schooners, each carrying six guns on a broadside; it is not known whether they have a long-tom, but the probability is that they have."

"They would be rather formidable opponents then if we caught them together, as they carry as many guns as we do, and those long-toms are vastly more powerful than anything we have. I think it is a pity that they don't furnish all ships on this station with a long twenty-four; it would be worth nearly all our broadsides."

"That is so, Mr. Farrance, but somehow the people at home

59

cannot get out of their regular groove, and fill up the ships with eight and ten-pounders, while, as you say, one long twenty-four would be worth a dozen of them. If we do catch one of these pirates I shall confiscate their long guns to our own use."

"It would be a capital plan, sir. Well, I am glad we shall have something to look for besides the French fleet, which may be a hundred miles away."

"Ay, or a thousand," the captain added.

Will had been standing not far from the captain, and heard this conversation. His heart beat high at the thought of the possibility of a fight with these murderous pirates.

For three weeks they cruised off the coast of Cuba. They saw no sign whatever of the French fleet, but from time to time they heard from native craft of the pirates. The natives differed somewhat widely as to the head-quarters of these pests, but all agreed that it was on an island lying in the middle of dangerous shoals.

One day they saw smoke rising some fifteen miles away and at once shaped their course for it. When they approached it they found that it rose from a vessel enveloped in flames.

"She is a European ship," the captain said as they neared her. "Send an officer in a boat to row round her and gather any particulars as to her fate. I see no boats near her, and I am afraid that it is the work of those pirates."

All watched the boat with intent interest as she rowed round the ship.

"I have no doubt whatever that it is the work of pirates," the officer said on his return. "Her bulwarks are burnt away, and I could make out several piles on deck which looked like dead men."

"Send a man up to the mast-head, Farrance, and tell him to scan the horizon carefully for a sail. I should say this ship can't have been burning above three hours at most."

No sooner had the man reached the top of the mast than he called down "Sail ho!"

"Where away?" Mr. Farrance shouted.

"On the port bow, sir."

"What do you make her out to be?"

"I should say she was a schooner by her topsails."

The ship's course was at once changed, and every rag of sail put upon her. The first lieutenant climbed to the upper crosstrees, and after a long look through his telescope returned to deck.

"I should say she is certainly one of the schooners that we are in search of, sir, but I doubt whether with this light wind we have much chance of overhauling her."

"We will try anyhow," the captain said. "She is probably steering for the rendezvous, so by following her we may at least get some important information."

All day the chase continued, but there was no apparent change in the position of the two vessels. The Furious was kept on the same course through the night, and to the satisfaction of all on board they found, when morning broke, that they had certainly gained on the schooner, as her mainsails were now visible. At twelve o'clock a low bank of sand was sighted ahead, and the schooner had entered a channel in this two hours later. The Furious had to be hove-to outside the shoal. The sand extended a long distance, but there were several breaks in it, and from the masthead a net-work of channels could be made out. It was a great disappointment to the crew of the Furious to have to give up the chase and see the schooner only some four miles off on her way under easy sail.

"This is an awkward place, Mr. Farrance," the captain said, "and will need a deal of examination before we go any farther. The first thing to do will be to sail round and note and sound the various channels. I wish you would go aloft with your glass and see whether there is any ground higher than the rest. Such a place would naturally be the point of rendezvous."

Lieutenant Farrance went aloft and presently returned.

"There is a clump of green trees," he said, "some ten miles off. The schooner is nearing them, and I think, though of this I am not certain, that I can make out the masts of another craft lying there."

"Well, it is something to have located her," the captain said. "Now we must find how we can best get there; that will be a work of time. We may as well begin by examining some of these channels."

Four boats were at once lowered and rowed to the mouths of those nearest. The sounding operations quickly showed that in three of them there was but two feet of water; the other was somewhat deeper, but there was still two feet less water than the Furious drew. The deep part was very narrow and winding.

"It may be this one that the schooner has gone up," the captain said. "I have no doubt she draws three or four feet less than we do, and, knowing the passage perfectly, she could get up it easily. I hope, however, we shall find something deeper presently."

The next three days were spent in circumnavigating the sand-banks and in sounding the various channels, but at last the captain was obliged to admit that none of them were deep enough for the Furious, although there were fully half a dozen by which vessels of lighter draught might enter.

"I am ready to run any fair risk, Mr. Farrance," he said, "but I daren't send a boat expedition against such a force as that, especially as they have no doubt thrown up batteries to strengthen their position. They must have any number of cannon which they have taken from ships they have captured."

"It would certainly be a desperate enterprise," the first lieutenant agreed, "and, as you say, too dangerous to be attempted now."

"Gilmore," Forster said, as the midshipmen met at dinner, "you are always full of ideas; can't you suggest any way by which we might get at them?"

"I am afraid not," Will laughed. "The only possible way that I can see would be to sail away, get together a number of native craft, and then make a dash at the place."

"What would be the advantage of native craft over our boats," one of the others said scoffingly.

"The great advantage would be that, if we had a dozen native craft, the men would be scattered about their decks instead of being crowded in boats, and would therefore be able to land with comparatively little loss."

"Upon my word," one of the seniors said, "I think there is something in Gilmore's idea. Of course they would have to be very shallow, and one would have to choose a night when there was just enough breeze to take them quietly along. At any rate I will run the risk of being snubbed, and will mention it to one of the lieutenants. 'Pon my word, the more I think of it the more feasible does it seem."

After dinner was over the midshipman went up to Mr. Peters, who was now third lieutenant, and saluted.

"What is it?" the lieutenant asked.

"Well, sir, it is an idea of Gilmore's. It may not be worth anything at all, but it certainly seemed to me that there was something in it."

"His ideas are generally worth something. What is it?"

The midshipman explained Will's plan.

"There is certainly something in it," Peters said. "What a beggar that boy is for ideas! At any rate, I will mention it to Mr. Farrance."

Mr. Farrance at first pooh-poohed the idea, but, on thinking it over, he concluded that it would be as well at any rate to lay it before the captain.

"'Pon my word it does seem feasible," the captain said. "They could tow the boats in after them, so that, when they came under the pirates' fire, the men could get into the boats and so be in shelter. Only one hand would be required to steer each vessel, and the rest would remain out of sight of the enemy until near enough to make a dash either for the shore or the pirates' craft, as the case might be. It is a good idea, a really brilliant idea, and well worth putting into effect. Besides, each of the vessels could carry one or two small guns, and so keep down the enemy's fire to some extent. Send for Gilmore."

In a few minutes Will entered the captain's cabin cap in hand.

"Mr. Farrance tells me, Mr. Gilmore, that you have an idea that by collecting a number of native craft of shallow draught we might attack the pirates with some hope of success."

"It was only an idea, sir, that occurred to me on the spur of the moment."

"Well, I am inclined to regard it as a feasible one," the captain said. "A dozen boats of that kind would carry the greater part of the ship's crew, and if each had a couple of light cannon on board they would be able to answer the enemy's fire. If I do attack in this manner I propose to send the boats in towing behind the native craft, so that when the enemy's fire becomes really heavy the men can take their places in these, and so be in shelter until close enough to make a dash. Is there any other suggestion you can offer I?"

"No, sir. The plan of taking the boats certainly seems to me to be a good one."

The captain smiled a little. He was not accustomed to have his plans approved of by midshipmen. However, he only said: "I think it will work. Should any other suggestion occur to you, you will mention it to Mr. Farrance. I am really obliged to you for the idea, which does great credit to your sharpness."

"Thank you, sir!" said Will, and retired.

An hour later the frigate was sailing away from the sand-banks.

"What did the old man say?" the midshipmen asked Will as he rejoined them.

"He thinks that there was something in the idea, but of course he has greatly improved it. He means to send the boats towing behind the native craft, so that if the fire gets very heavy the men can take to them and be towed in perfect shelter until near enough to make a rush. He intends to put a gun or two in each of the native boats, to keep down the enemy's fire a bit as they approach."

"That is an improvement," Forster said, "and it certainly seems, Gilmore, as if you had found a way out of our dilemma."

Those who had been most disposed to laugh at Will's suggestion were eager to congratulate him now that the captain had expressed his approval of it and had adopted it.

The Furious sailed direct for Port Royal. There was no fear that the pirates would abandon their island, for they would naturally take the retirement of the Furious as an admission of defeat. They were, of course, open to a boat attack, but they would consider themselves strong enough to beat off any such attempt without difficulty.

Arriving at Port Royal, Lieutenant Farrance went ashore in search of suitable craft. He had no difficulty in buying a dozen old native boats. He then procured a large quantity of cane, and lashed these in the bottom of the boats, using a sufficient quantity to keep them afloat even if they were riddled with balls. Then the carpenters set to work to make platforms in the bows of each to carry a seven-pounder gun. In three days the work was completed and the Furious started again, putting two men in each of the boats and taking them in tow.

Five days later they arrived off the sand-spits, and preparations were at once made for the attack. Lying low in the water, and keeping in a line behind the Furious, the native craft would be altogether invisible from the central islands, so that the pirates would not be aware of the method of attack. The greater portion of the men were told off to them, only forty remaining on board the Furious. All was ready an hour after nightfall, and the men took their places in the native craft, fastening their boats to the stern in each case. The sails were at once got up, and, following each other in single file, they entered the channel which had been found to be the deepest. The leading boat kept on sounding—an easy matter, as, the wind being light, the rate of progress did not exceed a mile an hour.

Will had been posted by the first lieutenant in his own boat, which was the leader, and Dimchurch and Tom Stevens were among the crew. Dimchurch had exchanged places with another seaman; Tom had been allowed a place by the special solicitation of Will.

"He fought stoutly in that fight on the Moorish prize, and he is very much attached to me. I should be obliged, sir, if you would take him."

"All right!" said the first lieutenant; "let him stow himself away in the bow till the fighting begins." Accordingly Tom curled himself up by the gun.

It was between two and three in the morning when the trees of the central island were made out; they were not more than five hundred yards away. Presently from a projecting point, where a heavy mass could be made out, a cannon was fired. The shot flew overhead, but the effect was instantaneous. Shouts were heard on shore and the sound of oars in rowlocks.

64

"Take to the boats!" the lieutenant shouted. The two lines of lights in the port-holes showed the positions of two vessels, and the men on the native craft left to work the guns at once opened fire at them. For a minute or two there was no return, and it was evident that the greater portion of the crew had been ashore. The battery that had first fired now kept up a steady discharge, but as the boats were almost invisible, the shot flew wildly overhead or splashed harmlessly in the water. The gunners on board disregarded it, and maintained a steady fire at the ports of the enemy's vessels. From these now came answering flashes, but the shot did little damage.

When the attacking party had got within a hundred yards of the pirate ships, the lieutenant gave the signal, and the boats, with a cheer, dashed forward at full speed. They had received instructions how to act in case two vessels were found, and, dividing, they made for their respective quarters.

The race was short and sharp, each officer urging his men to the fullest exertions. The instant they were alongside the oars were cast aside, and the men, drawing their cutlasses, leapt to their feet and endeavoured to climb up. They were thrust back with boarding-pikes, axes, and weapons of all kinds, but at last managed to get a foothold aft.

Will in vain endeavoured to get on deck; the sides were too high for him. Finding himself left with half the crew, he made his way in the boat forward along the side of the pirate vessel and clambered up by the bowsprit shrouds. Some of the men in the other boats, seeing what he was doing, followed his example. They were unnoticed. A fierce fight was raging on the quarter-deck, and the shouting was prodigious. When some thirty men were gathered Will led the way aft. Their arrival was opportune, for the attacking party, under the lieutenant, had been vastly outnumbered by the pirates, and although fighting stoutly, had been penned against the bulwark, where with difficulty they defended themselves.

With a cheer Will's party rushed aft, taking the pirates in the rear. Many of these were cut down, and the rest fell back confused by this unexpected attack.

"Now is your time, lads!" the lieutenant shouted. "Throw yourselves upon them and drive them back!"

Although the pirates still fought desperately, knowing that no mercy would be extended them, the steady valour of the sailors was too much for them. At last the pirate captain was cut down by Dimchurch, and with his fall his men entirely lost heart. Some threw down their arms, and many of them jumped overboard and swam ashore. A loud cheer burst from the sailors as the resistance came to an end.

65

The fight was still raging on board the other ship, and the lieutenant ordered the men of his own and another boat to row to it. Unseen by the pirates they reached the bow and climbed on deck. Then as soon as all had gained a footing they rushed aft. Here, too, the rear attack decided the struggle; in five minutes all was over.

Daylight was now breaking, and they were able to see that there was a line of storehouses on the islands together with a large number of huts. The greater portion of the men were ordered to land, and the fugitives from the ships were hunted down. Most of these had taken refuge in the battery at the mouth of the harbour, but as this was open on the land side it was soon stormed and the defenders all cut down. Then the huts were searched and burnt and the storehouses opened.

These were found to contain an enormous quantity of goods, the spoil evidently of many ships, and the men were at once set to work to transfer it to the prizes, and when these were full, to the native craft. A boat had been sent off, directly the fighting was over, with news to the captain of the success they had gained, and in the morning another message was sent saying that it would take four or five days to transfer the stores to the ships, and the Furious had in consequence hoisted anchor and gone for a short cruise away from the dangerous proximity of the sands.

On the afternoon of the third day a large cutter was seen approaching. Lieutenant Farrance ordered the native craft to be towed behind a small islet, where they were hidden from sight of a vessel entering the harbour, and the crews to take their places on the captured vessels. When this was done the guns were loaded and the men stood to their quarters. The new-comer approached without apparently entertaining any suspicion that anything unusual had happened, the huts that had been destroyed being hidden by the groves of trees.

As she came abreast of them the guns were run out and the lieutenant shouted: "I call upon you to surrender! These vessels are prizes of His Majesty's frigate Furious, and if you don't surrender we will sink you at once!"

There was a hoarse shout of fury and astonishment, and then the captain called back: "We will never surrender!"

Both the schooners at once poured in their broadsides, doing immense damage, and killing large numbers of the pirates. A few cannon were fired in answer, but in such haste that they had no effect. When two more broadsides had been fired into her, the cutter blew up with a tremendous explosion which shook both vessels to the keel and threw many of the men down. When the smoke cleared away the cutter had disappeared. Whether a shot had reached her magazine, or whether she was blown up by her desperate commander, was never known, as not a single survivor of the crew was picked up.

When the work of loading was completed, and the storehouses had been destroyed by fire, the two schooners sailed out, followed by the native craft with the boats towing behind.

The victory had been won at very little cost. Only three men had been killed and some seventeen wounded, while with the exception of some thirty prisoners, for the most part wounded, the whole pirate force had been annihilated.

The captain had already visited the scene, having rowed in as soon as he had received news of the success of the expedition. In Lieutenant Farrance's despatch several officers were noted for distinguished conduct. Among these was Will Gilmore, to whom the lieutenant gave great credit for the manner in which he had boarded the pirate, and by his sudden attack upon the rear of the enemy converted what was a distinctly perilous situation into a success.

"I tell you what it is, Gilmore," one of the midshipmen jestingly said, "if you go on like this we shall send you to Coventry. It is unbearable that you should always get to the front."

Great was the rejoicing among the merchants of Port Royal when the Furious returned with her two prizes and it became known that the third had been destroyed and the nest of pirates completely broken up.

On the following day Will was sent for by the admiral.

"My lad," he said, "I wish to tell you that although it is not usual for a captain to acknowledge in official despatches that he acted on the ideas of a young midshipman, Captain Marker has done full justice to you in his verbal report to me. Your idea showed great ingenuity, and although the surprise was so complete that even had the attack been made by ships' boats only it would probably have been successful, this detracts in no way from the merit of the suggestion. Of course you have some years to serve yet before you can pass, but I can promise you that as soon as you do so you shall, if you are still here, have your appointment at once as mate, with employment in which you can distinguish yourself."

"Thank you very much, sir!" Will said, and, saluting, retired.

In three days the ship's prizes and native craft were unloaded, and their contents were found to be of very great value, for by the marks upon the goods it was evident that at least twenty-three merchantmen must have been captured and pillaged, and as none of these were ever heard of after they had sailed it was reasonably concluded that all must have been burnt, and those on board murdered. The case was so atrocious that the prisoners were all tried, condemned to death, and executed in batches. There was little doubt that the pirates must have had agents in the various ports who had kept them informed of the sailing of ships, but there was no means of ascertaining who these parties were.

The Furious sailed four days after her return, and this time cruised on the northern coast of Cuba. One day, when sailing along by a stretch of high cliffs, a ship of war suddenly appeared from a narrow inlet; she was followed by two others. The Furious was headed round at once, and with the three French frigates in pursuit started on her way back. The wind was light, and though every stitch of canvas was set, it was evident, after an hour's sailing, that one, at least, of her pursuers gained steadily on her. The French ship would, indeed, have gained more than she had done had she not yawed occasionally and fired with her bow-chasers. The Furious had shifted two of her broadside guns to her stern to reply, but, although the aim was good, only one or two hits were made, the distance being still too great for accurate shooting.

"I wish the other two Frenchmen were a little slower," the captain said to the first lieutenant. "They are only a little farther behind her than when we started, and are, I think, only about half a mile astern of her. If she continues to travel at her present rate she will be close up to us by sunset. She is just about our own size, and I make no doubt that we should give a good account of her, but we could not hope to do so before her two consorts came up, and we could not expect to beat all three. If we could but fall in with one of our cruisers I would fight them willingly."

"Yes, the odds are too much against us at present, sir. I don't say that we could not fight them separately, but we could hardly hope to beat three of them at once. We can't make her go through the water faster than she is doing as far as I can see."

"No, every sail seems to be doing its best. There is nothing for it but to pray either for another frigate or for more wind. I am not sure that wind would help us, still it might."

"I think, sir," the lieutenant said, two hours later, "that one of your wishes is going to be fulfilled. There is a cloud rising very rapidly on the larboard bow, and from its colour and appearance it seems to me that we are going to have a tornado."

"It will be welcome indeed," the captain said. "We have been hit ten times in the last half-hour, and the nearest ship is not more than three-quarters of a mile away."

Five minutes later the captain said: "It is certainly a tornado.

All hands reduce sail. Don't waste a moment, lads; it will be on us in three minutes."

In a moment the vessel was a scene of bustle; the men swarmed up the rigging, urged to the greatest exertions not only by the voices of their officers but by the appearance of the heavens. The frigate behind held on three or four minutes longer, then her sheets were let fly, and immediately she was a scene of wild confusion.

"It will be on her before she is ready," the captain said grimly, "and if it is, she will turn turtle. It is as much as we shall do to be ready."

Just as a line of white foam was seen approaching with the speed of a race-horse, the last man reached the deck.

"I would give a great deal," the captain said, "to have time to get down all our light spars. Get ready your small fore try-sail, and a small stay-sail to run up on the mizzen."

A minute later the storm was upon them. A blinding sheet of spray, driven with almost the force of grape-shot, swept over the ship, followed by a deafening roar and a force of wind that seemed about to lift the ship bodily out of the water. Over and over she heeled, and all thought that she was about to founder, when, even above the noise of the storm, three loud crashes were heard, and the three masts, with all their lofty hamper, went over the side.

"Thank God," the lieutenant exclaimed, "that has saved her!"

All hands with axes and knives began cutting away the wreckage. At the same time the two try-sails were hoisted, but they at once blew out of the bolt-ropes.

"Don't you think, sir," the first lieutenant shouted, "that if we lash a hawser to all this hamper, and hang to it, it will act as a floating anchor, and bring her head up to the wind?"

"Very well thought of, Mr. Farrance," the captain shouted back; "by all means do so."

The order was given and immediately carried out. The tangle of ropes and spars, with the ship's strongest hawser attached, soon drifted past her, and as the cable tightened the vessel's head began to come slowly up into the wind.

"That will delay her fate for a bit," the captain said, "but we can't hope that it will more than delay it, unless we can get up some sail and crawl off the coast. Get ready the strongest try-sails we have in case they may be wanted."

In a few minutes the sails were got ready, but for the present there was nothing for it but to hang on to the wreckage. The shore was some miles away, but in spite of the floating anchor the drift was great. The crew of the Furious had now time to breathe, but it was pitch dark and nothing could be seen save the white heads of the waves which now every moment threatened to overwhelm them. Not a trace of the frigate which had so hotly pursued them could be seen.

"God rest their souls!" the captain said earnestly. "I am afraid she is gone. In fair fight one strives to do as much damage as possible, but such a catastrophe as this is awful. I trust the other two took warning in time."

"I hope so too. They were under the lee of that island we passed shortly before it began, so would be partially sheltered. There is no hope for the first, and their fate is terrible indeed, sir; all the more awful, perhaps, because we know that it may become ours before long."

"There is no doubt about that," the captain said. "Unless the wind drops or chops round our fate is sealed, and a few hours will see the ship grinding her bones on that rocky shore. It is too dark to see it, but we know that we are most surely approaching it."

As day broke the shore was made out a little more than half a mile away. The captain then called the crew together.

"My lads," he shouted, but in spite of his efforts his voice was heard but a few yards away, "everything has been done for the ship that could be done, but as you see for yourselves our efforts have been in vain. I trust that you will all get ashore, but as far as we can see at present the rocks are almost precipitous, and, high as they are, the spray flies right over them. I thank you all for your good conduct while the ship has been in commission, and am sure that you will know how to die, and will preserve your calm and courage till the end. Go to your stations and remain there until she is about to strike; then each man must make the best fight for life that he can."

The men went quietly off. Mr. Farrance stood watching the shore with his telescope. Presently he exclaimed: "See, sir, there is a break in the cliff! I do not know how far it goes in, but it looks to me as if it might be the opening to an inlet. We are nearly opposite to it, so if we shift the hawser from the bow to the stern she will swing round, and will probably drift right into the creek if that is what it is."

"By all means let us make the attempt," the captain said. "Thank God, there is a hope of escape for us all!"

The men sprang to their feet with alacrity when they heard the news. Another hawser was brought up and firmly spliced to the one in use just beyond the bulwark forward. Then it was led along outside the shrouds and fastened to the bitts astern and then to the

70

mizzen-mast. This done, the first hawser was cut at the bulwark forward, and the ship swung round almost instantly. As soon as she headed dead for shore the raffle that had so long served for their floating anchor was cut adrift and the try-sail was hoisted on the stump of the foremast, and with six good men at the wheel the vessel surged shorewards under the force of the gale, every man on board holding his breath. The opening was but a ship's-length across, but driven by the wind and steered with the greatest care the Furious shot into it as quickly and as surely as if she were propelled with oars. A great shout of relief burst from the whole crew when, after proceeding for a hundred yards along a narrow channel, the passage suddenly widened out into a pool a quarter of a mile across.

"Let go the anchor!" the captain cried, and he had scarce spoken when the great anchor went thundering down. "Pay out the chain gradually," was the next order, "and check her when she gets half-way across." The order was obeyed and the vessel's head swung round, and in less than a minute she was riding quietly over great waves that came rolling in through the entrance and broke in foam against the shore of the inlet. The quiet after the roar and din was almost startling. Above, the clouds could be seen flying past in rugged masses, but the breast of the pool, sheltered as it was from the wind by its lofty sides, was scarcely rippled, and the waves rolled in as if they were made of glass. Not a word was heard until the captain spoke.

"It is the least we can do, men, to thank God for this miraculous escape. I trust that there is not a man on board this ship who will not offer his fervent thanks to Him who has so wonderfully brought us out of the jaws of death."

Every head was bared, and for two or three minutes no sound was heard on board the ship. Then the captain replaced his hat, and the men went quietly off to their duties.

CHAPTER VI

A NARROW ESCAPE

They were hardly anchored before the gale showed signs of breaking, and in a few hours the sun shone out and the wind subsided. The destruction of the timber on the hillsides had been prodigious, and large spaces were entirely cleared.

The captain and first lieutenant had an anxious consultation. Every boat had gone, and all the masts and rigging. They were in what was practically a hostile country, for although Spain had not declared war against us, she gave every assistance to the French and left her ports open to them. In a few weeks probably she would openly throw herself into the scale against us.

"It is clear that we must communicate with Port Royal somehow," the captain said, "but it certainly isn't clear how we are to do it. Between this and the nearest port there may be miles and miles of mountain all encumbered by fallen trees, which it would be almost impossible to get through. Then again we have heard that there are always bands of fugitive slaves in the mountains, who would be sure to attack us. As to the sea, we might possibly make shift to build a boat. There is certainly no lack of timber lying round, and we have plenty of sail-cloth for sails, so we could fit her out fairly well. It would be a journey of fully a thousand miles, but that seems the most feasible plan. A small craft of, say, forty feet long might be built and got ready for sea in the course of a week."

"I should say so certainly, sir. With the amount of labour we have at our disposal it might be built even sooner than that. We have plenty of handy men on board who could give efficient help to the carpenter's gang."

"I suppose you would build it rather as a ship than as a boat?"

"Yes, I think so. We could build her of one-and-a-half-inch planks, fill the seams well with oakum, and give her a couple of coats of paint. Let her be of shallow draft with plenty of beam. She should, of course, be decked over, as she might meet with another tornado. The crew would consist of an officer and ten men. With such a vessel there should be no difficulty in reaching Port Royal."

The carpenters were at once told off to carry out the work.

"You can have as many hands to help you as you wish," the captain said to the head of the gang. "What will you do first?"

"I shall get some planks from below, sir, and make a raft. By means of that we can get on shore and choose the trunks that would be most suitable for the purpose; we are sure to find plenty about. Then we will find a suitable spot for a ship-yard, and at once start on the work. I will set a gang of men with axes to square the trunks and make them ready for sawing. They need not be more than six inches square when finished, and as I have a couple of double-handed saws we can soon rip these into planks."

"How long do you think you will be?"

"I should say, sir, with the help I can get, I ought to be ready to start in less than a week. Of course the ribs will take some time to prepare, but when I have them and the keel and stem- and stern-post in place the planking will not take us very long."

"She is to be decked, Thompson."

"All over, sir?"

"Yes, I think so. She may meet with weather like that we have just come through, and if she is well decked we may feel assured that she will reach Port Royal. I will leave Mr. Farrance and you to draw out her lines."

"I think," said the first lieutenant, "she should be like a magnified launch, with greater beam and a larger draft of water, which could, perhaps, best be gained by giving her a deep keel. Of course she must be a good deal higher out of the water than a launch, say a good four feet under the deck. There should be no need to carry much ballast; she will gain her stability by her beam."

"I understand, sir. The first thing to be done is to form the raft."

The ship's crew were soon at work, and it was not long before a raft was constructed. A rope was at once taken ashore and made fast to a tree, so that the raft could be hauled rapidly backwards and forwards between the ship and the shore.

The carpenter and his mates were the first to land, and while the chief selected a suitable point for a yard his assistants scattered, examining all fallen trees and cutting the branches off those that seemed most suitable. These were soon dragged down to the yard. Then strong gangs set to work to square them, and the carpenters to cut them into planks.

The first lieutenant remained with them, encouraging them at their work, while the junior officers and midshipmen were divided among the various gangs. By six o'clock, when the Furious signalled for all hands to come on board, they had indeed done a good day's work. A pile of planks lay ready to be used as required. The carpenters had made some progress with a keel, which they were laboriously chopping out from the straight trunk of a large tree. By evening of the next day this was finished and placed in position. On

73

the third day some started to shape the stem- and stern-posts, while the head-carpenter made from some thin planks templates of the ribs, and set others to chop out the ribs to fit.

In two more days all was ready for fastening on the planks. A hundred and fifty men can get through an amazing amount of labour when they work well and heartily. The planks were bent by main strength to fit in their places, and as there was an abundance of nails and other necessary articles on board, the sheathing was finished in two days. The rest of the work was comparatively easy. While the deck was being laid the hull was caulked and painted, and the two masts, sails, and rigging prepared. The boat had no bulwarks, it being considered that she would be a much better sea-boat without them, as in case of shipping a sea the water would run off at once. The hatchways fore and aft were made very small, with close-fitting hatches covered with tarpaulin.

The captain was delighted when she was finished.

"She is really a fine boat," he said, "with her forty feet of length and fifteen of beam. It has taken longer to build her than I had expected, but we had not reckoned sufficiently on the difficulties. Everything, however, has now been done to make her seaworthy, so those of us who remain here may feel sure that she will reach Port Royal safely. In case of a gale the sails must be lowered and lashed to the deck, and all hands must go below and fasten the hatchways securely. She has no ballast except her stores, but I think she will be perfectly safe; there is very little chance of her capsizing."

"With such beam and such a depth of keel," said the first lieutenant, "she could not possibly capsize. In case of a tornado the masts might very well be taken out of her and used as a floating anchor to keep her head to it."

"Now whom do you intend to send in her, sir?"

"I will send two officers," the captain said. "Peters, and a midshipman to take his place in case he should be disabled. I think it is Robson's turn for special service."

The next morning the boat started soon after daybreak, the ship's crew all watching her till the two white lug-sails disappeared through the opening.

"Now we will take a strong party of wood-cutters," the captain said, "and see if we can make a way to the top of the hill and get some idea of the country round. I don't expect we shall see much of interest, but it is just as well that we should be kept employed. By the way, before we do that, we will get hawsers to the shore and work the frigate round so as to bring her broadside to bear upon the opening; we ought to have done that at first. The French may know of this place, or if they don't they may learn of it from the Spaniards. Those two ships astern of us probably got themselves snug before the tornado struck them, and weathered it all right, though I doubt very much if they did so, unless they knew of some inlets they could run for. If they did escape, it is likely that they will be taking some trouble to find out what became of us. They may have seen their companion's fate, but they would hardly have made us out in the darkness. Still, they would certainly want to report our loss, and may sail along close inshore to look for timbers and other signs of wreck. I think, therefore, that it will be advisable to station a well-armed boat at this end of the cut, and tell them to row every half-hour or so to the other end and see if they can make out either sailing or rowing craft coming along the shore. If they do see them they must retire to this end of the opening, unless they can find some place where they could hide till a boat came abreast of them, and then pounce out and capture it."

"It would certainly be a good precaution, sir. I will see to it at once—but we are both forgetting that we have no boats."

"Bless me, I did forget that altogether! Well, here is that little dug-out the carpenters made for sending messages to and from the ship. It will carry three. I should be glad if you would take a couple of hands and row down to the mouth of the entrance and see if there is any place where, without any great difficulty, a small party with a gun could be stationed so as not to be noticed by a boat coming up."

"I understand, sir."

The lieutenant started at once, and when he returned, some hours later, he reported that there was a ledge some twenty feet long and twelve deep. "It is about eight feet from the water's edge and some twelve above it, sir," he said, "and is not noticeable until one is almost directly opposite it. If we were to pile up rocks regularly four feet high along the face, both the gun and its crew would be completely hidden."

"Get one of the hands on board, Mr. Farrance; I will myself go and see it with you."

One of the men at once climbed on deck, and the captain took his place in the little dug-out. When they reached the ledge he made a careful inspection of it.

"Yes," he said, "ten men could certainly lie hidden here, and with a rough parapet, constructed to look as natural as possible, they should certainly be unobserved by an incoming boat, especially as the attention of those in the stern would be directed into the inlet. Will you order Mr. Forster and one of the other midshipmen to go with as many men as the raft will carry, and build such a parapet. They had better take one of the rope-ladders with them and

75

fix it to the ledge by means of a grapnel. There is plenty of building material among the rocks that have fallen from the precipices above. I must leave it to their ingenuity to make it as natural as possible."

When they returned to the ship the first lieutenant called Forster and gave him the captain's orders.

"You can take young Gilmore with you," he said. "Your object will be to make it as natural as possible, so as to look, in fact, as if the rocks that had fallen out behind had lodged on the ledge. The height is not very important, for if a boat were coming along, the men would, of course, lie down till it was abreast of them, and the cannon would be withdrawn and only run out at the last moment."

"Very well, sir, I will do my best."

The raft was again brought into requisition, and it was found that it could carry twelve men. Dimchurch and nine others were chosen, and, using oars as paddles, they slowly made their way down to the spot.

"It will be a difficult job to make anything like a natural wall there," Forster said.

"Yes," Will agreed, "I don't see how it is to be managed at all. Of course we could pile up a line of stones, but that would not look in the least natural. If we could get up three or four big chunks they might do if filled in with small stones, but it would be impossible to raise great blocks to that shelf."

The ladder was fixed and they climbed up to the ledge. When they reached it they found that it was very rough and uneven, and consequently that the task was more difficult than it had seemed from below.

"The only way I see," Forster said, "would be to blast out a trench six feet wide and one foot deep, in which the men could lie hidden. The question is whether the captain will not be afraid that the blasting might draw attention to our presence here."

"They were just starting for the top of the hill when we came away," Will said, "and may be able to see whether there are any habitations in the neighbourhood. A couple of men in the dug-out would be able to bring us news of any craft in sight. I certainly don't see any other way."

When Forster made his report the captain said:

"I believe it will be the best plan. At the top of the hill we could see nothing but forests, for the most part levelled; we could make out no sign of smoke anywhere. The operation of blasting can be done with comparatively small charges, and occurring as it does at the foot of a gorge like that, the sound would hardly spread much over the surrounding country, and we could, of course, take care that there was no ship in sight when we fired the charges.

76

"Well, you can begin to-morrow. I believe there are some blasting-tools in the store. Take the gunner with you; this work comes within his province."

On the following morning the raft went off again, and at midday a number of sharp explosions told that the work was begun. In the evening another series of shots were fired, and the party returned with the news that the ground had been broken up to the depth of two feet and of ample size to give the men cover. The next morning the rocks were cleared out, and a seven-pounder and carriage, with tackle for hoisting it up, were sent over.

In the afternoon the captain went in the dug-out and inspected the work, and expressed himself as thoroughly satisfied with it. A garrison consisting of an officer and ten men was then placed in the fort. They remained there all day and returned to the ship as darkness fell, as it was thought pretty certain that no one would try to explore the inlet during the night. The next morning another party was told off to garrison duty, and so on, no man being given two consecutive days in the fort.

On the fourth day the dug-out returned in haste to the ship from its post at the mouth of the gap, and reported that two men-of-war were to be seen in the distance cruising close inshore. Mr. Farrance landed, and with difficulty made his way up the hill to a point near the mouth of the opening, which commanded a view over the sea. From that point he could easily see the hulls of the ships with his telescope, and had no doubt whatever that they were the former antagonists of the Furious. After watching for some time he made out four little black specks very close to the shore. He examined them closely and then hurried down to the cove.

"They are searching the coast with boats," he reported, "as I feared they would."

The news had been given to the little party at the battery as the dug-out came in, and they were at once on the alert. The carpenters, who after the departure of their first boat had been employed in building a large gig to pull twelve oars, were at once recalled to the ship, and the magazines were opened and the guns loaded. All the guns from the larboard main deck had been brought up to the upper deck and port-holes made for them, and a boom of trees had been built from the bow and stern of the ship to the shore, so as to prevent any craft from getting inside her. Thus prepared, the captain considered that he was fully a match for any two ships of his own size, but he knew, nevertheless, that, even if he beat them off, he might be exposed to attack from a still larger force unless assistance arrived from Jamaica.

But he did not think only of the ship. The dug-out, which had

77

brought Mr. Farrance back with his report, was at once sent off with orders to the party at the battery that they must, if possible, sink any boat or boats that entered, but that if ships of war came in they must not try to work their gun after the first shot, as if they did so they would simply be swept away by the enemy's fire. That one shot was to be aimed at the enemy's rudder; then they were to lie down, and if they had not disabled the ship they were to keep up a heavy musketry fire, aimed solely against her steersman. It was hardly likely that they would be attacked by boats, as the enemy would be fully engaged with the Furious; but even if they should, the Frenchmen would have no means of climbing the eight feet of precipitous rock.

The dug-out went to and from the entrance, bringing back news of the progress made by the enemy's boats. About three hours from the time when they had first been made out by Mr. Farrance the little boat reported that they were only two or three hundred yards from the entrance. On board the ship all listened anxiously, for a slight bend in the narrow passage prevented them from seeing the battery. Presently the boom of a cannon was heard, followed by a cheer, which told that the little garrison had been successful; then for two or three minutes there was a rattle of musketry. When this stopped, the dug-out at once went out to the fort, and returned with the news that two boats had come up abreast, that one of them had been sunk by the cannon at the fort, and that its crew had been picked up by the other boat, which had rowed hastily back, suffering a good deal from the musketry fire under which the operation was carried on.

"That is act one," the captain said; "now we shall have to look for act two. I will go up with you, Mr. Farrance, to the place whence you saw them; we may be sure that there will be a great deal of signalling and consultation before they make any further step."

Accordingly they landed and went up to the look-out. The two vessels were lying close to each other with their sails aback. The more fortunate of the two boats which had attempted to explore the passage had just returned to them with its load of wounded and the survivors of its late companion, and boats were passing to and fro between the two ships.

"It is an awkward question for them to decide," the captain said. "Of course they know well enough that a ship must be in here, the gun shows them that, but they cannot tell that we are capable of making any defence beyond the single gun battery on the ledge."

It was an hour before there was any change in the position, but at the end of that time the sails were filled and the two vessels headed for the mouth of the inlet. They had evidently concluded that the English ship was lying there disabled. The two officers hurried back to the Furious, and gave orders to prepare for the attack. The men at once stood to their posts. Presently the gun of the fort boomed out again, and by the cheering that followed the sound it was evident that the shot had taken effect and smashed the rudder of one of the French ships. Several guns were fired in reply, but a minute later the bowsprit of the leading ship came into view. The men waited until they could see the whole vessel, then a crashing broadside from every gun on board the Furious was poured into her bow.

The effect was tremendous; a hole ten or twelve feet wide was torn in her bow, and the ship was swept from end to end by balls and splinters, and the shrieks and groans that arose from her told that the execution was heavy. It was evident that the battle was already half-won as far as she was concerned. There was not room enough in the little inlet for her to manœuvre in the light wind so as to bring her broadside to bear on the Furious, and another crashing broadside from the latter vessel completed her discomfiture. The other vessel now came up by her side, but she had been disabled by the fort, and her helm would not act. Her captain at once lowered her boats and tried to get her head round, but these were smashed up by the fire of the Furious, and the two vessels lay together side by side, helpless to reply in any efficient way to the incessant fire kept up upon them. The Frenchmen did all that was possible for brave men to do in the circumstances, but their position was hopeless, and after suffering terribly for ten minutes, one after the other hauled down their flag.

A tremendous burst of cheering broke from the Furious. She had lost but two men killed and four or five wounded by the bullets of the French topmen. She had also been struck twice by balls from the bow-chaser of the second ship; but this was the extent of her damage, while the loss of life on board the French frigates had been frightful. Some sixty men had been killed and eighty wounded on the first ship, while thirty were killed and still more wounded in the boats of the second vessel.

Captain Harker went on board the captures to receive the swords of their commanders.

"You have done your best, gentlemen," he said; "no one in the circumstances could have done more. Had there been ten of you instead of two the result must have been the same. If your boats had got in and seen the situation you would have understood that the position was an impossible one. There was no room in here for manœuvring, and even had one of you not been damaged by the shot from that little battery of ours, your position would have been

79

practically unchanged, and you could not possibly have brought your broadsides to bear upon us."

The French captains, who were much mortified by the disaster, bowed silently.

"It is the fortune of war, sir," one of them said, "and certainly we could not have anticipated that you would be so wonderfully placed for defence. I agree with you that our case was hopeless from the first, and I compliment you upon your dispositions, which were certainly admirable."

"You and your officers will be perfectly at liberty," the captain said; "your crews must be placed in partial confinement, but a third of them can always be on deck. My surgeon has come on board with me, and will at once assist yours in attending to your wounded."

A considerable portion of the crew of the Furious were at once put on board the French frigate Eclaire, and set to work to dismantle her. The masts, spars, and rigging were transferred to the Furious and erected in place of her own shattered stumps, which were thrown overboard. Thus, after four days of the hardest work for all, the Furious was again placed in fighting trim.

Preparations were immediately made for sailing. The Furious led the way, towing behind her the dismantled hull in which the whole of the prisoners were carried. A prize crew of sixty were placed on board the Actif.

When they were about half-way to Jamaica a squadron of three vessels were sighted. Preparations were made to throw off the Eclaire if the ships proved to be hostile, but before long it was evident that they were English. They approached rapidly, and when they rounded-to near the Furious the crews manned the yards and greeted her with tremendous cheers. The officer in command was at once rowed to the Furious. As the boat neared the ship his friends recognized Mr. Peters and Robson sitting in the stern.

"What miracle is this, Captain Harker?" the officer cried as he came on deck. "Your lieutenant brought us news that you were dismasted and lying helpless in some little inlet, and here you are with what I can see is a French equipment and a couple of prizes! I can almost accuse you of having brought us here on a fool's errand."

"It must have that appearance to you; but the facts of the case are simple;" and he told the story of the fight. "The battle was practically over when the first shot was fired," he said. "The two French ships lost upwards of seventy killed and over a hundred wounded, while we had only four men killed and two wounded. If the place had been designed by nature specially for defence it could not have been better adapted for us."

"I see that," Captain Ingham said; "but you made the most of the advantages. Your plan of laying her broadside to the entrance, getting all your cannon on one side, and building a boom to prevent any vessel from getting behind you, was most excellent. Well, it is a splendid victory, the more so as it has been won with so little loss. The French certainly showed but little discretion in thus running into the trap you had prepared for them. Of course they could not tell what to expect, but at least, whatever it might have cost them, they ought to have sent a strong boat division in to reconnoitre. No English captain would have risked his vessel in such a way."

With very little delay the voyage to Jamaica was continued. Two of the relief party went straight on, the other remained with the Furious in case she should fall in with a French fleet. When the little squadron entered Port Royal they received an enthusiastic welcome from the ships on the station. Both prizes were bought into the service and handed over to the dockyard for a thorough refit. Their names were changed, the Eclaire being rechristened the Sylph, the Actif becoming the Hawke. Lieutenant Farrance was promoted to the rank of captain, and given the command of the latter vessel, and some of the survivors of a ship that had a fortnight before been lost on a dangerous reef were told off to her. He was, according to rule, permitted to take a boat's crew and a midshipman with him from his old ship, and he selected Will Gilmore, and, among the men, Dimchurch and Tom Stevens.

The planters of Jamaica were celebrated for their hospitality, and the officers received many invitations.

"You are quite at liberty to accept any of them you like," Captain Farrance said to Will. "Till the vessel gets out of the hands of the dockyard men there is nothing whatever for you to do. But I may tell you that there is a good deal of unrest in the island among the slaves. The doings of the French revolutionists, and the excitement they have caused by becoming the patrons of the mulattoes has, as might be expected, spread here, and it is greatly feared that trouble may come of it. Of course the planters generally pooh-pooh the idea, but it is not to be despised, and a few of them have already left their plantations and come down here. I don't say that you should not accept any invitation if you like, but if an outbreak takes place suddenly I fancy very few of the planters will get down safely. I mean, of course, if there is a general rising, which I hope will not be the case. Negroes are a good deal like other people. Where they are well treated they are quite content to go on as they are. Where they are badly treated they are apt to try and better themselves. Still, that is not always the case. There is no doubt that altogether the French planters of San Domingo are much gentler in their treatment of their slaves than our people are here.

Large numbers of them are of good old French families, and look on their slaves rather as children to be ruled by kindness than as beasts of burden, as there is no doubt some, not many, I hope, but certainly some of the English planters do. With San Domingo in the throes of a slave revolution, therefore, it will not be surprising if the movement communicates itself to the slaves here. I know that the admiral thinks it prudent to keep an extra ship of war on the station so as to be prepared for any emergency."

"Very well, sir. Then I will not accept invitations for overnight."

"I don't say that, Mr. Gilmore. In nine cases out of ten I should say it could be done without danger; for if a rebellion breaks out it will not at first be general, but will begin at some of the most hardly-managed plantations, and there will be plenty of time to return to town before it spreads."

As Will had no desire to mix himself up in a slave insurrection, he declined all invitations to go out to houses beyond a distance whence he could drive back in the evening. At all the houses he visited he was struck by the apparently good relations between masters and slaves. The planters were almost aggrieved when he insisted on leaving them in the evening, but he had the excuse that he was a sort of aide-de-camp to Captain Farrance, and was bound to be there the first thing in the morning to receive any orders that he might have to give. He generally hired a gig and drove over early so as to have a long day there, and always took either Dimchurch or Tom with him. He enjoyed himself very much, but was not sorry when the repairs on the Hawke were completed.

As the admiral was anxious for her to be away, some men were drafted from the other ships; others were recruited from the crews of the merchantmen in the port by Dimchurch, who spoke very highly of the life on board a man-of-war, and of the good qualities of the Hawke's commander. The complement was completed by a draft of fresh hands from England, brought out to make good the losses of the various ships on the station. Within three weeks, therefore, of her leaving the dockyard the Hawke sailed to join the expedition under Sir John Laforey and General Cuyler, to capture the island of Tobago, where, on 14th April, 1793, some troops were landed. The French governor was summoned to surrender, but refused, so the works were attacked and carried after a spirited resistance. But the attempt to capture St. Pierre in the island of Martinique was not equally successfully. The French defended the place so desperately that the troops were re-embarked with considerable loss.

CHAPTER VII

AN INDEPENDENT COMMAND

Will was hit by a musket-ball in the last engagement that took place, and was sent back with a batch of wounded to Port Royal. Three of the fingers of his left hand had been carried away, but he bore the loss with equanimity, as it would not compel him to leave the service. Tom, who went with him as his servant, fretted a good deal more over it than he himself, and was often loud in his lamentations.

"It would not have made any difference if it had been me," he said, "but it is awfully hard on you."

"What ridiculous nonsense, Tom!" Will said quite angrily, after one of these outbursts. "If it had been you it would have been really serious, for though an officer can get on very well without some of his fingers a sailor would be useless and would be turned adrift with some trifling pension. I shall do very well. I have been mentioned in despatches and I am certain to get my step as soon as I have served long enough to pass, so after a time I shall not miss them at all."

Tom was silenced, though not convinced. The wound healed rapidly, thanks to Will's abstemious habits, and in six weeks after entering the hospital he was discharged as fit for duty. The Hawke was not in harbour, so he went to an hotel. On the following day he received an order to call upon the admiral. When he did so that officer received him very kindly. "I am sorry," he said, "to learn that you have lost some fingers, Mr. Gilmore."

"I hope it will not interfere much with my efficiency, sir?"

"I think not," the admiral said; "I have received the surgeon's report this morning. In it he stated that your wound had from the first gone on most favourably, and that they had really kept you in hospital a fortnight longer than was absolutely necessary, lest in your anxiety to rejoin you might do yourself harm. Three days since a cutter of about a hundred tons was sent in by the Sylph. She was a pirate, and, like all vessels of that class, very fast, and would most likely have outsailed the Sylph had she not caught her up a creek. I have purchased her for the government service, and I propose to place you in command."

Will gave a start of surprise. At his age he could not have expected for a moment to be given an independent command.

"I have noted your behaviour here, and have looked through the records of your service since you joined, and I am convinced that you will do credit to the post. I shall give you a midshipman junior to yourself from the Thetis, and you will have forty hands before the mast. The Hawke is expected in in a few days, so you can pick five men from her. The rest I will make up from the other ships. The cutter will be furnished with four twelve-pounders, and the long sixteen as a bow gun, which she had when she was captured. Your duty will be to police the coasts and to overhaul as many craft as you may find committing depredations, of course avoiding a combat with adversaries too strong for you."

"I thank you most heartily, sir, for selecting me for this service, and will do my best to merit your kindness."

"That is all right, Mr. Gilmore. I have acted, as I believe, for the good of the service, and to some extent as an incentive to other young officers to use their wits."

Will went out with his head in a whirl. He could hardly have hoped, within a year of his term of service as a midshipman, to obtain a separate command, and he could have shouted with joy at this altogether unexpected promotion. The first thing he did was to take a boat and row off in it to his new command. She was a handsome boat, evidently designed to be fast and weatherly.

"These beggars know how to build boats much better than how to fight them," he said, when he had examined her. "Assuredly in anything like a light wind she would run away from the Sylph. The admiral was right when he said that it was only by chance that she was caught. I hope the fellow who is going with me is a good sort. It would be awkward if we did not pull well together. At any rate, as the admiral seems to have picked him out for the service, he must be worth his salt. Of course I shall have Dimchurch as my boatswain; he will take one watch and the youngster the other. It will be hard if we don't catch something."

Having rowed round the cutter two or three times he returned to the shore. As the little vessel had been taken by surprise, and had not been able to offer any resistance to a craft so much more powerful than herself, she was uninjured, and was in a fit state to be immediately recommissioned. She was called L'Agile, a name which Will thought very suitable for her.

"Forty men will be none too strong for her," he said, "for we shall have to work two guns on each side and that long one in the bow." He went to bed that night and dreamt of fierce fights and many captures, and laughed at himself when he awoke. "Still," he said, "I shall always be able to tackle any craft of our own size and carrying anything like our number of men."

84

Three days later the Hawke came in. Will at once rowed off to her and had a chat with his friends. When he mentioned his new command his news was at first received with absolute incredulity, but when at last his messmates came to understand that he was not joking, he was heartily congratulated on his good fortune. Afterwards he was not a little chaffed on the tremendous deeds he and his craft were going to perform. When at last they became serious, Latham, the master's mate, remarked: "But what is your new command like?"

"She is a cutter of about a hundred tons, carrying four twelve-pounders, and a sixteen-pounder long pivot gun at the bow. I am to have forty men and a young midshipman from the Thetis."

"A very tidy little craft, I should say, Gilmore, and you will probably get a good deal more fun out of her than from a frigate or line-of-battle ship. You will want a good boatswain to take charge of one of the watches."

"I shall have one, for I am to take five men out of the Hawke, and you may be sure I shall take Dimchurch as boatswain."

"You could not have a better man," Latham said; "he is certainly one of the smartest fellows on board the ship. He is very popular with all the men, and is full of life and go, and always the first to set an example when there is any work to be done. I suppose we shall also lose the services of that boy Tom?"

"I think so," Will laughed; "I should be quite lost without so faithful a hand, and indeed, though he still ranks as a boy, he is a big powerful fellow, and a match for many an A.B. at hauling a rope or pulling an oar."

"You are right. He is as big round the chest as many of the men, and though perhaps not so active, quite as powerful. When will you hoist your pendant?"

"I have to get the crew together yet. I am to have small drafts from several of the ships, and it may be a few days before they can be collected."

The next morning the Thetis arrived, and the young midshipman came on shore an hour later to report himself to Will. He looked surprised for a moment at the age of his new commander, but gravely reported himself for service. Will was pleased with his appearance. He was a merry-faced boy, but with a look on his face which indicated pluck and determination.

"You are surprised at my age, no doubt, Harman," Will said, "and I cannot be more than a year older than yourself, but I have been fortunate enough to be twice mentioned in despatches, indeed have had wonderful luck. I feel sure that we shall get on well together, and I hope both do well. We are to act as police on the coast of Cuba; it swarms with pirates, and it will be hard if we don't fall in with some of them. You will, of course, keep one watch, and the boatswain, who is a thoroughly good man, will take the other. I need hardly say that we shall have no nonsense about commanding officer. Except when on duty, I hope we shall be good chums, which means, of course, that when an enemy is in sight or the weather is dirty I must be in absolute command."

"Thank you, sir!" Harman said. "These are good terms, and I promise to obey your commands as readily as if you were old enough to be my father."

"That is good. Now I have dinner ordered and I hope you will share it with me. We can then talk over matters comfortably."

Before dinner was over, the lad was more than satisfied with his new chief, and felt sure that at any rate the cruise would be a pleasant one. Just as they had finished, Dimchurch and Tom came in to see Will. On finding that he was engaged they would have withdrawn, but Will called them in. "Sit down and join Mr. Harman and myself in a chat. This, Harman, is Bob Dimchurch, who is going to be our boatswain, and Tom Stevens, whom I have known since we were five years old, and although I have gone over his head we are as good friends as ever. Dimchurch took me under his wing when I first joined, and since then has fought by my side on several occasions."

"We came to wish you success in your new command, sir," Dimchurch said, "and should not have intruded had we known that you were not alone."

"It is no intrusion at all, Dimchurch. There is no man whose congratulations can be more pleasing to me. Have you seen the cutter?"

"Yes, sir. Tom and I noticed what a smart, likely craft she was when we came in and dropped anchor. I little thought that it was you who had command of her, but I have no fear but that you will do her full justice. I could hardly believe my ears when I was told this afternoon, and Tom was ready to jump out of his clothes with joy."

"It is wonderfully good fortune, Dimchurch; I can hardly believe it myself yet."

"I am sure you deserve it, sir. It was you who recaptured that prize in the Mediterranean; it was you who saved the first lieutenant's life; and it was you who suggested a plan by which we accounted for those three pirates. If that didn't deserve promotion, it is hard to say what would."

"I owe no small portion of it, Dimchurch, to the fact that I was able to take an observation so soon after I had joined, and that was due to the kindness of my good friend Miss Warden."

"Yes, sir, that goes for something, no doubt, but there is a good deal more than that in it." After some further talk both of the past and the future, Dimchurch sprang to his feet, saying: "Well, sir, I wish you success. But it is time we were off. I am told we are to remove our duds on board the new craft to-morrow."

"Yes, we are going to start manning her at once; I shall be on board with Mr. Harman directly after breakfast. I have not put foot upon her yet, and am most anxious to do so."

The craft fully answered Will's expectations. Her after-accommodation was exceedingly good; the cabin was handsomely fitted, and there were two state-rooms.

"We shall be in clover here, Harman," he said; "no one could wish for a better command. I must set to work to get stores shipped at once. How many of the crew are on board?"

"Twenty-three, sir, and I believe we shall have our full complement before night."

As they spoke a boat laden with provisions came alongside, and all hands were at once engaged transferring her load to the cutter. In the course of the forenoon the remainder of the men came on board in twos and threes. After dinner Will called the crew together and read out his commission. Then he made his maiden speech.

"My lads," he said, "I wish this to be a comfortable ship, and I will do my best to make it so. I shall expect the ready obedience of all; and you may be assured that if possible I will put you in the way of gaining prize-money. There are plenty of prizes to be taken, and I hope confidently that many of them will fall to our share." The men gave three cheers, and Will added: "I will order an extra supply of grog to be served out this evening."

On the following day L'Agile dipped her ensign to the admiral and set off on her voyage. Will was well pleased with the smartness the crew displayed in getting under weigh, and more than satisfied with the pace at which she moved through the water. For a month they cruised off the coast of Cuba, during which time they picked up eight small prizes. These were for the most part rowing-galleys carrying one large lateen sail. None of them were sufficiently strong to show fight; they were not intended to attack merchantmen, but preyed upon native craft, and were manned by from ten to twenty desperadoes. Most of them, when overhauled, pretended to be peaceful fishermen or traders, but a search always brought to light concealed arms, and in some cases captured goods. The boats were burned, and their crews, mostly mulattoes, with a sprinkling of negroes—rascals whose countenances were sufficiently villainous to justify their being hanged without trial,—were put ashore; for the admiral had given instructions to Will not to burden himself with prisoners, who would have to be closely guarded, and would therefore weaken his crew, and, if brought to Port Royal, would take up prison accommodation.

At last one day a schooner rather bigger than themselves was sighted. Her appearance was rakish, and there was little doubt as to her character. All sail was at once crowded on L'Agile. The schooner was nearly as fast as she was, and at the end of a six hours' chase she was still two miles ahead. Suddenly she headed for the shore and disappeared among the trees. L'Agile proceeded on her course until opposite the mouth of the inlet which the pirate had entered. It was getting dark, and Will decided to wait until morning, and then to send a boat in to reconnoitre.

"I have not forgotten," he said to Harman, "the way in which those two French frigates I have told you of ran into a trap, and I don't mean to be caught so if I can help it."

L'Agile remained hove to during the night, and in the morning lowered a boat, with four hands, commanded by Dimchurch, who was ordered to row in until he obtained a fair view of the enemy, and observe as far as possible what preparation had been made for defence. He was absent for half an hour, and then returned, saying that the schooner was lying anchored with her sails stowed at the far end of the inlet, which was about half a mile long and nearly as wide, with her broadside bearing on the entrance.

"If it is as large as that," Will said, "there will be plenty of room for us to manœuvre. Did you make out what number of guns she carried?"

"Yes, sir, she mounted four guns on each side; I should say they were for the most part ten-pounders."

"I think we can reckon upon taking her. Our guns are of heavier metal than hers, and the long-tom will make up for our deficiency in numbers."

L'Agile was put under as easy sail as would suffice to give her manœuvring powers, and then headed for the mouth of the inlet. She was half-way through when suddenly two hidden batteries, each mounting three guns, opened upon her.

"Drop the anchor at once," Will shouted; "we will finish with these gentlemen before we go farther." The schooner at the same time opened fire, but at half a mile range her guns did not inflict much damage upon the cutter. Lying between the two batteries she engaged them both, her broadside guns firing with grape, while the long-tom sent a shot into each alternately. In a quarter of an hour their fire was silenced, three of the guns were dismounted, and the men who had been working them fled precipitately.

"Take a boat and spike the remaining guns, Dimchurch," Will said; "I don't want any more bother with them."

In a few minutes Dimchurch returned to the cutter, having accomplished his mission. The anchor was then got up again, and she proceeded to attack the schooner. L'Agile's casualties had been trifling; only one had been killed and three wounded, all of them slightly. As she sailed up the inlet she replied with her pivot-gun to the fire of the enemy. At every shot the splinters were seen to fly from the schooner's side, much to the discomfiture of the pirate gunners, whose aim became so wild that scarcely a shot struck L'Agile. When within a hundred yards of the schooner the helm was put down, and the cutter swept round and opened fire with her two broadside guns.

The shots had scarcely rung out when Harman touched Will on the shoulder. "Look there, sir," he said. Will turned and saw a vessel emerging from a side channel, which was so closed in with trees that it had been unperceived by anybody aboard the cutter. Her aim was evidently to get between them and the sea. She was a cutter of about the same size as L'Agile, but carried six ten-pounders.

"The schooner has enticed us in here," Will said, "there is no doubt about that, and now there is nothing to do but to fight it out. Take her head round," he said, "we will settle it with the cutter first. The schooner cannot come to her assistance for some minutes as she has all her sails furled."

Accordingly he ranged up to the new-comer, and a furious contest ensued. He engaged her with two broadside guns and the long-tom, and at the same time kept his other two guns playing upon the schooner, the crew of which were busy getting up sail. The long-tom was served by Dimchurch himself, and every shot went crashing through the side of the pirate cutter, the fire of the two broadside guns being almost equally effective.

"Keep it up, lads," Will shouted; "we shall finish with her before the other can come up." As he spoke a shot from the long-tom struck the cutter's mainmast, which tottered for a moment and then fell over her side towards L'Agile, and the sails and hamper entirely prevented the crew from working her guns. For another five minutes the fire was kept up; then the crew were seen to be leaping overboard, and presently a man stood up and shouted that she surrendered. The schooner was now coming up fast.

"Don't let her escape," Will shouted; "she has had enough of it, and is trying to get away. Run her aboard!" In a minute the two vessels crashed together, and headed by Will, Harman, and Dimchurch, L'Agile's crew sprang on board the schooner.

The pirate crew were evidently discouraged by the fate of their consort and by the complete failure of their plan to capture L'Agile. The captain, a gigantic mulatto, fought desperately, as did two or three of his principal men. One of them charged at Will while he was engaged with another, and would have killed him had not Tom Stevens sprung forward and caught the blow on his own cutlass. The sword flew from the man's hand, and Tom at once cut him down. Dimchurch engaged in a single-handed contest with the great mulatto captain. Strong as the sailor was he could with difficulty parry the ruffian's blows, but skill made up for inequality of strength, and after a few exchanges he laid the man low with a clever thrust. The fall of their leader completed the discomfiture of the pirates, most of whom at once sprang overboard and made for the shore, those who remained being cut down by the sailors.

When at last they were masters of the ship the crew gave three lusty cheers. But Will did not permit them to waste precious time in rejoicing. He knew that, though they had accomplished so much, there was still a great deal to be done, for the prizes might even yet be recaptured before they got them out to sea. Without a moment's delay, therefore, he sent a boat to take possession of the cutter. The sail and wreckage were cleared away, and the boat proceeded to tow her out of the inlet. In the meantime a warp was taken from L'Agile to the schooner, the sails of the latter were lowered, and Will sailed proudly out with his second prize in tow. Once fairly at sea the crew began to repair damages. Five men in all had been killed and eleven were wounded. Several of the latter, however, were able to lend a hand. The shot-holes in L'Agile were first patched with pieces of plank, then covered with canvas, and afterwards given a coat of paint. Then the schooner was taken in hand, and when she was got into something like ship-shape order her sails were hoisted again, and ten men under Harman placed on board to work her. The cutter was taken in tow, only three men being left on board to steer.

It was late in the afternoon before all the repairs were completed. Before sailing, a rough examination was made of the holds of the two vessels, and to the great satisfaction of L'Agile's crew both were found to contain a considerable amount of booty.

"It is probable that there is a storehouse somewhere," Will

said; "but as we have under thirty available men it would be madness to try to land, for certainly two-thirds of the scoundrels escaped by swimming, and as each craft must have carried nearly a hundred men we should have been altogether overmatched. Well, they had certainly a right to count upon success; their arrangements were exceedingly good. No doubt they expected us to leave the batteries alone, and from the position in which they were placed they could have peppered us hotly while we were engaged with the schooner; in which case they would probably have had an easy victory. It was a cleverly-laid trap and ought to have succeeded."

"And it would, sir," Dimchurch said, "if you had not turned from the schooner and settled with the cutter before the other could come to her assistance."

"The credit is largely due to you," Will said; "that shot of yours that took the mast out was the turning-point of the fight. It completely crippled her, and as it luckily fell towards us it altogether prevented them from returning our fire."

Very proud were Will and his crew when they sailed into Port Royal with their two prizes. Will at once rowed to the flagship, where he received a very hearty greeting. "You have not come empty-handed, I see, Mr. Gilmore," the admiral said; "you were lucky indeed to take two ships of your own size one after the other."

"We took them at the same time, sir," Will said, "as you will see by my report."

The admiral gave a look of surprise and opened the document. First he ran his eye over it, then he read it more attentively. When he had finished he said: "You have fought a most gallant action, Mr. Gilmore, a most gallant action. It was indeed long odds you had against you, two vessels each considerably over your own size and manned by far heavier crews, besides the two batteries. It was an excellent idea to leave the vessel with which you were first engaged and turn upon the second one. If you had tried to fight them both at once you would almost certainly have been overcome, and you succeeded because you were cool enough to grasp the fact that the schooner at anchor and with her sails down would not be able to come to her friend's assistance for some minutes, and acted so promptly on your conclusions. The oldest officer in the service could not have done better. I congratulate you very heartily on your conduct. What are the contents of the cargoes of the prizes?"

"I cannot say, sir. With three vessels on my hands I had no time to examine them, but they certainly contain a number of bales of various sorts. I opened one which contained British goods."

"Then no doubt they are the pick of the cargoes they

captured," the admiral said; "I will go off with you myself and ascertain. I have nothing else to do this afternoon, and it will be a matter of interest to me as well as to you. You may as well let your own gig row back and I will take mine."

Accordingly the gig was sent back to L'Agile with orders for two boats to be lowered and twenty of the men to be ready to go to the two prizes. As soon as the admiral came on board the hatchways were opened, and the men brought up a number of the bales. These were found to contain fine cloths, material for women's dresses, china, ironmongery, carpets, and other goods of British manufacture. The other vessel contained sugar, coffee, ginger, spices, and other products of the islands. "That is enough," said the admiral; "I don't think we shall be far wrong if we put down the value of those two cargoes at £10,000. The two vessels will sell for about £1000 apiece, so that the prize-money will be altogether about £12,000, and even after putting aside my portion you will all share to a handsome amount in the proceeds. That is the advantage of not belonging to a squadron. In that case your share would not be worth anything like what it will now be. By the way, since you have been absent I have received the account of the prize-money earned by the Furious in the Mediterranean and by the capture of the French frigates. It amounts in all to £35,000. Of course as a midshipman your share will not be very large; probably, indeed, it will not exceed £250, so, you see, pirate-hunting in the West Indies, in command even of a small craft, pays enormously better than being a midshipman on board a frigate."

"It does indeed, sir, though £250 would be a fortune to a midshipman."

"Well, if our calculations as to the value of the cargoes and ships are correct, you will get more than ten times that amount now. And as there are only the flag and one other officer to share with you, the men's portion will be something like £100 apiece. A few more captures like this," and he laughed, "and you will become a rich man."

He then rowed away to his own ship, and Will returned to L'Agile and gladdened the hearts of Harman and the crew with the news of the value of their captures. L'Agile remained another week in harbour, during which time all signs of the recent conflict were removed, and he received a draft of men sufficient to bring his crew up to its former level. Then she again set sail.

They had cruised for about a fortnight when one morning, just as Will was getting up, Dimchurch ran down and reported that they had sighted two sails suspiciously near each other. "One," he said, "looks to me a full-rigged ship, and the other a large schooner."

"I will have a look at them," Will said, and, putting on his clothes, he ran on deck.

"Yes, it certainly looks suspicious," he said, when he had examined them through his telescope; "we will head towards them."

"She looks to me a very large schooner, sir," said Dimchurch.

"Yes, she is larger than these pirates generally are, but there is very little doubt as to her character. How far are they off, do you think?"

"Ten miles, sir, I should say; but we have got the land-breeze while they are becalmed. By the look of the water I should say we should carry the wind with us until we are pretty close to them."

Every sail the cutter could carry was hoisted, and she approached the two vessels rapidly. They were some four miles from them when the sails of the schooner filled and she began to move through the water.

"It will be a long chase now," Will said; "but the cutter has light wings, so we have a good chance of overhauling her."

"The sails of the ship are all anyhow, sir," Harman said.

"So they are, Mr. Harman; foul play has been going on there, I have not the least doubt. The fact that the crew are not making any effort to haul in her sheets and come to meet us is in itself a proof of it. I think it is our duty to board her and see what has taken place. Even if we allow the schooner to escape we shall light upon her again some day, I have no doubt."

"She is very low in the water," he said, after examining the merchantman carefully through his telescope, "and either her cargo is of no value to the pirates, and they have allowed it to remain in her, or they have scuttled her."

"I am afraid it is that, sir," Dimchurch said, "for she is certainly lower in the water than when I first saw her."

"You are right, Dimchurch, the scoundrels have scuttled her. Please God we shall get to her before she founders! Oh for a stronger wind! Do you think we could row there quicker than we sail?"

"No, sir. The gig might go as fast as the cutter, but the other boat would not be able to keep pace with her."

"Well, make all preparations for lowering. Heaven only knows what tragedy may have taken place there."

After all had been got ready, every eye on board the cutter was fixed on the vessel. There was no doubt now that she was getting deeper in the water every minute. When they got within a quarter of a mile of the ship she was so low that it was evident she could not float many minutes longer.

"To the boats, men," Will cried, "row for your lives."

A moment later three boats started at full speed. The gig, in which Dimchurch and Tom were both rowing, was first to search the sinking ship. Will leapt on board at once, and as he did so he gave an exclamation of horror, for the deck was strewn with dead bodies. Without stopping to look about him he ran aft to the companion and went down to the cabin, which was already a foot deep in water. There he found some fifteen men and women sitting securely bound on the sofas. Will drew his dirk, and running along cut their thongs.

"Up on deck for your lives," he cried, "and get into the boats alongside; she will not float three minutes."

At the farther end of the cabin a young girl was kneeling by the side of a stout old lady, who had evidently fainted.

"Come," Will said, going up to her, "it is a matter of life and death; we shall have the water coming down the companion in a minute or two."

"I can't leave her," the girl cried.

Will attempted to lift the old lady, but she was far too heavy for him.

"I cannot save her," he said, and raised a shout for Dimchurch. It was unanswered. "There," he said, "the water is coming down; she will sink in a minute. I cannot save her—indeed she is as good as dead already—but I can save you," and snatching the girl up he ran to the foot of the companion. The water was already pouring down, but he struggled up against it, and managed to reach the deck; but before he could cross to the side the vessel gave a sudden lurch and went down. He was carried under with the suck, but by desperate efforts he gained the surface just as his breath was spent. For a moment or two he was unable to speak, but he was none the less ready to act. Looking round he saw a hen-coop floating near, and, swimming to it, he clung to it with one arm while he held the girl's head above water with the other. Then, when he had recovered his breath, he shouted "Dimchurch!" Fortunately the gig was not far away, and his hail was at once answered, and a moment later the boat was alongside the hen-coop.

"Take this young lady, Dimchurch, and lay her in the stern-sheets. She can't be dead, for she was sensible when the ship went down, and we were not under water a minute."

After the girl had been laid down, Will was helped in.

"Did we save them all?" he asked.

"Yes, sir; at least I think so. They all came running on deck and jumped straight into the boats. I was busy helping them, and did not notice that you were missing. As the last seemed to have come up, I called to the other boats to make off, for I saw that she could only float a minute longer, and as it was we had only just got clear when she went down. Indeed we had a narrow escape of it, and the men had to row. I was standing up to look for you, and had just discovered that you were not in any of the boats, when I heard you call. It gave me a bad turn, as you may guess, sir, and glad I was when I saw you were holding on to that hen-coop."

"Now, let us try and bring this young lady round," Will said.

They turned her over first upon her face and let the water run out of her mouth. Then they laid her flat on her back with a jersey under her head, and rubbed her hands and feet and pressed gently at times on her chest. After five minutes of this treatment the girl heaved a sigh, and shortly afterwards opened her eyes and looked round in bewilderment at the faces of the men. Then suddenly she realized where she was and remembered what had happened.

"Oh, it was dreadful!" she murmured. "Poor Miss Morrison was lost, was she not?"

"If that was the name of the lady you were kneeling by I regret to say that she was. It was impossible to save her; for though I tried my best I could not lift her. As you call her Miss Morrison I presume she is not a close relation."

"No, she had been my governess since I was a child, and has been a mother to me. Oh, to think that she is dead while I am saved!"

"You must remember that it might have been worse," Will said; "you certainly cannot require a governess many more years, and will find others on whom to bestow your affection. How old are you?"

"I am fourteen," the girl said.

"Well, here is my ship, and we will all do our best to make you comfortable."

"Your ship!" the girl said in surprise; "do you mean to say that you are in command of her? You do not look more than a boy."

"I am not much more than a boy," he said with a smile, "but for all that I am the commander of this vessel, and this young gentleman is my second in command."

CHAPTER VIII

A SPLENDID HAUL

When all were got on board, and the boats hoisted to the davits, Will conducted the ladies down to the cabin, which he handed over to them. Then, having ordered the cook to prepare some hot soup for the girl he had rescued, he came on deck again and questioned the male passengers.

"We were all dressing for dinner," one said, "when we heard a shouting on deck. Almost immediately there was a great bump, which knocked most of us off our feet, and we thought that we had been run into, but directly afterwards we heard a great tumult going on above us, and we guessed that the ship had been attacked by pirates. The clashing of swords and the falling of bodies went on for two or three minutes, and then there was a loud savage yell that told us that the pirates had taken the ship. Next moment the ruffians rushed down upon us, took away any valuables we had about our persons, and then tied us up and threw us on the sofas. After scouring all the cabins they left us, and by the noise that followed we guessed that they had removed the hatches and were getting up the cargo.

"This continued all night, and some time this morning we heard the brutes going down to their boats, and thanked God that they had spared our lives. Presently all became still; but after a time we saw the water rising on the floor, and the dreadful thought struck us that they had scuttled the ship and left us to perish. One of us managed, in spite of his bonds, to make his way up the companion and endeavour to open the door. He found, however, to his horror that it was fastened outside. Time after time he flung himself against it, but it would not yield. The water rose higher and higher, and we were waiting for the end when, to our delight, we heard a bump as of a boat coming alongside the vessel, then the sound of someone running along the deck and of the companion door being hurriedly opened. You know the rest. The ship was the Northumberland of Bristol."

"Thank God we arrived in time!" Will said. "It was an affair of seconds. If we had been two minutes later you would all have been drowned."

"What has become of that terrible pirate?" asked one of the passengers.

"There he is, six miles away. I hope some day to avenge the murder of your captain and crew."

"But his ship looks a good deal larger than yours."

"Yes," Will said, "but we don't take much account of size. We captured two pirates in one fight, both of them bigger than ourselves."

"And your ship looks such a small thing, too, in comparison with our vessel!"

"Yes, your ship could pretty well take her up and carry her. Weight doesn't go for much in fighting."

"And are you really her commander?"

"I have that honour. I am a midshipman, and before I got command of L'Agile I was on board His Majesty's ships Furious and Hawke. I had a great deal of luck in several fights we came through, and as a result was entrusted by the admiral with the command of this vessel. As you say, she is small, but her guns are heavy for her size, and are more than a match for most of those carried by the pirates."

"Well, sir, in the name of myself and all my fellow-passengers I offer you my sincerest thanks for the manner in which you saved our lives. How close a shave it was is shown by the fact that you were yourself unable to get off the ship in time and were carried down with her."

"It was all in the way of business," Will laughed. "We were after the pirates, and when we saw the state of your vessel we reluctantly gave up the chase in order to see if we could be of any assistance. I expect the schooner wouldn't have run away from us had she not been so full of the cargo she got from your ship. They could not have had time to stow it all below, and it would have hampered them in working their guns, besides probably affecting their speed. I shall know her again when I see her, and then will try if these scoundrels are as good at fighting as they are at cold-blooded murder."

"Where are you going now, sir?"

"I am cruising at present, and am master of my own movements, so if you will let me know where you are bound for, I will try to set as many of you down at your destination as I can."

"Most of us are bound for Jamaica, sir, and the others will be able to find their way to their respective islands from there."

"Very well, then, I will head for Jamaica at once. In the

meantime my cabin and that of my second in command are at the service of the ladies. There are the sofas, too, in the saloon, and if these are not enough I will get some hammocks slung. I shall myself sleep on deck, and those of you who prefer it can do the same; for the others I will have hammocks slung in the hold."

Most of the ladies soon came up, but the girl Will had saved did not appear till the next morning. She was very pretty, and likely to be more so. If he had allowed her she would have overwhelmed him with thanks, but he made light of the whole affair. He learned from the other passengers that she was the daughter of one of the richest merchants in Jamaica. At the death of her mother, when she was five years old, she was sent home to England in charge of the governess who had been drowned in the Northumberland, and when this catastrophe occurred had been on her way to rejoin her father. Although saddened by the death of her old friend, she soon showed signs of a disposition naturally bright and cheerful. She bantered Will about his command, and professed to regard L'Agile as a toy ship, expressing great wonder that it was not manned by boy A.B.'s as well as boy officers.

"It must surely seem very ridiculous to you," she said, "to be giving orders to men old enough to be your father."

"I can quite understand that it seems so to you," he said, "for it does to me sometimes; but custom is everything, and I don't suppose the men give the matter a thought. At any rate they are as ready to follow me as they are the oldest veteran in the service."

Will carried all the sail he could set, as he was anxious to get the craft free from passengers and to be off in search of the schooner that had escaped him. He was again loaded with thanks by the passengers when they landed, and after seeing them off he went and made his report to the admiral.

"How is this, Mr. Gilmore?" the admiral said as he entered the cabin; "no prizes this time? And who are all those people I saw landing just now?"

Will handed in his report; but, as usual, the admiral insisted on hearing all details.

"But your uniform looks shrunk, Mr. Gilmore," he said when Will had finished. "You said nothing about being in the water!"

Will was then obliged to relate how he had rescued the girl from the cabin.

"Well done again, young sir! it is a deed to be as proud of as the capturing of those two pirates. Well done, indeed! Now I suppose you want to be off again?"

"Yes, sir, I should like to sail as soon as possible; in the first place, because I am most anxious to fall in with that schooner and bring the captain and crew in here to be hanged."

"That is a very laudable ambition. And why in the second place?"

"Because I want to get off before a lot of people come to thank me for saving their relatives, and so on, sir. If I get away at once, then I may hope that before I come back again the whole thing will be forgotten."

"It oughtn't to be, for you acted very wisely and gallantly."

"Well, sir, I don't want a lot of thanks for only doing what was my duty."

"Very good, Mr. Gilmore, I understand your feelings, but I quite expect that when you do return you will have to go through the ordeal of being presented with a piece of plate, and probably after that you will have to attend a complimentary ball. Now, you can go back to your ship at once. Here is a letter to the chief of the store department instructing him to furnish you with any stores you may want without waiting for my signature."

"Thank you very much, sir! I hope, when I return, that I shall bring that pirate in tow. Can I have three months from the present time?"

"Certainly, and I hope you will be able to make good use of it."

Returning to his ship, Will at once made out the list of the stores he required, and sent Harman on shore with it, telling him to take two boats and bring everything back with him. At five o'clock in the afternoon the two boats returned, carrying all the stores required. The water-tanks had already been filled up, and a quarter of an hour later the cutter was under sail and leaving the harbour.

Will, of course, had nothing whatever to guide him in his search for the schooner beyond the fact that she was heading west at the time when he last saw her. At that time they were to the south of Porto Rico, so he concluded that she was making for Cuba. Every day, therefore, he cruised along the coast of that island, sometimes sending boats ashore to examine inlets, at other times running right out to sea in the hope that the pirate, whose spies he had no doubt were watching his movements, might suppose he had given up the search and was sailing away. Nevertheless, he could not be certain that she would endeavour to avoid him should she catch sight of him, for with a glass the pirate captain could have made out the number of guns L'Agile carried, and would doubtless feel confident in his own superiority, as he would not be able to discover the weight of the guns. Will felt that if the pirate should fight, his best policy would be at first to make a pretence of running, in the hope that in a long chase he might manage to knock away some of the schooner's spars.

One day he saw the boats, which had gone up a deep inlet, coming back at full speed.

"We saw a schooner up there," Harman reported; "I think she is the one we are in search of. When we sighted her she was getting up sail."

"That will just suit me. We will run out to sea at once; that will make him believe we are afraid of him."

Scarcely had the boats been got on board, and the cutter's head turned offshore, when the schooner was seen issuing from the inlet. Will ordered every sail to be crowded on, and had the satisfaction of seeing the schooner following his example. He then set the whole of the crew to shift the long-tom from the bow to the stern. Its muzzle was just high enough to project above the taffrail, and in order to hide it better he had hammocks and other material piled on each side of it so as to form a breastwork three feet high.

"They will think," he said, "that we have put this up as a protection against shot from his bow-chasers."

After watching the schooner for a quarter of an hour, Will said:

"I don't think she gains upon us at all; lower a sail over the bow to deaden her way. A small topsail will do; I only want to check her half a knot an hour."

It was an hour before the schooner yawed and fired her bow-guns.

"That is good," Will said to Dimchurch; "it shows that she doesn't carry a long-tom. I thought she didn't, but they might have hidden it, as we have done. Don't answer them yet; I don't want to fire till we get within half a mile of her; then they shall have it as hot as they like."

The schooner continued to gain slowly, occasionally firing her bow-chasers. When she had come up to within a mile of L'Agile the cutter was yawed and two broadside guns fired; they were purposely aimed somewhat wide, as Will was anxious that the pirates should not suspect the weight of his metal, and did not wish, by inflicting some small injury, to deter her from continuing the chase. The schooner evidently depended upon the vastly superior strength of her crew to carry the cutter by boarding, and so abstained from attempting to injure her, as the less damage she suffered the better value she would be as a prize.

"They are not more than half a mile off now, I think, sir," Dimchurch said at last.

"Very well then, we will let her have it."

The gun was already loaded, so Dimchurch took a steady aim and applied the match. All leapt upon the bulwarks to see the effect of the shot, and a cheer broke from the crew as it struck the schooner on the bow, about four feet above the water. In return the schooner yawed so as to bring her whole broadside to bear on the cutter, and six tongues of flame flashed from her side. At the same moment L'Agile swung round and fired her two starboard guns. Both ships immediately resumed their former positions, and as they did so Dimchurch fired again, his shot scattering a shower of splinters from almost the same spot as the other had struck.

"You must elevate your gun a little more, Dimchurch," said Will, "and bring a mast about their ears. Get that sail on board!" he shouted; "I don't want the schooner to get any nearer."

The order was executed, and the difference in the speed of the cutter was at once manifest. Again and again Dimchurch fired. Several of the shot went through the schooner's foresail, but as yet her masts were untouched.

"A little more to the right, Dimchurch."

This time the sailor was longer than usual in taking aim, but when he fired the schooner's foremast was seen to topple over, and her head flew up into the wind, thus presenting her stern to the cutter.

"She is a lame duck now," Will said, "but we may as well take her mainmast out of her too. Fire away, and take as good aim as you did last time."

Ten more shots were fired, and with the last the pirate's mainmast went over the side.

"Well done, Dimchurch! Now we have her at our mercy. We will sail backwards and forwards under her stern and rake her with grape. I don't want to injure her more than is necessary, but I do want to kill as many of the crew as possible; it is better for them to die that way than to be taken to Jamaica to be hanged."

For an hour the cutter kept at work crossing and recrossing her antagonist's stern, and each time she poured in a volley from two broadside guns and the long-tom. The stern of the schooner was knocked almost to pieces, and the grape-shot carried death along her decks.

"I am only afraid that they will blow her up," Will said; "but probably, as they have not done so already, her captain and most of her officers are killed, for it would require a desperado to undertake that job."

At last the black flag was hoisted on a spar at the stern, and then lowered again. When they saw this the crew of L'Agile stopped firing, and sent up cheer after cheer.

"Now we must be careful, sir," Dimchurch said; "those scoundrels are quite capable of pretending to surrender, and then, when we board her, blowing their ship and us into the air."

"You are right, Dimchurch. They might very well do that, for they must know well enough that they can expect no mercy."

Bringing the cutter to within a hundred yards of the schooner, Will shouted:

"Have you a boat that can swim?" and receiving a reply in the negative, shouted back: "Very well, then, I will drop one to you."

He then placed the cutter exactly to windward of the schooner, and, lowering one of the boats, to which a rope was attached, let it drift down to the prize.

"Now," he shouted, "fasten a hawser to that boat; the largest you have."

There was evidently some discussion among the few men gathered on the deck of the pirate, and, seeing that they hesitated, Will shouted:

"Do as you are ordered, or I will open fire again."

This decided the pirates, and in a short time the end of a hawser was tied to one of the thwarts of the boat. The boat was then hauled back to L'Agile, and when the cable was got on board it was knotted to their own strongest hawser.

"That will keep them a good bit astern," Will said; "otherwise, if the wind were to drop at night, they might haul their own vessel up to us, and carry out their plan of blowing us up."

"It is wise to take every precaution, sir," Harman said; "but I don't think any trick of that sort would be likely to succeed. You may be sure we should keep too sharp a watch on them."

While the hawsers were being spliced, Will shouted to the pirates to cut away the wreckage from their ship, and when this was done he started with his prize in tow. As soon as they were fairly under weigh he hailed the prisoners through his speaking-trumpet and questioned them about their casualties. They replied that at the beginning of the engagement they had had one hundred and twenty men on board. The captain had been killed by the first volley of grape, and the slaughter among the crew had been terrible, all the officers being killed and eighty of the men. The remainder had run

102

down into the hold, and remained there until, after a consultation, one of them crawled up on deck and hoisted and lowered the black flag.

"I suppose," Will said, "your intention was to blow the ship and yourselves and us into the air as soon as we came on board."

"That is just what we did mean," one of them shouted savagely; "if we could but have paid you out we would not have minded what became of ourselves."

"It is well, indeed, Dimchurch, that you suggested the possibility of their doing this to us. But for that we should certainly have lost nearly all our number, for, not knowing how many of the crew survived, I could not have ventured to go on board without pretty nearly every man. It will be a lesson to me in future, when I am fighting pirates, to act as if they were wild beasts."

"Well, sir, I don't know that they are altogether to be blamed; it is only human nature to pay back a blow for a blow, and with savages like these, especially when they know that they are bound to be hanged, you could hardly expect anything else."

"I suppose not, Dimchurch, and certainly for myself I would rather be blown up than hanged. I suppose the reason why they did not blow up the ship when they found their plan had failed was that they clung to life even for a few days."

"I expect it is that, sir; besides, you know, each man may think that although no doubt the rest will be hanged, he himself may get off."

"Yes, I dare say that has something to do with it," Will agreed. "I don't think it likely, however, that any one of them will be spared after that affair of the Northumberland, and very probably that was only one of a dozen ships destroyed in the same way.

"Now, Harman, we will put her head round and sail back."

"Sail back, sir?"

"Certainly; I think there is no doubt that that inlet is the pirates' head-quarters, and that they are certain to have storehouses there choke-full of plunder. Some of their associates will in that case be on shore looking after it, and if their ship doesn't return they will divide the most valuable portion of these stores among themselves, and set fire to all the rest. We have done extremely well so far, but another big haul will make matters all the pleasanter."

"But what will you do with the prize?" asked Harman.

"I will cast her off eight or ten miles from the shore; they have no boats, and the schooner is a mere log on the water. When we see what plunder they have collected I shall be able to decide how to act.

The cutter can hold a great deal, but if we find more than she can carry we must load the schooner also."

"But what would you do with the pirates in that case, sir?"

"I should try to make them come off in batches, and then iron them; but if they would not do that, I should be inclined to tow the schooner to within half a mile of the shore, and so give all that could swim the chance of getting away. Those of them that are unable to do so would probably manage to get off on spars or hatchways. They have been richly punished already, and I fancy the admiral would be much better pleased to see the schooner come in loaded with valuable plunder than if she carried only forty scoundrels to be handed over to the hangman."

"But if we were to let them escape we should have to take great care on shore while we were rifling the storehouse."

"You may be sure that I should do that, Harman. The fellows could certainly take no firearms on shore, and I should keep ten men with loaded muskets always on guard, while those who are at work would have their firearms handy to them."

They towed the schooner to within seven or eight miles of the shore, and then cast her off and made for the creek from which the pirates had come out. As they entered the inlet, which was two miles long, they could see no signs of houses, so they sailed as far as they could and anchored. Will then landed with a party of ten well-armed men, and at once began to make a careful examination of the beach. In a short time they found a well-beaten path going up through the wood. Before following this, however, Will took the precaution to have fifteen more men sent ashore, as it was, of course, impossible to say how many of a guard had been left at the head-quarters. When the second party had landed, all advanced cautiously up the path, holding their muskets in readiness for instant action. They met, however, with no opposition; the pirates were evidently unaware of their presence. They had gone but a very short distance when they came to a large clearing, in the middle of which they saw several large huts and three great storehouses. They went on at the double towards them, but they had gone only a short distance when they heard a shout and a shot, and saw a dozen men and a number of women issue from the backs of the huts and make for the wood.

"Now, my lads," shouted Will, "break open the doors of those storehouses; there is not likely to be much that is of value in the huts. You had better take four men, Dimchurch, and set fire to them all; of course you can just look in and see if there is anything worth taking before you apply a light."

Will himself superintended the breaking open of the storehouses. When he entered the first he paused in amazement; it was filled to the very top with boxes and bales. The other two were in a similar condition.

"There is enough to fill the cutter and the prize a dozen times," Will said. "I expect they trade to some extent with the Spaniards, but they evidently had another intention in storing these goods. Probably they proposed, when they had amassed sufficient, to charter a large ship, fill her up to the hatchways, and sail to some American port or some other place where questions are not usually asked."

There was a safe in the corner of one of the storehouses; this they blew open, and when Will examined its contents he found that they consisted of the papers and manifests of cargoes of no fewer than eleven ships.

"My conjecture was right," he said. "They intended, no doubt, to keep some large merchantman they had captured, fill her with the contents of their prizes, and then with the papers and manifests of cargo they could go almost anywhere and dispose of their ill-gotten goods."

"I have no doubt that is so, sir," Dimchurch said; "I only wonder they did not set about it before."

"It is quite possible they have done so already," Will said, "but they may have taken prizes quicker than they could dispose of them, which would account for this immense accumulation. Now, Dimchurch, I will sit down and go through those bills of lading and pick out the most valuable goods. We will then take these off to begin with, and can leave it to the admiral to send a man-of-war or charter some merchantman to bring the rest. The schooner should carry between two and three hundred tons, and we could manage to cram eighty or a hundred into our hold. If we get all that safely to Jamaica, we need not grieve much if we find that the rest of the goods have been burned before the ships can come to fetch them."

It took him three hours to go through the bills of lading, making a mark against all the most valuable goods. Then some of the men were set to sort these out. There was no great difficulty about this, as the goods had been very neatly stored, those belonging to each ship being separated by narrow passages from the rest. The remainder of the men except two were meanwhile brought from the cutter. Sentries were then placed to watch all the approaches to the storehouses, and while ten men got out the bales and boxes, the remaining twenty-six carried them down the path. At night half the men remained in the storehouses, the other half returning to the cutter.

Before sunset Will went with a small escort to the top of a neighbouring hill to see that all was well with the hulk of the schooner. With the aid of his telescope he could see her plainly, and to his great satisfaction noted that she had made but little drift.

The next morning the work was resumed, and was carried on all day with only short breaks for meals, and so on the following two days. At the end of that time as much had been put on board the cutter as she could carry. Ten men were then left to guard the stores, and the rest, going on board, sailed out to the schooner and towed her in. They did not, as was at first intended, stop a mile outside the inlet, but came right into it and anchored opposite the path, as the labour of continually loading the cutter and then transferring her cargo to the hulk would have been very great. The next morning a party of twelve men went on board her, and found, as Will had expected, that she was entirely deserted.

"They will be too happy at having made their escape to do anything for the next day or two," Will said, "so we can go on working as usual. Fortunately the fellows who were left in the huts were taken so completely by surprise that they bolted at once and left their guns behind. If, therefore, they are joined by their friends from the schooner, and attack us, they will have no firearms with them, for, as the hulk is anchored about two hundred yards from shore, it would require a marvellously good swimmer to carry his musket and ammunition ashore with him. In future, however, we will leave twenty men to guard the storehouses at night; there is no boat in the inlet by means of which they could attack the cutter, and they are not likely to try to do so by swimming. At any rate, Harman, I will place you in command of her, and shall therefore feel perfectly confident that we shall not be taken by surprise."

"You can trust me for that, sir; I promise you that I will sleep with one eye open, though I don't think they would be likely to attempt such an enterprise. They are much more likely to attack you at the stores. I think it would be advisable to take twenty-five men with you and leave me with fifteen, which would be ample. I should divide them into two watches, so that there would always be seven on deck. Jefferson, who is an uncommonly sharp fellow, would be in charge of one of the watches, and Williams of the other; and as I should myself be up and down all night, there would be no chance of our being caught napping." Will agreed to this arrangement.

The prize was now brought close inshore, the water being

deep enough to allow of this. It was a great advantage, as the goods could be put on board direct, and the work was thereby greatly accelerated.

Behind a pile of goods another safe was discovered, and this was found to contain £8500 in money, nearly a hundred watches, and a large amount of ladies' jewellery. Many watches had also been found in the huts before these were burned. The bales and boxes contained chiefly spices, silks and sateens, shawls, piece-goods, and coffee.

On the night of the fourth day after the escape of the prisoners one of the sentries perceived a dark mass moving from the wood. He at once fired his musket, and in a minute Will and Dimchurch, with their five-and-twenty men, were all in readiness.

"Now, my men," Will said, "these fellows will attempt to rush us. We will divide into three parties and will fire by volleys; one party must not fire till they see that all are loaded. In that way we shall always have sixteen muskets ready for them. I have no fear of the result, and even if they close with us our cutlasses will be more than a match for their knives. Here they come! Get ready, the first section, and don't fire till I tell you."

The enemy, fully sixty strong, came on with fierce cries, knowing that the garrison were on guard, although they could not see them in the shadow of the storehouses. When they got within fifty yards Will gave the order to fire, and the first eight muskets flashed out. The second eight fired almost immediately after, and the third eight, waiting only till the first section had reloaded, followed suit. Nearly every shot told, and the shock was so great that it caused the advancing enemy to hesitate for a moment. This gave the second and third sections time to reload, so that, when the pirates again advanced, three more deadly volleys were poured into them in quick succession. The effect of these was instantaneous. Fully five-and-thirty had been brought to the ground by the six volleys; the remainder halted, swayed for a moment, then turned and fled at full speed, pursued, however, before they reached the wood, by another general discharge.

Will was well pleased with the tremendously heavy punishment he had inflicted.

"Out of the sixty men who attacked us," he said to Harman the next morning, "I calculate that forty belonged to the schooner. I don't suppose they were worse than the other twenty; but we had ourselves seen some of the crimes they had committed. We have accounted for forty in all, so of those who escaped from the

107

schooner probably some five- or six-and-twenty have been killed. After such a thrashing they are not likely to make another attempt."

He was right. The work now went on undisturbed, and at the end of a fortnight the schooner was laden. All the hatches had been closed and made water-tight; and so full was she that her deck was only two feet and a half above the water, although her guns had been thrown overboard or landed.

"Now I think we are all ready to sail," Harman said.

"Ready to sail! We have a fortnight's hard work before us," said Will. "You don't suppose I am going to leave all these hogsheads of sugar, puncheons of rum, and bales of goods to be burnt or destroyed by those scoundrels."

"How can you prevent it?"

"Very easily. There are plenty of materials on the spot to form four batteries, one on each side of the storehouses. We will drag up eight of the schooner's guns and mount two on each battery; they shall be loaded and crammed to the muzzle with grape-shot. The batteries shall be built clear of the storehouses and in echelon, so that if one is attacked it can be supported by the others. As a garrison I will leave sixteen men under Dimchurch."

Dimchurch was called up and the matter explained to him, and he readily agreed to take charge.

"Two men," he said, "can be on watch in each battery while the others sleep; so there will be no chance of being taken by surprise, and you may be quite sure that, no matter how strong a mob may come down, they won't stand the discharge of eight cannon loaded as you say. I suppose, sir, you mean to form the batteries of bales of cotton. There is a whole ship-load of them."

"That is my intention, Dimchurch; I have had it in my mind all the time."

The whole strength of the crew, with the exception of two to watch on board the cutter, now went up to the storehouses, and the men, delighted to know that all this booty was not to be lost, set to work with great vigour. Will marked out the sites for the batteries, and the bales of cotton were rolled to them and built up into substantial walls. It took ten days of hard labour to do this and haul up the guns.

When the work was completed Dimchurch chose sixteen of the crew. There was an ample supply of provisions, which had been taken out of the huts before they were burnt; so it was not necessary to draw upon the stores of the cutter. When all was ready the two parties said good-bye, and, with a mutual cheer, the cutter's crew went on board.

"It is a hazardous business, I admit," Will said, as, having got up sail, they moved down the inlet with the schooner in tow. "Of course I shall be a little uneasy until we can return from Jamaica and relieve Dimchurch; but I feel convinced that he will be able to hold his own and to give another lesson to the pirates if necessary. When they see us sail out they will naturally conclude that no great number can be left to guard the stores. Still, we may be sure that they have kept a watch on our doings from the edge of the forest, and that the sight of the guns will inspire a wholesome dread in them. I cannot but think that eight discharges of grape and langrage will send them to the right-about however strong they may be. Besides, we have given the men three muskets each, in addition to their own, from those we found on board the schooner; so if the enemy press on they will be able to give them a warm reception. And then, even if the attack is too much for them, they have still a resource, for we have left an exit in the rear of each battery by which they can retire to the storehouses. I have instructed them to carry all their muskets back with them; sixteen men with four muskets apiece could make a very sturdy defence. As you know, I had the doors repaired and strengthened and loopholes cut in the walls. Still, I don't think they will be needed."

"How much do you think the prize will be worth?" Harman asked.

"I have really no idea, but I am sure that what we have got here and in the schooner must be worth some thousands of pounds. What we have left behind must be the contents of about ten vessels, as all we have been able to take is only a full cargo for one good-sized ship."

CHAPTER IX

A SPELL ASHORE

Ten days later they arrived at Jamaica, and Will at once went to make his report to the admiral.

"Well," the admiral said heartily, "you have brought in another prize, Mr. Gilmore. She looks a mere hulk, and is remarkably deep in the water. What is she?"

"She is the schooner that sank the Northumberland."

"You must have knocked her about terribly, for she is evidently sinking."

"No, sir, she is all right except that the stern is shattered. We have covered it over with tarpaulins backed by battens; otherwise she is almost uninjured."

"I am glad, indeed, to hear that you have caught that scoundrel, Mr. Gilmore, but I hardly think she can be worth towing in."

"She is worth a good deal, sir, for both she and the cutter are choke-full of loot."

"Indeed!" the admiral said in a tone of gratification. "In that case she must be valuable; but let me hear all about it."

"I have stated it in my report, sir."

"But you always leave out a good deal in your report. Please give me a full account of it. First, how many guns did she carry?"

"Six guns a-side, sir."

"Then you must have done wonders. Now tell me all about it."

Will modestly gave a full account of the fight and of the steps he had afterwards taken to prevent them from playing a treacherous trick upon him, and of the land fight and the arrangements made to secure the goods he found at their head-quarters.

"And now, what have you brought home this time?" the admiral asked.

"This is the list, sir. I took it from the bills of lading which we found at the pirate head-quarters. Altogether the storehouses contained the cargoes of eleven ships. We picked out the most valuable goods and loaded the cutter and schooner with them, but that was only a very small portion of the total. I have left nearly half my crew there to guard the storehouses until you could send some

110

ships from here to bring home their contents. With the cutter to navigate and the schooner to tow I dared not weaken myself further. I have left sixteen of my men there under my boatswain, and have erected four batteries with cotton bales, each mounting two guns, which are charged to the muzzle with grape and langrage. I have every confidence, therefore, that the little garrison will be able to hold its own against a greatly superior force."

"It was a great risk," the admiral said gravely.

"I am aware of that, sir, but it was worth running the risk for such a splendid prize. The value of nearly eleven cargoes must be something very great."

"Indeed it must," the admiral said; "what are they composed of?"

"You will see the entire list in the bills of lading, sir. I should say that nearly half the goods are sugar, rum, and molasses; the other half are bales and boxes, of which the details are given. Those we have brought home are silks, satins, cloth, shawls, and other materials of female dress, coffee, and spices."

"Well, Mr. Gilmore, this certainly appears to be the richest haul that has ever been made in these islands, at any rate since the days of the Spanish galleons. I will lose no time in chartering some ships. How many do you think will be necessary?"

"I should say, sir, that if you had five vessels you could do it in two trips. Meanwhile I wish you would give me another thirty men to strengthen the garrison."

"Certainly I will do so. There are several vessels in the harbour which have discharged their cargoes and have not yet taken fresh ones on board, but are waiting to sail for England under a convoy. They will, no doubt, be glad of a job in the meantime."

Four days later the cutter again put to sea, with five merchantmen and a frigate, which was charged to act as a convoy. When they arrived off the inlet Will went ashore, and to his delight found the storehouses intact, and the little garrison all well. The crews of all the ships were at once landed, and in a short time the place was a scene of bustle and activity. In spite, however, of their exertions it was a fortnight before all the ships were loaded.

Before setting sail again Will told off the thirty additional men to remain, and Harman was left in command. Dimchurch had reported that only once had the pirates shown in force. He had allowed them to come within a hundred yards of the battery they were facing, and then poured the contents of both guns into them, whereupon they had at once fled, leaving ten killed behind them.

When the little fleet arrived at Jamaica again, Will found that the goods which he had brought in the cutter and schooner were valued at a far higher price than his estimate.

The merchantmen were unloaded as fast as possible, and started again for Cuba without delay. All was well with the garrison at the inlet. A serious attack had been made on the forts the day after the fleet had sailed for Jamaica, but the garrison had repulsed it so effectually that they had not seen a sign of the enemy since. Even the hope of plunder was not strong enough to induce the negroes to make another attempt, and as for the pirates, they had been almost entirely wiped out.

After the storehouses had been emptied they were burned, and Harman and his party returned to the cutter, and the fleet once more sailed for Jamaica.

Will immediately started again on a short cruise. This time he met with no adventures. At the end of three weeks he returned, and when he went to make his report the admiral told him that the total value of the capture amounted to £140,000.

"I must congratulate you," he said, "as well as myself, on this haul. I should say it would make you the richest midshipman in the service. My share, as you know, is an eighth. You, as officer in command, and altogether independent of the fleet, will get one quarter. Mr. Harman's share will be an eighth, and the rest will be divided among the crew, the boatswain getting four shares."

"I am astounded, sir," Will said, "it seems almost impossible that I can be master of so much money."

"You have the satisfaction at any rate, Mr. Gilmore, of knowing that you have earned it by your own exertions, courage, and skill. I think now that it is only fair that I should send you back to your ship when she next comes in, and give someone else a chance."

"I agree with you, sir, and I cannot but feel deeply indebted to you for having put me in the way of making a fortune."

"I little knew what was coming of it," the admiral said, "when I gave you the command of that little craft. If I had had the slightest notion I should assuredly have given it to an older officer."

Will returned to the cutter in a state of bewilderment at his good fortune. When he came on deck a little later he found waiting for him a gentleman who advanced with open arms.

"Mr. Gilmore," he said, "my name is Palethorpe. I am the father of the young girl whose life you so gallantly saved when the Northumberland sank. I have been trying to catch you ever since, but I live up among the hills, except when business calls me down here, and your stay here has always been so short that I never before heard of your arrival until you had started again. I cannot say, sir, how intensely grateful I feel. She is my only child, and you may guess what a terrible blow it would have been to me had she been lost."

"I only did my duty, sir, and I am glad indeed that I was able to save your daughter's life. Pray do not say anything more about it."

"But, my dear sir, that is quite impossible. One man cannot render so vast a service to another and escape without being thanked. I have driven down here to carry you off to my home whether you like it or not. I called on the admiral this morning, and he said that he would willingly grant you a week's leave or longer, and, in fact, that you would be unemployed until the Hawke came in, as a master's mate would take over your command."

Will felt that he could not decline an invitation so heartily given. Accordingly he packed up his shore-going kit, left Harman in temporary command, and went with his new friend ashore. A well-appointed vehicle with a pair of fine horses was waiting for them, and as soon as they were seated they at once started inland. After leaving the town they began to mount, and were soon high among the mountains. The scenery was lovely, and Will, who had not before made an excursion so far into the interior, was delighted with his drive. So much so, indeed, that Mr. Palethorpe gradually ceased speaking of the subject nearest his heart, and suffered Will to enjoy the journey in silence. At last they drove up to a handsome house which was surrounded by a broad veranda covered with roses and other flowers. As they stopped, a girl of fourteen ran out. Will would scarcely have recognized her. She was now dressed in white muslin, and her hair was tied up with blue ribbon, while a broad sash of the same colour encircled her waist. She had now also recovered her colour, which the shock of her adventure had driven from her cheeks, and she looked the picture of health and happiness.

"Oh, you dear boy!" she cried out, and to Will's astonishment and consternation she threw her arms round his neck and kissed him. "Oh, how much you have done for us! If it hadn't been for you father would have had no one to pet him and scold him. It would have been dreadful, wouldn't it, daddy?"

"It would indeed, my child," her father said gravely; "it would have taken all the joy out of my life, and left me a lonely old man."

"I have told you before," she said, "that you are not to call yourself old. I don't call you old at all; I consider that you are just in

113

your prime. Now come in, Mr. Gilmore, I have all sorts of iced drinks ready for you."

Alice and Will soon became excellent friends. She took him over the plantations and showed him the negro cabins, fed him with fruit until he almost fell ill, and, as he said, treated him more like a baby than as an officer in His Majesty's service.

"The stars don't look so bright to-night," Will said, as he stood on the veranda with Mr. Palethorpe on the last evening of his visit.

"No, I have been noticing it myself, and I don't like the look of the weather at all."

"No!" Will repeated in surprise; "it certainly looks as if there was a slight mist."

"Yes, that is what it looks like, but at this time of year we don't often have mists. I am afraid we are going to have a hurricane; it is overdue now by nearly a month. October, November, and the first half of December are the hurricane months, and I fear that, as it is late, we shall have a heavy one."

"I have seen one since I came out, and then we were at sea and were nearly wrecked. I saw its effects on land, however, for we spent some weeks ashore in consequence of it. The forest was almost levelled. I certainly should not care to see another one."

"No, it is not a thing that anyone would wish to see a second time. Words cannot describe how terrible they are. I hope, however, if we have one, that it will be a light one, but I am rather afraid of it."

Nothing more was said on the matter till they retired to bed, when Mr. Palethorpe said, half in fun and half in earnest: "I should advise you to have your clothes handy by your bedside, Mr. Gilmore, for you may want them quickly and badly if a hurricane comes."

Will laughed to himself at the warning, but nevertheless took the advice. He had been asleep for an hour when he felt the whole house rock. A moment later the roof blew bodily from over his head, and at the same time there was a roar so terrible that he did not even hear the crash of the falling timber. He leapt out of bed, seized his clothes, and hurried down. He met Mr. Palethorpe coming from his daughter's room, carrying her wrapped up in her bed-clothes. They went down together to the front door. Will turned the handle, and the door was blown in with a force that knocked him to the floor. He struggled to his feet again and tried to get out, but the force of the wind was so tremendous that for some time he could not stem it. When he did manage to get through the doorway he saw Mr. Palethorpe standing some distance from the house. He fought his way towards him against the wind.

114

"Are you not going to get into shelter?" he shouted in the planter's ear.

"It is safer here in the open," the planter said; "I dare not get below a tree, but I will put my daughter in a place where she will be safe."

Struggling along against the gale he led the way to a small shed where the gardener's tools were kept. It was about six feet long and three broad, and was built of bricks. The floor was some feet below the surface of the ground, so in entering one had to descend a short flight of steps.

"Just hold my daughter on her feet," the planter said, "while I clear this place out."

Much as he tried, Will was unable to keep the girl upright, and after a vain effort he allowed her to sink down on her knees and then knelt by her side. As soon as he had cleared away the tools Mr. Palethorpe came up and carried her down into the shed.

"I think we are quite safe here," he said; "the wall is only two feet above the ground, so even this gale will not shake us. The roof is strongly put together to keep out marauders. Now, Mr. Gilmore, there is room for us to crouch inside; it is the only place of safety I know of, for even in the open we might be struck by the flying branches torn from the trees. Besides, it will be a comfort to Alice to know that we are in safety beside her."

They spoke only occasionally, for the roar of the tempest was deafening. Every now and then they would hear a crash as some tree yielded to the force of the hurricane. Towards morning the gale abated, and soon after sunrise the wind suddenly stilled. When they looked out a scene of terrible devastation met their eyes. Some trees had been torn up by the roots, and branches twisted from others were strewed upon the ground everywhere. The house was a wreck; the whole of the roof was gone, and parts of the wall had been blown down. Inside there was utter confusion; the furniture was scattered about in all directions, and even looking-glasses had been torn from the walls and smashed. The planter, however, wasted but little time in looking at the wreck.

"You had better go up and dress at once, Alice," he said, "though you will have some trouble in finding your clothes. I have no doubt that all the loose ones are scattered about everywhere, and that some of the things are miles away. I will go down with Will at once to the slave-huts; I am afraid the damage and loss of life there has been great."

During his passage from the house to the shed the wind had

several times threatened to tear Will's clothes from his arms, but he had clung to them with might and main, and succeeded in carrying them safely into shelter. He had therefore been able to dress while they waited for the storm to abate. Mr. Palethorpe had felt so sure that a hurricane was impending that he had simply lain down on his bed without taking off his clothes. Accordingly they started at once for the slave-huts. As they had expected, the destruction there was complete. Every hut had been blown down. The negroes, who had fled to various places for shelter, were just returning, and Mr. Palethorpe soon learned from them that many were missing. He at once set all hands to remove the fallen timbers, and after two hours' work sixteen dead bodies were recovered, for the most part children, and nearly as many injured. Some, also, of those who had come in had broken limbs.

Alice came down as soon as she was dressed, and brought a bundle of sheets, needles, and thread, and Mr. Palethorpe took off his coat and set to work to bind and bandage the limbs and wounds. Alice suggested that a man on horseback should be sent down to the town for a surgeon, but her father pointed out that it would be absolutely useless to do so, as, judging by what they could see, the destruction wrought in the town would be terrible. Every surgeon would have his hands full, and certainly none would be able to spare time to come into the country. He decided to have all the worst cases carried down to the town and seen to there; slighter cases he could deal with himself.

"I don't know much about bandaging wounds," he said, "but I know a little, and some of the native women are very good at nursing."

Alice, aided by the negresses, tore up the linen into strips and sewed these together to make bandages. Canes split up formed excellent splints. Will rendered all the assistance in his power. Now he held splints in position while Mr. Palethorpe wound the bandages round them, and now he helped to distribute among the wounded the soothing drinks that the servants of the house brought down.

"What are you going to do now?" he asked as the last bandage had been applied.

"I will drive down to the town and see how things are doing there. Peter tells me that two of my horses are killed, but the other two seemed to have escaped without injury, as the part of the stable in which they stood was sheltered by a huge tree, which lost its head, but was fortunately otherwise uninjured. You had better come down with us, Alice; we must stop at our house in town till things are put straight here. I will, of course, ride backwards and forwards every day."

"Can't I be of some help here, father?"

"None at all; by nightfall the slaves will have built temporary shelters of canes and branches of trees. The overseer is among those who were killed; he was on his way from his house to the huts when a branch struck him on the head and killed him on the spot. I will put Sambo in his place for the present; he is a very reliable man, and I can trust him to issue the stores to the negroes daily. I am afraid it will be some time before we get the house put right again, as there will be an immense demand for carpenters in the town. We may feel very thankful, however, that we have got a house there. It is a good strong one, built of stone, so we may hope to find it intact."

The carriage was brought round and they took their seats in it. The planter ordered two strong negroes to get axes and to stand on the steps, and when all was ready they started. The journey was long and broken; at every few yards trees had fallen across the road, and these had to be chopped through and removed before the carriage could pass. It was therefore late in the day before they reached the town. Will could not help grieving at the terrible destruction wrought in the forest. In some places acres of ground had been cleared of the trees, in others the trunks and branches lay piled in an inextricable chaos. All the huts and cottages they passed on their way were in ruins, and their former inhabitants were standing listlessly gazing at the destruction. Mr. Palethorpe had placed in the carriage two gallon jars of spirits and a large quantity of bread, and these he had distributed among the forlorn inhabitants while his men were chopping a road through the trees.

When they arrived in the town they beheld a terrible scene of devastation. The streets occupied by the dwellings of well-to-do inhabitants had, for the most part, escaped, but in the suburbs, where the poorer part of the population dwelt, the havoc was something terrible. Parties of soldiers and sailors were hard at work here, clearing the ruins away and bringing out the dead and injured. Will, after saying good-bye to his friends at their door, joined one of these parties, and until late at night laboured by torchlight. At midnight he went to Mr. Palethorpe's house, to which he had promised to return, and slept till morning. Two long days were occupied in this work, and even then there was much to be done in the way of clearing the streets of the debris and restoring order. Not until this was finished did Will cease from his labours. He then

117

drove up with Mr. Palethorpe to his estate. They found that a great deal of progress had been made there, and that a gang of workmen were already engaged in preparing to replace the roof and to restore the house to its former condition. The slaves were still in their temporary homes, but with their usual light-heartedness had already recovered from the effects of their shock and losses, and seemed as merry and happy as usual.

On his return to Port Royal, Will was the object of the greatest attentions on the part of the other passengers of the Northumberland, and received so many invitations to dinner that he was obliged to ask the admiral to allow him to give up his leave and to take another short cruise in L'Agile, promising that if he did so he would take good care not to capture any more prizes. The admiral consented, and in a few days the cutter set sail once more.

After they had been out a month Will found it necessary to put in to get water. He chose a spot where a little stream could be seen coming down from the mountains and losing itself in the shingle, and he rowed ashore and set some of his men to fill the barrels. When he saw the work fairly under weigh he started to walk along the shore with Dimchurch and Tom. They had gone but a short distance when a number of negroes rushed suddenly out upon them. Will had just time to discharge his pistols before he was knocked senseless by a negro armed with a bludgeon. Tom and Dimchurch stood over him and made a desperate defence, and just before they were overpowered Dimchurch shouted at the top of his voice: "Put off, we are captured," for he saw that the number of their assailants was so great that it would only be sacrificing the crew to call them to their assistance. They were bound and carried away by the exulting negroes.

"This is a bad job," Will said when he came to his senses.

"A mighty bad job, Master Will. Who are these niggers, do you think?"

"I suppose they are escaped slaves; there are certainly many of them in the mountains of Cuba. I suppose they saw us sailing in, and came down from the hills in the hope of capturing some of us. It is likely enough they take us for pirates, who are a constant scourge to them, capturing them in their little fishing-boats and either cutting their throats or forcing them to serve with them. I am afraid we shall have but very little opportunity of explaining matters to them, for, of course, they don't speak English, and none of us understand a word of Spanish."

They were carried up the hill and thrown down in a small

clearing on the summit. Will in vain endeavoured to address them in English, but received no attention whatever.

"What do you think they are going to do with us, sir?" Dimchurch asked.

"Well, I should say that they are most likely going to burn us alive, or put us to death in some other devilish way."

"Well, sir, I don't think these niggers know much about tying ropes. It seems to me that I could get free without much trouble."

"Could you, Dimchurch? I can't say as much, for mine are knotted so tightly that I cannot move a finger."

"That won't matter, sir. If I can shift out of mine I have got my jack-knife in my pocket, and can make short work of your ropes and Tom's."

"Well, try then, Dimchurch. Half those fellows are away in the wood, and by the sounds we hear they are cutting brushwood; so there is no time to lose."

For five minutes no remark was made, and then Dimchurch said: "I am free." Immediately afterwards Will felt his bonds fall off, and half a minute later an exclamation of thankfulness from Tom showed that he too had been liberated.

"Now we must all crawl towards the edge of the forest," Will said, "and then, instead of going straight down the hill we will turn off for a short distance. They are sure to miss us immediately, and will believe that we have made direct for the sea."

They had barely got into the shelter of the forest when they heard a sudden shout, so they at once turned aside and hid in the brushwood. A minute or two later they had the satisfaction of hearing the negroes rushing in a body down the hill. They waited until their pursuers had covered a hundred yards, and then they jumped to their feet and held on their way along the hillside for nearly a quarter of a mile, after which they began to descend. Just as they changed their course they heard an outburst of musketry fire.

"Hooray!" Dimchurch exclaimed, "our fellows are coming up the hill in search of us. That's right, give it them hot! I guess they'll go back as quick as they came." They now changed their direction, taking a line that would bring them to the rear of their friends. The firing soon ceased, the negroes having evidently got entirely out of sight of the sailors, but by the shouting they had no difficulty in ascertaining the position of the party, who were pushing on up the hill, and presently Will hailed them.

"That is the captain's voice," one of the party exclaimed, and then a general cheer broke from the seamen. In another two minutes they were among their friends. Harman had landed with three-and-thirty men, leaving only five on board L'Agile. Great was their rejoicing on finding that the three missing men were all safe.

"We had better fall back now," Will said. "There must be at least three hundred negroes at the top, and though I don't say we would not beat them we should certainly suffer some loss which might well be avoided. There is no doubt they took us for pirates and believed they were going to avenge their own wrongs. So we may as well make our way down before their whole force gathers and attacks us."

They retired at once to the shore, and had but just taken their places in the boats when a crowd of negroes rushed down to the beach. Four or five shots were fired, but by Will's order no reply was made. They pushed off quietly and in a few minutes reached the cutter.

"That has been a narrow escape," Will said when he and Harman were together again on the quarter-deck; "as narrow as I ever wish to experience. If it hadn't been for Dimchurch I don't think you would have arrived in time, for they were cutting brushwood for a fire on which they intended to roast us. Fortunately he was not so tightly bound as we were, and so managed to free himself and us."

"I cannot say how thankful I was when I heard your voice. Of course we were proceeding only by guesswork, and could only hope that we should find you at the top of the hill. If they had carried you any farther away we could not have followed. I was turning this over in my mind as we advanced, when we heard the rushing of a large number of men down the hill towards us, and we at once concluded that you had escaped and that they were in pursuit, and as soon as the negroes appeared we opened fire."

"Well, all is well that ends well. It was very foolish of me to wander away from the men. Of course there was nothing whatever to tell us that we were being watched, but I ought to have assumed that there was a possibility of such a thing and not to have run the risk. I'll be mighty careful that I don't play such a fool's trick again. It was lucky that Dimchurch shouted when he did to the watering-party, otherwise we should have lost the whole of them, and with ten gone you would have found it very hazardous work to land a sufficiently strong party."

"I should have tried if I had only had a dozen men. I concluded that it must have been negroes who had carried you off, and my only thought was to rescue you before they set to work to torture you in some abominable manner."

"Well, I expect it would soon have been over, Harman, but certainly it would have been a very unpleasant ending. To fall in battle is a death at which none would grumble, but to be burnt by fiendish negroes would be horrible. Of course every man must run risks and take his chances, but one hardly bargains for being burnt alive. It makes my flesh creep to think of it, more now, I fancy, than when I was face to face with it. When I was lying helpless on the hill, there seemed something unreal about it, and I could not appreciate the position, but now that I think of it in cold blood it makes me shiver. I will take your watch to-night; I am quite sure that if I did get to sleep I should have a terrible nightmare."

"I can quite understand that you would rather be on deck than lying down and trying to sleep. I am sure I should do so myself, and even now the thought of the peril you were in makes me shudder."

For a time L'Agile cruised off the shore of Cuba, effecting a few small captures, but none of importance. Finally she fell in with three French frigates and was chased for two days, but succeeded in giving her pursuers the slip by running between two small islands under cover of night. The passage was very shallow, and the Frenchmen were unable to follow, and before they could make a circuit of the islands L'Agile was out of sight. When the cutter at length returned to Jamaica the admiral decided to lay her up for a time, and the crew was broken up and retransferred to the vessels to which they belonged.

Will was greeted with enthusiasm when he rejoined the Hawke.

"You certainly have singular luck, Gilmore," said Latham, who was the Hawke's master's mate. "Here we have been cruising and cruising, till we are sick of the sight of islands, without picking up a prize of importance, while you have been your own master, and have made a fortune. And now, just as there is a rumour that we are to go home you rejoin."

A few weeks after this conversation the Hawke received orders to sail for Portsmouth, and after a long and wearisome voyage arrived home late in the summer of the year 1793.

CHAPTER X

BACK AT SCARCOMBE

The news of their destination had created great satisfaction among the crew, as there was little honour or prize-money to be gained, and the vessel had been for some time incessantly engaged in hunting for foes that were never found. Not the least pleased was Will. He had left England a friendless ship's-boy; he returned home a midshipman, with a most creditable record, and with a fortune that, when he left the service, would enable him to live in more than comfort.

On arriving at Portsmouth the crew were at once paid off, and Will was appointed to the Tartar, a thirty-four gun frigate. On hearing the name of the ship, Dimchurch and Tom Stevens at once volunteered. They were given a fortnight's leave; so Will, with Tom Stevens, determined to take a run up to Scarcombe, and the same day took coach to London. Dimchurch said he should spend his time in Portsmouth, as there was no one up in the north he cared to see, especially as it would take eight days out of his fortnight's leave to go to his native place and back.

On the fourth day after leaving London the two travellers reached Scarborough. Tom Stevens started at once, with his kit on a stick, to walk to the village, while Will made enquiries for the house of Mrs. Archer, which was Miss Warden's married name. Without much trouble he made his way to it; and when the servant answered his knock he said: "I wish to see Mrs. Archer."

"What name, sir?" the girl said respectfully, struck with the appearance of the tall young fellow in a naval uniform.

"I would rather not say the name," Will said. "Please just say that a gentleman wishes to speak to her."

"Will you come this way?" the girl said, leading him to a sitting-room. A minute later Mrs. Archer appeared. She bowed and asked: "What can I do for you, sir?"

"Then you do not know me, madam?" said Will.

She looked at him carefully. "I certainly do not," she said, and after a pause: "Why, it can't be!—yes, it is—Willie Gilmore!"

"It is, madam, but no doubt changed out of all recognition."

"I have from time to time got your letters," said Mrs. Archer, "and learned from them with pleasure and surprise that you had become an officer, but never pictured you as grown and changed in this way. I hope you have got my letters in return?"

"I only got one, Mrs. Archer, and it reached me just before we sailed from the Mediterranean two years ago. I was not surprised, however, for of course the post is extremely uncertain. It is only very seldom that letters reach a ship on a foreign station."

"Dear, dear, you have lost some fingers!" Mrs. Archer cried, suddenly noticing Will's left hand. "How sad, to be sure!"

"That is quite an old story, Mrs. Archer. I lost them at the attempt to capture St. Pierre, and am so accustomed to the loss now that I hardly notice it. It is surprising how one can do without a thing. I have to be thankful, indeed, that it was the left hand instead of the right, as, had it been the other way, I should probably have had to leave the navy, which would have meant ruin to me."

"It is all very well to make light of it," she said, "but you must feel it a great drawback."

"Well, you see, Mrs. Archer, the loss of three fingers is of course terrible for a sailor, who has to row, pull at ropes, scrub decks, and do work of all sorts; but an officer does not have to do manual work of any kind, and hardly feels such a loss, except, perhaps, at meals. I am going to sea again almost directly, but the first time I have a long holiday I shall have some false fingers fitted on, more for the sake of avoiding being stared at than for anything else."

"Well, I am more than pleased at seeing you again, Willie. It is so natural for me to call you that, that it will be some time before I can get out of it. So you have got on very well?"

"Entirely owing to you, Mrs. Archer, as I told you in the first letter I wrote to you after I got my promotion. You taught me to like study, and were always ready to help me on with my work, and it was entirely owing to my having learned so much, especially mathematics, that I was able to attract the attention of the officers and to get put on the quarter-deck. I have, I am happy to say, done very well, and I am sure of my step as soon as I have passed.

"I had the extraordinary good fortune," he said, after chatting for some time, "to be put in command of a prize that had been taken from some pirates, and was thus able to earn a good deal of prize-money. But nothing has given me greater pleasure since I went away than the purchasing of this little present for you as a token, though a very poor one, of my gratitude to you for your kindness;" and he handed her a little case containing a diamond brooch, for which he had paid one hundred and fifty pounds as he came through London.

"Willie!" she exclaimed in surprise as she opened it, "how could you think of buying such a valuable ornament for me?"

"I should have liked to buy something more valuable," he said. "If I had paid half my prize-money it would only have been fair, for I should never have won it but for you."

"I have nothing nearly so valuable," she said. "Well, now, you must take up your abode with us while you stay here. How long have you?"

"I have a fortnight's leave, but it has taken me four days to come down here, and of course I shall have to allow as many for the return journey. I have therefore six days to spare, and I shall be very pleased indeed to stay with you. I must, of course, spend one day going over to the village to see John Hammond and his wife. I am happy to say that I shall be able to make their declining days comfortable. Your father is, I hope, well, Mrs. Archer?"

"Yes, he is going on just as usual. I was over there a fortnight ago. I am sure he will be very glad to see you; he always enquires, when I go over, whether I have had a letter from you, and takes great interest in your progress."

"Tom Stevens has come back with me, and has gone on to-day to the village. I told him not to mention about my coming, as I want to take the old couple by surprise."

"That you certainly will do. Of course they have aged a little since you went away, but there is no great change in them. Ah, there is my husband's knock! Lawrence," she said, as he entered, "this is the village lad I have so often spoken to you about. He has completely changed in the three years and a half he has been away. We heard, you remember, that he had become an officer, but I was quite unprepared for the change that has come over him."

"I am glad to see you, Mr. Gilmore. My wife has talked about you so often that I quite seem to know you myself, but, of course, as I did not know you in those days I can hardly appreciate the change that has come over you. One thing I can say, however, and that is that you bear no resemblance whatever to a fisher lad."

Will was soon quite at home with Mr. and Mrs. Archer, who introduced him with pride as "our sailor boy" to many of their friends. On the third day of his stay he hired a gig and drove over to Scarcombe. Alighting at the one little inn, he walked to John Hammond's cottage, watched on the way by many enquiring eyes, the fisher folk wondering whether this was a new revenue officer. He knocked at the door, lifted the latch, and entered. The old couple were sitting at the fire, and looked in surprise at the young officer standing at the door.

"Well, sir," John asked, "what can I do for you? I have done with smuggling long ago, and you won't find as much as a drop of brandy in my house."

"So I suppose, John," Will said; "your smuggling didn't do you much good, did it?"

"Well, sir, I don't see as that is any business of yours," the old man answered gruffly. "I don't mind owning that I have handled many a keg in my time, but you can't bring that against me now."

"I have no intention of doing so, John. I dare say you gave it up for good when that dirty little boy who used to live with you chucked it and got into trouble for doing so. You recollect me, don't you, mother?" he said, as the old woman sat staring at him with open eyes.

"Why, it is Willie himself!" she exclaimed; "don't you know him, John, our boy Willie, who ran away and went to sea?"

"You don't say it is Will!" the old man said, getting up.

"It is Will sure enough," the lad said, holding out his hand first to one and then to the other. "He has come back, as you see, an officer."

"Yes, Parson told us that. Well, well! Why, it was only two days ago that Tom Stevens came in. He has growed to be a fine young fellow too, and he told us that you were well and hearty and had been through lots of fights. But he didn't say nothing about your having come home."

"Well, here I am, John; and what is better, I have brought home some money with me, and I shall be able to allow you and the mother a guinea a week as long as you live."

"You don't mean it, lad!" the old man said with a gasp of astonishment; "a guinea a week! may the Lord be praised! Do you hear that, missis? a guinea a week!"

"Lord, Lord, only to think of it; why, we shall be downright rich!" said his wife. "Plenty of sugar and tea, a bit of meat when we fancy it, and a drop of rum to warm our old bones on Saturday night. It is wonderful, John. The Lord be praised for His mercies! But can you afford it, Will? We wouldn't take it from you if you can't, not for ever so."

"I can afford it very well," Will said, "and it will give me more pleasure to give it you than to spend it in any other way. Now, mother, let us say no more about it. Here is a guinea as a start, and I wish you would go to the shop and get some tea and sugar and bread and butter and a nice piece of bacon, and let us have a meal just as we used to do when we had made a good haul, or taken a hand in a successful run."

125

"It is three years and a half since I saw a golden guinea," the old woman said as she put on her bonnet, "and they won't believe their eyes at the shop when I go in with it. You are sure you would like tea better than beer?"

"Much better, though if John would prefer beer, get it for him; but I think we had better put that off till this evening, then we will have a glass of something hot together before I start."

"You are not going away so soon as that, Will, surely?" the old man said when his wife had left them.

"Yes, John, this is a short visit. I have only four days, and am staying with Miss Warden; that is to say, Miss Warden that was. I must go in and see her father for a few minutes. We'll have plenty of time to talk over everything before I leave, which I won't do till eight o'clock. I don't suppose you have much to tell me, for there are not many changes in a place like this. This man, perhaps, has lost his boat, and that one his life, but that is about all. Now I have gone through a big lot, and have many adventures to tell you."

"But how did you come to be made an officer, Will? That is what beats me."

"Entirely owing to my work at books, which you used always to be raging about. But for that I should have remained before the mast all my life. Now in a couple of years or so I'll be a lieutenant."

"Well, well! one never knows how things will turn out. I did think you were wasting your time in reading, and reading, and reading. I didn't see what good so much book-learning would do you; but if it got you made an officer, there is no doubt that you were right and I was wrong. But you see, lad, I was never taught any better."

"It has all turned out right, John, and there is no occasion for you to worry over the past. I felt sure that it would do me good some day, so I stuck to it in spite of your scolding, and you will allow that I was never backward in turning out when you wanted me for the boat."

"I will allow that, Will, allow it hearty; for there was no better boy in the village. And so you have been fighting, I suppose, just like Tom Stevens."

"Just the same, father. We have been together all the time, and we have come back together."

"And he didn't say a word about it!" the old man said. "He talked about you just as if you were somewhere over the sea."

"I told him not to tell," Will said, "as I wanted to take you by surprise."

"But he is not an officer, Will. He is just a sailor like those revenue men. How does that come about? Didn't he fight well?"

126

"Yes, no one could fight better. If he had had as much learning as I had he would have been made an officer too; but, you see, he can hardly read or write, and, fight as he may, he will always remain as he is. A finer fellow never stepped; but because he has no learning he must always remain before the mast."

"And you have lost some fingers I see, Will."

"Yes, they were shot off by a musket-ball in the West Indies. Luckily it was my left hand; so I manage very well without them."

"I hope you blew off the fingers of the fellow that shot you."

"No, I can't say who did it, and indeed I never felt anything at all until some little time after."

"I wish I had been there," John said, "I would have had a slap at him with a musket. That was an unlucky shot, Will."

"Well, I have always considered it a lucky one, for if it had gone a few inches on one side it would have probably finished me altogether."

"Well, well, it is wonderful to me. Here am I, an old man, and never, so far as I can remember, been a couple of miles from Scarcombe, and you, quite a young chap, have been wandering and fighting all over the world."

"Not quite so much as that, John, though I have certainly seen a good deal. But here is mother."

Mrs. Hammond entered with a face beaming with delight.

"You never saw anyone so astonished as Mrs. Smith when I went in and ordered all those things. Her eyes opened wider and wider as I went on, and when I offered her the gold I thought she would have a fit. She took it and bit it to make sure that it was good, and then said: 'Have you found it, Mrs. Hammond, or what good fortune have you had?'

" 'The best of fortunes, Mrs. Smith,' says I. 'My boy Will has come back from the wars a grand officer, with his pocket lined with gold, so you will find I'll be a better customer to you than I have been.'

" 'You don't say so, Mrs. Hammond!' says she. 'I always thought he was a nice boy, well spoken and civil. And so he is an officer, is he? Only to think of it! Well, I am mighty pleased to hear it,' and with that I came off with my basket full of provisions. The whole village will be talking of it before nightfall. Mrs. Smith is a good soul, but she is an arrant gossip, and you may be sure that the tale will gain by the telling, and before night people will believe that you have become one of the royal family."

In half an hour a meal was ready—tea, crisp slices of fried bacon, and some boiled eggs—and never did three people sit down to table in a more delighted state of mind.

"My life," the old woman said, when at last the meal was finished, "just to think that we'll be able to feed every day of the year like this! Why, we'll grow quite young again, John; we sha'n't know ourselves. We had five shillings a week before, and now we'll have six-and-twenty. I don't know what we'll do with it. Why, we didn't get that on an average, not when you were a young man and as good a fisherman as there was in the village. We did get more sometimes when you made a great haul, or when a cargo was run, but then, more often, when times were bad, we had to live on fish for weeks together."

"Now, missis, clear away the things and reach me down my pipe from the mantel, and we'll hear Will's tales. I'll warrant me they will be worth listening to."

When the table was cleared the old woman put some more coal on the fire and they sat round it, the old folk one on each side, with Will in the middle. Then Will told his adventures, the fight with the French frigate, the battle with the three Moorish pirates, how he had had the luck to save the first lieutenant's life and so obtained his promotion, and how the next prize they took was recaptured, but that he and a portion of the crew again overcame the Moors. Then he related how he had had the good fortune to obtain the command of a prize, with forty men and another midshipman under him, and gave a vivid account of the adventures he had gone through while cruising about in her.

"Well, well!" John Hammond said, when he brought his story to a conclusion, "you have had goings-on. To think that a boy like you should command a vessel and forty men, and should take three pirates."

"But the most awful part of it all," the old woman said, "is about them black negroes that carried you off and were going to burn you alive. Lor', I'll dream of it at nights."

"I hope not, missis," John said. "You dream more than enough now, and wake me up with your jumps and starts, and give me a lot of trouble to pacify you and convince you that you have only been dreaming. I am sorry, Will, that you told us about those niggers. I know I'll have lots of trouble over it. Generally all she has had to dream about has been that my boat was sinking, or that the revenue officers had taken me and were going to hang me; but that will be nothing to this 'ere negro business."

"They are terrible creatures these negroes, ain't they?" the old woman said. "I have heard tell that they have horns and hoofs like the devil."

"No, no, mother, they are not so bad as that, and they don't

128

have tails, either. They are not good-looking men for all that, and they look specially ugly when they are gathering firewood to make a bonfire of you."

"For goodness sake don't say more about them; it makes me all come over in a sweat to think about them."

Just at this moment Tom Stevens came in and sat and chatted for some time. Will asked him to come in again later and to bring with him a bottle of the best spirits he could find in the village.

"I'll warrant I will get some good stuff," Tom said. "There are plenty of kegs of the best hidden away in the village, and I think I know where to lay my hand on one of them."

Will then went to the rectory and had a chat with Mr. Warden, who was unaffectedly glad to see him.

"I never quite approved," he said, "of my daughter's hobby of educating you, but I now see that she was perfectly right. I thought myself that at best you would obtain some small clerkship, and that your life would be a happier one as a fisherman. It has, however, turned out admirably well, and she has a right to be proud of her pupil. After the way you have begun there is nothing in your own line to which you may not attain."

"I wanted to ask you, Mr. Warden, what you could remember about my father. My own recollection of him is very dim. I am going to sea again in a week, but next time I return I'll have a longer spell on shore, and I am resolved to make an effort to discover who he was."

"I fear that is quite hopeless, but I will certainly tell you all I know about him. I saw him, of course, many times in the village. He was a tall thin man with what I might call a devil-may-care, and at the same time a mournful expression. I have no doubt that had his death not been so sudden he would have told you something about himself. I have his effects tied up in a bundle. I examined them at the time, but there was nothing of any value in them except a signet-ring. It bore a coat-of-arms with a falcon at the top. I intended to hand this to you when you grew up, but of course you left so suddenly that I had no opportunity to do so. I will give you the bundle now."

"Thank you very much, sir! That ring may be the means of discovering my identity. Of course I have no time to make enquiries now, but when I next return I will advertise largely and offer a reward for information. It is not that I want to thrust myself on any family, or to raise any claim, but I should like, for my own satisfaction, to know that I come of a decent family."

"That is very natural," the clergyman said; "but were I you I should not hope to be successful. You see, nearly thirteen years have elapsed since his death, and he may have been wandering about for three or four years before. That is a long time to elapse before making any enquiries."

"That may be so, but if these arms belong, as I suppose, to a good family, there must be others bearing them, and an advertisement of a lost member of it might at once catch their eye, and might very possibly bring a reply. Besides, surely there must be some place where a record is kept of these things."

"I do not know that, but I am sure I wish you success in your search, and can well understand that, now you are an officer in His Majesty's navy, you would like to claim relationship with some big family."

"Quite so, sir. Of course I cannot imagine how it was my father came to be in such reduced circumstances."

"I should say, Will, that he quarrelled with his father, perhaps over his marriage, and left home in a passion. He was a man who, I could well imagine, when he once quarrelled, would not be likely to take the first step to make it up."

"Perhaps that was it, sir. Well, I am exceedingly obliged to you, and will, you may be sure, investigate the contents of the bundle carefully."

Returning to the cottage, Will found Tom Stevens already there with a small keg of brandy.

"This is good stuff, Will," he said; "it has been lying hidden for eight years, and was some of the choicest landed. I got it as a favour, and had to pay pretty high for it; but I knew you would not stick at the price."

"Certainly not, I wanted the best that could be got. Now, mother, mix us three good stiff tumblers, and take a glass for yourself."

"It is twenty year since I tasted spirits," the old woman said, "though John has often got a drop after a successful run; but this afternoon I don't mind if I do try a little, if it is only to put the thought of them bonfiring negroes out of my mind."

"I hope it will have that effect," Will laughed.

"Now, John, I told you about my adventures; let me hear a little village gossip."

John's tale was not a very long, nor, it must be owned, a very interesting one. Mary Johnson, Elizabeth Cruikshank, Mary Leaper, and Susie Thurston had all had boys, while there had been five girls born. It was not necessary, however, to specify the names of their mothers, as girls were considered quite secondary persons in

Scarcombe. One small cargo had been run, but the revenue people were so sharp that the French lugger had given up making the village a landing-place. John Mugby and his two sons had been drowned, and John Hawkins's boat had been smashed up. As a result of the decline of smuggling there had been a revulsion of the feeling against Will, and the four men who had been the ringleaders in the movement had made themselves so generally obnoxious that they had had to leave the village.

At seven o'clock Will said:

"Now, father, I must be moving. Here are fifty guineas. They will last you for nearly a year. I'll hand another fifty to Mr. Archer, and ask him to send you twenty pounds at a time. I'll probably be back in England before it has all gone, and if not I will manage to find a means of sending more over to you."

"I sha'n't sleep," the old woman said; "I never shall sleep with all that money in the house. It is sure to get known about, and I should never feel safe."

"Very well, mother, take the money up to Mr. Warden, and ask him to hand you a guinea every Monday."

"Tom Stevens," said the old woman, "I will ask you to go up to the rectory with me this very evening. I daren't keep it here, and I daren't carry it through the village, for there might be a pedlar about, and everybody knows that pedlars are apt to be thieves."

"Very well," Tom said with a smile, "I will go with you, missis, when Will has left. I am big enough to tackle a pedlar if we meet one on the way."

"Thank you very heartily, Tom! I'll be comfortable now; but I should never get a wink of sleep with fifty gold guineas in the house."

Will had noticed that the old couple's clothes were sorely patched, and the next morning he purchased a complete new outfit for both. These he sent over by a carrier, with a note, saying: "My dear father, it is only right that you should start with a fair outfit, and I therefore send you and the missis a supply that will last you for some time."

Tom Stevens came over two days later, and he and Will started together for London. On their arrival at Portsmouth they at once joined the Tartar, which was quite ready to sail, and which was under orders to join Lord Hood's fleet in the Mediterranean.

CHAPTER XI

CAPTIVES AMONG THE MOORS

A week later the Tartar proceeded to the Mediterranean. One morning after cruising there for some weeks, when the light mist lifted, a vessel was seen some three miles away. The captain looked at her through his telescope.

"That is a suspicious-looking craft," he said to the first lieutenant, Mr. Roberts. "We will lower a cutter and overhaul her."

The cutter's crew were at once mustered. Will was the midshipman in charge of her, and took his place by the side of the third lieutenant, Mr. Saxton. The lieutenant ordered the men to take their muskets with them.

"May I take Dimchurch and Stevens?" Will asked.

"Yes, if you like. There is room for them in the bow, and two extra muskets may be useful."

The two men, who were standing close by, took their places when they heard the permission given.

"I certainly don't like her appearance, Gilmore," the lieutenant said. "I cannot help thinking that she is an Algerine by her rig; and though every Algerine is not necessarily a pirate, a very large number of them are. I fancy a breeze will spring up soon, and in that case we may have a long row before we overtake her."

The breeze came presently, and the Algerine began to slip away. It was, however, but a puff, and the boat again began to gain on her. When they were five miles from the ship they were within a quarter of a mile from the chase.

"Confound the fellow!" the lieutenant muttered; "but I think I was mistaken, for there are not more than half a dozen men on her deck."

At length the boat swept up to the side of the craft. As the men leapt to their feet a couple of round shot were thrown into the boat, one of them going through the bottom. The cutter immediately began to fill, and the men as they climbed up were confronted by fully a hundred armed Moors. Lieutenant Saxton was at once cut down, and most of the sailors suffered the same fate. As usual, Will, Dimchurch, and Stevens held together and fought back to back. The contest, however, was too uneven to last, and the Moorish captain came up to them and signed to them that they must lay down their arms.

"Do it at once," Will said. "They evidently prefer to take us prisoners to killing us, which they could do without difficulty. We have been caught in a regular trap, and must make the best of it."

So saying he threw down his cutlass, and the others followed his example.

They were taken down below with three other unwounded sailors, and the wounded and dead were at once thrown overboard.

"This is the worst affair we have been in together," said Dimchurch, "since we fell into the hands of those negroes. Unless the Tartar overtakes us I am afraid we are in for a bad time."

"I am afraid so, Dimchurch, and I fear that there is little chance indeed of the frigate overtaking us. In such a light wind this craft would run away from her, and with fully five miles start it would be useless for the boats to try to overtake her."

"What are they going to do with us?"

"There is very little doubt about that. They will make slaves of us, and either set us to work on the fortifications or sell us to be taken up-country."

"I don't expect they will keep us long," Dimchurch said grimly.

"I don't know; they have great numbers of Christians whom they hold captive, and it is rare indeed that one of them escapes. I suppose some day or other we'll send a fleet to root them out, but our hands are far too full for anything of that sort at present. If we have a chance of escape you may be sure that we'll take it, but we had better make up our minds at once to make the best of things until opportunity offers."

"I only hope we'll be kept together, sir. I could put up with it if that were so, but it would be awful if we were separated; for even if one saw a chance for escape he could not let the others know."

"You may be sure, Dimchurch, that whatever opportunity I might see I would not avail myself of it unless I could take you both off with me."

"The same here, sir," Dimchurch said; and the words were echoed by Tom.

Six days later they heard the anchor run down, and presently the hatchway was lifted and they were told to come on deck. They found, as they had expected, that the craft was lying in the harbour of Algiers. At any other time they might have admired the city, with its mosques and minarets, its massive fortifications, and the shipping in the port, but they were in no humour to do so now. They regarded it as their jail. They and the three sailors were put into a boat and rowed ashore, the captain of the craft going with them. They were met at the wharf by a Moor, who was evidently an official

133

of rank. He and the captain held an animated conversation, and by their laughter Will had no doubt whatever that the captain was telling the clever manner in which he had effected their capture. Then the official said something which was not altogether pleasing to the captain, who, however, crossed his hands on his breast and bowed submissively. The official then handed the six prisoners over to some men who had accompanied him, and they were immediately marched across to a large barrack-like building, which was evidently a prison. Two hours afterwards a great troop of captives came in. These were so worn and wearied that they asked but few questions of the new-comers.

"Don't talk about it," one said in answer to a question from Will. "There is not one of us who would not kill himself if he got the chance. It is work, work, work from daybreak till sunset. We have enough to eat to keep us alive; we are too valuable to be allowed to die. We get food before we start in the morning, again at mid-day, and again when we get back here. Oh, they are very careful of us, but they don't mind how we suffer! The sun blazes down all day, and not a drop of drink do we get except at meals. In spite of their care we slip through their hands. Sunstroke and fever are always thinning our ranks. That is the history of it, mate, and if I were to talk till morning I could not tell you more. I suppose by your cut that you are a man-of-war's-man?"

"You're right," Dimchurch said. "We got caught in a trap, and our nine mates were killed without having a chance to fire a shot."

"Ah!" the man said with a sigh, "I wish I had had their luck, and you will wish so too before you have been here long."

Rough food was served out, and then the slaves, after eating, lay down without exchanging a word, anxious only to sleep away the thought of their misery. The three friends lay down together. To each prisoner a small rug had been served out, and this was their only bedding.

"We are certainly in a bad corner," Dimchurch said, "but the great point will be to keep up our spirits and make the best of it."

"That is so," Will agreed. "I am convinced that, however sharp a watch they may keep, three resolute men will find some way of escape. We'll know a little more about it to-morrow. If there are windows to this building we ought to be able to get out of them, and if it is surrounded by walls we ought to be able to scale them. Besides, if we are set to work in the city we might find an opportunity of evading the diligence of our guards. For one thing, we must assume an air of cheerfulness while we work. In time, when they see that we do our work well and are contented and obedient,

134

their watch will relax. Above all, we must not, like these poor fellows, make up our minds that our lot is hopeless. If we once lose hope we shall lose everything. At any rate, for the present we must wait patiently. We have still got to find out everything; all we know is that we are confined in a prison, and that we shall have to do some work or other during the day.

"We have got to find out the plan of the city and its general bearings, to learn something, if we can, of the surrounding country, and to see how we should manage to subsist if we got away. Of course the natural idea would be to make for the sea and steal a boat. But we came up from the shore through an archway in the wall; it was strongly guarded, and I fear it would be next to impossible to get down to the port. Our best plan, I think, would be to take to the country if we can, and go down to the shore some distance from the city. We might then light upon a boat belonging to some fisherman. Of course all this is pure conjecture, and all we can arrange is that we shall keep our eyes about us, and look for an empty house in which we might hide and discover how we might leave the town on the land side, where it is not likely the fortifications will be nearly so strong as on the sea-face."

The next morning the captives were deprived of their clothes, and in their place were given dirty linen jackets and loose trousers. Their shoes were also taken away. They then fell in with the rest of the captives. On leaving the prison they were formed into companies, each of which, under a strong guard, marched off in different directions. The three friends kept close together, and were assigned to a company which was told off to clean the streets of a certain quarter of the town. They were furnished with brooms and brushes, and were soon hard at work. As the morning went on, the heat became tremendous. Several men fell, but the overseers lashed them until they got upon their feet again.

"My eye! this is like working in an oven," Dimchurch muttered; "the dust is choking me. We must certainly get out of this as soon as we can, sir."

"I agree with you, Dimchurch. I feel as if I were melting away. If I were to put a bit of food in my mouth I believe the heat would bake it in no time."

"I couldn't swallow anything," Tom said, "not even a mackerel fresh out of the sea."

"You know we agreed that we must make the best of everything," Will said. "If we work as we are doing we can't but please our overseers, and shall save ourselves from blows."

"They had better not strike me," Dimchurch said; "the man that did it would never live to strike another."

135

"That might be," Will said, "but it would be a small satisfaction to you if you were to be flogged to death afterwards."

"No, I suppose not, sir; but flesh and blood can't stand such a thing as being struck by one of these yellow hounds."

At twelve o'clock the gang returned, and the men drank eagerly from a fountain in the courtyard of the prison.

"Take as little as you can," Will said; "if you drink much it will do you harm. You can drink often if you like, provided that you only take a sip at a time."

"It is easy to say, Mr. Gilmore, but it is not so easy to do. I feel as if I could drink till I burst."

"I dare say you do; I feel the same myself; but I am sure that to take a lot of water just now would do us harm instead of good."

Their abstinence so far benefited them that they felt their work in the afternoon less than they had done in the morning, though the heat was, if anything, greater.

That evening they examined their prison. It consisted of one great hall supported by rows of pillars. Here the whole of the prisoners were confined. It was lighted by windows five-and-twenty feet from the ground. There was no guard inside, but fifty men, some of whom were always on sentry, slept outside the hall. It was clear to them, therefore, that no escape could be made after they were once locked up, and that if they were to get away at all they must make the attempt when they were employed outside.

On the third day one of the sailors from the Tartar, who had disregarded Will's advice to drink sparingly, fell down dead after drinking till he could drink no more. Scarcely a day passed without one or more of the captives succumbing; some of them went mad and were at once despatched by their guards.

After working for a fortnight in the streets the gang were marched in another direction, and were put to labour on the fortifications. This was a great relief. They were now free from the choking dust of the streets, and obtained a view of the surrounding country. The three, as usual, laboured together, and showed so much zeal and activity that they pleased the head of their guard. They had the great advantage that they were accustomed to work together, while the majority of the gang had no such experience. There were men of all nationalities—French, Spanish, Italians, Maltese, and Greeks, and though most of them were accustomed to a warm climate, they had nothing like the strength of the three Englishmen. In moving heavy stones, therefore, the three friends were able to perform as much work as any dozen other prisoners. They were the only Englishmen in the gang, for the other two sailors had been from the first placed with another party.

136

On the march to their work they passed by a palace of considerable extent, surrounded by grounds which were entered on that side by a small postern gate. "I would give a good deal to know if that gate is locked," Will said.

"What good would that do, sir?"

"Well, if we could get in there we might hide in the shrubbery, and stop there till the first pursuit was over. No one would think of searching there. I should say we might, if we had luck, seize and bind three of the gardeners or attendants, and so issue from one of the gates dressed in their clothes without exciting suspicion."

"What should we do for grub, sir?"

"Well, for that we must trust to chance. There are houses that might be robbed, and travellers who might be lightened of their belongings. I can't think that three active men, though they might be unarmed, would allow themselves to starve. Of course we should want to get rid of these clothes, and find some weapons; but the great point of all is to discover whether that door is locked."

"All right, sir! I am ready to try anything you may suggest, for I am sick to death of this work, and the heat, and the food, and the guard, and everything connected with it."

They looked at the door with longing eyes each time they passed it. At last one day a man came out of the gateway just as they were passing, and, pulling the gate to behind him, walked away without apparently thinking of locking it.

"That settles that point," Will said. "The next most important question is, Are there people moving about inside? Then how are we to slip away unseen? To begin with, we will manage always to walk in the rear of the gang. There are often rows; if some poor wretch goes mad and attacks the guard there is generally a rush of the others to his assistance. If such a thing were to happen near this gate we might manage to slip in unnoticed. Still, I admit the chances are against anything of the sort taking place just at that point, and I expect we must try and think of something better."

A fortnight later, just as they were passing the door, a small party of cavalry, evidently the escort to some great chief, came dashing along at full speed. The road being somewhat narrow the slaves and guards scattered in all directions, several of them being knocked down.

"Now is our chance!" Will exclaimed; and the three ran to the gate and entered the garden. There was no one in sight; evening was coming on, and any men who might have been working in the garden had left. They closed the gate behind them and turned the key in the lock, then ran into a shrubbery and threw themselves down. They trusted that in the confusion their absence would not be noticed, and this seemed to be the case, for they heard loud orders given and then all was quiet.

"So far so good," Will said. "The first step is taken, and the most difficult one. To-morrow, when the gardeners come, we will spring upon three of them and bind them. I should not think that there will be more than that."

Fortune favoured them, however, for an hour later three servants came along, laughing and talking together. The sailors prepared to act, and as the men passed their hiding-place Will gave the word, and, leaping out upon them, they hurled them to the ground. Tom and Dimchurch both stunned their men, and then aided Will to secure the one he had knocked down. Without ceremony they stripped off the clothes of the fallen men, tore up their own rags, and bound the captives securely, shoving a ball of the material between the teeth of each, and then secured them to three trees a short distance apart.

"That is good," said Will, as they put on the servants' clothes; "they are safe till they are found in the morning. In these clothes we can boldly venture out from the town gate as soon as it is opened. There is always the risk that our colour may betray us, but we are all burnt nearly as dark as mahogany and may very well pass."

"Shall we start now, sir?"

"No, they will find out when they get to the prison that we are missing, and there will be a keen hunt for us. And now I come to think of it, the guards at the gate will be warned of our escape, and will probably question us, particularly as these bright-coloured garments would attract their attention. I really think our best plan would be to go out into the town at once and try to get hold of other disguises."

"It would be a good thing if we could do so, sir."

"Dear me, how stupid I am!" exclaimed Will after a pause. "You know that wall we were repairing to-day? It was only about fourteen feet above the ground outside, so we should have no difficulty in dropping down."

"That is so, sir. It is an easy drop, and by leaving in that way we'll avoid being questioned, and get well away before the alarm is given."

"Then we will lose no time," said Will. "We have to pass through a busy quarter, but if we go separately we shall attract no notice, though no doubt by this time the search will have begun. They will be looking, however, for three men together. Of course they will not so much as cast an eye upon the servants of this palace, for they will know nothing of our doings here till to-morrow morning. I will go first when we get into the street. You, Dimchurch, follow me forty or fifty yards behind, and Tom the same distance behind you."

"I hardly think they will be in search of us yet," Dimchurch said. "It is little more than an hour since we escaped, and they won't find out till they get to the prison and count the gang. When they have done that they would have to see who it was that was missing, and then they would take some time to organize the search."

"That is so, Dimchurch; still, we will take every precaution."

So saying they started. When they were half-way to the wall they saw a number of soldiers and convict guards come running along, questioning many people as they passed. They trembled lest they should be discovered, but fortunately no question was put to any of them, and they kept on their way. Presently Will emerged upon the open space of ground between the wall and the houses, and when Dimchurch and Tom had come up they went together along the foot of the wall until they came to the place where they had been working.

"Keep your eyes open," Will said as they climbed up, "there are crowbars and hammers lying about, and, where the stone-cutters were working, chisels. A crowbar or a heavy hammer is a weapon not to be despised."

In a few minutes each was armed with a chisel and a light crowbar. They then went to the edge of the wall, and, throwing these weapons down, lowered themselves as far as they could reach and dropped to the ground.

"Thank God we are out of that place!" Will said fervently; "we won't enter it again alive. Now, the first thing is to get as far away as possible, keeping as nearly parallel to the line of the coast as we can, but four or five miles back, for we may be sure that when they cannot find us in the town they will suspect that we have made for the coast, and a dozen horsemen will be sent out to look for us along the shore. It is no use our thinking of trying to get to sea until the search has been given up. Our principal difficulty will be to live. From the walls the country looked well cultivated in parts, and even if we have to exist on raw grain we shall not be much worse off than when we were in prison."

"I don't care what it is," Tom said, "so long as there is enough of it to keep us alive; but we must have water."

"I don't think there will be much difficulty about that, Tom, as every one of the houses scattered over the plain will have wells and fountains in their gardens. Thank goodness, they won't miss any we

139

take, and we could go every night and fetch water without exciting any suspicion that we had been there!"

"One of the first things we must do," said Will, "is to dirty these white jackets and trousers so that we may look like field labourers, for then if anyone should catch sight of us in the distance we should attract no attention."

They walked all night, and just as morning was breaking they saw a large country house with the usual garden. They climbed over the wall, which was not high, and drew some water in a bucket which they found standing at the mouth of the well.

"This bucket we will confiscate," Will said; "we can hardly lie hidden all day without having a drink. Of course they will miss it; but when they cannot find it they will suppose that it has been mislaid or stolen. One of the gardeners will probably get the blame, but we can't help that. Now we will go another mile and then look for a hiding-place. There are a lot of sand-hills scattered about, and if we can't find a hole that will suit us we must scoop one out. I believe they are pretty hard inside, but our crowbars will soon make a place large enough."

After an hour's walk they fixed upon a spot on the shady side of a hill and began to make a cave that would allow the three to lie side by side. The work was completed in less than an hour, and they crawled in and scraped up some of the fallen sand so as partially to close the mouth behind them.

"Thank goodness, we have got shelter and water!" Will said. "As for food, we must forage for it to-night."

"I am quite content to go without it for to-day," Dimchurch said, "and to lie here and sleep and do nothing. I don't think anything would tempt me to get up and walk a mile farther, not even the prospects of a good dinner."

"Well, as we are all so tired we shall probably sleep till evening."

In a few minutes all were asleep. Once or twice in the course of the day they woke up and took a drink from the bucket and then fell off again. At sunset all sat up quite refreshed.

"I begin to feel that I have an appetite," Will said; "now I think, for to-night, we will content ourselves with going into one of the fields and plucking a lot of the ears of maize. Messages may have been sent out all over the country, and the people may be watchful. It will be wise to avoid all risk of discovery. We can gather a few sticks and make a fire in there to roast the maize; there are sand-hills all round, so what little flame we make would not be noticed."

"But how about a light?" Dimchurch asked.

"I picked up a piece of flint as we came along this morning," Will said, "and by means of one of these chisels we ought to be able to strike a light; a few dead leaves, finely crumbled up, should do instead of tinder."

"It is a good thing to keep one's eyes open," Dimchurch remarked. "Now if I had seen that piece of stone I should not have given it a thought, and here it is going to give us a hot dinner!"

As there were numbers of fields in the neighbourhood they soon returned with an armful of maize each. Dried weeds and sticks were then collected, and after repeated failures a light was at last obtained, and soon the grain was roasted. A jacket was stretched across the entrance of their den so that, should anyone be passing near, they would not observe the light.

"Now," Will said as they munched some maize the next evening, "we must start foraging. We will go in opposite directions, and each must take his bearing accurately or we'll never come together again."

They were out for some hours, and when they returned it was found that Will had come across four fowls, Tom had gathered a variety of fruit, consisting chiefly of melons and peaches, while Dimchurch, who was the last to come in, brought a small sheep.

"We only want one thing to make us perfect," Will said, "and that is a pipe of 'bacca."

"Well, that would be a welcome addition," Tom admitted, "but it does not do to expect too much. I should not be at all surprised if we were to light upon some tobacco plants in one of the gardens, but of course it could hardly be like a properly dried leaf. I dare say, though, we could make something of it."

So they lived for a month, sometimes better, sometimes worse, but with sufficient food of one sort or another. So far as they knew no suspicion of their presence had been excited, though their petty robberies must have been noticed. One evening, however, Will, on going to the top of the sand-hill, as he generally did, saw a large detachment of soldiers coming along, searching the ground carefully. He ran down at once to his companions.

"Take your weapons, lads," he said, "and make off; a strong party of soldiers are searching the country, and they are coming this way. No doubt they are looking for us."

They had run but a few hundred yards when they heard shouts, and, looking round, they saw a Moorish officer waving his hands and gesticulating. This was alarming, but they reckoned that they had fully five hundred yards start.

"Keep up a steady pace," Will said; "I don't expect the beggars can run faster than we can. It will be pitch dark in half an hour, and as, fortunately, there is no moon, I expect we'll be able to give them the slip."

As they advanced they found that the vegetation became scarcer and scarcer.

"I am afraid we are on the edge of a desert," Will said, "which means that there are no more fowls and fruit for us. I see, Dimchurch, that you have been the most thoughtful this time. That half sheep and those cakes will be very valuable to us."

"I wasn't going to leave them for the soldiers if I knew it, sir; they wouldn't have gone far among them, while they will last us some time with care."

They changed their course several times as soon as it became quite dark, and presently had the satisfaction of hearing the shouts of their pursuers fade away behind them.

"Now we can take it quietly, lads. We can guide ourselves towards the sea by means of the stars. I fancy it must be fully twenty miles away. We must hold on till we get to it, and then gradually work our way along among the sand-hills or clumps of bush bordering it till we come to a village. Then we must contrive to get a good supply of food and water, steal a boat, and make off. If galleys were sent out to search for us they must have given it up long ago. As for other craft, we'll have to take our chance with them."

They kept steadily north and at last came down to the coast. As it was still dark they lay down till morning. When the sun rose they thought they could make out a village some eight miles away.

"Now it will be quite safe to cook our breakfast," Dimchurch said.

"Yes, I think so," Will answered, "but we must be sparing with the mutton; that is our only food at present, and it may be some little time before we get hold of anything else."

After breakfast they lay down among the bushes and slept till evening. Then they started along the shore towards the village. When they got within half a mile of it they halted. They could see some boats on the shore, so they felt that the only difficulty in their way was the question of provisions. When it was quite dark they went into the village and started to forage, but on meeting again they had very little to show. Between them they had managed to take five fowls; but the village was evidently a poor place, for with the exception of a few melons there was no fruit.

"The beggars must have grain somewhere," said Will. "They can't live on fowls and melons."

"I expect, sir, they live very largely on fish."

142

"That is likely enough," Will agreed. "Let us put down these fowls and melons under this bush, and have a nap for a couple of hours, till we are sure that everyone is asleep. We can then go down and have a look at the boats. Those of them that come in late may probably leave some of their catch on board."

When they went down to the boats they found that three of them contained a fair quantity of fish. They helped themselves to some of these, and then retreated some distance from the village, picking up the other provisions on the way, and then, going into a clump of bushes, cooked a portion of the fish.

"That pretty well settles the question of provisions," Will said. "We must choose a night when there is a good wind blowing offshore, so that we may run a good many miles before morning. Then we must trust to falling in with one of our cruisers."

"Fish won't keep long in this climate," suggested Tom.

"No," said Will, "but we can dry some of them in the sun and they will then keep good for some time. Then we might clean half a dozen fowls and cook them before we start."

"The great difficulty will be water."

"Yes, but we can get over that by stripping the gardens clean of their melons. They weigh four or five pounds apiece and would supply us with fluid for a week easily."

The next evening they went down and made a more careful examination of the boats. One in particular attracted their attention. She was nearly new, and looked likely to be faster than the rest. She was anchored some fifty yards from the shore. Three more evenings were spent in prowling about the village collecting food. It was evident that the villagers were alarmed at their depredations, for on the third evening they were fired at by several men. In consequence of this they moved a mile farther away, in case a search should be made, and the next night carried the provisions down to the shore. As they were all expert swimmers they were soon alongside the chosen craft. They pushed the provisions before them on a small raft, and when they had put them on board they made a trip to one or two of the other boats and brought away some twenty pounds of fish. Then they cut the hawser and hoisted sail. As they did so they heard a great tumult on shore, and the villagers ran down to the water's edge and opened fire upon them. The shooting, however, was wild, and they were very soon out of range. Several boats put off in pursuit. This caused them some uneasiness, and they watched them somewhat anxiously, for the wind, though favourable, was light, and they felt by no means certain that they would be able to keep ahead of the rowers. The stolen craft, however, proved

143

unexpectedly fast, and the boats, after following fifteen miles without sensibly gaining, at last gave up the chase. About this time, too, the wind, to their great relief, became stronger, and the little vessel flew more and more rapidly over the sea.

"She is a fine craft," Dimchurch said; "these Moors certainly know how to build boats. It would require a smart cutter to hold her own with us."

Dimchurch kept at the helm and the other two investigated their capture. She was three parts decked. In the cabin they came upon a lantern and flint and steel, and soon had light, which helped them greatly in their work. In the bow ropes were stored away, while in a locker they found some bread, which, although stale, was very acceptable. They also unearthed two or three suits of rough sea clothes with which they were glad to replace the light clothes they had carried away with them from the palace grounds, for though the weather on shore was warm the sea-breeze was chilly. Among other useful things they also discovered several long knives, and axes, and a flat stone for cooking upon.

"Now it is all a question of luck," Will said; "the danger will be greater when we get a bit farther out. All vessels going up and down the Mediterranean give the Barbary coast a wide berth. Of course those pirate fellows are most numerous along the line of traffic, but they are to be found right up to the Spanish, French, and Italian coasts, though of late, I fancy, they have not been so active. There are too many of our cruisers about for their taste, and the Spaniards, when they get a chance, show the scoundrels no mercy."

When morning broke not a sail was visible.

"I think, sir," Dimchurch said, "that there is going to be a change of weather, and that we are in for a gale."

"It does not matter much. I fancy this boat would go through it however severe it might be."

"Yes, sir, but it would check our progress, and we want to run north as fast as we can. I see, by the line you are making, that you are aiming at Toulon, and at our present pace it would take us something like four days to get there. If we are caught in a gale we may take two days longer."

"That is so," Will agreed; "but on the other hand, if the wind becomes much stronger we'll have to take in sail, and in that case we should have more chance of escaping notice if we come near any of those Moorish craft. Besides, if the sea were really rough it would be difficult for them to board us even if they did come up with us."

"You are right, sir; still, for myself, I should prefer a strong southerly wind and a clear sky."

144

"Well, I am afraid you will not get your wish, for the clouds certainly seem to be banking up from the north, and we'll get a change of wind ere long."

By night the wind was blowing fiercely and the sea rapidly rising. The sails were closely reefed, and even then they felt with pleasure that the little craft was making good way. The wind increased during the night, and was blowing a gale by morning. Just at twelve o'clock a craft was seen approaching which all were convinced was an Algerine. She changed her course at once and bore down upon them, firing a gun as a signal for them to stop.

"She is rather faster than we are," Dimchurch said, "but we'll lead her a good dance before she gets hold of us. She could not work her guns in this sea, and if she is the faster, at least we are the handier."

For three hours the chase continued. Again and again the Algerine came up on them, but each time the little boat, turning almost on her heel, so cleverly was she handled, glided away from underneath the enemy's bows. Each time, when they saw the chase slipping away from them, the angry Moors sent a volley of musketry after her, but the fugitives took refuge in the cabin, or lay down on the deck close under the bulwarks, and so escaped.

Soon the Moors were so intent on the chase that they began to take great risks with their own vessel. In fact, they became positively reckless. For this they paid very heavily. After many disappointments they felt that the fugitives were at last in their clutches, and were preparing to board her when suddenly Dimchurch put down his helm sharply. He nearly capsized the little craft, and indeed they would rather have gone down with her than fall into the hands of the Moors again, but she righted immediately, and once more skimmed away from her pursuers. In the excitement of the moment the Moorish steersman attempted the same manœuvre. If he had succeeded he would probably have run down the cockle-shell that had baffled him so long. But at that moment a violent squall struck his ship with its full force, and her mainmast snapped a few feet above the deck. The three fugitives jumped to their feet and cheered, and then calmly proceeded on their way.

CHAPTER XII

BACK ON THE "TARTAR"

The next morning broke fair. Their late foe had dropped out of sight on the previous evening, but now, when the sun rose, Tom made out the top-sails of a large ship on the horizon.

"She is coming towards us, lads, and by the course she is steering she will pass within three miles of us. Is she English or French?"

"She is too far away yet to be certain," Dimchurch said, "but I can't help thinking she is French."

"At any rate, Dimchurch, our best course will be to lower the sail, shake the reef-points out, and have it ready for hoisting at a moment's notice. Now that the wind is light again I should fancy we could get away from her; with a start of two or three miles she would have no chance whatever of catching us."

Suddenly Tom Stevens exclaimed:

"There is a sail coming up from behind. She looks to me close-hauled. If both ships come on they are bound to meet; if one is French and the other is English they are likely to have a talk to each other. In that case we should be able to tell friend from foe by the colours, and could then make for the English ship."

They sat anxiously watching the two ships, and soon they saw that the point of meeting must be very near their own position. Presently their hulls became visible, and Dimchurch pronounced one to be a thirty-two-gun frigate, and the other a forty or forty-two. They then made out that the one coming up from the south was flying the white ensign, and at once they hoisted their sail and made for her. Equally intent upon a fight, the two vessels approached each other without paying the slightest attention to the little craft.

"The Frenchman means fighting, and as he has ten guns to the good he may well think he is more than a match for our ship. Do you know her, Dimchurch?"

"I think she is the Lysander, sir, though I can't be sure; there are so many of these thirty-twos."

The vessels, as they passed, exchanged broadsides. Then both tacked, but the Englishman was the quicker, and he raked the French frigate as she came round. Then they went at it hammer and tongs. The Frenchman suffered very heavily in spars and rigging, but at last the foremast of the English ship fell over her side. The Frenchman at once closed with her, and after pouring in a broadside, tried to board her.

The little boat bore up to the stern of the English ship. A desperate conflict was going on at that point, and failing to get up they moved along the side. Here a rope, which had been cut by the French fire, was hanging overboard, and, grasping this, they climbed up to a port-hole. The deck was deserted, all hands having rushed up to meet the attack of the French boarders. Without a moment's delay they snatched cutlasses from a rack and ran up the companion to the upper deck.

Here things were going somewhat badly. The French were much more numerous than the English, and were forcing them back by sheer weight of numbers. The new-comers rushed at once into the fray, and laid about them lustily. The force and suddenness of the onslaught caused the enemy to hesitate, and at the same time it had the effect of inspiring to fresh efforts the English crew, who, having lost their captain and first lieutenant, were beginning to lose heart. They answered the cheers of their strangely-clad allies, and with one accord charged to meet them. At that moment Dimchurch almost severed the French captain's head from his body by a sweeping blow, and the French, being disheartened by the loss of their leader, gave way. The English sailors redoubled their efforts, and after ten minutes of desperate fighting succeeded in driving their foes back to their own ship. Then the men ran to their guns again and the cannonade recommenced. But the spirit of the two crews had changed. The French were discouraged by their failure, and the British were exultant over their success. Consequently the guns of the English ship were fired with far more rapidity and precision than those of the French. Several of the port-holes of the French ship were knocked into one, and when at last her mainmast, which had been hit several times, fell over her side, her flag was run down amidst tremendous cheering from the English ship.

Immediately all hands were engaged in disarming and securing the French prisoners. When these had been sent below, the decks of both ships were cleared of the dead. Then the bulk of the crew set to work to cut away the wreckage, secure damaged spars, and stop holes near the water's edge. At last the second lieutenant, who was now in command, had time to turn to the strangers. Will was superintending the work, while Dimchurch and Tom were working hand in hand with the crew.

"May I ask," said the lieutenant, addressing Will, "who it is that has so mysteriously come to our assistance?"

"Certainly," said Will, laughing; "I had quite forgotten that I am clothed in strange garments. I am a midshipman belonging to the Tartar. One of my companions is a boatswain's mate, and the other is an A.B. on the same ship. We were sent with a lieutenant and ten men to overhaul a craft which, though she was somewhat suspicious looking, seemed to have but a small crew. When we got alongside her, however, we found to our disgust that she was manned by at least a hundred Algerines. The lieutenant and seven of the crew were killed, and three others, my two companions, and myself were made prisoners and carried to Algiers. We three escaped, and, capturing the small craft which you will see lying by the side of your ship, made for the open sea. An Algerine nearly recaptured us in the gale yesterday, but fortunately she carried away her mast and we again escaped. This morning we saw two ships approaching us, and when we made out their nationalities we knew there was bound to be a fight. Naturally we made for your ship, and when we found that the French had boarded you we did our best to aid you to drive them back. My name is Gilmore."

"Well, Mr. Gilmore, I have to thank you most heartily for the very efficacious aid you have rendered us. Things were going very badly, but your unexpected appearance, your strange attire, and the strength and bravery with which you fought, quite turned the tables. I think," he said with a laugh, "the French must have taken you for three devils come to our assistance, and certainly you could not have fought harder if you had been. You will, I hope, give us your assistance until we reach Malta, to which port, of course, I shall carry the prize. Our third lieutenant is severely wounded, and I have lost two of my midshipmen."

"Certainly, sir, and I will place myself at once under your orders."

"The two midshipmen who have fallen were the seniors," the lieutenant said, "and as you must be two or three years older than the others I'll appoint you acting-lieutenant. Our first duty here will be to rig up a jury foremast. I'll appoint you, however, temporary commander of the Camille, which is, I see, the name of our prize. I can only spare you forty men. We have lost forty-three killed and at least as many wounded, and I have therefore only a hundred and ten altogether fit for service, and must retain seventy for the work of refitting. I should not attempt to get up a jury mainmast on the Camille. It will be better to clear away the wreckage and secure her other two masts in case we meet with another squall."

"I understand, sir. If either of the midshipmen that have been killed is about my size, I should be glad to rig myself out with a suit from his chest, for my appearance at present is rather undignified for a British officer. I should also be glad if the purser's clerk would issue a couple of suits for my two men. I may tell you that they have been with me in every ship in which I have served, and indeed entered the navy with me. I therefore regard them quite as personal friends. The bigger of the two held the position of boatswain under me in a small craft of which I had command in the West Indies, as well as on the Tartar."

"Very well, then, by all means give him the temporary rank of boatswain on board the Camille, and you can appoint the other as boatswain's mate."

"Thank you, sir! I am very much obliged. It would be difficult to find two better men."

In ten minutes Will was attired in a midshipman's uniform, and his two companions, to their great relief, in the clothes of British seamen. They then crossed to the Camille with the forty men whom the lieutenant had told off as a prize crew. Work was at once begun, and before sundown the fore and mizzen masts were as firmly secured as if the mainmast were still in its place. Will felt that they could now meet a storm without uneasiness. Next morning the repairs to the hull were begun, pieces of plank covered with tarred canvas being nailed over the shot-holes, and ere the day was done the Camille had a fairly presentable appearance. Meanwhile the crew of the Lysander had been hard at work, and had got the jury-foremast into position and securely stayed.

"You have made a very good job of the prize, Mr. Gilmore," the lieutenant said. "Of course she is a lame duck without her mainmast, but we'll sail together, and so will show a good face to any single ship we may meet."

"I should certainly think so, sir. Should any ship heave in sight I will get all the guns loaded on both broadsides. Of course, I should only be able to work one side at a time, but with forty good men I could keep up a pretty hot fire."

"I will give you ten more, Mr. Gilmore. Now that our repairs are finished I can manage that easily, and as the Camille is a bigger ship than the Lysander you ought certainly to have as many as can be spared."

"Thank you, sir! I am sure I could make a good fight with that number, and as we have covered all the shot-holes with canvas, and so do not appear to be injured in the hull, I don't think any one ship would think of meddling with us, unless, of course, she were a line-

149

of-battle ship. In that case our chance would be a small one, although, by presenting a resolute front, we might cause her to sheer off without engaging us."

Fortunately they fell in with no enemy on their way to Malta. When they arrived in port the lieutenant went to the flag-ship with his report. The admiral was greatly pleased at the capture, and he was specially interested when he learned the share that Will and his two companions had taken in the fight, and the manner in which Will had performed his duties while in command of the Camille.

"Gilmore?" he asked. "That is the name of a young midshipman who was on board the Furious. Is that the man?"

"I believe he is, sir."

"Well, tell him to come and see me when he is disengaged."

The lieutenant reported this when he returned, and a little later Will went on board the flag-ship.

"Well, Mr. Gilmore," said the admiral, "so you are still to the fore. I read some time ago the official report of a midshipman of your name in the West Indies who had captured two vessels, each larger than the craft he commanded, and I wondered whether it was the lad I had met here."

Will acknowledged that he had commanded on that occasion.

"It shows that the admiral there was as struck as I was myself with your doings, that he should have appointed you to command that craft, when he must have had so many senior midshipmen to select from. What had you done?"

"It was really nothing, sir. We were lying off a pirate stronghold, but could not get at it, as our ship was too deep for the shallow approaches. In the course of conversation in the midshipmen's mess I happened to suggest that if we got hold of some native craft we might be able to beard the lion in his den, and one of the elder midshipmen reported the idea to one of the lieutenants, who passed it on to the captain, who put it into execution. The result was that we captured two vessels and a very large amount of plunder which they had stored on an island. I got a great deal more credit than was due to me, for I had only suggested the plan when joking with my companions, and the captain improved upon it greatly in carrying it out. It was very good of him to mention in his report that the original idea was mine."

"It was a good plan," the admiral said, "and you well deserve the credit you got. And so it was for that that you got the command of the cutter! Tell me about the capture of those two pirate vessels."

Will related the story of the trap that had been formed for L'Agile, and the manner in which he had captured his two opponents.

"Admirably managed, Mr. Gilmore," the admiral said. "How much longer have you to serve?"

"I have another year yet, sir."

"Well, a commission is to sit here next week to pass midshipmen. I will direct them to examine you, and will see that you get your step the day you finish your term of service. If I had the power I would pass you at once, but that is one of the things an admiral cannot do. But how was it that you got on board the Lysander?"

Will related the story of his captivity with the Algerines and his escape.

"Just what I should have expected of you," the admiral said. "I fancy it would take a very strong prison to hold you. Well, tell Lieutenant Hearsey that I shall expect him to dinner to-day, and that he is to bring you with him. I'll ask two or three other officers to meet you, and you shall then tell the story of your adventures."

A post-captain and three other captains dined that evening with the admiral, and when Will had modestly related his adventures they complimented him highly. Two of them happened to be on the examining committee, and consequently Will passed almost without question. A few days later he was appointed temporarily to a ship bound for the blockading fleet of Toulon, where he was informed he would probably find his own ship. When he and his two companions rejoined the Tartar they were warmly congratulated on their escape from Algiers.

"I am sorry for the loss of Lieutenant Saxton," the captain said, when Will had reported the manner in which they had been captured. "He was a good officer, and in this case he was not to blame. With our telescopes we could only see a few men on board the Algerine, and they must have kept up the deception till the last. It is to be regretted that you followed her so far out of reach of our guns, though, so far as his fate was concerned, we could not have altered it even if we had been within easy range.

"At any rate, Mr. Gilmore, you were by no means to blame in the affair, and I congratulate you on having effected your escape with your two followers."

They had only rejoined the Tartar a short time when, on the 5th February, 1794, the captain was signalled to proceed with a small squadron that was to sail, under Captain Linzee of the Alcide, as commodore, to Corsica, where a force under General Paoli had asked for assistance in their endeavours to regain their freedom.

The chief strongholds of that island were the fortified towns of San Fiorenzo, Bastia, and Calvi. These towns are near each other, and as the troops scornfully rejected his summons to surrender, the commodore was placed in a difficulty. The force under his command was not strong enough to blockade the three forts at once, while they were so near each other that to blockade one or two and leave the entrance to the other open would have been useless. He determined at first to take Forneilli, a fortified place two miles from San Fiorenzo, but when he opened the attack he found that it was so much more strongly fortified than he had anticipated that its capture could not be effected without more loss than the gain of the position would justify.

Lord Hood then placed a squadron of frigates under Captain Nelson's command to cruise off the north-western coast of the island so as to prevent supplies being introduced, and he also sailed there himself with some of his seventy-fours and a body of soldiers under Major-general Dundas. Before he arrived, Nelson had done something towards facilitating his enterprise, for, having learned that the French in San Fiorenzo drew their supplies of flour from a mill near the shore, he landed a body of seamen and soldiers and burnt the mill, threw into the sea all the flour contained in it and in a large storehouse close to it, and regained his ship without the loss of a man.

When Lord Hood arrived he ordered Nelson to land on the island to prevent supplies from getting into Bastia, and took charge of the siege of San Fiorenzo himself. On his way Nelson captured the town of Maginaggio, routed the garrison, and destroyed a great quantity of provisions which were being prepared for a number of French vessels in the harbour. Lord Hood commenced the siege by attacking the town of Mortella. The garrison fought with great bravery and inflicted heavy loss upon the Fortitude, seventy-four guns, to which the task of battering was assigned. As she was evidently getting the worst of it the Fortitude was withdrawn, but the shore batteries were more successful, and the place being set on fire the garrison surrendered.

The Convention redoubt was the next place to be attacked. It was fortified in a most formidable manner, and indeed was so strongly constructed as to withstand any ordinary attack. A short distance away, however, was a rock rising seven hundred feet above the level of the sea, which entirely commanded it. This the enemy had left unfortified and unguarded because they believed it was inaccessible. In many places it was almost perpendicular, and though there was a path leading to the summit, this was in very few places wide enough to allow more than one person to ascend at a time. Admiral Hood in person reconnoitred and decided that a battery could be formed on the summit.

152

The next day Will was on shore in command of a party of thirty men who were to start getting up the guns. The sailors looked at the rock and at the guns in dismay.

"La, Mr. Gilmore," one of them said, "we can never get them up there! In the first place it is too steep, and in the second it is too rough. It would take two hundred men to do it, and even they would not be much good, for the path winds and twists so much that they could not put their strength on together."

Will looked at the path, and at the hill on which the new battery was to be formed.

"You see, sir," another said, "the path would have to be blasted in lots of places to make room for the guns, and we have got no tools for the job."

Will did not answer. He saw that what the men said was correct. Presently, however, his eye fell upon an empty rum puncheon, and at once his thoughts flashed back to the West Indies.

"Wheel that puncheon here, men."

Much surprised, the men did as they were ordered.

"Now knock out both ends, and when you have tightened the hoops again, fill the barrel about a third full with sticks, grass, bits of wood, anything you can come across."

The men scattered at once to collect the ballast, with some doubts in their minds as to whether the midshipman had not gone out of his senses. In about fifteen minutes they had carried out his instructions.

"Dismount the gun," he then ordered, "and put it inside the barrel."

When this had, with some difficulty, been accomplished, and the barrel surrounded the centre of the gun, he said: "Now fill up the barrel with the rest of that rubbish."

The sailors had now caught the idea, and very soon they had the gun tightly packed into its novel carriage. Two long ropes were then passed round the puncheon, the ends being carried a little way up the hill. This formed a parbuckle, and when the men hauled upon the upper lengths of the ropes the cask easily rolled up to the ends of the lower lengths. This operation was repeated again and again, and gradually the cask moved up the rock. At places it had to be hauled up lengthways, boards being placed underneath it to give it a smooth surface over which to glide instead of the rough rock, and men encouraging it from behind with levers. While they were at work Nelson came up and stood watching them for some minutes without speaking.

"Where did you learn how to do that?" he said to Will at last.

"I heard of it at the siege of St. Pierre, sir."

"Well, you profited by your lesson. It is a pleasure to see a young fellow use his wits in that way. But for your sharpness I question whether we should ever have got the guns up there. I was looking at it myself yesterday, and I doubted then whether it was at all practicable. You have settled the question for me, and I'll not forget you. What is your name, sir?"

"Gilmore of the Tartar."

Nelson made a note of it and walked away.

The work took two days of tremendous labour, the seamen being relieved three times a day. Will was constantly on the spot directing and superintending the operations, and had the satisfaction at last of seeing six guns placed on the summit of the rock.

Next morning the besieged were astonished when the guns opened fire upon them from the rock, for, the path being at the back, they had not seen what was going on. As they could obtain no shelter from this attack, and there was no possibility of silencing the guns, they hastily abandoned the post and retreated on San Fiorenzo. The battery on the rock, however, also commanded the town, which, accordingly, had to be abandoned on the following day, the garrison retiring to the adjoining ridge of ground and to Bastia, which was considered the strongest place in the island.

The capture of San Fiorenzo was the more valuable, inasmuch as in the harbour were two frigates, the Minerve and La Fortunée, both of which became our prizes. The Minerve, thirty-eight guns, was sunk by the French, but was weighed by our men and taken into the service, when she was renamed the San Fiorenzo.

Nelson was immensely pleased with the manner in which the operation of getting the guns up the rock had been performed, and requested the captain of the Tartar that Will should be permanently stationed on shore to act as his own aide-de-camp, a request which was, of course, complied with.

In the meantime Nelson had reconnoitred Bastia and the neighbouring coast, and recommended that troops and cannon be disembarked, for he was convinced that a land force of about a thousand, in co-operation with a few ships, would be sufficient to reduce the place. Unfortunately the general commanding the troops was one of the most irresolute of men, and when, after a few days, he resigned the command, in consequence of his differences with Lord Hood, his successor, General D'Aubant, was still more incapable. He pronounced at once that, though the force at his command was almost double that which Nelson asked for, it was insufficient for the work required of it. Nelson, burning with indignation, decided that the attempt to take Bastia must be made, and that if the army would not do it the navy must.

Lord Hood agreed with him, but even when it was decided to undertake the siege, D'Aubant insisted on their doing without a single soldier or a single cannon, and, retiring to San Fiorenzo, kept his men inactive while the sailors were performing the work. On the 17th of February, 1794, the fortified town of Mareno, a little to the north of Bastia, was captured, and four days later a reconnaissance was made. Nelson's ship, the Agamemnon, was supported by the Tartar and the frigate Romulus. As they passed slowly in front of the town thirty guns opened upon them with shot and shell. Nelson lowered his sails, and for an hour and three-quarters peppered the forts so warmly that at last the French garrison deserted their guns. One battery, containing six guns, was totally destroyed. The citizens of Bastia were eager to surrender, but the governor declared that he would blow up the city if such a step were taken. Two days later Nelson was preparing to repeat the blow, but a sudden calm set in, and he could not get near the town. In a short time the opportunity for carrying the place by assault passed away, as the French officers were indefatigable in strengthening their fortifications, and soon rendered the town practically impregnable.

Nelson, however, maintained the blockade in spite of heavy weather, and in the middle of March provisions were so short in the place that a pound of bread was selling for half a crown. Nelson himself was almost as much straitened for provisions, but the admiral contrived to send him a supply.

Nelson pitched a tent on shore and personally superintended all the operations. A considerable body of seamen were landed, and worked like horses, dragging guns up heights that appeared inaccessible, making roads, and cutting down trees with which to build abattis.

CHAPTER XIII

WITH NELSON

One day during the siege Nelson said to Will: "I'll be glad, Mr. Gilmore, if you will accompany me on an excursion along the shore. I have my eye on a spot from which, if we could get guns up to it, we should be able to command the town. From what I have seen of you I believe you know more about mounting guns than anyone here, so I'll be glad to have your opinion of the position."

Will of course expressed his willingness to go, and they at once started in the gig. They rowed on for some time, keeping a sharp look-out for suitable landing-places. At last Nelson bade the men lie on their oars, and pointed to the ridge of which he had spoken.

"Well, what do you say?" he asked, after Will had made a careful examination of it from the boat.

"I am afraid it would not be possible, sir, to carry out your plan. The labour of getting the guns up from the shore would be enormous, and considering the rugged state of the country I question if they could be taken across to the ridge when they were up."

"No; I agree with you. I did not examine it so closely before; and at any rate, underhanded as we are, we could not spare enough men for the business. We may as well, however, row a bit along the shore. I am convinced that if we could land three or four hundred men within five or six miles of the town, and attack it simultaneously on both sides, we should carry it without much trouble. The French have been fighting well, but they must have been losing heart for some time. A Frenchman hates to be cornered, and as they see our batteries rising they cannot but feel that sooner or later they must give in. I fancy by this time they are asking each other what use it is to keep on being killed when they must surrender in the end."

They had rowed on for a couple of hours without fixing on a suitable place, when Nelson exclaimed: "We are going to be caught in a fog. That is distinctly unpleasant. Have we a compass in the boat?" he said, turning to the coxswain.

"No, sir. I thought you were only going to row out to the ship, and did not think of bringing one with me."

156

"Never forget a compass, my man," Nelson said, "for though the sky may be blue when you start, a sudden storm may overtake you and blow you far from your ship. However, it can't be helped now."

In less than ten minutes the boat was enveloped in a dense fog. The position was decidedly awkward. Had there been any wind they could have steered by the sound of the surf breaking at the foot of the cliffs, but the sea was absolutely calm, and they could hear nothing. They rowed on for some time, and then Nelson said: "Lay in your oars, men, we may be pulling in the wrong direction for all we know. We'll have to remain here till this fog lifts, even if it takes a week to clear. This is a northerly fog," he said to Will. "Cold wind comes down from the Alps and condenses when it reaches the sea. These fogs are not very common, but they sometimes last for a considerable time."

The afternoon passed, and presently night fell. There was no food of any kind in the boat. The men chewed their quids, but the two officers could not indulge in that relief. At night Nelson and Will wrapped themselves in their boat-cloaks and made themselves as comfortable as they could, getting uneasy snatches of sleep. Morning broke and there was no change; a white wall of fog rose all round the boat.

"This is awkward," Nelson said. "I wish one of the batteries would fire a few guns; that might give us some indication as to our position, though I am by no means sure that in this thick atmosphere the sound would reach so far. I think we were about eleven miles away when the fog caught us."

In the afternoon a breeze sprang up.

"God grant that it may continue!" Nelson said. "Slight as it is, two or three hours of it might raise a swell, and we might then hear the wash of the waves on the rocks."

Hour after hour passed, but at last the coxswain said: "I think I hear a faint sound over on the right."

"I have thought so some little time," Will said, "but I would not speak until I was sure."

"Out oars," Nelson ordered, "and row in that direction." The sound became more and more distinct as they proceeded, and soon they were satisfied that they were heading for the land. In a quarter of an hour the boat ran up on a sandy beach.

"I have not seen this spot before, it must therefore be farther away from the town than the point we had reached, and as we have been nearly twenty-four hours in the fog the current may have taken us a good many miles. However, we will land. I am parched with thirst, and you must be the same, lads. Leave two men in the boat; the rest of us will go in search of water and bring some down to those left behind when we find it. I think we had better scatter and look for some way up the cliff. If we can find a path we must follow it until we come to some house or other. Where there is a house there must be water. Mr. Gilmore and I will go to the right. If any of you find water, shout; we will do the same. But whether you find water or not, come down to the boat in three hours' time. Thirsty or not thirsty we must row back to the town this evening. Now, Mr. Gilmore, we will walk along the beach until we come to a path, or at any rate some place where we can climb. I hope, as we get higher, the fog will become less dense."

For an hour they groped their way along the foot of the cliff, and then, finding a place where it seemed not so steep as elsewhere, began to climb. When they had reached a height of some three or four hundred feet they emerged from the fog into bright sunshine. Below them stretched a white misty lake. On all sides rose hill above hill, for the most part covered to the top by foliage.

"I see some smoke rising from among the trees over there to the right, sir, a mile or a mile and a half away."

"I will take your word for it, Mr. Gilmore. As you know, my sight is not at all in good condition. Let us be off at once, for the very thought of water makes me thirstier than ever."

Half an hour's walking brought them to the hut of a peasant. The owner came to the door as they approached. He was a rough-looking man in a long jacket made of goat-skin, coarse trousers reaching down to the knee, and his legs bound with long strips of wadding. "Who are you," he asked in his own language, "and how come you here?" As neither of the officers understood one word of the patois of the country they could only make signs that they wanted something to eat and drink. The peasant understood, and beckoned to them to come into the hut. As they entered he gave some instructions to a boy, who went out and presently returned with a jug of water. While the officers were quenching their thirst the boy went out again, and the man brought from a cupboard some black bread and goats'-milk cheese, which he set before them.

"I don't altogether like that man's movements, sir. He crawls about as if he were trying to put away as much time as possible. The boy, too, has disappeared."

"Perhaps he has gone to get some more water," Nelson suggested.

"He could have gone a dozen times by now, sir. It is possible that he takes us for French officers. A peasant living in such a spot as this, sixteen or twenty miles from a town, might not even know that there are English troops in the country."

Having satisfied their hunger and thirst, they tried to make the man understand that they were willing to buy all the bread and cheese he had, together with a large jar for carrying water.

The man showed a prodigious amount of stupidity, and although his eyes glistened when Nelson produced gold, he still seemed unable to understand that, having had as much as they could eat, they wanted to buy more. At last Nelson, in a passion, said: "Look here, my man, there is a sovereign, which is worth at least twenty times your miserable store of bread and cheese. If you don't choose to accept the money you needn't, but we will take the food whether or no," and he pointed to his store. As he spoke there was a sound of footsteps outside, and a moment later the door was darkened by the entry of a dozen wild figures, who flung themselves upon the two officers before they had time to make any effort to defend themselves.

In vain Nelson attempted in French and Italian to make himself understood. The men would not listen, but poured out objurgations upon them whenever they attempted to speak. The word Français frequently occurred in their speeches, mixed up with what were evidently expressions of hatred.

"This is awkward, Mr. Gilmore," Nelson said quietly as they lay bound together in a corner of the hut. "A more unpleasant situation I was never in."

"I was in one as bad once before. I was captured by a band of negroes in Cuba, and they were preparing to burn me alive when I managed to escape."

"I should not be at all surprised if that is what these gentlemen are preparing to do now, Gilmore. I am sorry I have brought you into this."

"It cannot be helped, sir," Will said cheerfully; "and if they do kill us, my loss to the nation will be as nothing compared with yours. There is no doubt they take us for French officers who have lost their way in the mountains, and they are preparing to punish us for the misdeeds of our supposed countrymen. There are only two things that could help us out of this plight so far as I can see. One is the arrival of a priest; I suppose they have priests hereabouts with a knowledge of French or Italian. The other is the appearance on the scene of our boat's crew."

"Both are very unlikely, I am afraid. The crew, you know, all went the other way."

"Yes, sir; but it is just possible that they may have seen the smoke of this hut also, and be making their way here. Though I looked carefully on all sides I could see no other signs of life."

"It is possible," Nelson said; "but for my part I think the priest the more likely solution, if there is to be a solution. Well, it is a comfort to know that we have eaten a hearty meal and shall not die hungry or thirsty. It was foolish of us to come up here alone, knowing what wild savages these people in the mountains are. It would have been better to have gone on suffering ten or twelve hours longer, and to have made our way to the fleet by following close in by the foot of the rocks."

"I don't think we could have done it in that time, sir. We should have had to keep within an oar's-length of the rocks, and so must have progressed very slowly. Besides, we might have staved in the boat at any moment."

"That is so. Still, we were only drifting for about twenty-four hours, and we shouldn't have taken so long to go back. Even twenty-four hours of hunger and thirst would have been better than this. It is useless, however, to think of that now."

In the meantime the men were engaged in a noisy talk, each one apparently urging his own view. At last they seemed to come to an agreement, and four of them, going to the corner, dragged the two officers to their feet, and hauled them out of the cottage. Then they bound them to trees seven or eight feet apart, and piled faggots round them. When this was done they amused themselves by dancing wildly round their prisoners, taunting them and heaping execrations upon them.

"The sooner this comes to an end the better," Nelson said quietly. "Well, Mr. Gilmore, we have both the satisfaction of knowing that we have done our duty to our country. After all, it makes no great difference to a man whether he dies in battle or is burnt, except that the burning method lasts a little longer. But it won't last long in our case, I fancy. Do you notice that these faggots are all lately cut? We'll probably be suffocated before the flames touch us."

"I see that, sir, and am very grateful for it."

The dance was finished, and two men brought brands from the cottage.

"Listen, Mr. Gilmore," said Nelson at this moment. "I think I can hear footsteps; I am sure I heard a branch crack."

Brands were applied to the faggots, but these were so green that at first they would not catch. At this, several of the peasants rushed into the cottage, and were returning with larger brands, when some figures suddenly appeared at the edge of the little clearing in the direction from which Nelson had heard sounds. They stood silent for a minute, looking at the scene, and then with a loud shout they rushed forward with drawn cutlasses and attacked the natives. Four or five of the peasants were cut down, and the remainder fled in terror.

"Thank God, your honour, we have arrived in time!" the coxswain said as he cut Nelson's bonds, while another sailor liberated Will.

"Thank God indeed! Now, my lads, we have not a moment to lose. Those fellows are sure to gather a number of their comrades at the nearest village, and I have no wish to see any more of them. Go into that hut; you will find enough bread and cheese there to give you each a meal, and there is a spring of water close by."

The sailors scattered at once, and were not long in discovering the spring. There they knelt down and drank long and deeply. Then they went into the cottage and devoured the bread and cheese, which, although far from being sufficient to satisfy them, at least appeased their hunger for a time. After they had finished they all went back to the spring for another drink. Then, taking some bread and cheese and a large jug of water for the boat keepers, they followed Nelson and Will from the place which had so nearly proved fatal to their officers. They went down the hill at a brisk pace until they reached the top of the fog. After this they proceeded more cautiously. They had no longer any fear of pursuit, for, once in the fog, it would require an army to find them. At last they reached the strand and found the boat. When the two men who had been left in charge had finished their share of the food and water, Nelson said:

"Now, my lads, we must row on. If we keep close to the foot of the rocks, that is, within fifty yards of them, the noise of the waves breaking will be a sufficient guide to prevent our getting too far out to sea."

"May I be so bold as to ask how far we'll have to row?" the coxswain said.

"That is more than I can tell you. It may be a little over eleven miles, it may be twice or even three times that distance. Now, however, that you have had something to eat and drink you can certainly row on until we reach the ships."

"That we can, sir. We feel like new men again, though we did feel mighty bad before."

"So did we, lads. Now it is of no use your trying to row racing pace; take a long, quiet stroke, and every hour or two rest for a few minutes."

"It will be dark before very long," Nelson remarked quietly to Will when the men began to row; "but fortunately that will make no difference to us, as we are guided not by our eyes but by our ears. There is more wind than there was, and on a still night like this we can hear the waves against the rocks half a mile out, so there is no fear of our losing our way, and it will be hard indeed if we don't reach the ships before daylight. The boat is travelling about four knots an hour. If the current has not carried us a good deal farther than we imagine, five or six hours ought to take us there."

The hours passed slowly. Sometimes the men had to row some distance seaward to avoid projecting headlands. At last, however, about twelve o'clock, Will exclaimed:

"I hear a ripple, sir, like the water against the bow of a ship."

"Easy all!" Nelson said at once.

The order was obeyed, and all listened intently. Presently there was a general exclamation as the sound of footsteps was heard ahead.

"That is a marine pacing up and down on sentry. Give way, lads."

In a few minutes a black mass rose up close in front of them. The coxswain put the helm down, and the boat glided along the side of the ship. As she did so there came the sharp challenge of a sentry:

"Who goes there? Answer, or I fire."

"It is all right, my man; it is Captain Nelson."

"Wait till I call the watch, Captain Nelson," the sentry replied in the monotonous voice of his kind.

"Very well, sentry, you are quite right to do your duty."

In half a minute an officer's voice was heard above, and a lantern was shown over the side.

"Is it you, sir?" he asked.

"Yes; what ship is this?"

"The Romulus."

"Can you lend me a compass?"

"Yes, sir, I will fetch one in a moment."

"Thank you!" Nelson said when the officer returned with the instrument. "I have lost my bearings in the fog, and I want to get to my tent on shore. I know its exact bearings, however, from this ship."

Twenty minutes' row brought them to the landing-place. Nelson's first thought was for the crew, and, going to the storehouse close at hand, he knocked some of the people up, and saw that they were supplied with plenty of food and drink. Then he went into his tent. Here the table was spread, with various kinds of food standing on it. His servant being called up, a kettle was boiled, and he and Will sat down to a hearty meal.

"Do you know what has been said about us in our absence, Chamfrey?" Nelson asked his servant.

"No, sir; everything has been upset by this fog. They sent down from the batteries to enquire where you and Mr. Gilmore were, and we could only say that we supposed you were on board the ship. They sent from the ships to ask, and we could only say that we didn't know, but supposed that you were somewhere up in the batteries. Some thought, when you did not return this afternoon, that you had lost your way in the fog; but no one seemed to think that anything serious could have happened to you."

Nelson got up and went to where the boat's crew were sitting after having finished their meal.

"Coxswain, here are two guineas for yourself and a guinea for each of the men. Now I want every man of you to keep his mouth tightly shut about what has happened. I promise you that if any man blabs he will be turned out of my gig. You understand?"

"Yes, sir," they replied together. "You can trust us to keep our mouths shut. We will never say a word about it."

"That is a good thing," Nelson remarked when he returned to Will. "If what has happened came to be known, I should get abused by Lord Hood for having gone so far away and run so great a risk. Of course, as you and I are aware, there would have been no risk at all if that fog had not set in and we had not forgotten to bring a compass. But, you know, a naval man is supposed to foresee everything, and I should have been blamed just as much as if I had rowed into the fog on purpose. I should have had all the captains in the fleet remonstrating with me, and they would be saying: 'I knew, Nelson, the way you are always running about, that you would get into some scrape or other one of these days.' A report, indeed, might be sent to England, enormously magnified, of course, with the headings: 'Captain Nelson lost in a fog!' 'Captain Nelson roasted alive by Corsican brigands!' I would not have the news get about for five hundred guineas. I don't suppose my absence was noticed the first day. It was known, of course, that I went off in my gig; but as I sometimes sleep here and sometimes on board my ship, the fact that I was not in either place would not cause surprise. As for to-day, if any questions are asked, I'll simply say that I lost my way in the fog and did not return here until late at night, a tale which will have the advantage of being true."

163

"You may be sure, sir, that no word shall pass my lips on the matter."

"I am quite sure of that, Mr. Gilmore. I shall never forget this danger we have shared together, nor how well you bore the terrible trial. I shall always regard you as one of my closest comrades and friends, and when the time comes will do my best to further your interests. I have not much power at present, as one of Lord Hood's captains, but the time may come when I shall be able to do something for you, and I can assure you that when that opportunity arrives I shall need no reminder of my promise."

By the 11th of April, 1794, the three batteries were completed, and they at once opened fire on the town. The garrison vigorously replied with hot shot, which set fire to a ship that had been converted into a battery. Still D'Aubant remained inactive. The sailors, fired with indignation, worked even harder than before. Nelson now felt confident of success. He predicted that the place would fall between the 11th and 17th of May, and his prediction was fulfilled almost to the letter, for at four o'clock on the afternoon of the 11th a boat came out from the town to the Victory offering to surrender. That afternoon, General D'Aubant, having received some reinforcements from Gibraltar, arrived from San Fiorenzo only to find that the work he had pronounced impracticable had been done without his assistance.

Will had spent the whole of his time during the siege on shore. He had laboured incessantly in getting the guns up to their positions, and had been placed in command of one of the batteries. Nelson specially recommended him for his services, and Lord Hood mentioned him in his despatches to the Admiralty at home.

No sooner had Bastia fallen than the admiral determined to besiege Calvi, the one French stronghold left in the island. The news came, however, that a part of the French fleet had broken out of Toulon, and Lord Hood at once started in pursuit, leaving Nelson to conduct the operations.

Taking the troops, which were now commanded by General Stuart, a man of very different stamp from D'Aubant, Nelson landed them on the 19th June without opposition at a narrow inlet three miles and a half from the town. A body of seamen were also landed under Will. These instantly began, as at Bastia, to get the guns up the hills to form a battery.

The enemy were strongly protected with four outlying forts. There were also in the harbour two French frigates, the Melpomene and the Mignonne. The proceedings resembled those at Bastia. The work accomplished was tremendous, and batteries sprang up as if by magic.

At the end of June Lord Hood returned from watching the French, and the work proceeded even more vigorously than before. As at Bastia, Nelson animated his men by his energy and example. He himself was wounded by some stones which were driven up by a shot striking the ground close to him, and lost the sight of his right eye for ever. But although his suffering was very severe he would not interrupt his labours for a single day. Presently the batteries opened fire, and one by one the outlying forts were stormed, and the town itself attacked. At last, on the 1st of August, the enemy proposed a capitulation. This was granted to them on the terms that if the Toulon fleet did not arrive in seven days they would lay down their arms, and surrender the two frigates. The Toulon fleet was, however, in no position to risk a battle with Lord Hood's powerful squadron, and accordingly on the 10th the garrison surrendered and marched out of the great gate of the town with the honours of war. Nelson was exultant at the thought that the capture of this town, as well as Bastia, was the achievement of his sailors, that the batteries had been constructed by them, the guns dragged up by them, and with the exception only of a single artillery-man all the guns also fought by them.

Will gained very great credit by his work. He had a natural gift for handling heavy weights, and he had thoroughly learnt the lesson that the power and endurance of English sailors could surmount obstacles that appeared insuperable.

CHAPTER XIV

THE GLORIOUS FIRST OF JUNE

It was while besieging Calvi that the news came of the great sea-battle fought in the Channel by Lord Howe, and very much interested were the sailors on shore in Corsica at hearing the details of the victory. A vast fleet had assembled at Spithead under the command of the veteran Lord Howe. It had two objects in view besides the primary one of engaging the enemy. First, the convoying of the East and West India and Newfoundland merchant fleets clear of the Channel; and next, of intercepting a French convoy returning from America laden with the produce of the West India Islands. It consisted of thirty-four line-of-battle ships and fifteen frigates, while the convoy numbered ninety-nine merchantmen.

On 2nd May, 1794, the fleet sailed from Spithead, and on the 5th they arrived off the Lizard. Here Lord Howe ordered the convoys to part company with the fleet, and detached Rear-admiral Montagu with six seventy-fours and two frigates with orders to see the merchantmen to the latitude of Cape Finisterre, where their protection was to be confided to Captain Rainier with two battle-ships and four frigates.

Lord Howe now proceeded to Ushant, where he discovered, by means of his frigates, that the enemy's fleet were quietly anchored in the harbour of Brest.

He therefore proceeded in search of the American convoy. After cruising in various directions for nearly a fortnight he returned to Ushant on the 18th May, only to find that Brest harbour was empty. News was obtained from an American vessel that the French fleet had sailed from that harbour a few days before. It afterwards turned out that the two fleets had passed quite close to each other unseen, owing to a dense fog that prevailed at the time. They were exactly the same strength in numbers, but the French carried much heavier guns, and their crews exceeded ours by three thousand men.

For more than a week the two fleets cruised about in the Bay of Biscay, each taking many prizes, but without meeting. At last, early on the morning of the 28th of May, they came in sight of each other. The French were to windward, and, having a strong south west wind with them, they came down rapidly towards us, as if anxious to fight. Presently they shortened sail and formed line of battle. Howe signalled to prepare for battle, and having come on to the same tack as the French, stood towards them, having them on his weather quarter. Soon, however, the French tacked and seemed to retreat. A general chase was ordered, and the English ships went off in pursuit under full sail. Between two and three o'clock the Russell, which was the fastest of the seventy-fours, began to exchange shots with the French, and towards evening another seventy-four, the Bellerophon, began a close action with the Révolutionnaire, one hundred and ten guns. The Bellerophon soon lost her main top-mast, and dropped back; but the fight with the great ship was taken up, first by the Leviathan and afterwards by the Audacious, both seventy-fours, which, supported by two others, fought her for three hours. By that time the Révolutionnaire had a mast carried away and great damage done to her yards, and had lost four hundred men. When darkness fell she was a complete wreck, and it was confidently expected that in the morning she would fall into our hands. At break of day, however, the French admiral sent down a ship which took her in tow, for her other mast had fallen during the night, and succeeded in taking her in safety to Rochefort. The Audacious had suffered so severely in the unequal fight that she was obliged to return to Plymouth to repair damages.

During the night the hostile fleets steered under press of canvas on a parallel course, and when daylight broke were still as near together as on the previous day, but the firing was of a desultory character, Lord Howe's efforts to bring on a general engagement being thwarted by some of the ships misunderstanding his signals. The next day was one of intense fog, but on the 31st the weather cleared, and the fleets towards evening were less than five miles apart. A general action might have been brought on, but Lord Howe preferred to wait till daylight, when signals could more easily be made out. Our admiral was surprised that none of the French ships showed any damage from the action of the 29th. It was afterwards found that they had since been joined by four fresh ships, and that the vessels that had suffered most had been sent into Brest.

During the 31st various manœuvres had been performed, which ended by giving us the weather-gage; and the next morning, the 1st of June, Lord Howe signalled that he intended to attack the enemy, and that each ship was to steer for the one opposed to her in the line. The ships were arranged so that each vessel should be opposite one of equal size. The Defence led the attack, and came under a heavy fire. The admiral's ship, the Queen Charlotte, pressed forward, replying with her quarter-deck guns only to the fire of some of the French ships which assailed her as she advanced, keeping the fire of her main-deck guns for the French admiral, whom he intended to attack. So close and compact, however, were the French lines that it was no easy matter to pass through. As the Queen Charlotte came under the stern of the Montagne she poured in a tremendous fire from her starboard guns at such close quarters that the rigging of the two vessels were touching. The Jacobin, the next ship to the Montagne, shifted her position and took up that which the Queen Charlotte had intended to occupy. Lord Howe then engaged the two vessels, and his fire was so quick that ere long both had to fall out of the fight. A furious combat followed between the Queen Charlotte and the Juste, in which the latter was totally dismasted. The former lost her main-topmast, and as she had previously lost her fore-topmast she became totally unmanageable.

Thus almost single-handed, save for the distant fire of the Invincible, Lord Howe fought these three powerful ships. At this time a fourth adversary appeared in the Républicain, one hundred and ten guns, carrying the flag of Rear-admiral Bouvet. Just as they were going to engage, however, the Gibraltar poured in a broadside, bringing down the main and mizzen-masts of the Frenchman, who bore up and passed under the stern of the Queen Charlotte, but so great was the confusion on board her that she neglected to rake the flagship.

The Montagne, followed by the Jacobin, now crowded on all sail; and Lord Howe, thinking they intended to escape, gave the order for a general chase, but they were joined by nine other ships, and wore round and sailed towards the Queen. This craft was almost defenceless, owing to the loss of her mainmast and mizzen-topmast.

Seeing her danger, Lord Howe signalled to his ships to close round her, and he himself wore round and stood to her assistance.

He was followed by five other battle-ships, and Admiral Villaret-Joyeuse gave up the attempt and sailed to help his own crippled ships, and, taking five of them in tow, made off.

Six French battle-ships were captured, and the Vengeur, which had been engaged in a desperate fight with the Brunswick, went down ten minutes after she surrendered.

The British loss in the battle of the 1st of June, and in the preliminary skirmishes of the 28th and 29th of May, was eleven hundred and forty-eight, of whom two hundred and ninety were killed and eight hundred and fifty-eight wounded.

The French placed their loss in killed and mortally wounded at three thousand, so that their total loss could not have been much under seven thousand.

Decisive as the victory was, it was the general opinion in the fleet that more ought to have been done; that the five disabled ships should have been taken, and a hot chase instituted after the flying enemy. Indeed, the only explanation of this inactivity was that the admiral, who was now an old man, was so enfeebled and exhausted by the strain through which he had gone as to be incapable of coming to any decision or of giving any order.

One of the most desperate combats in this battle was that which took place between the Brunswick, seventy-four guns, under Captain John Harvey, and the Vengeur, also a seventy-four. The Brunswick had not been engaged in the battles of the 28th and 29th of May, but she played a brilliant part on the 1st of June. She was exposed to a heavy fire as the fleet bore down to attack, and she suffered some losses before she had fired a shot. She steered for the interval between the Achille and Vengeur. The former vessel at once took up a position closing the gap, and Captain Harvey then ran foul of the Vengeur, her anchors hooking in the port fore channels of the Frenchman.

The two ships now swung close alongside of each other, and, paying off before the wind, they ran out of the line, pouring their broadsides into each other furiously.

The upper-deck guns of the Vengeur got the better of those of the Brunswick, killing several officers and men, and wounding Captain Harvey so severely as to compel him to go below.

At this moment the Achille bore down on the Brunswick's quarter, but was received by a tremendous broadside, which brought down her remaining mast, a foremast. The wreck prevented the Achille from firing, and she surrendered; but as the Brunswick was too busy to attend to her, she hoisted a sprit-sail—a sail put up under the bowsprit—and endeavoured to make off.

Meantime the Brunswick and Vengeur, fast locked, continued their desperate duel. The upper-deck guns of the former were almost silenced, but on the lower decks the advantage was the other way. Alternately depressing and elevating their guns to their utmost extent, the British sailors either fired through their enemy's bottom or ripped up her decks.

Captain Harvey, who had returned to the deck, was again

knocked down by a splinter, but continued to direct operations till he was struck in the right arm and so severely injured as to force him to give up the command, which now devolved on Lieutenant Cracroft, who, however, continued to fight the ship as his captain had done.

After being for some three hours entangled, the two ships separated, the Vengeur tearing away the Brunswick's anchor. As they drifted apart, some well-aimed shots from the Brunswick smashed her enemy's rudder-post and knocked a large hole in the counter. At this moment the Ramillies, sailing up, opened fire at forty yards' distance at this particular hole. In a few minutes she reduced the Vengeur to a sinking condition, and then proceeded to chase the Achille. The Vengeur now surrendered. The Brunswick, however, could render no assistance, all her boats being damaged, but, hoisting what sail she could, headed northward with the intention of making for port. During the fight the Brunswick lost her mizzen, and had her other masts badly damaged, her rigging and sails cut to pieces, and twenty-three guns dismounted. She lost three officers and forty-one men killed; her captain, second lieutenant, one midshipman, and one hundred and ten men wounded. Captain Harvey only survived his wounds a few months.

The greater portion of the crew of the Vengeur were taken off by the boats of the Alfred, Culloden, and Rattler, but she sank before all could be rescued, and two hundred of her crew, most of whom were wounded, were drowned. Among the survivors were Captain Renaudin and his son. Each was ignorant of the rescue of the other, and when they met by chance at Portsmouth their joy can be better imagined than described.

The Tartar returned to the blockade of Toulon after the work in Corsica was done. When she had been there some time she was ordered to cruise on the coast, where there were several forts under which French coasting-vessels ran for shelter when they saw an English sail approaching, and she was, if possible, to destroy them. There was one especially, on one of the Isles d'Hyères, which the Tartar was particularly ordered to silence, as more than any other it was the resort of coasters. The Tartar sailed in near enough to it to exchange shots, and so got some idea of the work they had to undertake; then, having learned all she could, she stood out to sea again. All preparations were made during the day for a landing; arms were distributed, and the men told off to the boats. After nightfall she again sailed in, and arrived off the forts about midnight. The boats had already been lowered, and the men took

170

their places in them while the Tartar was still moving through the water, and, dividing into three parties, made respectively for the three principal batteries.

Dimchurch was not in the boat in which Will had a place, as he rowed stroke of the first gig and Will was in the launch. Tom was also in another boat, but was in the same division. No lights were to be seen, and absolute silence reigned. Noiselessly the men landed and formed up on the beach. To reach the batteries they had to climb the cliff by a zigzag pathway, up which they were obliged to go in single file. They arrived at the summit without apparently creating a suspicion of their presence, and then advanced at a run. Suddenly three blue lights gleamed out, illuminating the whole of the ground they had to traverse, and at the same moment a tremendous volley was fired from the battery. Simultaneously fire opened from the other batteries, showing that the boats' crews had all arrived just at the same instant, and that while the French were supposed to be asleep they were awake and vigilant. Indeed, from the heaviness of the fire there was little question that the force on the island had been heavily reinforced from the mainland.

Numbers of the men fell, but nevertheless the sailors rushed forward fearlessly and reached the foot of the fort. This was too high to be climbed, so, separating, they ran round to endeavour to effect an entrance elsewhere. Suddenly they were met by a considerable body of troops. The first lieutenant, who commanded the division, whistled the order for the sailors to fall back. This was done at first slowly and in some sort of order, but the fire kept up on them was so hot that they were compelled to increase their pace to a run. A stand was made at the top of the pass, as here the men were only able to retreat in single file. At length the survivors all reached the beach and took to the boats again under a heavy fire from the top of the cliffs, which, however, was to some extent kept down by the guns of the Tartar. The other divisions had suffered almost as severely, and the affair altogether cost the Tartar fifty killed and over seventy wounded. Will was in the front rank when the French so suddenly attacked them, and was in the rear when the retreat began. Suddenly a shot struck him in the leg and he fell. In the confusion this was not noticed, and he lay there for upwards of an hour, when, the fire of the Tartar having ceased, the French came out with lanterns to search for the wounded. Will was lifted and carried to some barracks behind the fort, where his wound was attended to. They asked whether he spoke French, and as, though he had studied the language whenever he had had time and opportunity and had

171

acquired considerable knowledge of it, he was far from being able to speak it fluently, he replied that he did not, a French officer came to him.

"What is your name, monsieur?" he asked.

"William Gilmore."

"What is your rank?"

"Midshipman."

"Age?"

"Nearly nineteen."

"Nationality, English" was added.

"What ship was that from which you landed?"

There was no reason why the question should not be answered, and he replied: "The Tartar, thirty-four guns."

"Ah, you have made a bad evening's business, monsieur!" the officer said. "When the ship was seen to sail in and sail away again, after firing a few shots, we felt sure that she would come back to-night, and five hundred men were brought across from the mainland to give you a hot reception. And, parbleu, we did so."

"You did indeed," Will said, "a desperately hot reception. I cannot tell what our loss was, but it must have been very heavy. You took us completely by surprise, which was what we had intended to do to you. Well, it is the fortune of war, and I must not grumble."

"You will be sent to Toulon as soon as you can be moved, monsieur."

Three other wounded officers had fallen into the hands of the enemy, and these were placed in the same room as Will. One was the third lieutenant, another the master's mate, and the third was a midshipman. They were well treated and cared for and were very cheery together, with the exception of the lieutenant, whose wound was a mortal one, and who died two days after the fight.

A month after their reception into the hospital all were able to walk, and they were taken across in a boat to the mainland and sent to Toulon. They were all asked if they would give their parole, and though his two companions agreed to do so, Will refused. He was accordingly sent to a place of confinement, while the other two were allowed to take quarters in the town.

Will was privately glad of this, for, though both were pleasant fellows, he thought that if he were to make his escape it must be alone, and had the others been quartered with him he could not well have left them. His prison was a fort on a hill which ran out into the sea, and Will could see the sails of the blockading vessels as they cruised backwards and forwards. He also commanded a view over the town, with its harbour crowded with shipping, its churches, and fortifications. He longed continually for the company of his two faithful followers, Dimchurch and Tom. They had been with him in all his adventures, and he felt that if they were together again they would be able to contrive some plan of escape. At present no scheme occurred to him. The window of the room in which he was confined was twenty feet from the ground, and was protected by iron bars. In front was a wall some twelve feet high, enclosing a courtyard in which the garrison paraded and drilled. At night sentinels were planted at short intervals, from which Will concluded that there must be many other prisoners besides himself in the fort. He was attended by an old soldier, with whom he often had long chats.

"They certainly know how to make prisons," he grumbled to himself. "If it was not that I shall never lose hope of something turning up, I would accept my parole."

After he had been there for three months he was one day led out and, with three other midshipmen, taken down to a prison in the town. He had no doubt that prisoners of more importance had arrived, and that he and the others had been moved to make way for them. A month later they were again taken out, and, having been joined by a hundred other prisoners under a strong guard, were marched out of the town. There were five officers among them, and the rest were seamen. All were glad of the change, though it was not likely to be for the better. Will was sorry, inasmuch as at Toulon he could always hope that if he escaped from prison he would be able to get hold of a boat and row out to the blockading squadron. Inland he felt that escape would be vastly more difficult. Even if he got out of prison he knew but little French, and therefore could hardly hope to make his way across country. They trudged along day after day, each according to his fancy, some sullen and morose, others making the best of matters and trying to establish some speaking acquaintance with their guards, who evidently regarded the march as a sort of holiday after the dull routine of life in a garrison town. Will, who had during his imprisonment at Toulon studied to improve his French to the best of his ability by the aid of some books he had obtained and by chatting with his jailer, worked his hardest to add to his knowledge of the language, and as the French soldiers were quite glad to beguile the time away by talking with their captives, he succeeded at the end of the journey, which lasted nearly a month, in being able to chat with a certain amount of fluency. Verdun was one of the four places in which British prisoners were confined. At that time France had fifteen thousand prisoners, England forty thousand. By an agreement between the governments these were held captive in certain prisons, so that they could, when occasion offered, be exchanged; but owing to the vastly greater number of English prisoners the operation went on very slowly. The health of the prison was bad, the large number confined in the narrow space, and the lack of sanitary arrangements, causing a vast amount of fever to prevail.

When he got to Verdun, Will continued to devote himself to the study of French. He knew that, should he escape, he could have no hope of finding his way across country unless he could speak the language fluently, and accordingly he passed the whole day in conversation with the guards and others employed about the prison. These were inclined to regard his anxiety to become proficient in the language as a national compliment. Some of the prisoners also knew French well, so that at the end of four months he could talk with perfect fluency. He was a good deal laughed at by the English officers for the zeal he was displaying in studying French, for, as they said, he might as well try to get to the moon as out of Verdun. He accepted their chaff good-humouredly, and simply said: "Time will show, but for my part I would as soon be shot as continue to live as prisoner here."

Many of the prisoners passed their time in manufacturing little trifles. The sailors, for the most part, made models of ships; some of them were adepts at sewing patchwork quilts, and got their warders to purchase scraps of various materials for the purpose. The soldiers were also, many of them, skilled in making knick-knacks. These were sold in the town, chiefly to country people who came in to market, and so their makers were able to purchase tobacco and other little luxuries. A few of the prisoners were allowed every day to go into the town, which, being strongly walled, offered no greater facility for escape than did the prison itself. They carried with them and sold their own manufactures and those of other prisoners, and with the proceeds purchased the things they required.

Several times Will was one of those allowed out, and he set himself to work to make the acquaintance of some of the townspeople. As he was one of the few who could speak French, he had no difficulty in getting up a chatty acquaintance with several people, among them a young girl living in a house close to the wall. She had looked pitifully at him the first time he had come out with a small load of merchandise.

"Ah, my poor young fellow," she said in French, "how hard it is for you to be thus kept a prisoner far from all your friends!"

"Thank you, mademoiselle," he said, "but it is the fortune of war, and English as well as French must submit to it."

"You speak French!" she said. "Yes, yes, monsieur, I feel it as much as any. There is one who is very dear to me a prisoner in England. He is a soldier."

"Well, mademoiselle, it is a pity that they don't exchange us. We give a lot of trouble to your people, and the French prisoners give a lot of trouble to ours, so it would be much better to restore us to our friends."

"Ah! that is what I say. How happy I should be if my dear Lucien were restored to me."

So the acquaintance became closer and closer, and at last Will ventured to say: "If I were back in England, mademoiselle, I might perhaps get your Lucien out. You could give me his name and the prison in which he is confined, and it would be hard if I could not manage to aid him to escape."

"Ah, monsieur, that would be splendid!" the girl said, clasping her hands. "If you could but get away!"

"Well, mademoiselle, I think I could manage to escape if I had but a little help. For example, from the top window of this house I think I could manage to jump upon the wall, and if you could but furnish me with a rope I could easily make my escape. Of course I should want a suit of peasant's clothes, for, you see, I should be detected at once if I tried to get away in this uniform. I speak French fairly now, and think I could pass as a native."

"You speak it very well, monsieur, but oh, I dare not help you to escape!"

"I am not asking you to, mademoiselle; I am only saying how it could be managed, and that if I could get back to England I might aid your lover."

The girl was silent.

"It could never be," she murmured.

"I am not asking it, mademoiselle; and now I must be going on."

The next time he came she said: "I have been thinking over what you said, monsieur, and I feel that it would be cowardly indeed if I were to shrink from incurring some little danger for the sake of Lucien. I know that he would give his life for me. We were to have been married in a fortnight, when they came and carried him off to the war. Now tell me exactly what you want me to do."

"I want a disguise, the dress of a travelling pedlar. I could give you two English sovereigns, which would be ample to get that. I want also a rope forty feet long. Then you must let me go up through your house to the top story. I have been looking at it from behind, and see that from the upper window I could climb up to the roof, and I am sure that from there I could easily jump across the narrow lane to the wall."

"I will do it, monsieur, partly for Lucien and partly because you are kind and gentle and," she added with a little blush and laugh, "good-looking."

"I thank you with all my heart, mademoiselle, and I swear to you that when I get to England I will spare no pains to find Lucien and aid him to escape."

"When will you be out again, monsieur?"

"This day week."

"I will have everything ready by that time," she said. "You will come as late as you can?"

"Yes, I will come the last thing before we all have to return to the prison. It will be dark half an hour later."

"But there are sentries on the walls," she said.

"Yes, but not a large number. The prison is strongly guarded at night, but not the outer walls; I have often watched. There is one other thing which I shall want, and that is a sack in which to put this long box. I carry it, as you see, full of goods, but to-day I have intentionally abstained from selling any of them. I will leave the things with you if you have any place in which to hide them."

"I will put them under my bed," the girl said. "My grand'mère never goes into my room. Besides, she is generally away at the time you will arrive, and if she is not she will not hear you go upstairs, as she is very deaf. My father is one of the warders of the prison, and only comes home once a week."

Will then returned to the prison. When the appointed day arrived he put only a few small articles into his box. For these he paid cash. Then he said good-bye to four or five of the officers with whom he was most friendly.

"You are mad to try to escape," one of them said, "there is no getting over the walls."

"I am going to try at any rate. I am utterly sick of this life."

"But you may be exchanged before long."

"It is most improbable," he said. "Only a few are exchanged at a time, and as I have not a shadow of influence my name would not be included in the list."

"But how are you going to attempt it?"

"Now that I must keep to myself. A plan may succeed once,

but may fail if it is tried again. I really think I have a chance of getting through, but of course I may be caught. However, I am going to take the risk."

"Well, I wish you luck, but I can hardly even hope that you will succeed."

After going about the town as usual, without making any serious effort to sell his goods, Will made his way, towards the end of the day, to the house in the lane. Marie was standing at the door. As he approached she looked anxiously up and down the street, to be certain that there was no one there, and then beckoned to him to enter quickly. He obeyed at once, and she closed the door behind him. "Are you sure no one saw you enter, monsieur?" she said.

"Yes," he said, "I am quite certain."

"Now," said Marie, "you must go at once up to the attic in case my grand'mère should come in. I have everything ready for you there. It will be dark in half an hour. I hear the prison bell ringing for the return of the prisoners who are out, but the roll-call is not made until all have returned to their cells and are locked up for the night, which will not be for an hour and a half, so you have plenty of time."

"I thank you with all my heart, mademoiselle."

He went up with her to the attic and looked out at the wall. The lane was only some twelve feet across, and he was convinced that he could leap it without difficulty. He emptied his box and repacked it, selecting chiefly articles which would take up the smallest amount of room. He made quite sure how he could best climb from the window to the roof above it, then he waited with what patience he could until it was absolutely dark. When he was ready to start he fastened the rope firmly round the box and said good-bye to Marie.

His last words were: "I will do my very best for Lucien, and when the war is over I will send you a gold watch to wear at your wedding."

Then he got upon the window-sill, with the end of the rope tied round his waist, and with some little difficulty climbed to the roof of the house, and when he had got his breath began to pull at the rope and hoisted up the box. He had, before starting, put on the disguise Marie had bought for him, and handed her the remains of his uniform, telling her to burn it at once, and to hide away the buttons for the present, and throw them away the first time she left the town. "There will be a strict search," he said, "for any signs of me, and those buttons would certainly betray you if they were found."

177

When he got the box up he listened attentively for a little, and as, to his great joy, he could not hear the footsteps of a sentinel, he threw it on to the wall and jumped after it. He landed on his feet, and, picking up the box, ran along the wall till he came to a gun. He tied the end of the rope round this and slipped down. Then without a moment's delay he slung the box over his shoulder and walked away. He had two or three outworks to pass, but luckily there were no guards, so he made his way through them without difficulty. All night he tramped on, and by morning was forty miles away from Verdun. He did not want to begin to ply his assumed trade till he was still farther away, so he lay down to sleep in a large wood. He had saved from his rations during the week a certain amount of bread, and he had bought a couple of loaves while wandering with his wares through the town. He slept for the best part of the day, and started again at night. Beyond making sure that he was going west he paid but little attention to the roads he followed, but, keeping steadily in that direction, he put another forty miles between him and Verdun by the following morning. Then after a few hours' sleep he boldly went into a village and entered an inn.

"You are a pedlar," the landlord said, "are you not?"

"Yes," he said, "I am selling wares manufactured by the prisoners at Verdun."

The news spread and the villagers flocked in to look at these curiosities.

"I bought them at a low price, and will sell at the same. They could not be made by ordinary labour at ten times the price I charge for them."

The bait took, and soon a good many small articles were sold. Two hours later he again started on his way.

CHAPTER XV

ESCAPED

So he travelled across France, avoiding all large towns. Once or twice he got into trouble with a pompous village official on account of his not holding a pedlar's permit; but the feeling of the people was strong in favour of a man who was selling goods for the benefit of poor prisoners, and, of course, he always had some plausible story ready to account for its absence. At last he came to Dunkirk. He had saved money as he went, and on his arrival there had eight louis in his pocket. He took up a lodging at a little cabaret, and, leaving his box, which was now almost empty, strolled down to the harbour. Fishing-boats were coming in and going out. Observing that they were not very well manned, probably because many of the men had been drafted into the navy, he selected one which had but four men, a number barely sufficient to raise the heavy lug-sail, and when she made fast alongside the quay he went on board.

"Do you want a hand?" he said, "I am not accustomed to the sea, but I have no doubt I could haul on a rope as well as others."

"Where do you come from," one asked, "and how is it that you have escaped the conscription?"

"I am exempt," he said, "as the only son of my mother. I come from Champagne."

"But why have you left?"

"I came away because the girl I was engaged to jilted me for a richer suitor, and I could not stop there to see her married; I should have cut his throat or my own. So I have tramped down here to see if I can find some work for a time."

"You are a fool for your pains," the skipper said. "No girl is worth it."

"Ah, you never could have been jilted! If you had been you wouldn't think so lightly of it."

"Well, mates, what do you say? Shall we take this young fellow? He looks strong and active, and I dare say will suit us."

"At any rate we can give him a trial for a voyage or two."

"Well, you may begin by helping us up into the town with our fish. We have had a heavy catch to-day."

Will at once shouldered a basket and went up with them to the market-place.

179

"We are going to get a drink," the fisherman said. "Let us see how well you can sell for us. You must get a franc a kilogramme. Here are scales."

For a couple of hours Will sold fish, attracting, by his pleasant face, buyers who might otherwise have passed him; and when the fishermen returned they were pleased to find that he had almost sold out their stock, and accounted for his take to the last sou.

"I have been watching you all the time," the captain said, "though you did not know. I wanted to see if you were honest, and, now that I have a proof of it, will take you willingly. The pay is twelve francs a week and a tenth share in the sales. The boat takes a third, I take two, and the sailors take one apiece, and you will have half a share besides your pay till you know your business. Do you agree to that?"

"Yes," Will said.

Accordingly he settled down to the work of a fisherman, and gave great satisfaction. His mates were indeed astonished at the rapidity with which he learned his work, and congratulated themselves upon the acquisition of so promising a recruit.

A month after he had joined the smack a ship-of-war was seen sailing along three miles from shore. The fishermen were half-way between her and the land, and paid no great attention to her, knowing that British men-of-war did not condescend to meddle with small fishing-boats. Will waited until the captain and one of the men were below; then, suddenly pushing the hatch to and throwing a coil of rope over it, he produced from his pockets a brace of pistols which he had bought at Dunkirk out of the stock of money he had had in his pocket when he was captured, and ordered the man at the helm to steer for the frigate. The man let go the tiller at once, and he and his companion prepared to make a rush upon Will. But the sight of the levelled pistols checked them.

"You will come to no harm," Will said. "You have but to put me on board, and I warrant you shall be allowed to depart unmolested. I am an English officer. Now, down with the helm without hesitation, or I will put a bullet through your head; and do you, Jacques, sit down by his side."

Sullenly the men obeyed his orders, and the boat went dancing through the water in a direction which, Will calculated, would enable him to cut off the frigate. In the meantime the captain and his companion, unable to understand what was going on, were thumping at the hatchway. Will, however, paid no attention to them, but stood on it, keeping his eye upon the men in the stern.

Twenty minutes brought them close to the frigate, which, on seeing a small boat making for her, threw her sails aback to wait for it. As they came close a rope was thrown; Will grasped it and swung himself up the side, leaving the boat to drift away. The sailors stood looking in surprise at him, but Will went straight up to the first lieutenant.

"I beg to report myself as having come on board, sir. I am, or rather was, a midshipman on board the Tartar. I have just escaped from Verdun."

"Do you really mean it?" the lieutenant said. "I thought only one or two English prisoners had ever made their escape from there."

"That is so, sir, and I am one of the fortunate ones."

"But how on earth have you managed to pass right through France?"

"I was detained three months at Toulon, sir, and there was allowed to buy some French books. I was then a month on the way to Verdun, and five months there. During that time I practised French incessantly, and picked up enough to pass muster. At last, thanks to a French girl, I succeeded in getting a disguise and climbing over the wall, and passed through France as a pedlar with wares made by the prisoners."

"Come with me to the captain's cabin. He will, I am sure, be glad to hear your story. How were you captured?"

"In the attack the Tartar made on a battery on one of the Isles d'Hyères I was shot through the leg and left behind in the retreat."

"Yes, I heard of that affair, and a most unfortunate one it was. You caught it hot there, and no mistake!"

The captain listened to the story with great interest, and then said: "Well, Mr. Gilmore, I congratulate you very heartily on getting out of that terrible prison. I am rather short of officers, and will rate you as midshipman until I have an opportunity of sending you home. I have no doubt your brother officers will manage to rig you out."

The lieutenant went out with Will and introduced him to the officers of the ship, to whom he had again to tell the tale of his adventure. "Now come down below to our berth," the senior midshipman said, "and we will see what we can do to rig you out. We lost one of our number the other day, and I have no doubt the purser's clerk will let you take what you require out of his kit if you give him a bill on your paymaster."

Fortunately the clothes fitted Will, so he took over the whole of the effects, as there was sufficient standing to his account on the Tartar to pay for them, in addition to the pay that would accrue during the time of his captivity.

He learned that they were on their way to the Texel, where they were to cruise backwards and forwards to watch the flotilla of boats that Napoleon was accumulating there for the invasion of England. It was arduous work, for the heavy fogs rendered it necessary to use the greatest caution, as there were many dangerous shoals and currents in the vicinity.

One dark night, when they thought that they were in deep water, the ship grounded suddenly. The tide was running out, and though they did everything in their power they could not get her off.

"If we have but another couple of hours," the first lieutenant said, "we shall float, as the tide will be turning very soon. But it is getting light already, and we are likely to have their gun-boats out in no time."

His anticipation turned out correct, for six gun-boats were soon seen making their way out of the Texel. When within range they opened fire. The Artemis replied with such guns as she could bring to bear on them. She suffered a good deal of damage, but the tide had turned and was flowing fast. Hawsers had been run out at the stern and fastened to the capstan, and the bars were now manned, and the sailors put their whole strength into the work. At last there was a movement; the ship quivered from stem to stern, and then slipped off into deep water. A joyous cheer burst from the crew. But they did not waste time. They ran at once to their guns, and opened a broadside fire on the gun-boats. One was disabled and taken in tow by two others; and the rest, finding themselves no match for the frigate, sheered off and re-entered the Texel.

The Artemis continued to cruise to and fro for upwards of a month. One evening the first lieutenant said to Will: "The captain is worried because we were told to expect a messenger with news as to the state of affairs at Amsterdam and in Holland generally, and none has arrived. There is no doubt that they are adding to the number of gun-boats there, and also to the flat-bottomed boats for the conveyance of troops. The delay is most annoying, especially as we have orders to sail for England with the news as soon as we get it, and we are all heartily sick of this dull and dreary work."

"I will volunteer to land and communicate with some of the country-people near Amsterdam," Will said, "if the captain would like it. We know that their sympathies are all with us, and I have no doubt that I could get what information is required. If my offer is accepted I should greatly prefer to go in uniform, for, while I am quite ready to run the risk of being taken prisoner, I have certainly no desire to be captured out of uniform, as I should be liable to be hanged as a spy."

The first lieutenant mentioned the matter to the captain, who at once embraced the offer, for he, too, was sick of the work, in which no honour was to be obtained, and in which the risks were great, as the coast was a dangerous one. He sent for Will and said: "I hear, Mr. Gilmore, that you are willing to volunteer to land and gain information. Have you considered the risks?"

"I know that, of course, there is a certain amount of danger, sir, but do not consider it to be excessive. At any rate I am ready to try it."

"I am very much obliged to you," the captain said, "for we are all anxious to get away from this place; but mind, I cannot but consider that the risk is considerable. With our glasses we constantly see bodies of horsemen riding along the sands, and have sometimes noticed solitary men, no doubt sentinels; and it is probably because of them that the messenger we expected has not been able to put out. I will give you his address. He lives within half a mile of Amsterdam, in a house near the shore of the Texel. When are you prepared to start?"

"This evening if you wish it, sir."

"Well, I think the sooner you go the better. If you land to-night I will send the boat ashore to the same spot to-morrow night. They will lie off two or three hundred yards, and come to your whistle."

"Very well, sir."

Will had no preparations to make for his journey. He received a letter from the captain authorizing the man to give every information in his power to the bearer, and with this in his pocket he took his place in the boat after dark and was rowed towards the shore. The Artemis was four miles from the land when he embarked in the gig, the oars were muffled, and the men were enjoined to row with the greatest care when they approached the land. An officer went in charge, and the Artemis was to show a light an hour after they started, so that they could find their way back to her. Will chatted in a whisper to the officer till they were, he judged, within half a mile of the land. Then they rowed on in perfect silence till the keel grated on the sands. At that moment a musket shot was heard from a sand-hill a couple of hundred yards away. Will leapt out and ran at full speed for some little distance, and then threw himself down. The shots were repeated from point to point, and men ran down to the water's edge and fired after the retiring boat.

Presently the noise ceased. Whether he had been seen or not he could not say, but he hoped that, although the sentinel had made out the boat against the slight surf that broke on the beach, he had not been able to see him leave it. He got up cautiously, and, stooping low, moved off until he was quite certain that he was well beyond the line of sentries. Once or twice he heard the galloping of parties of men, evidently attracted by the sound of firing, but none of them came very near him, and he ran on without interruption. In two hours he saw lights before him, and knew that he was approaching Amsterdam. He turned to the right, and went on until he came to a wide sheet of water, which must, he knew, be the Texel. Then he lay down and slept for some hours. At the first gleam of dawn he was on his feet again, and made his way to a farmhouse which exactly agreed with the description that had been given him. He knocked at the door, and it was presently opened by a man in his shirt-sleeves.

"Are you Meinheer Johan Van Duyk?" he asked.

"I am," the man said. "Who are you?"

"I am the bearer of this letter from the captain of the Artemis, who had expected you to communicate with him."

"Come in," the man said. "We are early risers here, and it is advisable that no one should see you. Yes," he went on when the door was closed, "I have been trying to communicate, but the cordon of sentries along the shore has been so close, and the watch so vigilant, that it has been quite impossible for me to come out. I suppose you are an officer of that ship?"

"Yes."

"Do you speak Dutch?"

"No, I speak French."

The man read the letter.

"That is all right; I can furnish you with all these particulars when you leave to-night, but of course in that uniform you must lie dark until then. For some reason or other the French have suspicions of me, and they have paid me several visits. Were you seen to land last night?"

"I do not know. They fired on the boat, and I expect they have a shrewd idea that somebody was put on shore."

"In that case," the man said, "it is probable that they will search my house to-day. By this time they know every little corner of it, so I cannot see where I am to conceal you."

184

"I observed a stack behind your house," suggested Will.

"Yes, there is one."

"Well, if you would at once get a ladder, and take off some of the thatch and make a hole, I could get into it, and you could then replace the thatch long before the soldiers are likely to come out from Amsterdam."

"Yes, I could do that, and I could hand you in a bottle of schnapps and some water and bread and meat."

"That will do very well. I suppose you have men?"

"Yes, I have two, and both of them are true Dutchmen, and may be trusted. I will give you at once the list of the gun-boats and flat-boats I have made ready to send on the first opportunity. I shall be glad to get it out of the house, for, though it is well hidden, they search so strictly that they might find it. They broke all my wainscots, pulled up the flooring, and almost wrecked the house the last time they came; and I don't suppose they will be less vigilant this time."

He went to the cupboard and brought out some food and drink.

"Now, sir," he said, "if you will eat this I will call up my two men and set to work at once to get your hiding-place made, so that you may be safely lodged in it before any people are about."

Will was by no means sorry to take breakfast. He ate the food leisurely, and just as he had finished Van Duyk came in to say that the place was ready for him.

It was not a large hole, but sufficient to let him lie down at full length under the thatch. He climbed up the ladder the men had used and got into his nest, and after Van Duyk had handed him in the provisions he had promised, the two men set to work with all speed to replace the thatch. It was made thin, so that he had no difficulty in raising it, and could even with his finger make a tiny opening through which he could look. The hay that had been removed to make room for him was carried away and thrown down in the mangers for the cows, so that there was nothing to show that the stack had recently been touched.

Two hours later Will heard the trampling of horses, and two officers, with a troop of cavalry, rode up.

"I bear a warrant to search your house, Van Duyk," Will heard one of them say.

"You have searched it three times already, meinheer, but you can, of course, search it again if you wish. You will certainly find no more now than you did then."

"A spy landed last night, Van Duyk, and it is more than probable that he is taking shelter here."

"I don't know why you should suspect me more than anyone else. I am a quiet man, meddling in no way with public matters, and attending only to my own business."

"It is all very well to say that; we have certain information about you."

"I am well known to my neighbours as a peaceable man," Van Duyk repeated, "and think it monstrous that I should be so interfered with and harried."

"Well, we don't want any talk. Now, men, set to work and search every corner of the house, not only where a man could be hidden, but even a paper. These Dutchmen are traitors to a man, and if this fellow is no worse than others he is at least as bad."

For an hour and a half Will, in his hiding-place, heard the sound of smashing panels and furniture, and the pulling up of floors. At the end of that time the troopers left the house and mounted, the officer saying: "You have deceived us this time, old traitor, but we will catch you yet."

"Catch me if you can. I tell you that if you level the house to the ground you will find nothing."

After they had ridden off, Van Duyk went out to the haystack.

"They have gone for the present, meinheer, but you had better stay where you are. They are quite capable of coming back again in the hope that you may have come out from some hiding-place they may have overlooked."

Indeed, an hour later the troop galloped up again, only to find the Dutchman smoking placidly on a seat before his house. Another search was made, but equally without success, and then, with much use of strong language, the party rode off.

"I think you can come down safely now," the Dutchman said to Will.

"Thank you, but I don't wish to run the least risk. I will remain where I am till it gets dark; I can very well sleep the time away till then. I sha'n't get much sleep to-night."

Not until it was quite dark did Van Duyk and his men come with a ladder to remove the thatch again. It took but a minute to extricate Will from his hole.

"We will get that filled up and mended before morning," Van Duyk said. "Now, can I let you have a horse?"

"No, thank you, I have but twelve miles to walk. I noted the road as I came, and can find the spot where I landed without difficulty."

186

With thanks for the Dutchman's kindness, and handing him the reward with which the captain had entrusted him, Will started on his walk. When he approached the spot it was still four hours from the time at which the boat was to arrive, and seeing a light in a cottage he went and looked in at the window. Only a girl and an old woman were there, so he lifted the latch and went in. "I am an English officer," he said, "will you let me sit down by your fire for a couple of hours? The cold is piercing outside."

The old woman answered in broken French, bidding him welcome, and he sat down and began to talk to her. Her stock of French was small, and the conversation soon languished. Presently the girl leapt to her feet and exclaimed in Dutch: "Soldiers!" The old woman translated, and Will then heard the trampling of horses. He jumped up, snatched a long cloak of the old woman's from the wall, and threw it round him. He also took one of her caps that hung there and put it on his head. It was large, with frills, and almost covered his face. He had but just time to reseat himself by the fire and cower over it, as if warming his hands, when the door opened and a French officer entered. At the sight of the two apparently old women bending over the fire, and the girl sitting knitting, he stopped.

"Madam," he said courteously, "it is my duty to search your house. It is believed that a spy who landed here last night may be returning to-night."

"You can look," the old woman said in her quavering voice, "as much as you like; you will not find any spy here."

As the cottage consisted of only two rooms the search was quickly effected.

"Thank you, madam!" the French officer said; "I am quite satisfied, and am sorry I have incommoded you."

"That is a civil fellow," Will said, as the sound of the retreating hoofs was heard. "Some of these fellows would have blustered and sworn and turned the whole place upside down. Well, madam, I am deeply obliged to you for the shelter you have given me and the risk you have run for my sake. Here is a guinea; it is all the gold I have with me, but it may buy some little comfort for you."

"It will buy me enough turf to last me all the winter," the old woman said. "My son is a fisherman who is sometimes weeks from home, and our supply of turf is running low. Thank you very much! though I would gladly have done it without reward, for we all hate the French."

Will went out cautiously and made his way down to the shore, listening at every step for some sound that would tell of the presence of a sentry. He lay down near the edge of the sea and watched. At last he saw a dim shape lying stationary a hundred yards out. He gave a low whistle, but this was almost instantaneously followed by the report of a musket within fifty yards of him. He did not hesitate, but with a shout to the boat ran into the water and struck out towards it. Another musket was fired, fifty yards to the left, and the signal was, as before, repeated by sentry after sentry till the sound died away in the distance. Almost immediately the galloping of horses could be heard. The boat rowed in to meet him, and as he scrambled on board a volley of carbines rang out from the shore. The sailors bent to their oars and, although the firing continued for some time, they knew that the enemy had lost sight of them. A quarter of an hour later the sound of oars was heard. "Stop rowing," the lieutenant in command of the boat ordered, "and don't move."

In about three minutes a large rowing-boat, manned by a number of oars, could be made out passing across ahead of them. The ship's boat, however, was so small an object in comparison that it remained unnoticed. They waited till the beat of oars ceased in the distance and then rowed on again.

"That was a narrow escape," the lieutenant muttered. "Evidently she was lying in wait to catch you, and if she had been fifty yards nearer to us she must have made us out. I think we are safe now, for the course she was taking will not carry her anywhere near the frigate. At any rate we have a good start, and I have a lantern here to show in case we are chased."

They had rowed two miles farther when they again heard the sound of oars.

"We must row for it now," the lieutenant said. "The frigate is not much more than a mile away."

The men bent to their oars, and the lieutenant raised and lowered his lantern three times. This signal was almost immediately answered by the boom of a gun from the frigate. For a time the enemy continued the pursuit, but on a second gun being fired they ceased rowing.

"They must know that the frigate can't see them," the lieutenant said, "but they have no doubt come to the conclusion that they cannot overtake us before we get to her. Anyhow it is certain that they have given it up as a bad job."

In ten more minutes they were alongside the frigate.

"Is Mr. Gilmore with you?" a voice asked from above.

"Yes, I am here, sir, safe and sound."

"That is good news," the first lieutenant said, as Will stepped on deck. "The captain was afraid, after he had let you go, that he had sacrificed you, and that, going as you did in your uniform, you would be certain to be captured."

"No, sir; I had two narrow escapes, but got off all right, and have brought you the list of gun-boats and row-boats that you required. I am afraid, though, that it will require careful opening, for I had to swim off to the boat."

"That will not matter as long as we can read it," the lieutenant said. "Now you had better come to the captain and hand it to him."

"I am heartily glad to see you, Mr. Gilmore," the captain said. "I have been very uneasy about you, and I really hardly expected you to return to-night. We knew that the boat was being chased, by the lights Lieutenant Falcon showed, but I feared that she was coming back without you. Now tell me what has happened to you. We knew by the firing that French sentries saw the boat come to land last night."

Will gave a full account of his adventures.

"Well done indeed, Mr. Gilmore! I shall have much pleasure in reporting your conduct. Now let us examine the list."

The words were a good deal blurred by water, but were still quite legible.

"They are stronger in gun-boats than I expected," the captain said when he had read it. "If they had had an ounce of pluck about them they would have come out and fought us. A thirty-two-gun frigate is no match for sixteen gunboats. Well, now that we have got this despatch, we can make for Sheerness at once. Have her headed for that port, Mr. Falcon, if you please. We won't lose a moment before making for England."

CHAPTER XVI

A DARING EXPLOIT

On reaching Sheerness the captain at once went ashore, accompanied by Will, and they proceeded to London. Will took up his quarters at the Golden Cross, and next day called at the Admiralty, where he sent in his name to the First Lord.

"I have received a most favourable report from Captain Knowles of your conduct in landing on the coast of Holland, and of obtaining despatches of much value. How were you taken prisoner?"

"At the attack by a force from the Tartar on some batteries on one of the Isles d'Hyères. I was hit in the leg, and, being left behind in the confusion of the retreat, fell into the hands of the French. I was imprisoned for four months at Toulon, and then sent to Verdun. Six months after leaving Toulon I effected my escape in a disguise procured for me by a French girl. I had learned the language while in prison, and, travelling through France in the disguise of a pedlar, reached Dunkirk. There I worked in a fishing-boat for a month, and then, seeing the Artemis cruising off the town, I shut up two of the sailors in their cabin, and frightened the other two into taking me off to her."

"In consideration of the valuable services you have rendered I have much pleasure in appointing you master's mate."

"Thank you, sir! but I own I had rather hopes of obtaining a lieutenancy."

"A lieutenancy!" the admiral said in a changed tone. "I am surprised to hear you say so, when you have had no service as a master's mate. What makes you entertain such a hope?"

"My past services, sir," Will said boldly.

"Captain Purfleet, will you hand me down the volume of services under the letter G. Ah! here it is."

He glanced at it cursorily at first, and then read it carefully.

"You were right, Mr. Gilmore, in entertaining such a hope. I see that you have been highly spoken of by the various officers under whom you have served; that you were most strongly recommended by the admirals both at Malta and in the West Indies for your singular services, and also by Lord Hood for your conduct in Corsica. You were in command of a small craft for nearly a year, and in that capacity you not only took a number of prizes, some of them valuable, but actually captured, in one hard-fought action, two pirates, each of which was stronger than yourself. You have, therefore, well shown your capacity to command. Captain Purfleet, have any appointments been made yet to the Jason?"

"No, sir."

"Very well, then appoint Mr. Gilmore to be second lieutenant of her. You need not thank me, sir; you owe your commission to your own gallantry and good conduct. I don't know that I have at any time seen such strong testimonials and so good a record for any officer of your age and standing. I am quite sure that you will do full justice to the appointment that I have made. As the Jason will not be ready for two months I can grant you six weeks leave."

No sooner was this matter settled than Will took the coach to Fairham. Thence he drove to the village of Porchester, where Marie's fiancé was confined. Here he put up at a little inn. He had, before starting from London, bought and put on the disguise of a countryman, as he could hardly have stayed in the village as a gentleman without exciting remark or suspicion. He had, however, brought other clothes with him, so that if necessary he could resume them, and appear either as a naval officer or as a civilian. His first step was to make a tour of the great wall which enclosed the castle and the huts in which the prisoners were confined. He saw at once that any attempt to scale the wall would be useless. At the inn he gave out that by the death of a relative he had just come into a few pounds and meant to enjoy himself.

The inn he had selected was scarcely more than a tavern, and he had chosen it because he thought it probable that it would be frequented by the soldiers whose camp stood near the walls, and who supplied the guards in the castle. This expectation was fulfilled a short time after his arrival by four or five soldiers coming in.

"Will you drink a glass with me?" he said. "I have been telling the landlord that I have come into a little brass, and mean to spend it."

The soldiers, not unwillingly, accepted the invitation, and sat down at a table with him.

"It must be slow work," he said, "keeping guard here, and I expect you would sooner be out at the war."

"That we should," one of them replied; "there is nothing to do here but to drill all day, and stare across the water when we are off duty, and wish we were at Portsmouth, where there is something to do and something to amuse one. This is the dullest hole I ever was quartered in. Cosham on one side and Fairham on the other are the only places that one can walk to. We expect, however, to be relieved before long, and I never want to see the place again."

"I suppose you take recruits here?" Will said.

"Oh yes, we take recruits when we can get them."

"How long is a recruit before he begins to be a soldier, and takes his regular turn as guard and so on?"

"Two or three months," the man said; "that is long enough to get them into something like shape."

"I should like to go in and have a look at the prisoners," Will said after a little chat.

"Well, there is no chance of your doing that," the soldier replied. "Orders are very strict, and only three or four hucksters are allowed to go in, to sell things to them."

"How many are there of them?"

"About three thousand."

He chatted for some time, and then, after calling for another pint of beer all round, sauntered out, leaving the soldiers to finish it. He saw at once that his only possible plan in the time he had at his command was either to bribe some of the guards, which appeared to him too hazardous a plan to adopt, and not likely to lead to success, or to get at one or other of the people who were allowed in.

He spent two days watching the gate of the prison. During that time five people in civilian dress went in. One of these was a short fat woman, who carried a large basket with cakes and other eatables. Another was similarly laden. A third, a man of about his own height, took in a variety of material used by the prisoners for making articles for sale. He had needles and thread, scraps of materials of many colours for making patchwork quilts, blocks of wood for carving out model ships, straw dyed various colours for making fancy boxes, glass beads, and other small articles. Will at once fixed on him as being the most likely of the visitors to serve his purpose. He spoke to him after he had left the prison.

"My friend," he said, "do you want to earn fifty pounds?"

The man opened his eyes in surprise.

"I should certainly like to," he said, "if I could see my way to do it."

"Well, I will double that if you do as I tell you. I want you, in the first place, to find out the hut in which Lucien Dupres is confined, and give him a letter."

"There will be no great difficulty about that," the man said. "I only have to whisper to the first prisoner I meet that I want to find a

192

man, and have got a letter from his friends for him, and if he doesn't know him he will find him out for me. That is not much to do for a hundred pounds."

"No; but in the next place I want you to keep out of the way for a week, and to lend me your clothes and pass. I want to go in and see the man."

"Well, that is a more dangerous business. How could you pass for me?"

"I think I could do that without fear. We are about the same height. I should have a wig made to imitate your hair, and should, I imagine, have no difficulty in getting my face made up so as to be able to pass for you. You must be so well known that they will do no more than glance at me as I go in. The only alternative to that will be for you to take to him a rope and other things I will give you. I tell you frankly I want to aid his escape. Mind, a hundred pounds is not to be earned without some slight risk."

"Of the two things I would rather risk carrying the rope and the tools, if they are not too bulky. Mind you, it is a big risk, for I should be liable to be shot for aiding in the escape of a prisoner."

"Well, look here," Will said, "I will go into Portsmouth this afternoon and find some man who can fake me up. There are sure to be two or three men who make that their business, for young naval officers are constantly getting into scrimmages, and must want to have their eyes painted before they go back on board. Do you go to the prison to-morrow morning. Find out the man, and deliver this letter to him. Then come into Portsmouth in the coach. I will be waiting there till it arrives, and you can go with me, and when I have got myself made up you shall judge for yourself whether I shall pass muster for you. There will be no difficulty in getting whiskers to match yours."

"Very well," the man said, "I will be on the coach to-morrow."

Will at once changed his clothes to an ordinary walking suit, and went into town. On making enquiries he found that there was a barber who made it his business to paint black eyes and to remove the signs of bruises. He went to him and said: "I hear you are an artist in black eyes."

The man smiled.

"You don't look as if you wanted my services, sir."

"No, not in that way, but I suppose you could make up a face so as to resemble another."

"Yes, sir, I was at one time engaged at a theatre in London in making up the performers, and feel sure that I could accomplish such a job to your satisfaction."

193

"I have made a bet," Will said, "that I could disguise myself as a certain man so well that I could take my friends in. Have you a sandy wig in your shop?"

"Yes, sir, half a dozen."

"And whiskers?"

"I have several sets, sir, and I dare say one would be the right colour."

"Very well, then, I will bring the man here to-morrow, and you shall paint me so as to resemble him as closely as possible. I don't mind giving you a five-pound note for the job."

"Well, sir, if I am not mistaken I can paint you so that his own mother wouldn't know the difference."

Will took a bed at the George, and at mid-day went to the inn where the coach stopped. The man was on the outside.

"Well, sir, I have found the Frenchman, and given him the letter, so that part of the business is done."

"That is good. What is the number of the man's hut?"

"Number sixty-eight;" and the man carefully described its position.

"Very well. Now we will set about the second part."

When they arrived at the shop the barber seated them in two chairs next to each other, in a room behind the shop, and set to work at once. He first produced a wig and whiskers, which, with a little clipping, he made of the size and shape of the hair on the huckster's face. Then he set to work with his paints, first staining Will's face to the reddish-brown of the man's complexion, and then adding line after line. After two hours' work he asked them to stand together before a glass, and both were astonished; the resemblance was indeed perfect. Will's eyebrows had been stained a grayish white, and some long hairs had been inserted so as to give them the shaggy appearance of the pedlar. A crow's foot had been painted at the corner of each eye, and a line drawn from the nose to the corners of the lips. The chin and lower part of the cheeks had been tinted dark, to give them the appearance of long shaving. Both of them burst into a laugh as they looked at the two faces in the mirror.

"You will do, sir," the man said. "It would need a sharp pair of eyes to detect the difference between us."

"Yes, I think that will do," Will said, "and to aid the deception I will, as I go in, use my handkerchief and pretend to have a bad cold."

"Is there a basket-maker's near?" Will asked the barber.

"Yes, sir, first turning to the right, and first to the left, two or three doors down, there is a small shop."

"I want you at once to go and choose one the size and shape of your own," Will said to his companion. "When you see one, set the man to work to weave a false bottom to it. I want it to lodge so as to leave a recess four or five inches deep. Have it made with two handles, so that it can be lifted in and out. How long would he be doing it, do you think?"

"About an hour and a half, I should say."

"Very well; order the man to send it round to the George, wrapped up in paper, to the address of Mr. Earnshaw. When you have done this, come back here. We cannot go into the street together; our singular resemblance would at once be noticed."

"Now," Will said to the pedlar when he returned, "meet me on the road a hundred yards from where it turns down to Porchester; bring a stock of goods with you, and I will put them in my basket. Of course you will bring your pass, and the clothes you now have on in a bundle. I will change there; as far as I have seen it is very seldom that anyone passes that way."

Will then went for a walk, and when it became quite dark he took off his wig and whiskers and went into the town again. Here he bought a long rope, very slender, but still strong enough to support a man's weight, and a grapnel which folded up flat when not in use. Then he went to the George, having wrapped a muffler round his face as if he were suffering with toothache. His basket was standing in the hall.

"I shall not return this evening," he said, "so I will pay my bill."

Then, having bought a suit of ready-made sailor's clothes, with hat complete, he put them into his basket, hired a vehicle, and drove to Fairham. In the morning at nine o'clock he walked along the main road towards Cosham till he reached the turning to Porchester, went down it a couple of hundred yards, and sat on a grassy bank till he saw the pedlar approaching.

"It is a foggy morning," the huckster said when he came up.

"So much the better. I hope it will last over to-morrow, and then they won't be able to signal the news of the prisoner's escape. It is only in clear weather that the semaphores can be made out from hill to hill."

The goods were changed from the pedlar's basket to the one Will had brought.

"There, then, is the hundred pounds I promised you; I hope you are perfectly satisfied?"

"Perfectly, sir; it is the best two days' work I have ever done."

195

"Now for my clothes," Will said; and no one being in sight he quickly changed into the clothes the pedlar had brought.

"We are more alike than ever," the man said with a laugh, "but you will have to remember that I walk with a limp. I got a ball in my leg in the fighting at Trinidad, and was discharged as being unfit for service. But I got a small pension, and the right to sell things to the prisoners in Porchester Castle."

"I noticed the limp when I saw you first," Will said, "and there will be no great difficulty in copying it. I regarded it as rather fortunate, as when the soldiers see me limp along they will not look farther."

"Well, sir, I wish you luck. You are the freest-handed gentleman I ever came across."

Will hid his own clothes in a neighbouring bush, and then started, imitating the pedlar's limp so exactly that the man laughed as he looked after him before starting for Fairham.

There were few people in the streets of the quiet little village as Will passed through it. When he neared the castle he overtook the fat apple-woman, who hailed him as a friend, and they walked together into the castle. They showed their passes to the guard at the gate, but he scarcely looked at them. They then separated, and Will, stopping now and then to sell small articles, made his way at last to Lucien's hut. He had in his letter informed Lucien of his reasons for trying to get him free, and had directed him to be leaning at that hour against the corner of the hut. When Lucien saw the pedlar approaching, if all was clear he was to retire into it, but if there were others inside he was to shake his head slightly. As Will approached the hut he saw a prisoner standing there according to his instructions, but he gave the danger signal and Will passed on. This he did twice, but when Will returned the third time the man went quietly into the hut.

"There is not a moment to lose," Will said as he followed, and he at once lifted up the false bottom and pulled out the rope and grapnel. He had knotted the rope about every foot, to assist the prisoner in climbing, and had covered the iron of the grapnel with strips of flannel so that it would make no noise when it struck the wall.

"Hide them in your bed. It will be a very dark night, and you must steal out and make your way to the middle of the south wall. There fling your grapnel up and scale the wall. I shall be there waiting for you. It looks as if it will be very wet as well as very dark, so you ought to be able to avoid the sentinel."

At this moment he heard someone at the door, and adroitly changing his tone said: "You do not like these colours for a bed-quilt? Very well, I am getting a fresh stock from London in a few days, and I have no doubt you will be able to suit yourself. Good-morning!"

He then turned and offered some of his goods to the new-comer, who bought a block for carving out a ship, and some twine and other things for rigging her. When he left the hut he went about the yard till he had disposed of a considerable amount of his goods, and then left the prison and made his way back to the spot where he had hidden his clothes. On arriving there he changed at once, rubbed the pigment from his face, threw away the wig and whiskers, hid the basket in a place which he and the pedlar had agreed upon, with the clothes in it and the pass in one of the pockets, and then went back into the village, where he hired a chaise and drove to Fairham.

"Landlord," he said, as he drew up at the principal hotel, "I shall want a post-chaise to-night for London. I shall be at a party to-night and cannot say at what time I may get away, but have the horses ready to put in at twelve o'clock. If they have to wait an hour or two you shall not be the loser."

After ordering dinner, he strolled about the town till he thought it would be nearly ready. Then he asked for a room, and there changed into his naval uniform, which he had brought with him. He ate a good dinner, and then, putting on his cloak, started to walk back to Porchester, carrying with him a bag in which was the sailor's suit he had bought for Lucien. The night was pitch dark, and the rain had set in heavily, but although his walk was not an agreeable one he was in high spirits. In his letter to Lucien he had told him that if anything should prevent him from making his way to the wall that night he would expect him on the following one. Nevertheless he felt sure that in such favourable circumstances he would be able to get through the sentries without difficulty. He took up a position as near as he could guess at the centre of the south wall, on the narrow strip of ground between it and the lake. He had waited about an hour when he heard a slight noise a few yards on one side of him. He moved towards the sound, and was just in time to see Lucien alight. He grasped him by the hand.

"Thank heaven," he said in French, "that I have got you free, as I promised your sweetheart I would! Now let us first make our way up the village. I have a suit of sailor's clothes for you in this bag; you can change into them when we get beyond the houses, and

197

throw those you are wearing into the pond there, with a few stones in them to make them sink."

"Ah, monsieur, how can I thank you?" Lucien said.

"I am only paying a debt. Marie risked a good deal to aid me, and I promised solemnly that I would, if it were at all possible, get you out of prison in return, so there is no occasion for any thanks."

Few words passed between them as they walked through the village, and when they had left it behind, Lucien changed his clothes and disposed of his old ones as Will had suggested.

"It was necessary to get rid of them," Will said, "because if they were found in the morning it would show that you had got a change, and instead of looking for someone in a well-worn uniform they would direct their attention to other people."

They tramped along to Fairham, and reached the hotel just as it was about to be shut up, the stage-coach having passed a few minutes before. They had some refreshments, and then took their seats in the chaise. At once the postilions cracked their whips, and the four horses started at a gallop.

"We are absolutely safe now," Will said; "they will not discover that you have gone until the roll-call in the morning, and by that time we shall be within a few miles of London. In such weather as this they will be unable to signal. Before we arrive I will put on civilian clothes again, and as soon as we have discharged the chaise we will go to a clothier's and get a suit for you. There are so many emigrants in London that your speaking French will attract no attention."

The journey was quickly accomplished. Will was very liberal to the postilions at the first stage, and these hurried up those who were to take the next, and so from stage to stage they went at the top of the horses' speed, the ninety miles being covered in the very fast time, for the period, of ten hours. At the last stage Will asked for a room to himself for a few minutes and there changed his clothes. They were put down in front of a private house, and, having seen the post-chaise drive off, took their bags and walked on until they reached a tailor's shop.

"I want to put my man into plain clothes while he is with me in town," Will said to the shopman.

"Yes, sir. What sort of clothes?"

"Oh, just private clothes, such as a valet might wear when out of livery!"

Lucien was soon rigged out in a suit of quiet but respectable garments, and, putting his sailor suit into his bag, they went on.

They looked about for a considerable time before they found a suitable lodging, but at last they came upon a French hotel. Entering, Will asked in French for two rooms. They were at once accommodated, and after washing and dressing they went down to the coffee-room, where several French gentlemen were breakfasting. It had been arranged that Will should say that they were two emigrants who had just effected their escape from France.

The next day they took the coach to Weymouth, the port from which at that time communication was kept open with France by means of smugglers and men who made a business of aiding the French emigrants who wanted to escape, or the Royalists who went backwards and forwards trying to get up a movement against the Republic. On making enquiries they heard of a man who had a very fast little vessel, and they at once looked him up. "This gentleman wants to go across," Will said. "What would you do it for?"

"It depends whether he will wait till I get some more passengers or not."

"He is pressed for time," Will said; "what will you run him over for alone?"

"Fifty pounds," the man said. Will thought it advisable not to appear to jump at the offer.

"That is rather stiff," he said; "I should think thirty-five would be ample."

"It seems a good sum," the man said; "but you see there are dangers. I might be overhauled by a British cruiser."

"You might," Will said; "but when they learned your business they would not interfere with you."

"Then there are the port authorities," the man said.

"Yes, but a few francs would prevent them from asking inconvenient questions. Besides, my friend is not a royalist, he is only going over to see his friends."

"Well, we will say thirty-five," the man said with a smile. "When will you want to start?"

"He doesn't care whether he sails this evening or to-morrow morning."

"Well, we will say to-morrow morning at daybreak."

"Where will you land him?"

"At Cherbourg or one of the villages near; most likely at Cherbourg if the coast is clear, for I have friends there who work with me."

They went to an hotel for the night. In the morning Will gave Lucien a small package containing a very handsome gold watch and chain which he had bought in London.

"Give this to Marie from me," he said; "I promised that she should have one for her wedding-day. Here are a thousand francs of French money, which will carry you comfortably from Cherbourg to Verdun and give you a bit of a start there. No, you need not refuse it, I am a rich man, and can afford it without in the least hurting myself. Give my love to Marie," he said, "and tell her that I shall never forget her kindness."

Lucien was profuse in his gratitude, but Will cut him short by hurrying him down to the boat, which was lying at the quay with her sails already hoisted. Will watched the boat till it was well out to sea, and then took the next coach back to London, filled with pleasure that he had been able to carry out his plan and to repay the kindness that Marie had shown him.

He had given Lucien the address of his London agent, so that on his arrival at Verdun he could write him a letter saying how he had fared, and when he and Marie were to be married. This letter he received on his return from the next cruise. It contained the warmest thanks of Marie and her lover, and the information that they were to be married the following week, and that the young man had an offer of good employment in the town.

When he reached London, Will obtained the address of a respectable solicitor, and called upon him to ask his advice as to advertising to try to discover a family bearing the arms on his seal.

"I should advise you," the lawyer said, "to leave the matter until you return from sea again. Questions of this sort always require a good deal of time to answer. You would have to be present to give information, and when the matter is taken up it should be pressed through vigorously. Of course there would be difficulties to face. The mere fact of this seal being in the possession of your father, that is, if he was your father, would not be sufficient to prove his identity, and there would be all sorts of investigations to make, which would, of course, take time. If you will leave the matter in my hands I will cause enquiries to be made as to the arms. That will probably only take a day or two, and it would perhaps be a satisfaction to you to know the family with which you might be connected. It will be in the subsequent steps that delays will occur."

"Thank you, sir! I should certainly like to know, though I quite see that, as you say, it will be very difficult for me to establish my connection."

The lawyer then took down what particulars Will could give him of his early history. When he returned a week later the lawyer gave him a cordial reception.

"I congratulate you, Mr. Gilmore," he said. "The head of the family carrying those arms is Sir Ralph Gilmore, one of our oldest baronets. He has no male issue. He had one son who died six years ago. There was another son, a younger one, of whom there is no record. He may be alive and he may be dead; that is not known. It is, of course, possible that you were stolen as a child by your reputed father, and that he gave you the family name in order that when the time came he could produce you, but of course that is all guesswork. When you return from sea again I will set people to work to trace, if possible, the wanderings of this person; but as I said, this will take time, and as you will be going to sea in a fortnight the matter can very well stand over. So long as you are on board a ship your parentage can make very little difference to you."

Will had still a fortnight of his leave remaining. He wandered about London for a couple of days, but he found it rather dull now that he had finished his business, as he had no friends in town. On the second day he was walking along one of the fashionable streets of Bloomsbury, considering whether he should not go down by the next coach to Portsmouth, where he was sure of meeting friends, when a carriage passed him, drawn by a pair of fine horses. A young lady who was sitting in it happened to notice him. She glanced at him carelessly at first, and then with great interest. She stopped the carriage before it had gone many yards, and when Will came up, looked at him closely. "Excuse me, sir," she said as he was passing; "but are you not Mr. Gilmore?" Greatly surprised he replied in the affirmative.

"I thought so!" she exclaimed. "Do you not remember me?"

He looked at her hard. "Why—why," he hesitated, "surely it is not—"

"But it is!" she cried. "I am Alice Palethorpe!"

"Miss Palethorpe!" he exclaimed, grasping the hand she held out. "Is it possible?"

"Not Miss Palethorpe," she said. "To you I am Alice, as I was nearly four years ago. Get into the carriage. My father will be delighted to see you. We have talked of you so often. He made enquiries at the Admiralty when he came home, but found that you were a prisoner in France, and he has been trying to get your name down in the list of those to be exchanged, but he had so little interest that he could not succeed, and, indeed, for the past two years no exchange had taken place."

By this time he was in the carriage, and they were driving rapidly along the busy streets. Presently they stopped before a large house in Bedford Square.

"This is our home, for the present at any rate," she said. "Now come in."

She ran upstairs before him and signed to him to wait at the top. "Father," she said, bursting into a room, "I have taken a captive; someone you certainly don't expect to see. Now, you must guess."

"How can I, my dear, when you say I don't expect to see him? Is it—?" and he mentioned five or six of his friends in Jamaica, any of whom might be returning.

"No, father. You are out altogether."

"Then I give it up, Alice."

"It is Will," she said.

Will heard him spring to his feet and hurry to the door.

"My dear young friend!" he exclaimed. "At least I suppose it is you, for you have grown out of all recognition."

"Ah, father!" the girl broke in. "You see, he hadn't changed so much as to deceive me. I felt sure of him the moment I set eyes upon him."

"Well, then, your eyes do you credit," her father said. "Certainly I should not have recognized him. He has grown from a lad into a man since we saw him last. He has widened out tremendously. He was rather one of the lean kind at that time."

"Oh, father, how can you say so? I consider that he was just right."

"Yes, my dear, I quite understand that. At that time he was perfect in your eyes, but for all that he was lean."

"You are quite right, sir, I was, and I really wonder that I have put on flesh so much. The diet of a French prisoner is not calculated to promote stoutness. But your daughter was not only sharper-sighted than you, but even than myself. Till she spoke to me I had not an idea who she was. I saw that she thought she recognized me, but I was afraid it would be rude on my part to look at her closely. Of course now I do see the likeness to the Alice I knew, but she has changed far more than I have. She was a little girl of fourteen then, very pretty, certainly, I thought, but still quite a girl—" and he stopped.

"Now, you mean that I have grown into a young woman, and have lost my prettiness?"

"I think your looking-glass tells you another story," he laughed. "If it doesn't, it must be a very bad one."

"Well, now, do sit down," her father said. "You must have an immense deal to tell us."

"It is a longish story," Will replied, "too long to tell straight off. Besides, I want to ask some questions. When did you come home? Have you come for good? If not, how long are you going to stay? though I am sorry to say that the length of your visit can affect me comparatively little, for I am appointed second-lieutenant of the Jason, and must join in a few days."

"I congratulate you very heartily, Will," Mr. Palethorpe said. "You are fortunate indeed to get such promotion so early."

"I am most fortunate, sir. Though just at present I feel inclined to wish that it hadn't come quite so soon."

"In answer to your question, Will, I can say that we are home for good. I have disposed of my estate and wound up my business, principally, I think, because this little girl had made up her mind that she should like England better than Jamaica."

"I am glad to hear that, sir. I shall have something to look forward to when I return to England."

"Where are you staying?"

"At the Golden Cross."

"Well, then, you must go and fetch your luggage here at once. It would be strange indeed if you were to be staying at any house but mine while you are in London."

As he saw that the planter would not hear of a refusal, Will gladly accepted the invitation, and, taking a fly, drove to the hotel, paid his bill, and took his things away.

CHAPTER XVII

ON BOARD THE "JASON"

"I won't ask you for your story till after dinner," Mr. Palethorpe said. "To enjoy a yarn one needs to be comfortable, and I feel more at home in my arm-chair in the dining-room than I do in this room, with all its fal-lals. You see, I have taken the house furnished. When I settle down in a home of my own, I can assure you it will look very different from this. In fact I have one already building for me. It is at Dulwich, and will be as nearly as possible like my house in Jamaica. Of course there will be differences. I at first wished to have the same sort of veranda, but the architect pointed out that while in Jamaica one requires shade, here one wants light. So they are getting large sheets of glass specially made for putting in instead of wood above the windows. Then, of course, we want good fireplaces, whereas in Jamaica a fire is only necessary for a few days in the year. There are also other little differences, but on the whole it will remind me of the place I had for so many years."

"The house will have one advantage over that in Jamaica, Mr. Palethorpe."

"What is that?" he asked.

"You will be able to go to bed comfortably without fear of having the roof taken from over your head by a hurricane."

"Ah! that is indeed a matter to which I have not given sufficient consideration, but it is certainly a very substantial advantage, as we have all good reason to know."

"I never think of it without shuddering," Alice said. "It was awful! It seemed as if there was an end of everything! I think it was the memory of that night that first set me thinking of going to England."

"Then I cannot but feel grateful to that hurricane, for if you had remained out there it is probable that I should never have met you again."

"I am having a large conservatory built so that we can have greenness and flowers all the year," Mr. Palethorpe remarked presently.

"I should think that would be charming. I hope you will be settled at Dulwich long before I come back from my next cruise."

"Well, I don't know that I can say the same, Will. I hope your next cruise will be a short one."

When dinner was over, the chairs were drawn up to the fire, and Will related his adventures since his return from the West Indies.

"Have you heard of your two favourite sailors?" Alice interrupted.

"Dimchurch and Tom Stevens? No, I have not. I shall feel lost without them at sea, and sincerely hope that I may some day run against them, in which case I am sure, if they are free, they will join my ship."

"How terribly cut up they must have been," the girl said, "when they got down to the beach and found that you were missing!"

"I am sure they would be," he replied. "I expect the rest of the men almost had to hold them back by force."

"Well, go on. You were hit and made prisoner."

Will went on with his story till he came to his escape from Verdun.

"What was she like?" the girl asked. "I expect she was very pretty."

"No, not particularly so. She was a very pleasant-looking girl."

"I can imagine she seemed very pleasant to you," the girl laughed; "and, of course, before you got out of the window and climbed to the top of the house you kissed her, didn't you?"

"Yes, I did," Will said. "Of course she expected to be kissed. I am not at all used to kissing. In fact, I only experienced it once before, and then I was a perfectly passive actor in the affair."

The girl flushed up rosily.

"You drew that upon yourself, Alice," her father said. "If you had left him alone he would not have brought up that old affair."

"I don't care," she said. "I was only thirteen, and he had saved my life."

"You didn't do it again, my dear, I hope, when you met him in the street to-day."

"Of course not!" she exclaimed indignantly. "The idea of such a thing!"

"Very well, let this be a lesson to you not to enquire too strictly into such matters."

"Ah! I will bear it in mind," she said.

"I can assure you, Alice, that it was a perfectly friendly kiss. She was engaged to be married to a young soldier who was a prisoner at Porchester, and during the past week I have been employed in setting him free, as you will hear presently. I promised her I would do so if possible, and of course I kept my word."

"What! you, an English officer, set a French prisoner free! I am shocked!" Mr. Palethorpe said.

"I would have tried to set twenty of them free if twenty of their sweethearts had united to get me away from prison."

They laughed heartily at the story of his escape as a pedlar, and were intensely interested in his account of the manner in which he succeeded in getting a despatch from the agent of the British Government at Amsterdam. He continued the narrative until his arrival in England.

"Now we shall hear, I suppose, how this British officer perpetrated an act of treason against His Most Gracious Majesty."

"Well, I suppose it was that in the eyes of the law," Will laughed. "Fortunately, however, the law has no cognizance of the affair, at any rate not of my share in it. I don't suppose it has been heard of outside Porchester. As His Gracious Majesty has some forty thousand prisoners in England, the loss of one more or less will not trouble his gracious brain."

He then related the whole story of Lucien's escape.

"I should have liked to see you dressed up like a pedlar, with your face all painted, and a wig and whiskers," the girl said, "though I don't suppose I should have recognized you in that disguise to-day."

"It was a capitally-managed plan, Will, and had it been for a legitimate object I should have given it unstinted praise. And so you saw him fairly off from England?"

"Yes; and by this time I have no doubt he is on the top of a vehicle of some sort, going as fast as horses can gallop to join his sweetheart."

"I wonder," Alice said mischievously, "whether she will ever tell him of that kiss at the window."

"I dare say she will," laughed Will, "but perhaps not till they are married. I sent her the gold watch I promised her, and when she holds it up before his eyes I think he won't grudge her the kiss. Still, I believe these things are not always mentioned."

"No, I suppose not," she said, with an affectation of not understanding him. "Why should they be?"

"I can't say indeed, if you can't."

"Well, I am not ashamed of it one little bit, though I own that I never have told anybody. But I don't see why I shouldn't. I am sure there were at least half a dozen ladies in Jamaica who would willingly have kissed you for what you did for them."

"Thank you! I should certainly not have willingly submitted to the ordeal."

It was late when the story was finished, and they soon afterwards went to bed.

Will spent a delightful week with his friends. Alice had grown up into a charming young woman, full of life and vivacity, and even prettier than she had promised to be as a girl. They went about together to all the sights of London, for Mr. Palethorpe said that he didn't care about going, and young people were best left to themselves. When the time came for parting, Will for the first time experienced a feeling of reluctance at joining his ship. He and Alice were now almost on their old footing, and Will thought that she was by far the nicest girl he had ever seen; but it was not until he was on the top of the Portsmouth coach that he recognized how much she was to him. "Well," he said to himself, "I never thought I should feel like this. Some young fellows are always falling in love. I used to think it was all nonsense, but now I understand it. I do not know why her father should object to me, as I am fairly well off. I must see as much of her as I can when I land next time. I hope she won't meet anyone in the meantime she likes better."

The Jason was now lying out in the harbour, and the riggers had taken possession of her. Will at once reported himself and went on board. The other officers had not yet joined, but he at once took up his work with his usual zeal, and spent a busy fortnight looking after the riggers, and seeing that everything was done in the best manner. He was, however, somewhat angry to find that Alice's face and figure were constantly intruding themselves into the cordage and shrouds. "I am becoming a regular mooncalf," he said angrily to himself. "It is perfectly absurd that I can't keep my thoughts from wandering away from my work, and for a girl whom I can hardly dare hope to win. I shall be very glad when we are off to sea. I'll then have, I won't say something better, but something else to think of. If this is being in love, certainly it is not the thing a sailor should engage in. I have often heard it said that a sailor's ship should be his wife, and I have no longer any doubt about it. But I know I'll get over it when I hear the first broadside fired."

A week later the first lieutenant joined. His name was Somerville.

"Ah, Mr. Gilmore," he said, "I see you have taken time by the forelock and given an eye to everything! I only received my appointment two days ago or I should have joined before. There is nothing like having an officer to superintend things, and I feel really very much obliged to you for not having extended your leave, which, of course, you could have done, especially as, so far as I know, no boatswain has yet been appointed."

207

"I was glad to get back to work, sir, and it is really very interesting seeing all the rigging set up from the very beginning."

"That is so, but for all that men don't generally want to rejoin," the first lieutenant said with a smile. "The difficulty is to get young officers on board. They hang back, as a rule, till the very last moment. Well, if you will dine with me this evening, Mr. Gilmore, at the George, I shall be glad to hear of some of your services. That they are distinguished I have no doubt, for nothing but the most meritorious services or extraordinary interest could have gained you at your age the appointment of second lieutenant in a fine ship like this. I think it a very good thing for the first lieutenant to know the antecedents of those serving with him. Such knowledge is very useful to him in any crisis or emergency."

After dinner that evening Will gave an account of his services, the lieutenant at times asking for more minute details, especially of the capture of the two pirates.

"Thank you very much!" Lieutenant Somerville said when he had finished. "Now I feel that I can, in any emergency, depend upon you to second me, which I can assure you is by no means commonly the case, for promotion goes so much by influence, and such incapable men are pushed up in the service that it is a comfort indeed to have an officer who knows his work thoroughly. I hope to goodness we shall have the captain so fine a ship deserves."

"I hope so indeed, sir. I have hitherto been extremely fortunate in having good captains, as good as one could wish for."

"You are fortunate indeed, then. I have been under two or three men who, either from ignorance or ill-temper or sheer indifference, have been enough to take the heart entirely out of their officers."

On the day when the Jason was ready for commission the captain came down to Portsmouth and put up at the George, and Mr. Somerville and Will called upon him there. He was a young man, some years younger than the first lieutenant.

"Gentlemen," he began, "I have pleasure in making your acquaintance. I saw the admiral this morning, and he assured me that I could not wish for better officers. I hope we shall get on pleasantly together, and can assure you that if we do not it will not be my fault. We have as fine a ship as men could wish to sail in, and I will guarantee that you will not find me slack in using her. As you may guess by my age, I owe my present position partly to family interest, but my object will be to prove that that interest has not been altogether misplaced. I have already had command of a frigate, and we had our full share of hard service. I am afraid that with a seventy-four we shall not have quite so many opportunities of distinguishing ourselves, but shall generally have to work with the fleet and fight when other people bid us, and not merely when we see a good chance. There is, however, as much credit, if not as much prize-money, to be gained in a pitched battle as in isolated actions. I was kindly permitted by the admiral to read both your records of service, and I cannot say how gratified I was to find that I had two such able and active officers to second me."

"I am sure we are much obliged to you, sir," Lieutenant Somerville replied, "for speaking to us as you have done. I can answer for it that we will second you to the very best of our power, and I am glad indeed to find that we have a commander whose sentiments so entirely accord with our own."

"Now, gentlemen, we have done with the formalities. Let us crack a bottle of wine together to our better acquaintance, and I hope I shall very often see you at my table on board, for while I feel that discipline must be maintained, I have no belief in a captain holding himself entirely aloof from his officers, as if he were a little god. On the quarter-deck a captain must stand somewhat aloof, but in his own cabin I cannot see why he should not treat his officers as gentlemen like himself."

They sat and chatted for an hour, and when they left, Lieutenant Somerville said to Will: "If I am not much mistaken, we shall have a very pleasant time on board the Jason. I believe Captain Charteris means every word he says, and that he is a thoroughly good fellow. He has a very pleasant face, though a firm and resolute one, and when he gives an order it will have to be obeyed promptly; but he is a man who will make allowances, and I do not think the cat will be very often brought into requisition on board."

One day Will was sauntering down the High Street when he saw two country-looking men coming along. One of them looked at him and staggered back in astonishment.

"Why," he exclaimed, "it is Mr. Gilmore! We thought you were in prison in the middle of France, sir."

"So I was, Dimchurch; but, as you see, I have taken leg-bail."

"That was a terrible affair, sir, at them French batteries. When I got down to the shore, and found you were missing, it was as much as they could do to keep Tom here and me from going back. You mayn't believe me, Mr. Gilmore, but we both cried like children as we rowed to the Tartar."

"I am indeed glad to see you again, and you too, Tom. I guessed that if I ever came across the one I should meet the other also. What are you doing in those togs?"

"Well, sir, we put them on because we did not want to be impressed by the first ship that came in, but preferred to wait a bit till we saw one to suit us. I see, sir, that you have shipped a swab. That means, of course, that you have got a lieutenancy. I congratulate you indeed, sir, on your promotion."

"Yes, I got it a month ago, and to a fine ship, the Jason."

"She is a fine ship, sir, and no mistake. Tom and I were watching her lying out in the harbour yesterday, and were saying that, though we have always been accustomed to frigates, we should not mind shipping in her if we found out something about the captain."

"Well, I can tell you, Dimchurch, that he is just the man you would like to serve under, young and dashing, and, I should say, a good officer and a fine fellow."

"And who is the first lieutenant, sir, because that matters almost as much as the captain."

"He is a good fellow too, Dimchurch, a man who loves his profession and has a good record."

"And who is the second, sir? not that it matters much about him if the captain and first luff are all right. I suppose she has four on board, as she is a line-of-battle ship?"

"Yes, she carries four. As to the second, I can only tell you that he is one of the finest fellows in the service, and you will understand that when I say that I am the second lieutenant."

"What, sir!" Dimchurch almost shouted, "they have made you second lieutenant on a line-of-battle ship! Well, that is one of the few times I have known promotion go by merit. I am glad, sir. Well, I will go and sign articles at once, and so, of course, will Tom; and what is more, I will guarantee to find you a score of first-rate hands, maybe more."

"That is good indeed," Will said. "I will speak to the first lieutenant and get you rated as boatswain, if possible. You have already served in that capacity, and unless the berth is filled up, which is not likely, I have no doubt I can get it for you."

"Well, sir, if you can, of course I shall be glad; but I would ship with you if it was only as loblolly boy."

"The same here," Tom said; "you know that, sir, without my saying it."

"Is there any berth that I could get you, Tom?"

"No, sir, thank you! A.B. is good enough for me. I am not active enough to be captain of the top, but I can pull on a rope, or row an oar, or strike a good blow, with any man."

"That you can, Tom; but I do wish I could get you a lift too. How about gunner's mate?"

"No, thank you, sir! I would rather stop A.B. I should like to be your honour's servant, but, lor', I should never do to wait in the ward-room. I am as clumsy as a bear, and should always be spilling something, and breaking glasses, and getting into trouble. No, sir, I will be A.B., but of course I should like to be appointed to your boat."

"That is a matter of course, Tom. Well, I will go round to the dockyard at once and see you sworn in, and then gladden the first lieutenant's heart by telling him that you will bring a good number of men along with you, for at present we are very short-handed."

"You trust me for that, sir. I know where lots of them are lying hid, not because they don't want to serve, but because they want a good ship and a good captain. When I tell them that it is a fine ship, and a good captain, and a good first and second, they will jump at it."

Dimchurch was as good as his word, and the following week persuaded thirty first-class seamen to sign on.

"At the same time, sir," he said as they went towards the harbour, "I would rather she had been a frigate. One has always a chance of picking up something then, as one gets sent about on expeditions, while on a battle-ship one is just stuck blockading."

"That is just what I think," Tom said. "There are no boat expeditions, no chances of picking up a prize every two or three days, or of chasing a pirate. Still, though the Tartar was a frigate, we did not have much fun in her, except when we were on shore. That was good enough, though it would not have been half so good if the sailors had not done it alone. We wanted to show these redcoats what British seamen could do when they were on their metal. I know I never worked half so hard in my life."

"Well, I quite agree with you. It is more pleasant commanding a small craft than being second officer in a large one, although I must say I could not have had a more pleasant captain and first lieutenant than I have now if I had picked them out from the whole fleet. I am sorry that I cannot get leave at present, for I want to make researches about my father. According to what my lawyer said it is likely to be a long job. I hope, however, to get it well in trim on my next spell ashore. It makes really no difference to me now who or what my father was. I have a good position, and what with the prize-money I made before, and shall gain now by my share of the sale of the frigates we took at Corsica, to say nothing of the guns and stores we captured, I have more than enough to satisfy all my wants."

"I have done extraordinarily well too, Mr. Gilmore," Dimchurch said. "I took your advice, and Tom and I have put all our prize-money aside. He has over a thousand saved, and I have quite sufficient to keep me in idleness all my life, even if I never do a stroke of work again."

Mr. Somerville, on Will's recommendation, at once appointed Dimchurch boatswain, and he soon proved himself thoroughly efficient. "He is a fine fellow, that sailor of yours," the lieutenant said, "and will make a first-rate boatswain. He has done good service in bringing up so many hands, and good ones too, and he is evidently popular among the men."

"He is a thoroughly good man, sir. He attached himself to my fortunes when I was but a ship's boy, and has stuck to me ever since. He and Tom Stevens are, with one exception, the greatest friends I have ever had, and both of them would lay down their lives for me."

"A good master makes a good man," Lieutenant Somerville said with a smile. "Your greatest friend was, of course, the lady who pushed you on with your education."

"Yes, sir, certainly I regard her as the best friend I ever had."

"Well, there is no better friend for a lad than a good woman, Gilmore. In that sense my mother was my greatest friend. Most mothers are against their sons going to sea. In my case it was my father who objected, but my mother, seeing how I was bent upon it, persuaded him to let me go."

Three weeks after being commissioned the complement of the Jason was complete, and she was ordered to proceed to the West Indies, to which place they made a fast passage. To their disappointment they fell in with none of the enemy's cruisers on their way. The voyage, however, sufficed to give the crew confidence in their commander. He was prompt and quick in giving orders, and at the same time pleasant in manner. He paid far more attention than most captains to the comfort of his crew, and, while he insisted upon the most perfect order and discipline, abstained from giving unnecessary work. In cases where punishments were absolutely necessary he punished severely, but when it was at all possible he let delinquents off with a lecture. So, while he was feared by the rougher spirits of the crew, he was regarded with liking and respect by the good men.

On their arrival at Carlisle Bay, Barbados, they found that they were in time to join a naval expedition whose object was to recover the islands of St. Lucia, St. Vincent, and Grenada, which had been captured by the French the previous year.

A fleet had been sent from England under the command of Rear-admiral Christian, consisting of two ships of the line and five frigates, convoying a large fleet of transports with a strong body of troops on board under the command of Sir Ralph Abercrombie.

At Carlisle Bay this fleet were joined by most of the ships on the West Indian station, and on the 21st April, 1796, the augmented fleet, under the command of Sir John Laforey, sailed to Marin Bay, Martinique, where they anchored. On the following day Sir John Laforey resigned his command to Admiral Christian and sailed for England. The fleet then stood across to St. Lucia. The troops were landed at three different points under the protection of the guns of the fleet.

The first point was protected by a five-gun battery. The fire of the ships, however, soon silenced it, and the first division made good its landing. The seventy-four-gun ship Alfred was to have led the second division, supported by the fifty-four-gun ship Madras and the forty-gun frigate Beaulieu, but the attempt was thwarted by lightness of wind and a strong lee current. On the next day, however, a landing was effected with little opposition. Eight hundred seamen, under the command of Captains Lane of the thirty-two-gun frigate Astrea and Ryves of the bomb-vessel Bulldog, were landed to co-operate with the troops. Morne Chabot was attacked and carried that night with the loss of thirteen officers and privates killed, forty-nine wounded, and twelve missing.

On the 3rd of May an attempt was made to dislodge the enemy from their batteries at the base of the mountains, but was repulsed with loss, as was an attack on the 17th on the place called Vigie.

In the meantime the men had been busy building batteries and planting guns, and when these opened fire on the evening of the 24th of May the enemy capitulated, two thousand marching out and laying down their arms. A great quantity of guns, together with stores of every description, were found in the different forts, and some small privateers and merchantmen were captured in the offing. Eight hundred seamen and three hundred and twenty marines had been landed from the ships of war, and had behaved with their usual courage and promptitude. The manner, indeed, in which they established batteries and planted guns in places deemed almost impracticable astonished the troops, unused as they were to exercises demanding strength and skill.

As soon as St. Lucia had surrendered, the expedition moved to St. Vincent. The defence here was decidedly weak, and after some skirmishing, the enemy, composed chiefly of negroes and Caribs, capitulated. Our loss amounted to thirty-eight killed and one hundred and forty-five wounded. Grenada offered a comparatively slight resistance. The monster, Fedon, who was in command there, massacred twenty white people who were in his power in full view of the British, who were on the plain below. He and his men, however, were hotly pursued through the forest by a detachment of German riflemen, and the greater portion of them killed without mercy.

A detachment of British and colonial troops from the garrison of Port au Prince in St. Domingo proceeded to besiege the town of Leogane in that island. Covered by the guns of the fleet the troops were landed in two divisions, while the Swiftsure, seventy-four, cannonaded the town, and the Leviathan and Africa the forts. The place, however, was too strong for them, and at nightfall the ships moved off to an anchorage, while those who had landed were withdrawn on the following morning. Two of the frigates were so much damaged that they were compelled to return to Jamaica to refit. An attack was next made upon the fort of Bombarde, which stood at a distance of fifteen miles from the coast. Will and a detachment from his ship formed part of the force engaged. The road was extremely rough, and was blocked by fallen trees and walls built across it. The labour of getting the cannon along was prodigious.

"I must say," Will said to Dimchurch, who was one of the party, "I greatly prefer fighting on board to work like this. We have to labour like slaves from early morning till late in the evening; but I don't so much mind that, as the fact that at night we have to lie down with only the food that remains in our haversacks, and what water we may have saved, for supper. Now in a fight at sea one at least gets as much to drink as one wants."

"I quite agree with you, Mr. Gilmore. It's dog's work without dog's food. I don't mind myself working here with a chopper eight or ten hours a day, but I do like a good supper at the end of it. The worst of it is, that when it is all over it is the troops who get all the credit, while we poor beggars do the greater part of the work. The soldiers are well enough in their way, but they are very little good for hard work. How do you account for that, sir?"

"I can only suppose, Dimchurch, that while they get as much food as we do, they have nothing like the same amount of hard work to do."

"That's it, sir. Why, look at them at Portsmouth! They just go out of a morning and drill on the common for a bit, and then they have nothing else to do all day but to stroll about the town and talk to the girls. How can you expect a man to have any muscle to speak of when he never does a stroke of hard work? I don't say they don't fight well, for I own they do their duty like men in that line; but when it comes to work, why, they ain't in it with a jack-tar. I do believe I could pull a couple of them over a line."

"I dare say you could, Dimchurch, but you must remember that you are much stronger than an ordinary seaman."

"Well, sir, I grant I am stronger than usual, but I should be ashamed of myself if I could not tackle two of them soldiers."

"Yes, but don't forget they have been cooped up on board a ship for a month, with nothing to keep them in health, and certainly no exercise, while you are constantly doing hard work. If you were to put these men into sailors' clothes, and give them sailors' work for six months, they would be just as strong and useful."

"Well, sir, if they are that sort of men why do they go and enlist in the army instead of becoming sailors. It stands to reason that it is because they know that they cannot do work."

"Why, Dimchurch, I have heard that in the great towns girls think as much of soldiers as of sailors."

"Well, that shows how little they know about them. In a seaport, what girl would look at a soldier if she were pretty enough to get a sailor for a sweetheart."

"You are a prejudiced beggar," Will laughed, "and it is of no use arguing with you. If you had gone as a soldier instead of taking to the sea you would think just the other way."

On the next morning the march was renewed, and in the evening they reached the fort. They had had several severe skirmishes during the day, losing eight killed and twenty-two wounded, but the garrison, consisting of three hundred, surrendered without further resistance as soon as the place was surrounded, and the sailors then rejoined their ships.

"Well, I am mighty glad I am back on board," Dimchurch said to Will the evening they re-embarked. "This marching, and chopping trees, and being shot at from ambushes, doesn't suit me. There is nothing manly or straightforward about it. Hand to hand and cutlass to cutlass is what I call a man's work."

"That is all very well, Dimchurch, but though you may capture ships you will never get possession of islands or colonies in that way. If you want them you must land and fight for them."

"Yes, sir, that is all very good, but it seems to me that the hard work of making batteries and mounting guns falls on the sailor, while the soldier gets all the credit. It is not our admiral who sends the despatches, it is the general. He may speak a few good words for the sailors, as a man speaks up for a dog, but all the credit of the fighting, and the surrender, and all that business goes to the soldiers. The sooner we sail away from here, and do some fighting nearer home, where there are no soldiers, and where the sailors get their due, the better pleased I shall be."

"Well, Dimchurch, I hope our turn out here is nearly finished. We may have to take part in a few more attacks on French

215

possessions, but as soon as that work is over I have great hopes that we shall get sailing orders for home again."

Indeed, late in August a fast cruiser arrived with orders that the Jason was at once to return to Brest and join the Channel fleet. To the great delight of everyone the wind continued favourable throughout the whole voyage, and after an exceptionally speedy passage they joined Admiral Bridport, who was cruising off Ushant on the look-out for the French fleet that was preparing for the invasion of Ireland.

The French fleet, under Admiral Morard-de-Galles, got under weigh from Brest on 26th December, 1796. It consisted of seventeen ships of the line, thirteen frigates, six corvettes, seven transports, and a powder-ship, forty-four sail in all, conveying eight thousand troops under the command of Generals Grouchy, Borin, and Humbert. Misfortune, however, dogged the fleet from the very commencement, for the Séduisant, a seventy-four-gun battle-ship, got on shore shortly after leaving Brest, and out of thirteen hundred seamen and soldiers on board six hundred and eighty were drowned.

They were noticed by Vice-admiral Colpoys' fleet, who sent off two frigates to warn Lord Bridport, and after chasing the French for some distance himself, sailed for Falmouth to report the setting out of the expedition.

Admiral Bouvet, with thirty-two sail, managed to reach the mouth of Bantry Bay, but the weather was so tempestuous that he was unable to land his troops. After struggling for some days against this boisterous weather, the fleet scattered, and the majority of the ships returned to Brest. The rest reached the coast of Ireland, but not finding the main portion of their fleet there, they returned to France.

The failure of the expedition was as complete as was that of the Spanish Armada, and was due greatly to the same cause. Out of the forty-four ships that sailed from Brest only thirty-one managed to return to France. The British frigates, by the vigilance they displayed, had done good service, cutting off four transports and three ships of war; but the stormy weather had dispersed the expedition, and was accountable for the loss of two battle-ships, three frigates, and a transport. It was curious that although Lord Bridport's fleet was constantly patrolling the Channel during this time, the two fleets never came in contact.

CHAPTER XVIII

ST. VINCENT AND CAMPERDOWN

On the 19th of January, 1797, Lord Bridport detached Rear-admiral Parker with five battle-ships—among them the Jason—and one frigate, to Gibraltar, and on the 6th of February they joined Admiral Sir John Jervis off Cape St. Vincent.

They were cruising along the Portuguese coast when, on the morning of the 13th of February, Nelson brought Admiral Jervis the long-expected news of the approach of the Spanish fleet. Its exact strength he had not discovered, but it was known to exceed twenty sail of the line, while Jervis had but fifteen, two of which had been greatly injured by a collision the night before. The repairs, however, were quickly executed, and they fell into their positions. Jervis made the signal to prepare for action. During the night the signal guns of the Spaniards were heard, and before daylight a Portuguese frigate came along and reported that they were about four leagues to windward. At that time the fleet were south-west of Cape St. Vincent. The Spaniards, who had hitherto been prevented by an adverse wind from getting into Cadiz, were ready to meet us, not knowing that the British admiral had been reinforced, and believing that he had but some ten ships.

The wind, however, changed during the night, and, acting in strict obedience to his orders, the Spanish commander-in-chief determined to set sail for Cadiz. When day broke, his fleet was seen about five miles off, the main body huddled together in a confused group, with one squadron to leeward. It was then seen what a formidable fleet lay before us. The admiral's flag was carried by the Santissima-Trinidada, one hundred and thirty, and he had with him six three-deckers of one hundred and twelve guns each, two of eighty, and eighteen seventy-fours. Our fleet had scarcely half the ships and guns. We had two ships of one hundred guns, three of ninety-eight, one of ninety, eight seventy-fours, and a sixty-four. There was, however, no comparison between the men. Our own were for the most part tried and trained sailors, while a considerable proportion of the Spaniards were almost raw levies.

The morning of the 14th February was foggy, and neither the number nor the size of our ships could be made out by the

Spaniards until we were within a mile of them. Then, as mid-day approached and the fog cleared off, they saw Jervis bearing down upon them in two lines. His object was to separate the Spanish squadron to leeward from the main body, and in this he completely succeeded.

The Culloden led the way, and the greater part of the fleet followed, opening a tremendous fire as they came up with the Spaniards, and receiving their broadsides in return. The Spanish vice-admiral attempted to cut through the British line, but was thwarted by the rapid advance of the Victory, which forced the admiral's ship, the Principe de Asturias, to tack close under her lee, pouring in a tremendous raking broadside as she did so. Fortunately at this moment Commodore Nelson was in the rear, and had a better view of the movements of the enemy than had the commander-in-chief. He perceived that the Spanish admiral was beginning to bear up before the wind, with the object of uniting the main body with the second division. Accordingly he ordered his ship the Captain to wear.

Up to this time she had hardly fired a gun, but this movement gave her the lead of the fleet, and brought her at once into action with the enemy. In a few minutes she was attacked by no fewer than four first-raters and two third-raters. The Culloden, however, bore down with all speed to her assistance, and some time afterwards the Blenheim came up to take a share in the fight. Two of the Spanish ships dropped astern to escape the tremendous fire of the three British seventy-fours, but they only fell in with the Excellent coming up to support the Captain, and she poured so tremendous a fire into them both that one of them struck at once. She left the other to her own devices and pressed on to join Nelson, who greatly needed help, for the Captain was now little better than a wreck.

Her chief antagonist at this time was the San Nicholas. Into that ship she poured a tremendous fire, and then passed on to the San Isidro and Santissima-Trinidada, with which the Captain had been engaged from the beginning. The fire of the Excellent had completed the work done by the Captain, and the San Nicholas and the San Josef had collided with each other. Nelson, being in so crippled a state that he could no longer take an active part in the action, laid his ship alongside the San Nicholas and carried her by boarding; and after this was done the crew crossed to the San Josef, and carried her also. Other prizes had been taken elsewhere; the Salvador Del Mundo and Santissima-Trinidada surrendered, as did the Soberano. The Santissima-Trinidada, however, was towed away by one of her frigates. Evening was closing in, and as the Spanish fleet still greatly outnumbered the British, Jervis made the signal to discontinue the action, and the next morning the fleets sailed in different directions, the British carrying their four prizes with them. Considering the desperate nature of the fighting the British loss was extraordinarily small, only seventy-three being killed and two hundred and twenty-seven wounded. Of these nearly a third belonged to the Captain, upon which the brunt of the fight had fallen. For this victory Admiral Jervis was made an earl, and two admirals baronets. Nelson might have had a baronetcy, but he preferred the ribbon of the Bath. Also, he shortly afterwards was promoted to the rank of Rear-admiral. Captain Calder received the ribbon of the Bath, and all the first lieutenants were promoted.

The captain of the Jason had earned golden opinions from his crew by the manner in which he had fought his vessel and the careless indifference he had shown to the enemy's fire as he walked up and down on the quarter-deck issuing what orders were necessary. Their losses had not been heavy, but among them, to Will's deep regret, the first lieutenant had been killed by a cannon-ball.

"I am grieved indeed," the captain said the next morning to Will, "at the death of Mr. Somerville. He was an excellent officer and a most worthy man. It is, however, a consolation to me that I have a successor so worthy to take his place. Since we have sailed together, Mr. Gilmore, I have always been gratified by the manner in which you have done your duty, and by the skill you have shown in handling the ship during your watch. It is a great satisfaction to me that I have so good an officer for my first lieutenant."

It was but a few months after the battle of St. Vincent that a greater danger threatened England than she had ever before been exposed to. The seamen in the navy had long been seething with discontent, and all their petitions had been neglected, their remonstrances treated as of no account.

Rendered desperate, they at last determined to mutiny, and the first outbreak occurred on the 15th April in the Channel fleet, which was at the time anchored at Spithead. On Admiral Lord Bridport giving the signal to weigh anchor, the seamen of the flagship, instead of proceeding to their stations, ran up the rigging and gave three cheers, and the crews of the rest of the ships at once did the same. The officers attempted to induce the men to return to their duty, but in vain. The next day two delegates from each ship met on the Queen Charlotte, the flagship, to deliberate, and the day after all the men swore to stand by their leaders, and such officers as had rendered themselves obnoxious to the men were put on shore.

The delegates then drew up two petitions, one to Parliament the other to the Admiralty, asking that their wages should be increased—they had remained at the same point since Charles II was king,—that the pound should be reckoned at sixteen ounces instead of fourteen, and that the food should be of better quality. Further, that vegetables should be occasionally served out, that the sick should be better attended and their medical comforts not embezzled; and, finally, that on returning from sea the men should be allowed a short leave to visit their friends.

On the 18th a committee of the Board of Admiralty arrived at Portsmouth, and in answer to the petition agreed to ask the king to propose to Parliament an increase of wages, and also to grant them certain other privileges; but these terms the sailors would not accept, and expressed their determination not to weigh anchor till their full demands were granted.

The committee now sent, through Lord Bridport, a letter to the seamen granting still further concessions, and promising pardon to all concerned; but the sailors answered expressing their thanks for what had been granted, but reiterating their demands.

On the 21st Vice-admirals Sir Allen Gardner and Colpoys and Rear-admiral Pole went on board the Queen Charlotte to confer, but they were informed that until the reforms were sanctioned by the king and Parliament they would not be accepted as final. This so angered Admiral Gardner that he seized one of the delegates by the collar and swore he would hang the lot, and every fifth man in the fleet. The delegates at once returned to their ships, and the seamen of the fleet proceeded to load the guns. Watches were set as at sea, and the ships were put into a complete state of defence.

On the 22nd Lord Bridport, having received a letter from the mutineers explaining the cause of the steps they had taken, went on board, and after a short deliberation his offers were accepted, and the men returned to their duty.

The fleet was detained at St. Helens by a foul wind until the 7th of May, when news was received that the French were preparing to sail. Lord Bridport made the signal to weigh, but the crews again refused to obey orders, alleging that the silence that Parliament had observed respecting their grievances led them to suspect that the promised redress was to be withheld.

For four days matters continued in the same state, but on the 14th Admiral Lord Howe arrived from London with full powers to settle all disputes with an Act of Parliament which had been passed on the 9th, and a proclamation granting the king's pardon to all who should return at once to their duty.

After various discussions the men agreed to the terms, and on the 16th May, all matters having been amicably settled, Lord Bridport put to sea with his fleet of fifteen sail of the line.

Notwithstanding these concessions the sailors of the ships lying at the Nore broke into mutiny on the 20th of May, their ringleader being a seaman of the name of Richard Parker, one of a class of men denominated sea-lawyers. The delegates drew up a statement of demands containing eight articles, most of which were perfectly impossible, and the Admiralty replied by pointing out the concessions the Legislature had recently made, and refusing to accede to any more, but offering to pardon the men if they would at once return to their duty. The mutineers refused, and hoisted the red flag. They landed at Sheerness and marched through the streets, and in many ways went to greater lengths than their comrades at Spithead. They even flogged and otherwise ill-treated some of the officers.

This outbreak now assumed the most alarming proportions. Eleven ships belonging to the North Sea fleet, on the way to blockade the Texel, turned back and joined Parker, and the greatest alarm was felt in London, the Funds falling to an unheard-of price. The Government acted, however, with vigour; buoys were removed, and the forts were manned and the men ordered to open fire should the fleet sail up the river. Bills were rushed through Parliament in two days, authorizing the utmost penalties on the mutineers and on all who aided them.

This had the desired effect, and early in June the fleets at Portsmouth and Plymouth disavowed all complicity with Parker, and two ships—the Leopard and Repulse—hauled down the red flag and retreated up the Thames, being fired on by the rest of the fleet. The example was, however, contagious, and ship after ship deserted until, on the 14th, the crew of the Sandwich handed over Parker to the authorities.

He was tried, convicted, and hanged on board that ship on the 29th of June. Some of the other leaders were also hanged, some were flogged through the fleet, and some sent to prison.

The mutiny was not confined to the ships on the home stations, but it never became serious at any point, and a display of timely severity soon brought matters back to their usual condition of discipline and obedience to orders.

A mutiny of a different character, as it was caused by the tyranny of the captain, and had very different results, took place in the West Indies.

On the night of the 21st of September the thirty-two-gun frigate Hermione was cruising off Porto Rico. Its captain, Pigot, was known to be one of the most harsh and brutal officers in the navy. On the previous day, while the crew were reefing topsails, he had called out that he would flog the last man down. The poor fellows, knowing well that he would keep his word, hurried down; and two of them, in trying to jump over those below them, missed their footing and were killed. When this was reported to the captain he simply said: "Throw the lubbers overboard." All the other men were severely reprimanded. The result of this, the last of a succession of similar acts of tyranny, was that the crew broke into mutiny. The first lieutenant went to enquire into the disturbance, but he was killed and thrown overboard. The captain, hearing the tumult, ran on deck, but he suffered the same fate as his second in command. The mutineers then proceeded to murder eight other officers, two lieutenants, the purser, the surgeon, the captain's clerk, one midshipman, the boatswain, and the lieutenant of marines. The master, a midshipman, and the gunner were the only officers spared. They then carried the ship into the port of La Guayra, representing to the Spanish governor that they had turned their officers adrift. The real circumstances of the case were explained to the governor by the British admiral, but he insisted upon detaining the vessel and fitting her out as a Spanish frigate.

Many of the perpetrators of this horrible crime were afterwards captured and executed. Had they contented themselves with wreaking their vengeance on their captain, some excuse might have been offered for them when the catalogue of his brutalities was published, but nothing could be said in condonation of the cold-blooded murder of the other officers, including even a midshipman and the young captain's clerk, neither of whom could have in any way influenced their commander's conduct.

The Hermione, however, was of but little use to the Spaniards. Sir Hyde Parker, in October, 1799, hearing that she was about to sail from Porto Cabello, in Havana, detached the Surprise under Captain Hamilton, to attempt to obtain possession of her. On arriving off Porto Cabello he found the Hermione, which was manned by four hundred men, moored between two strong batteries at the entrance to the harbour, but, nothing daunted, Captain Hamilton resolved to cut her out. At eight o'clock in the

222

evening he pushed off from the Surprise with all his boats, manned by one hundred officers and men.

Undeterred by a heavy fire, the boats made for the Hermione and were soon alongside. The main attack at the gangways was beaten off, but the captain, with his cutter's crew, made good his footing on the forecastle, and here he was joined by the crew of the gig and some of the men from the jolly-boat. He then fought his way to the quarter-deck, where he was soon reinforced by the crews of the boats that had at first been repulsed. In a very short time, after some desperate fighting, the Hermione was captured. The cables were now cut and the sails hoisted, and under a heavy fire from the batteries the frigate was brought off, though much damaged both in rigging and hull. A few days later she anchored in Port Royal.

This feat stands perhaps unparalleled in naval history for its audacity and success. The victors had only twelve wounded; the enemy lost one hundred and nineteen killed and ninety-seven wounded. Captain Hamilton was knighted for this achievement, the legislature of Jamaica presented him with a sword valued at three hundred guineas, and on his arrival in England after his exchange, for he was taken prisoner on his way home, the common council of London voted him the freedom of the city. He was, however, much injured in the attack, and was to the end of his life under medical treatment.

After the battle of St. Vincent the Jason required some repairs to her hull, but as her spars were uninjured she was ordered by Admiral Jervis to proceed to Portsmouth with despatches. Here, to Will's great joy, he was confirmed in his position as first lieutenant. He was unable to get leave, as it was found the repairs would take but a short time, and after ten days' stay in port the Jason sailed to join Lord Bridport's fleet. On doing so, she was at once despatched to reinforce the North Sea fleet under Admiral Duncan, then blockading the Texel.

It was while engaged in this monotonous work that the news came of Admiral Nelson's disastrous attack on Santa Cruz. The expedition was a complete failure, one hundred and forty-one being killed or drowned, and one hundred and five wounded or missing. Among the wounded was Admiral Nelson himself, who lost his arm.

The news of the mutinies taking place at Spithead and the Nore was a source of great anxiety to the officers, but the men were so attached to them that there was no real cause for uneasiness with regard to their own ship, and when the eleven ships of Duncan's fleet joined the mutineers at the Nore, the Jason was one of the few that remained with the admiral.

During the equinoctial gales many of the ships were so badly strained that Admiral Duncan returned to Yarmouth Roads to gather and repair his fleet, leaving the Jason and two other ships to watch the enemy. De Winter lost not a moment in taking advantage of his absence, and on the 7th of October sailed out with his whole fleet, chasing the watch vessels before him. On their way, however, they met a squadron under Captain Trollope, consisting of Duncan's ships which had been refitted. The Dutch fleet, on seeing them, thought that the whole British fleet was behind, and not at the time wishing to engage, went about and steered again for the Texel. On the 9th the Active came in sight off Yarmouth Roads with the signal flying that the enemy were at sea. At once a general chase was ordered, and by the time the Active joined them the whole fleet was under way. Her captain was hailed and ordered to guide the fleet to the precise spot where he had last seen the enemy.

Captain Trollope had, as soon as the Dutch fleet went about, started in chase of them, and kept them in sight until they approached the Texel, when he steered to meet Admiral Duncan. He was therefore able to give the exact position of the enemy, and at once the fleet sailed towards them. On the morning of the 11th October, 1797, the admiral came in sight of the enemy about nine miles from shore and nearly opposite the village of Camperdown. The fleet, however, was greatly scattered owing to the different speeds of the ships. De Winter, as soon as he saw the British coming, got up his anchors and made for shore, hoping that he might be able to get so close in among its shoals and sand-banks, which were much better known to him than to his antagonists, as to deter Duncan from pursuing him. He was, above all things, anxious to avoid action; not so much because his fleet was slightly inferior to the British, as because his instructions enjoined him to regard his junction with the French at Brest as his chief object.

The British admiral, seeing his arrangements and divining his object, pressed on, regardless of the scattered state of his fleet, and made the signal for each ship to attack as she came up. Another signal intimated that he should attempt to break the enemy's line, so as to get between it and the land. But this signal was not generally seen by the fleet. It was, however, seen and acted upon by the second in command, Admiral Onslow, in the Monarch, who soon after led the larboard division through the Dutch line, three ships from the rear, and then closely engaged the Jupiter. Duncan's own ship, the Venerable, the leading ship of the starboard division, marked out the Vryhide, De Winter's flagship, as his own antagonist.

The Dutch ship States-general, the flagship of their rear-admiral, seeing his design, pressed so close up to his chief that the British admiral was compelled to change his course and pass astern of her; but as he did so he poured so terrible a fire into her stern that she was glad to fall back and leave the Venerable free to attack the Vryhide. Others of our ships followed the example of their chief, breaking the Dutch line at several points. At one o'clock the battle became general, and was carried on with unsurpassed courage on both sides. The two biggest Dutch frigates, which carried as heavy guns as the British line-of-battle ships, crept forward into the fight and fought gallantly, the Mars raking the Venerable severely while she was engaged with no fewer than three Dutch line-of-battle ships.

The crew of the Venerable had been particularly anxious to fight, their ship having been for the past five months engaged in the dreary work of blockading the Texel; and when they had seen the Dutch with their topsails bent, as if intending to come out, they had offered to advance into the narrow entrance to the Texel, and in that position stop the way against the whole fleet, or at least fight their ship till she sank. Now they proved that their offer had been no empty boast, for, although fighting against overwhelming odds, they stuck to their guns with unexampled devotion.

More than once every flag they hoisted was shot away, and at last one of the sailors went aloft and nailed the admiral's colours to the stump of the main topgallant mast. The Vryhide also fought with desperate courage. Other British ships, however, came up, and the disparity in numbers turned the other way. The Ardent attacked her on the other side, and the Triumph and Director poured a raking fire along her decks. One after another her masts fell, and the wreck rendered half her guns unworkable. Her crew were swept away, until De Winter was left alone on her quarter-deck, while below there were hardly enough men left to man the pumps. Then the gallant admiral with his own hand hauled down his colours, having fought to the admiration of the whole British fleet. The States-general, almost disabled by the fruitless attempt to foul the Venerable, maintained a vigorous conflict for some time against a succession of adversaries, during which she lost above three hundred men killed and wounded, until at last her captain was compelled to strike. No one, however, attempted to take possession of her, and, gradually dropping astern until clear of both fleets, she rehoisted her colours and made off to the Texel.

Ship after ship struck, and of the whole Dutch fleet but six ships of the line and two frigates managed to reach the Texel, and this was only due to the fact that several of the Dutch vessels, knowing that the orders had been that they were not to fight, stood aloof and disregarded their admiral's signal to engage. The entire casualties among our men exceeded a thousand. Many of the ships were completely riddled by shot, and on some of them the men were employed day and night at the pumps to keep them afloat till they could cross the Channel to our own harbours. Two seventy-fours, five fifty-fours, two gun-ships, and two frigates remained in our hands, but all were so battered that not one of them could ever be made fit for service. The two fleets were nearly equal in strength, the British being about one-twelfth the stronger. Some of the Dutch ships took no share in the action, but the same is true of the British. Some of them arrived too late, the hazy weather having prevented the signals of the Venerable from being seen by them. For one of them, however, the Agincourt, no excuse could be found, so her captain was tried by court-martial and declared incapable of serving in the navy for the future.

The Jason had taken her share in the battle. She had at once placed herself alongside the Brutus, a battle-ship of the same size as herself. All the afternoon the duel was continued, and both ships lost some masts and spars and had their hulls completely shattered. It was not until the engagement had almost ceased elsewhere that the enemy hauled down her colours. The battle was a desperate one, and Will had felt the strain greatly; there was comparatively little for him to do, for both ships sailed along side by side, and there was no attempt at manœuvring. He had, therefore, simply to move about, encouraging the sailors and directing their fire. So incessant was the cannonade that it was with difficulty he could make his orders heard, and, cool as he was, he was almost confused by the terrible din that went on around. It was found, after the Brutus surrendered, that her loss had been one hundred and twenty killed and wounded, while on board the Jason little over half that number had suffered.

As soon as the prize surrendered, parties were put on board to take possession, while the rest of the men were engaged in attending to their own and the Dutch wounded. The next day jury-masts were got up, and the Jason, with her prize in tow, sailed with the rest of the fleet for England. When they arrived at Sheerness the Jason was found to require a complete refit. The crew were therefore ordered to be paid off, and Will was promoted to the rank of captain, and at once appointed to the command of the frigate Ethalion, thirty-four guns, which had just been fitted ready for sea.

226

He had no difficulty in manning his ship, as a sufficient number of the Jason's old crew volunteered, and he was soon ready for service.

He was at once despatched to join Lord Bridport's fleet, and for nearly nine months was engaged in the incessant patrolling which at that time the British frigates maintained in the Channel.

Towards the end of July, 1798, the vigilance of the frigates, if possible, increased, for it became known that two French squadrons were being prepared with the intention of landing troops in Ireland. On the 6th of August a small squadron slipped out of Rochefort, and, eluding the British cruisers, succeeded, on the 22nd, in landing General Humbert and eleven hundred and fifty men at Killala Bay, and then at once returned to Rochefort.

The attempt ended in failure; the peasantry did not join as was expected, and on the 8th of September General Humbert surrendered at Ballinamuck to Lieutenant-general Lake.

Another fleet sailed from Brest on the 16th of September, 1798, consisting of one ship of the line, the Hoche, and eight frigates, under Commodore Bompart. It had on board three thousand troops, a large train of artillery, and a great quantity of military stores. It had set sail for Ireland before the news of the failure of Humbert's expedition had arrived, and it was certain that as soon as it reached its intended place of landing in Ireland it would endeavour to return without delay. Two or three days earlier the Ethalion and the eighteen-gun brig Sylph had joined the thirty-eight-gun frigate Boadicea, which was watching Brest. At daybreak a light breeze sprang up, and the French made sail. Leaving the Ethalion to watch the French fleet, the Boadicea sailed to carry the news of the start of the expedition to Lord Bridport.

At two o'clock on the 18th the Ethalion was joined by the Amelia, a thirty-eight-gun frigate, and at daylight the French directed their course as if for the West Indies. At eight o'clock they bore up, and five of their frigates chased the English ships. Presently, however, finding that they did not gain, they rejoined the squadron, which bore away to the south-west. On the 20th the two frigates were joined by the forty-four-gun frigate Anson. At noon the French were nearly becalmed. There was now no doubt that the destination of the squadron was Ireland, and the news was despatched by the Sylph to the commander-in-chief of the Irish station.

On the 26th the French ships turned on the frigates, but gave this up about noon, and proceeded on their way. The sea now became so rough that all the ships shortened sail. On the 29th the weather moderated, and the French squadron again started in chase. About nine o'clock the French battle-ship, the Hoche, sprung her main-topmast, and one of the French frigates carried away her top-sail yard. At this both the French and the British ships shortened sail. The French ships wore away to the north-west, and the British again followed them; but the Anson had sprung her topmast, and in the evening the Hoche lowered hers. The weather now became very bad, and the frigates hauled up and soon lost sight of the enemy. A week later the Amelia left them, but three days after, they fell in with the squadron that had been despatched from Cawsand Bay when the Boadicea arrived with news of the start of the French squadron from Brest. They were also joined by the frigates Melampus and Doris, which while at Lough Swilly had received news from the Sylph of the destination of the French squadron. The whole were under the command of Sir John Warren.

With the hope that he had now shaken off his pursuers, Admiral Bompart bore away for Killala Bay, but as he neared the land his leading frigate signalled the appearance of the British squadron. Sir John Warren immediately gave the signal for a general chase, but a heavy gale set in that evening, during which the Anson carried away her mizzen-mast main-yard and main-topsail-yard. The Hoche, however, was even more unfortunate, for she carried away her main-topmast, and this in its fall brought down the fore and mizzen-topgallant-masts. A few hours later the Résolue signalled that she had sprung a leak which she could not stop, and the admiral signalled orders to her captain to sail towards the coast, and by burning blue lights and sending up rockets to endeavour to lead the British squadron after him, and so allow the rest of the fleet to make off.

Admiral Bompart now changed his course, but at daybreak found himself almost surrounded by the British vessels. Both squadrons waited, but with very different feelings, the order to commence action. The Robust led the way, followed closely by the Magnanime, and was received with a fire from the stern-chasers and the quarter guns of the French frigates Embuscade and Coquille. A few minutes later the Robust returned the fire, and bore down to leeward for the purpose of engaging the Hoche, which, like herself, was a seventy-four-gun ship. In half an hour all the French frigates that could get away were making off. The Hoche by this time was a mere wreck, having suffered terribly from the fire of the Robust; her hull was riddled with shot, she had five feet of water in her hold, twenty-five of her guns were dismounted, and a great portion of her crew were killed and wounded. After the battle had raged for three hours she struck her colours. The Embuscade had also surrendered. The other British vessels set out in pursuit of the fugitives. The Coquille, after a brave resistance, was forced to haul down her colours, and the Ethalion pursued and captured the Bellone. Five French frigates attempted to escape, and in doing so sailed close to the Anson, which had been unable to take part in the action owing to the loss of her mizzen-mast, and as they passed ahead of her, poured in such destructive broadsides that she lost her fore and main masts, and had much other serious damage. Of the ships that had escaped, the Résolue was captured two or three days later. The Loire made a good fight; she was pursued by the Mermaid, and Kangaroo. The latter, which was an eighteen-gun brig, engaged her, but lost her fore-topmast. The Mermaid, a thirty-two-gun frigate, continued the pursuit.

At daybreak the Loire, seeing that her pursuer was alone, shortened sail. As the Loire was a forty-gun ship the fight was a desperate one, and both vessels were so badly injured that by mutual consent they ceased fire. The Mermaid lost her mizzen-mast, main topmast, and had her shrouds, spars, and boats cut to pieces. She was also making a great deal of water, and was therefore necessarily obliged to discontinue the fight. The Loire, however, was out of luck, for a day or two later she fell in with the Anson and Kangaroo, and in consequence of her battered condition she had to surrender without resistance. Similarly, the Immortalité, while making her way to Brest, fell in with the Fisgard, a vessel of just the same size. The Immortalité's fire was so well aimed that in a short time the Fisgard was quite unmanageable. Repairs, however, were executed with great promptness, and after a chase the action was recommenced. At the end of half an hour the Fisgard had received several shots between wind and water and she had six feet of water in her hold. Nevertheless she continued the fight, and at three o'clock the Immortalité, which was in a semi-sinking state, and had lost her captain and first lieutenant, hauled down her colours.

Thus seven out of the ten vessels under the command of Commodore Bompart were captured.

In the combat with the Bellone Will had been slightly wounded, and as he was most anxious to proceed with his investigation with regard to his relations, he applied for leave on his arrival at Portsmouth.

This was at once granted, and at the same time he received his promotion to post rank in consequence of his capture of the Bellone.

CHAPTER XIX

CONCLUSION

Will's first visit, after arriving in London, was to Dulwich. He had visited the house with Mr. Palethorpe when it was in progress of building, and had been favourably impressed with it, but now that it was complete he thought it was one of the prettiest houses that he had ever seen. The great conservatory was full of plants and shrubs, which he recognized as natives of Jamaica, and the garden was brilliant with bright flowers.

"I am delighted to see you again, Will," Mr. Palethorpe said, as he was shown in. "Alice is out at present, but she will be back before long. I must congratulate you on your promotion, which I saw in the Gazette this morning."

"Yes, sir, my good fortune sticks to me, except for this wound, and it is nothing serious and will soon be right again."

"Don't say good fortune, lad. You have won your way by conduct and courage, and you have a right to be proud of your position. I believe you are the youngest captain in the service, and that without a shadow of private interest to push you on. I am very glad to hear that your wound is so slight."

"You are not looking well, sir," Will said, after they had chatted for a time.

"No, I have had a shock which, I am ashamed to say, I have allowed to annoy me. I came home with £70,000. Of that I invested £40,000 in good securities, and allowed the rest to remain in my agent's hands until he came upon some good and safe security. Well, I was away with Alice in the country when he wrote to me to say that he strongly recommended me to buy a South Sea stock which everyone was running after, and which was rising rapidly. I must own that it seemed a good thing, so I told him to buy. Well, it went up like wildfire, and I could have sold out at four times the price at which I bought. At last I wrote to him to realize, and he replied that it had suddenly fallen a bit, and recommending me to wait till it went up again, which it was sure to do. I didn't see a London paper for some days, and when I did get one I found, to my horror, that the bubble had burst, and that the stock was virtually not worth the paper on which it was printed. The blow has affected

230

me a good deal. I admit now that it was foolish, and feel it so; but when a man has been working all his life, it is hard to see nearly half of the fortune he has gained swept away at a blow."

"It is hard, sir, very hard. Still, it was fortunate that you had already invested £40,000 in good securities. After all, with this house and £40,000 you will really not so very much miss the sum you have lost."

"That is exactly what I tell myself, Will. Still, you know, a dog with two bones in his mouth will growl if he loses one of them. Nevertheless £40,000 is not to be despised by any means, and I shall have plenty to give my little Alice a good portion when she marries."

"That will be comfortable for her, sir, but I should say that the man would be lucky if he got her without a shilling."

"Well, well, we'll see, we'll see. I have no desire to part with her yet."

"That I can well understand, sir."

"Ah, here she is!"

A rosy colour spread over the girl's face when she saw who her father's visitor was.

"I expected you in a day or two," she said, "but not so soon as this. When we saw your name in the Gazette we made sure that it would not be long before you paid us a visit. I am glad to see that your wound has not pulled you down much."

"No indeed. I am all right; but it was certain that I should come here first of all."

"And what are your plans now?" Mr. Palethorpe asked.

"I am going to set to work at once to discover my family. I have not been to my lawyer yet, so I don't know how much he has done, but I certainly mean to go into the business in earnest."

"Well, it doesn't matter to you much now, Will, whether your family are dukes or beggars. You can stand on your own feet as a captain in the royal navy with a magnificent record of services."

"Yes, I see that, sir; but still I certainly do wish to be able to prove that I come of at least a respectable family. I have not the least desire to obtain any rank or anything of that kind, only to know that I have people of my own."

"I do not say that it is not a laudable ambition, but I don't believe that anyone would think one scrap better or worse of you were you to find that you were heir to a dukedom."

Will slept there that night, and the next morning drove into the city to his lawyer's office. "Well, Captain Gilmore?" said that

231

gentleman as Will entered his private room. "I am glad to see you. I have been quietly at work making enquiries since you were last here. I sent a man down to Scarcombe some months ago. He learned as much as he could there, and since then has been going from village to village and has traced your father's journeyings for some months. Now that you are home I should suggest employing two or three men to continue the search and to find out if possible the point from which your father started his wanderings. Assuming, as I do, that he was the son of Sir Ralph Gilmore, I imagine that he must have quarrelled with his father at or about the time of his marriage. In that case he would probably come up to London. I have observed that most men who quarrel with their parents take that step first. There, perhaps, he endeavoured to obtain employment. The struggle would probably last two, or three, or four years. I take the last to be the most likely period, for by that time you would be about three years old. I say that because he could hardly have taken you with him had you been younger.

"It is evident that he had either no hope of being reconciled to his father or that he was himself too angry to make advances. I therefore propose to send men north from London to enquire upon all the principal roads. A man with a violin and a little child cannot have been altogether forgotten in the villages in which he stopped, and I hope to be able to trace his way up to Yorkshire. Again, I should employ one of the Bow Street runners to make enquiries in London for a man with his wife and child who lived here so many years ago, and whose name was Gilmore. I am supposing, you see, that that was his real name, and not one that he had assumed. I confess I have my doubts about it. A man who quits his home for ever after a desperate quarrel is as likely as not to change his name. That of course we must risk. While these enquiries are being made I should like you to go back to your old home; it is possible that other mementoes of his stay there may have escaped the memory of the old people with whom you lived. Anything of that kind would be of inestimable value."

"I will go down," Will said. "I am afraid there is little chance of my finding them both alive now. I fancy they were about fifty-five when I went to live with them, which would make them near eighty now. One or other of them, however, may be alive. I have not been to my agent yet, and therefore do not know whether he still sends them the allowance I made them."

After leaving the lawyer he went to his agent and found that the allowance was still paid, and regularly acknowledged by a receipt from the clergyman. He supposed, therefore, that certainly one, if not both, of the old people were still alive. He went back to Dulwich and said that he had taken a seat on the north coach for that day week. "I could not bring myself to leave before," he said, "and I knew you would keep me."

"Certainly, my boy. I don't think either Alice or myself would forgive you were you to run away the moment you returned."

When the time came Will started for the north, though he felt much reluctance to leave Alice. He acknowledged now to himself that he was deeply in love with her. Though from her father's manner he felt that when he asked for her hand he would not be refused, about Alice herself he felt far less confident. She was so perfectly open and natural with him that he feared lest she might regard him rather as a brother than as a lover, and yet the blush which he had noticed when he first met her on his return gave him considerable hope.

On arriving at Scarborough he stopped for the night at the house of his old friend Mrs. Archer. She and her husband listened with surprise and pleasure to his stories of his adventures in spite of his assurances that these were very ordinary matters, and that it was chiefly by luck that he had got on. He was a little surprised when, in reply to this, Mrs. Archer used the very words Mr. Palethorpe had uttered. "It is of no use your talking in that way, Will," she said. "No doubt you have had very good fortune, but your rapid promotion can only be due to your conduct and courage."

"I may have conducted myself well," he said warmly, "but not one bit better than other officers in the service. I really owe my success to the fortunate suggestion of mine as to the best method of attacking that pirate hold. As a reward for this the admiral gave me the command of L'Agile, and so, piece by piece, it has grown. But it was to my good fortune in making that suggestion, which really was not made in earnest, but only in reply to the challenge of another midshipman, that it has all come about. Above all, Mrs. Archer, I shall never forget that it was the kindness you showed me, and the pains you took in my education, that gave me my start in life."

The next day he drove over to Scarcombe, and to his pleasure, on entering the cottage, found John and his wife both sitting just where he had last seen them. They both rose to greet him.

"Thank God, Will," John said, "that we have been spared to see you alive again! I was afraid that our call might come before you returned."

"Why, father, I don't think you look a year older than you did

233

when I last saw you. Both you and mother look good for another ten years yet."

"If we do, Will, it will be thanks to the good food you have provided for us. We live like lords; meat every day for dinner, and fish for breakfast and supper. I should not feel right if I didn't have a snack of fish every day. Then we have ale for dinner and supper. There is no one in the village who lives as we do. When we first began we both felt downright fat. Then we agreed that if we went on like that we never could live till you came back, so we did with a little less, and as you see we both fill out our clothes a long way better than we did when you were here last."

"Well you certainly do both look uncommonly well, father."

"And you ain't married yet, Will?"

"No, I've not done anything about that yet, though perhaps it won't be very long before I find a wife. I am not going to apply to go on service again for a time, so I'll have a chance to look round, though I really have one in my mind's eye."

"Tell us all about it, Will," the old woman said eagerly; "you know how interested we must be in anything that affects you."

"Well, mother, among the many adventures I have been through I must tell you the one connected with this young lady."

He then told her of his first meeting, of his stay at her father's house, and of the hurricane which they experienced together.

"Well, mother, I met her again unexpectedly more than two and a half years ago in London. Her father had come over here to live, and has a fine house at Dulwich. I have just been staying there for a week, and I have some hope that when I ask her she will consent to be my wife."

"Of course she will," the old woman said quite indignantly. "How could she do otherwise? Why, if you were to ask the king's daughter I am sure she would take you. Here you are, one of the king's captains, have done all sorts of wonderful things, and have beaten his enemies all over the world, and you are as straight and good-looking a young gentleman as anyone wants to see. No one, who was not out of her mind, could think of saying 'No' to you."

"Ah, mother, you are prejudiced! To you I am a sort of swan that has come out of a duck's egg."

They chatted for some time, and then Will said:

"Are you quite sure, John, that the bundle the clergyman handed over to me contained every single thing my father left behind him?"

"Well, now I think of it, Will, there is something else. I never remembered it at the time, but when my old woman was sweeping a cobweb off the rafters the other day she said: 'Why, here is Will's father's fiddle', and, sure enough, there it was. It had been up there from the day you came into the house, and if we noticed it none of us ever gave it a thought."

"I remember it now," Will exclaimed. "When I was a young boy I used to think I should like to learn to play on it, and I spoke to Miss Warden about it. But she said I had better stick to my lessons, and then as I grew up I could learn it if I still had a fancy to do so."

He got on to a chair, and took it from the rafter on which it had so long lain. Then he carefully wiped the dust off it.

"It looks a very old thing, but that makes no difference in its value to me. I don't see in the least how this can be any clue whatever to my father's identity. Still, I will take it away with me and show it to my lawyer, who is endeavouring to trace for me who my father was."

"And do you think that he will succeed, Will?"

"I rather believe he will. At any rate he has found a gentleman, a baronet, who has the same name and bears the same coat of arms as is on the seal which was in my father's bundle. We are trying now to trace how my father came down here, and where he lived before he started. You see I must get as clear a story as I can before I go to see this gentleman. Mind, I don't want anything from him. He may be as rich as a lord for anything I care, and may refuse to have anything to do with me, but I want to find out to what family I really belong."

"He must be a bad lot," John said, "to allow your father to tramp about the country with a fiddle."

"I would not say that," Will said; "there are always two sides to a story, and we know nothing of my father's reasons for leaving home. It may have been his fault more than his father's, so until I know the rights and wrongs of the case I will form no judgment whatever."

"That is right, my boy," the old woman said. "I have noticed that when a boy runs away from home and goes to sea it is as often his fault as his father's. Sometimes it is six of one and half a dozen of the other; sometimes the father is a brute, but more often the son is a scamp, a worthless fellow, who will settle down to nothing, and brings discredit on his family. So you are quite right, Will, not to form any hard judgment on your grandfather till you know how it all came about."

"I certainly don't mean to, mother. Of course I have so little recollection of my father that it would not worry me much if I found

235

that it were his fault, though of course I would rather know that he was not to blame. Still, I should wish to like my grandfather if I could, and if I heard that my poor father was really entirely to blame I should not grieve much over it."

"I can't help thinking that he was to blame, Will. He was a curious-looking man, with a very bitter expression at times on his face, as if he didn't care for anyone in the world, except perhaps yourself, and he often left you alone in the village when he went and wandered about by himself on the moor."

"Well, well," Will said, "it matters very little to me which way it is. It is a very old story now, and I dare say that there were faults on both sides."

Will spent a long day with the old people and then returned to Scarborough, taking the violin with him. When he told how he had found it Mr. Archer took the instrument and examined it carefully.

"I think really," he said at last, "that this violin may prove a valuable clue, as valuable almost as that coat of arms. That might very well have been picked up or bought for a trifle at a pawnshop, or come into the hands of its possessor in some accidental way. But this is different; this, unless I am greatly mistaken, is a real Amati, and therefore worth at least a couple of hundred guineas. That could hardly have come accidentally into the hands of a wandering musician; it must be a relic of a time when he was in very different circumstances, and may well have been his before he left the home of his childhood."

"Thank you very much for the information, Mr. Archer! I see at once that it may very well be a strong link in the chain."

Two days later he returned to London. Mr. Palethorpe was greatly pleased to hear that he had found so valuable a clue.

"I don't care a rap for family," he said, "but at the same time I suppose every man would like his daughter—" Here he stopped abruptly. "I mean to say," he said, "would like to have for his son-in-law a man of good family. I grant that it is a very stupid prejudice, still I suppose it is a general one. You told me, I think, that your lawyer had found out that this Sir Ralph Gilmore had only two sons, and that one of them had died suddenly and unmarried."

"That is so, sir."

"Then in that case, you see, if you prove your identity you would certainly be heir to the baronetcy."

"I suppose so, sir. I have never given the matter any thought. It is not rank I want, but family. Still, I might not be heir to the baronetcy, for even supposing that my father was really the other son, he might have had children older than I am who remained with their grandfather."

"That is possible," Mr. Palethorpe said, "though unlikely. Why should he have left them behind him when he went out into the world?"

"He might not have wished to bother himself with them; he might have intended to claim them later. No one can say."

"Well, on the whole, I should say that your chance of coming into the baronetcy is distinctly good. It would look well, you know—Captain Sir William Gilmore, R.N."

"We mustn't count our chickens too soon, Mr. Palethorpe," Will laughed; "but nevertheless I do think that the prospects are favourable. Still, I must wait the result of the search that my lawyer has been carrying on."

"Well, you know my house is your home as long as you like to use it."

"Thank you, sir! but I don't like to intrude upon your kindness too much, and I think that I will take a lodging somewhere in the West End, so that I may be within easy reach of you here."

"Well, it must be as you like, lad. In some respects, perhaps, it will be best so. I may remind you, my boy, that it is not always wise for two young people to be constantly in each other's society." And he laughed.

Will made no answer; he had decided to defer putting the question until his claim was settled one way or the other.

In a few days he again called upon his lawyer.

"I have found out enough," the latter said, "to be certain that your father started from London with his violin and you, a child of three. I have considerable hopes that we shall, ere long, get a clue to the place where he lived while in London. The runner has met a woman who remembers distinctly such a man and a sick wife and child lodging in the house of a friend of hers. The friend has moved away and she has lost sight of her, but she knows some people with whom the woman was intimate, and through them we hope to find out where she lives."

"That is good news indeed," Will said. "I had hardly hoped that you would be so successful."

"It is a great piece of luck," the lawyer said. "I have written to my other agents to come home. It will be quite sufficient to prove that he journeyed as a wandering musician for at least fifty miles from London. Of course if further evidence is necessary they can resume their search."

"I have found a clue too, sir," Will said; and he then related the discovery of the Amati, the possession of which showed that the minstrel must at one time have been in wealthy circumstances.

"That is important indeed," the lawyer said, rubbing his hands. "Now, sir, if we can but find out where the man lived in London I think the chain will be complete, especially if he was in comparatively good circumstances when he went there. The woman will also, doubtless, be able to give a description of his wife as well of himself, and with these various proofs in your hand I think you may safely go down and see Sir Ralph Gilmore, whom I shall, of course, prepare by letter for your visit."

Four days afterwards Will received a letter by an office-boy from his lawyer asking him to call.

"My dear sir," he said as Will entered, "I congratulate you most heartily. I think we have the chain complete now. The day before yesterday the Bow Street runner came in to say that he had found the woman, and that she was now living out at Highgate. Yesterday I sent my clerk up to see her, and this is his report. I may tell you that nothing could possibly be more satisfactory."

The document was as follows:

"I called on Mrs. Giles. She is a respectable person who lets her house in lodgings. Twenty-five years ago she had a house in Westminster, and let the drawing-room floor to a gentleman of the name of Gilmore. He was rather tall and dark, and very variable in his temper. He had his wife with him, and two months afterwards a child was born. It was christened at St. Matthew's. I was its godmother, as they seemed to have very few friends in the town. Mr. Gilmore was out a good deal looking for employment. He used to write of an evening, and I think made money by it. He was very fond of his violin. Sometimes it was soft music he played, but if he was in a bad temper he would make it shriek and cry out, and I used to think there was a devil shut up in it. It was awful! When he came to me he had plenty of money, but it was not long before it began to run short, and they lived very plain. He had all sorts of things, whips and books and dressing-cases. These gradually went, and a year after the child was born they moved upstairs, the rooms being cheaper for them. A year later they occupied one room. The wife fell ill, and the rent was often in arrears. He was getting very shabby in his dress too. The child was three years old when its mother died. He sold all he had left to bury her decently, and as he had no money to pay his arrears of rent, he gave me a silver-mounted looking-glass, which I understood his mother had given him, and he said:

'Don't you sell this, but keep it, and one day or other I will come back and redeem it.'"

"This is the glass, sir," the lawyer said. "My clerk redeemed it after telling her that her lodger had died long ago. He went round to St. Matthew's Church and obtained the certificate of the child's baptism. So I think now, Mr. Gilmore, that we have all the evidence that can be required. Mrs. Giles, on hearing that the child was alive, said she would be happy to come forward and repeat what she had said to my clerk. She seemed very interested in the affair, and is evidently a kindly good-hearted woman. I fancy the silver frame is of Italian workmanship, and will probably be recognized by your grandfather. At any rate, someone there is sure to know it. Now I think you are in a position to go down and see him, and if you wish I will write to him to-day. I shall not go into matters at all, and shall merely say that the son of his son, Mr. William Gilmore, is coming down to have an interview with him, and is provided with all necessary proofs of his birth."

The next morning Will took the coach and went down to Radstock, in Somersetshire. He put up at the inn on his arrival, and next morning hired a gig and drove to the house of Sir Ralph Gilmore. It was a very fine mansion standing in an extensive park.

"Not a bad place by any means," Will said to himself; "I should certainly be proud to bring Alice down here."

He alighted at the entrance and sent in his name, and was immediately shown into the library, where a tall old man was sitting.

"I understand, sir," he said stiffly, "that you claim to be the son of my son, William Gilmore?"

"I do, sir, and I think the proofs I shall give you will satisfy you. You will understand, sir, please, before I do so, that I have no desire whatever to make any claim upon you; I simply wished to be recognized as a member of your family."

The old man looked him up and down, and then motioned him to take a seat.

"And what has become of your father, supposing him to be your father?" he asked with an evident effort.

"He died, sir, nearly twenty years ago."

The old man was silent for some little time, and then he said: "And you, sir, what have you been doing since then? But first, in what circumstances did he die?"

"In the very poorest. For the last two years of his life he earned his living and mine as a wandering fiddler."

"And what became of you?"

"I was brought up, sir, by a fisherman in the village in Yorkshire in which my father died."

"Your manner of speech does not at all agree with that, sir," the old man said sharply.

"No, sir," Will said quietly. "I had the good fortune to attract the interest of the clergyman's daughter, and she was good enough to assist me in my education and urge me on to study."

"And what is your trade or profession, sir?"

"I have the honour, sir, to be post-captain in His Majesty's navy."

"You a post-captain in His Majesty's navy!" the old man said scornfully. "Do you think to take me in with such a tale as that? You might possibly be a very junior lieutenant."

"I am not surprised that you think so, sir. Nevertheless I am indeed what I say. My name appeared in the Gazette a month ago."

"I remember now," the baronet said, "there was a William Gilmore appointed to that rank. The name struck me as I glanced through the Gazette. I had noticed it before on several occasions, and I sighed as I thought to myself how different must have been his career from that of my unfortunate son. Now, sir, I beg that you will let me see your proofs."

"In the first place, sir, there is this seal with your armorial bearings, which was found upon him after his death. This is a looking-glass, one which I believe was given to him by his mother. This is the violin with which he earned his living."

The old man stretched his hand out for the violin, with tears in his eyes.

"I gave it to him," he said, "when he was eighteen. I thought it a great piece of extravagance at the time, but he had such a taste for music that I thought he deserved the best instrument I could get. The looking-glass I also recognize, and of course the seal. Is there anything more, sir?"

"This, sir, is the certificate of my baptism at St. Matthew's Church, Westminster. This is a statement of my lawyer's clerk, who interviewed the woman in whose house my father and mother lived, and my mother died."

The baronet took it and read it in silence.

"I can produce also," Will went on, as the old man laid it down with a sigh, "the evidence of the lady who educated me, and to whom I owe all the good fortune that has befallen me. The old fisherman and his wife who brought me up are still alive, though

240

very old. I have means of obtaining abundant evidence from my shipmates in the various vessels in which I have sailed that I am the boy who left that village at the age of fifteen, and entered as a ship's boy in one of His Majesty's vessels."

"And you are now—?" the baronet asked.

"I am now twenty-three, sir."

"And a captain?"

"That is so, sir. I was made a midshipman before I had been three months on board, partly because I saved the first lieutenant's life, and partly because I understood enough mathematics to take an observation. Of course I served my time as a midshipman, and a year after passing I was made a second lieutenant. By the death of my first lieutenant at the battle of St. Vincent I succeeded to his post, and obtained the rank of captain for my share in the battle of Camperdown. I received post rank the other day when, in command of the Ethalion, I brought the Bellone, a frigate of Admiral Bompart's fleet, a prize to Portsmouth."

"Well, sir, your career has indeed been creditable and successful, and I am proud to acknowledge, as my grandson and heir to my title, a young gentleman who has so greatly distinguished himself. For I do acknowledge you. The proofs you have given me leave no doubt in my mind whatever that you are the son of my second son. You were, of course, too young to remember whether he ever spoke to you of me."

"Yes, sir. I was but five at the time of his death, and have but a very faint recollection of him."

"Of course, of course," the baronet said; "it was a sad affair. Perhaps I was to blame to some extent, though I have never thought so. Your father was, as doubtless you know, a second son. Although somewhat eccentric in disposition, and given to fits of passion, I had no serious occasion to complain of him until he went up to Oxford. There he got into a wild and dissipated set, and became the wildest and most dissipated among them. His great talent for music was his bane. He was continually asked out. After being two years up there, and costing me very large sums in paying his debts, he was sent down from the university. He would not turn his hands to anything, and went up to London with the idea of making his way somehow. He made nothing but debts, got into various scandalous affairs, and dragged our name through the dust. At last he came home one day and calmly informed me that he had married a woman in a rank of life beneath him. She was, I believe, the daughter of a horse-dealer of very doubtful character. He also said that he wanted £1200 to

241

enable him to start fair. I lost my temper and said that he should not have another pound from me. We had a desperate quarrel, and he left the house, taking with him all his belongings. It was four years before I took any steps to bring him back. Then his elder brother died, and on that I took every means to find him out. That he would ever be a credit to me I did not even dare to hope, but at least he could not be allowed to live in poverty. I advertised widely and employed detectives for months, but all without result. I have long since given up any hopes of ever seeing him again. I am glad, indeed, to find that the title, at my death, will not go to a distant cousin, but to my grandson, a gentleman in every way worthy of it. You are not married, I hope?"

"I am not married, sir; but I think, if you had asked the question, I should have replied that I was engaged, or rather had hopes of being engaged soon."

"Who is she?" the baronet asked quickly.

"She is the only daughter of a successful West Indian planter, a man of the highest standing in the colony, who has now returned and settled here."

The baronet heaved a sigh of relief.

"That is well," he said; "and considering that you have been all your life at sea, and have had no opportunity of making the acquaintance of ladies of titled families, it is better than I could have expected. As I do not know the procedure in these matters I had better consult my lawyer as to the best way of using these relics and the proofs you have given me that you are my grandson. It may be that my recognition of you is sufficient, but it would be as well to make sure that at my death there will be no opposition to your succession. You will stop here for a day or two, I hope, before going up to town to arrange the little affair you spoke of, and I think if your chances were good before, they will be still better now that you are recognized as heir to a baronetcy and one of the finest estates in England."

"I have never thought of that, sir. I have my profession and nearly £40,000 of prize-money, which will enable us to live in great comfort; and indeed I anticipate that her father will wish us to reside with him, or, at any rate, that she shall do so while I am away on service."

"I hope you will not think of remaining at sea. It would be monstrous for a man heir to £10,000 a year, besides very large accumulations, to be knocking about the world and running the risk of having his head taken off with a round-shot every day. I earnestly entreat you not to dream of such a thing."

242

"I will think it over. I am fond of the sea, but shall certainly be fonder of my wife, and I feel that your wishes in the matter should weigh with me."

"Well, I hope you will at least spend a portion of your time here. It will be your future home, and it is well that you should acquaint yourself with your duties. Besides, remember the years that I have been a lonely man."

"I would rather not give a promise, but I shall certainly take your wishes into consideration."

"Well, I am content with that, my boy. You will stay here now a few days, I hope. I have so much to hear of your life, and of course I wish to become better acquainted with you."

Will remained a week, during which time he made a great advance in the baronet's affections, and the old man seemed to gain some years of life as he walked in the garden and drove through the country with his young heir, whom he was delighted to introduce to everyone.

When he returned to London he at once drove over to Dulwich.

"Well, Will, what is the result of it all?" Mr. Palethorpe asked, for Will had purposely abstained from going to their house after his last interview with his lawyer. "Alice has been imagining all sorts of things: that you had been run over, or had run away with some girl."

"Father! I never thought that for a moment," his daughter said indignantly, "though I have been very anxious, for it is nearly a fortnight since he was here."

"I have done a good deal in the time," Will said. "I did not write to you, because I wanted to tell you. I am acknowledged as the grandson and heir to the title and estates of Sir Ralph Gilmore."

Both gave an exclamation of pleasure.

"And now," he said, taking her hand, "I only need one thing to complete my happiness, and that is, that you will share my good fortune with me. May I hope that it will be so?"

"Certainly you may, Will. I think I have loved you ever since I was a little girl, and acknowledge that my principal reason for inducing father to come to live in England was that I believed I should have more chance of meeting you again here than in Jamaica."

"I am heartily glad, too, that it is all settled," Mr. Palethorpe said. "I have seen it coming on ever since you met us the first time in London, and I may say that I have seen it with pleasure, for there is no one to whom I would sooner trust her happiness than you. Now I will leave you to yourselves."

It need hardly be said that Alice was as anxious as Sir Ralph Gilmore that Will should quit the navy, and he consequently yielded to their entreaties. He wrote to his grandfather to tell him of his engagement, and the baronet wrote back by return of post to Mr. Palethorpe, begging him to come down with his daughter and Will for a time.

"I only half know him at present," he said, "and as I understand that just at present he will not want to leave the young lady of his choice, you will gladden an old man if you will all three come down to stay with me."

Three months later the marriage took place from the house at Dulwich. Sir Ralph Gilmore came up for the ceremony, and the change that the three months had effected in him was extraordinary. He was the gayest of the party.

Among those present at the ceremony were also Will's two devoted friends, Dimchurch and Tom Stevens. The baronet was greatly pleased with their affection and pride in Will, and offered both good posts on the estate. So none of the comrades went to sea again.

The baronet gave into Will's hands the entire management of the estate and house, so his death, seven years later, made practically no difference to Will's position. Will took to country pursuits, and became one of the most popular landlords in Somersetshire, while his wife was quite one of the most popular ladies in the county. Her father, up to the time of his death, spent most of his time down there, and they used the house at Dulwich as their abode when they stayed in London during the season. Mrs. Archer came more than once to stay with them, as their most honoured guest. Stevens and Dimchurch both married. The former became head-gamekeeper on the estate, a post in which he showed great talent. The latter took a small cottage with a bit of land just outside the park gates, for he was able to live very comfortably on the interest of his prize-money. He had no children of his own, and his great pleasure was to wander about with Will's, telling them of their father's adventures in the great war.

It was not till well on in the sixties that Sir William Gilmore, captain, R.N., departed this life, a few weeks after the death of his wife, leaving behind him a large family to carry on the old name.

THE END

244

www.ingramcontent.com/pod-product-compliance
Lightning Source LLC
Chambersburg PA
CBHW020637260626
47157CB00008B/2787